HIS TEMPORARY ASSISTANT

A GRUMPY BOSS OFFICE ROMANCE

TARYN QUINN

His Temporary Assistant
© 2021 Taryn Quinn
Rainbow Rage Publishing

Cover by Najla Qamber Designs
Photo by Lindee Robinson Photography
Models Alyse & David

First print edition: November 2021
ISBN Print edition: 978-1-940346-69-4

AUTHOR NOTE

To whom it may concern…Ryan has many typos, but we (and PMS) love her anyway.

FYI - His Temporary Assistant overlaps with Luna's story in WRONG BED BABY. So…you know. Spoiler-ish. Though if you know what Crescent Cove is about, you won't be surprised. ***winky face***

Sometimes we make up fictional places that end up having the same names as actual places. These are our fictional interpretations only. Please grant us leeway if our creative vision isn't true to reality.

*We've always had a special place in our hearts for the mystical. Naturally, our favorite place is Salem, MA. We've always wanted to play with a little of the **other** in our world and finally took the leap.*

We hope you love Miss Moon & PMS as much as we did.

CHAPTER ONE

PRESTON

JUST WHEN I thought my day—week, month, life—couldn't get any worse, my assistant said she was taking a vacation.

In a week.

Not a year.

Not a month.

A week.

"Look, sir, I'm really sorry. I never expected to get this opportunity. My grandmother was supposed to go to Fiji on her honeymoon, but they broke up, and Biff is taking the Tahoe so she's taking the vacation."

I pressed a fingertip to my aching temple. "Biff? Your grandmother? Fiji?"

"He's taking the Tahoe," my assistant April repeated slowly, leaning forward. Her blond hair fell down around her shoulders, escaping whatever pinned-up thing she'd done in the back. Unless that was the style.

Must be. April Finley was never anything but perfectly put together.

Before today, she'd also never been late. Or taken a vacation

1

beyond a standard and reasonable long weekend. She'd called in sick precisely twice and worked from home.

"We had an agreement." My voice remained even. "I hired you on the spot approximately eighteen months ago on the condition you realized this was not a position that afforded you—"

"What, I can't take some time for myself?" Unlike my own, her voice rose in pitch to match the lifting asymmetrical hem of her dress. Not to indecent levels, mind you, because April was always proper.

Yet somehow my lack of sleep and brewing tension headache was bringing to mind ocean waters creeping higher on the Titanic.

The dress was sea blue too. Or hmm, was that more of a blue-green? I never did get why women had so many colors for things.

Look at my closet. I had black and navy suits. More navy than black because it was less severe for court. My tie collection was more colorful, but I certainly didn't know the names for the damn shades. Who had time for all that nonsense?

Not me. I didn't even have time to complete the work on my plate. I also didn't have time to further engage in this conversation.

April was still blathering on about mud masks and self-care and did I realize how long it had been since she'd even slept in?

No, I could honestly say I didn't.

"What exactly does that mean? I rise every day at precisely four."

She stopped mid-tirade and stared. "You what—why?" She tapped a glossy pale nail against her mouth. "Actually, that's better than I assumed. Rising means you sleep."

"Not necessarily," I said under my breath.

That certainly wasn't the case this month. My father was on the verge of retirement, which meant we would be looking to hire a new partner soon, and my brother and I were overloaded with work. Well, I was overloaded. Dex was strictly a nine-to-fiver—sometimes a ten-to-twoer if the water looked good. In the winter, he was all about the slopes.

I wasn't just talking about skiing. He made just as good use of the lodge as he did the hills. The guy dated more women in a year than I had in my entire life.

I was too busy working. And that was when I'd had an assistant.

Dear God, how was I going to get through a week without April? She kept my life running smoothly. Or at least it was less bumpy than it could've been without her.

"You remind me to eat," I said accusingly.

She frowned. "No, I don't. You just saw me with a donut or a sandwich a few times."

"Right, but seeing you with food reminds me I haven't eaten."

"Sir, your growling stomach should do that without my help."

As if I paid attention to such physical cues.

I would soon find out exactly how good I'd had it before.

Before vacations.

Before retirements.

Before I'd succumbed to a life of no meals and no sleep.

I grunted. "This is not enough notice. How am I supposed to hire a temp in," I consulted my Apple watch, "six days, eighteen hours, and eleven minutes?"

"I know it's short notice."

"Short? Try minuscule."

"But I have the perfect solution."

My shoulders unknotted for the first time since she'd walked into my office. "You've decided to cancel?"

April scowled. Until today, I'd never seen anything but a serene, unruffled expression on my assistant's face. That was one reason I appreciated her so much. She wasn't prone to mood swings.

Mood swings were a good part of why I was single. My mother had enough of them to change the weather from across town.

I didn't need any additional stress in my life. The calmer a woman was, the better. That went for men too, although that was a different dynamic because I didn't get naked with them.

For that matter, I didn't get naked with women much recently either.

Moving on.

"I can't cancel. My grandmother needs me. She and Biff were together for two years."

It took everything I possessed not to give a mock shudder. "I'm grievously sorry for her loss, but why does her misfortune have to become mine?"

April huffed out a breath. "Biff isn't dead. Have you been listening at all?"

"Of course I have." I adjusted my cuff links. "You're cruising to Alaska?"

"Seriously?"

"Look, I have back-to-back meetings this afternoon." Normally, at this point in a conversation I did not want to have, I would text my assistant to call me with a made-up appointment. That was hard to do when she was the one seated across from me.

One more reason I hated unplanned, unnecessary vacations.

"Not according to your Daytimer."

"There were a few last minute additions."

"Mmm-hmm. You know, I'm beginning to rethink my backup plan."

Hope bloomed inside me like a daisy in spring. "You are?"

"I always thought you were a fair, equitable boss who didn't play power games."

"I do not. Ever."

"You never so much as pinched my ass—rump," she corrected, thereby putting the image of an ass-rump in my head—luckily, not hers.

I had never so much as glimpsed her backside. I wasn't that sort of employer.

"Of course not."

"You don't take advantage of your position, and you see everyone as equals."

I couldn't help preening. Slightly. "I am careful to do exactly that."

"So, naturally, I figured Ryan would be the perfect choice to assist you while I'm away. I would never introduce you to a friend if I didn't believe you were fair-minded. Some look at having an assistant as an opportunity to lord their elevated status over them."

Why did it sound as if she was lecturing me? "I have never done such and I never will."

She rose. "Good. It's settled. Ryan will start for you next Monday at nine. Possibly nine-fifteen. No more than nine-thirty. Mornings are iffy." She crossed the office to the door. "Oh, and thanks! I'll bring you back a souvenir."

The door clicked shut on my curses.

I stalked over to the coffeemaker and discovered I was down to five pods—inhumane considering my current level of tension.

I popped one in the brewer and returned to my desk to stab the intercom button on the phone.

"Yes?"

"I'm almost out of coffee. Can you kindly place an order before your vacation?" The question held the same level of wrath as a death threat.

Preston Michael Shaw was not someone to tangle with without his caffeine.

"Already taken care of two days ago. Tracking says it should arrive by Monday afternoon. Your preferred flavor of Columbian coconut-caramel was backordered."

"Of course." I had no reason to feel ashamed I enjoyed coconut and caramel. Those were extremely manly flavors.

And Monday afternoon meant I would have to deal with April's friend who was "iffy about mornings" without the benefit of my early morning pick-me-up unless I grabbed one on the way in. My own kitchen at home was stocked with an assortment of possibilities that I rarely took time to actually make there, other than my restorative Friday night meal. For the most part, I only used my place to shower and sleep.

"I actually paid for rushed shipping."

"Why, does Ryan enjoy coffee too?" There was no keeping the edge of sarcasm out of my voice.

"Hardly. Tea is much more Ryan's speed. Coffee is a dangerous stimulant and can lead to hallucinations."

"Such as fantasizing about murdering someone when you don't have any?"

"You have five pods left," April said crisply. "Ration."

She hung up before I could reply.

In the old days before vacation, April never hung up without making sure I had everything I needed. Now she seemed dismissive. Perhaps this was her way of weaning me off the teat of capable assistantship before she took her leave.

It was hard to imagine Ryan, with his inconsistent start times and love of tea, could measure up.

Maybe I was being unfairly judgmental. Usually, water seeking its own level was a factor in friendships, but I had no idea if this was a former ex of April's or someone she merely had an acquaintance with. Many people today called everyone their friend, from the mailman to the barista who made their latte. I was far more selective.

My old school buddy, Bishop, counted as a close friend. I also had numerous acquaintances. I wasn't looking to add to the roster.

I grabbed my coffee from the brewer and disposed of the pod before sitting at my desk. I slipped on my glasses then typed a missive to April.

Memo: Ryan Moon

Ms. Finley,

Upon further reflection, while your effort to provide someone in your stead while you are vacationing is commendable, I need more information before I blindly accept someone into my employ, even temporarily. Does this individual have a CV? A work history? Applicable skills? References? I will need to see these materials before I hire anyone.

Yours,

Preston Michael Shaw, Esquire

Addressing her as Ms. Finley was a bit much, as was signing my full name and using Esquire. I was annoyed on multiple levels and needed an outlet.

I didn't believe in gyms—communal sweating had never been my kink—so I'd be going for a nice long run tonight to get out my frustrations. God knows I didn't have any other healthy outlets, other than playing Mario Kart on my ancient Super Nintendo system.

Vintage. Not ancient. I needed to learn the lingo so I didn't sound like someone caught in the past.

I drank a mouthful of hot coffee and flicked through screens until I came to my notes about one of my biggest cases, Terrance vs. Yorn, a multi-million dollar divorce with drama worthy of *Judge Judy.* I did not do drama. I also didn't relish reviewing notes that amounted to little more than a record of personal attacks rather than anything based on legal precedent.

I had pulled up my email program to dash off another email, this time to Donald Terrance, when said program dinged.

I frowned. I had turned off all notifications. How had one gotten through?

The frown grew as the most recent email in my box seemed to loom larger than all of the others. The sender? Ryan Moon.

Mental note: tell Ms. Finley not to share my email address with outsiders before asking.

Narrowing my eyes, I clicked it open.

To whom it may concern:
   I have attached my resume. References are at the bottom. The first one is the person who got me this gig.
   Sincerely,
   Ryan G. Moon

I cocked a brow. *Gig?* That was a new one.

Rather than reply to Ryan G. Moon, I opened my email to send another memo to April.

Ms. Finley,

I just received correspondence from one Ryan G. Moon. Kindly do not share my email with strangers in the future. Also, did you make clear what sort of position this is? Your friend referred to it as a "gig."

Yours,

Preston Michael Shaw, Esquire

I'd barely hit send and sat back to drink smugly from my rapidly disappearing coffee when my email dinged.

Yet again it had bypassed my no notifications setting. How was this happening? I did not want unanticipated noises interrupting my blessed silence.

To whom it may concern:

I am well aware what kind of position this is, as April (Ms. Finley to you) has told me all about her job many, many times. I am also well-versed in the likes of you.

Sincerely,

Ryan G. Moon

I set my coffee mug down with a snap. My gaze narrowed on the jaunty saying on the side of the cup, a gift from my last secretary right before I'd fired her.

Lawyers do it in their briefs.

She'd laughed uproariously upon handing me this item at the

company Christmas party. Then she'd pinched my ass. I'd been quite certain she'd dipped into the punch, but I couldn't have the other employees thinking I'd crossed a line.

As if I'd willingly have sex with a woman with nails as long as tongue depressors.

I begun to type again. Forget Ms. Finley. Evidently, Ryan G. Moon and I were meant to communicate solely with each other.

> **Ryan G. Moon,**
> **What do you mean by 'the likes of me'? If you have formed a bias against me due to Ms. Finley's description of her workplace, perhaps you would like to seek employment elsewhere. Ms. Finley should also discuss any concerns she may have with me herself rather than through a questionable intermediary.**
> **With all due respect,**
> **Preston Michael Shaw, Esquire**

I wasn't even surprised when the reply came through before I'd managed to finish even half my email to Donald. At this point, the resulting ding was also anticlimactic.

Clearly, my notifications setting had gone as rogue as my obviously displeased assistant.

> **To whom it may concern:**
> **April actually loves her job. I find it hard to believe, since my interactions with lawyers over the years haven't led to a feeling warmer than luke at best, but she is more generous than I. She has no concerns. I just read between the lines.**
> **So, have you checked out my resume or what?**
> **Sincerely,**
> **Ryan G. Moon**

. . .

What kind of feeling was *luke*? The word lukewarm was not meant to be split as if the first half counted as an adjective on its own.

I rubbed the knot in my forehead. If this was an example of Ryan's grammatical skills, I was nearly giddy with anticipation.

Also, I had forgotten to download Ryan's résumé. But I had one other salient point to attend to first.

> **Ryan G. Moon,**
> **The word is resumé with the accent mark over the e. Without it, the word is simply resume. Which the dictionary defines as: to take up or go on with again after interruption; continue. Example: to resume a journey.**
> **Sincerely,**
> **Preston Michael Shaw, Esquire**

Her response took all of three-point-five minutes.

> **To whom it may concern:**
> **You forgot the accent mark on the first e. It should be résumé.**
> **Insincerely,**
> **Ryan G. Moon**

This time, I did not answer the missive. Instead, I summoned Ms. Finley via the phone's intercom. "My office, please."

That *please* constricted my throat.

She knocked and appeared in my doorway, without seeming the slightest bit contrite. "Yes?"

"Sit."

She sat. Waited. Blinked innocently.

"Do you have some rapid-fire system that allows you to forward my emails to your friend in an instant? I've never seen anyone reply so quickly."

April's lips twitched. "She's very conscientious."

Now there was no doubting my throat was tight. "She?"

"Why, yes. Didn't you realize? Ryan is a woman." Now she did smile, widely. "She can't wait to meet you."

CHAPTER TWO

PRESTON

"Are you sure you won't take a kitten?"

I forced myself to smile for Tracy, one of the head volunteers at Kitten Around, one of our local cat shelters. "You know my lifestyle isn't conducive to pets, unfortunately."

That didn't seem likely to change.

It had been four days since April's surprise vacation announcement and my introduction to Miss Moon—I still hadn't gotten over the fact she was female, which said something about me I didn't care to entertain—and subsequent email exchange.

Since then, April had not decided to cancel her vacation. She hadn't decided to select another, likely more suitable friend to fill in for her.

All she'd done was clock out for the week with a jaunty smile, a wave, and a promise to send a postcard. Yippee.

And Ryan was still coming to work for me on Monday. Assuming she could make it in eventually, since mornings were so *iffy* and all.

"I know, since you're so busy. You have so many high-powered cases. So much responsibility and influence." Tracy's smile turned feral at the edges, accompanied by a lot of blinking her clearly faux eyelashes. "No time for a wife either?"

If I'd had a tie, she might've reached out and stroked it. Not the first time from her or others. My tie seemed to be a magnet for wandering female hands. Probably because I tended to wear ones in bright colors that drew the eye.

I'd pocketed today's tie on the walk in from my car. I'd had a very long day, and the shelter was about to close. If I'd been thinking sensibly, I would've just gone home for a burger on the grill and my requisite single glass of Maker's Mark every Friday evening. Never two. Always just one, no matter how arduous the week had been.

Or the year.

"I don't date."

"Really? Never?"

"No."

She exhaled. "Wow," she said under her breath.

Every time, the response was the same. Wide eyes. A hand lifted to the chest. Then sympathy, oozing out around a smile.

Did you get your heart broken? Poor thing.

No. You have to have one for it to break.

In my case, I was fairly certain the fluid in my veins was a mix of ice water and coconut-caramel coffee.

With what I dealt with day in and day out, who could blame me? Saying I witnessed love gone wrong was putting a positive spin on it. In truth, many of our clients had never loved each other at all. They married for lots of reasons, but affection wasn't at the top of the list. Or if it had been once, the feeling had dissipated quickly.

Some said love and hate were opposite sides of the same coin. So were infatuation and love. And it was far too easy to confuse one for the other.

Before Tracy started the usual spate of questions, I whipped out my platinum card and slapped it on the counter. Her eyes widened for an entirely different reason.

We'd done this dance before, minus the dating questions. But she'd just started volunteering a few months ago and had been tiptoeing to this point all this time.

"I'd like to make a donation." I named a figure ten percent higher than my usual and her throat bobbed. "The wing probably needs improvements."

In truth, I didn't care what they used the donation for. The wing that bore my name was new and they used it to care for the most critical cases. It seemed improbable that it would require anything this soon. But the shelter always needed supplies. Food, medication, incubators for the ill kittens, stuffed mama cats with soothing heartbeats, toys. The list was endless. Donations also went toward the cost of spaying and neutering and vaccines so when they had low-cost adoption events, the kittens were ready to go to their new homes right away.

"Oh, we appreciate this so much. You have no idea how many kittens you're helping. How many families will gain treasured pets because of your kindness." She couldn't swipe and type fast enough. "We have coffee and donuts," she added hastily. "Take anything you'd like."

Probably leftover from earlier in the day. My mouth watered just the same. I did enjoy the occasional sugary treat, and I hadn't eaten since breakfast. I'd avoided April all week so I hadn't had much opportunity to be tempted by her lunches.

That perfectly grilled burger and glass of Scotch would go down smooth.

I signed the credit card slip and made small talk for a few more minutes before I went out to my Lexus. Slipping behind the wheel into the cool air-conditioned silence normally soothed me. Eased some of the jagged edges of a tedious work week dealing with irate spouses and innumerable facets of marital law.

Add in a good bit of disgust at how humans treated other humans they'd once claimed to care about, and it was no surprise I made no time for relationships.

I'd wanted to go into entertainment law once upon a time. Preferably on the west coast where the sun never set and winter was rarely any colder than light jacket weather. LA had once lured me, the home of the fascinating world of the music and film industry.

Instead, I'd ended up working in my father's firm handling cases where I made more money the more I screwed over the other client. Meanwhile, my carefree younger brother did the bare minimum and lived his own sun-soaked life no matter the season in central New York. Dex never seemed to notice the rain or the cold. In fact, he loved both. Loved every damn thing.

I was the grump tapping my thumbs on the steering wheel as I sat at a light on another lonely Friday night in my silent, barely driven car. I didn't have time for leisurely drives anymore. I spent my life shackled to a desk.

And that was quite enough of my morose thoughts. I was free—for two days at least.

A short while later, I parked at the end of the long driveway of my home on the outskirts of Crescent Cove. On a clear night, I could see the glimmer of the lake from the second-floor balcony. I had a telescope out there and liked to check out the stars before bed. Sometimes I'd lower the scope and study the flickering lights in homes around the lake, wondering who lived there. What they were doing.

If anyone was looking out at me.

Blowing out a breath, I loosened the top couple buttons on my shirt and climbed out to walk up to my big, quiet house, looming in the near darkness with lights glowing against the glass. Every lamp in the place was lit, thanks to timers. I couldn't stand coming back to a dark place.

I stepped onto the huge wraparound porch and debated sitting on the swing for a few minutes before heading in. It was a gorgeous August night, with the hint of chill in the air that reminded the summer-weary the sweetness of fall would soon be here.

And after that, the isolation of a frigid winter. The lake would be a gleam of ice then, deceptively beautiful.

My stomach growled as I gave the swing one last long look as it drifted in the slight breeze.

Later, I promised myself.

Dinner and Scotch first. A shower after that. Then I'd come out here and hope the creak of the swing could drown out my restless thoughts.

I went inside and poured my drink before heading out to grill on the back half of the porch. Soon, the scent of sizzling meat and vegetables filled the air, and the Scotch settled warmly in my belly.

Everything seemed a little easier when the edges disappeared.

When I'd sated my hunger and cleaned the kitchen—God knows I didn't ever leave a dirty dish behind—I finally found my way to the swing. That shower was sounding better and better, but I needed the crisp breeze against my skin. The air was tinged with a hint of woodsmoke now.

Finally, I could fully unwind in peace.

So, why did I pull out my phone and scroll to a document I had deliberately not looked at all week?

Possibly boredom. Maybe self-destruction. Or my endless desire to prepare for what lay ahead.

As if I even could.

There wasn't much on the page. Three references on the bottom, starting with April Finley. Her name and address on top.

Ryan Goddess Moon.

Alone in the darkness, I laughed out loud. I'd wondered if her last name was fictitious before. Now I knew it had to be.

Or my name was really Preston Lovechild Shaw.

The apartment she listed was a couple miles from here, closer to Syracuse and just outside Kensington Square, where my office was located. Well, wasn't that handy?

Yet April had warned me she probably wouldn't be on time. How late would she be if she lived farther away?

Luckily, not my problem. I had enough of them.

Her job history was sparse. She had some experience at an insurance agency. A brief position as the front desk greeter for some hotel. A few lines about her past as a "curator of crystals and metaphysical goods" for an eclectic shop.

Currently, she was part of a podcasting duo. But it got even better.

Her show was about "exploring your inner earth goddess through Tarot, palmistry, auras, and astrology."

The name? Tarot Tramps.

I laughed again, hard enough my side cramped.

Then I zeroed in on the cell number listed beneath her address. A quick check of my phone said it was nearing ten pm. Way past a reasonable time for a work-related text.

Or any sort of text with a woman who'd pissed me off so much with her additional accent mark rejoinder that I hadn't deigned to reply all week. Mainly because I was impressed. She'd sent volley after volley back at me when normally, people deferred to whatever I said.

I was used to that treatment. Expected it.

Ryan Goddess Moon did not give one good crap what I expected.

I typed in the number and a quick text. The time, the method of delivery, and maybe even the message was inappropriate for a future associate. But she'd inadvertently made me laugh on a night when it seemed out of reach. So, I owed her my kind of thank you.

ME:

> Where did you come up with the name Tarot Tramps?

I'd grown so used to her rapid-fire email responses that I figured she would text the same way. Then again, it was late in the evening on a Friday.

Some people had social lives. She might be on a date. With her boyfriend. Or husband.

My shoulders tightened. So what? I was just asking a simple question. She could respond if and when she chose.

Which apparently wasn't right now.

I jerked the swing into motion and tipped back my head as it creaked and squeaked. It probably needed WD-40 or whatever one did to aging porch swings. I could get someone out here to fix it, but this was my sanctuary. I didn't want to deal with more people.

Except, oddly enough, the one I'd just voluntarily texted during my free time. But that was different. She was going to be working for me.

Sure, I'd demanded her work history and not looked at it for four days. That seemed illogical. Wholly unlike me. As if it hadn't mattered if she was competent, because she'd intrigued me.

But I didn't operate that way. Besides, I'd been busy.

Right.

The vibration in my hand broke into my thoughts. I glanced down and swiped to see the full message.

MISS MOON:

Who this?

This was going to be my assistant for a week? Her command of the English language concerned me. Then again, maybe she was in a hurry. In the middle of…something.

What I wasn't going to dwell on.

This is Preston Shaw. Your new boss.

Another delay, this one longer than the last. I tapped my foot while I waited.

MISS MOON:

Did you lose your watch? You're past business hours.

I am, unavoidably so. Are you engaged?

MISS MOON:

Like to be married? Hell no. Why?

There was no stopping my smirk. Or my sense of relief. Wasn't going to try to explain that one.

Some things defied all sense.

I meant are you currently engaged in an activity that precludes you from speaking to me.

MISS MOON:

Yes.

That was it. Just yes. No explanation. No apology. I hadn't apologized for texting so late either.

We were just a pair of unapologetic, inappropriate individuals.

Was that why I'd sought her out tonight? Because I was tired of coloring within the lines, and I could already tell Ryan Goddess Moon did not let anything stop her, let alone rules.

But apparently, she wasn't going to talk to me now. And if I was disappointed, I would just turn off my damn phone and go take a shower.

I certainly wasn't going to swallow hard when an audio file appeared on my screen some ten minutes later. I still hadn't moved.

I pressed play and sinuous, sexy music started to play. After about thirty seconds, feminine laughter rolled over the track.

Hey there, gods and goddesses. It's time for another episode of the Tarot Tramps. Featuring me, la-la-Luna, and...

My forearm tensed where it rested on the arm of the swing. Husky laughter joined the lighter, frothier version from la-la-Luna.

Ryan Moon, goddess of all things creative, sexual and free.

I wasn't smirking now. Her voice on the podcast was a seductive tease. Low, deep, with a bit of a rasp as if she'd smoked a full pack of Camels and followed them up with a whisky chaser.

I pushed a hand through my hair. Shifted on the swing. Wanted to turn off the damn audio because it was getting hot out here and not even the chilly breeze could cool me off.

How did April think a woman who sounded like *this* could work for me? It wasn't right.

I wasn't supposed to notice her voice. In fact, I'd felt a hell of a lot more comfortable when Ryan had been a man.

Or so I'd believed.

I gripped the back of my neck to keep myself from hitting pause.

And possibly setting my phone on fire so I wasn't tempted to *ever* listen to this again.

She continued talking and I found myself leaning toward her voice. Desperate for more even as I knew I should turn it off.

So, what's new with you, baby? Tell us all about your new job.

La-la-Luna—that could not be her real name—laughed and tapped her mic.

Is this thing on?
You know it is. Stop stalling.
Okay, okay, the new job is fab. I forgot how much I liked retail.
People are so fun, you know?

I definitely did not know. If Luna knew some fun people, I suspected they probably weren't the ones coming to me for assistance with their contentious divorces.

Really? Since when? People come in all flavors and some of them I don't want to try.

Ryan's sarcastic response made me grin. That was more like it.

Oh, stop being such a bitter Betty. You're just pissy because of what happened at the bar last week.

I cocked a brow. Do tell.

Oh, shut up.

Thankfully, Luna did not listen to Ryan.

Your girl, Miss Goddess Moon here, was line dancing on the bar during Country Chaos night and she was getting down, let me tell you. Then she really got down. As in fell off the bar. I'm surprised she didn't snap her ankle.

I rubbed my now bristly jaw. Weekends were the only time I allowed myself not to shave. But I couldn't claim much interest in the current state of my facial hair when I had an image of the faceless Ryan G. Moon line-dancing on a bar. Probably dressed in something short and skimpy.

Then again, maybe that wasn't her aesthetic at all. She could be the sort who preferred long skirts and flowy tops with plunging necklines.

Yes, turning this off would soon be an imperative.

You know I pivoted at the last moment. Do not deny my grace, you wench.

Their laughter was impossible to listen to and not smile. Since that was better than imagining Ryan in whatever she wore to dance in, I was all for joviality.

I think Ryan needs a reading to cheer her up today. What do you all think? We'll do a quick three card spread for her and then we'll dive into our Trampbox and see what you all have for us this week.

Ryan sighed. Heavily. The sound verged on a sexual noise that required a rating. Was there such a thing as an X label for a podcast? If not, they might need to create it for this one.

I don't need to be cheered up. Hello, you know my vibe is permanently set on glow. Okay, okay, fine. Hit me.

I frowned until I heard the unmistakable sound of cards being shuffled.

Also, these cards better tell me I'm going to get laid soon. If not, keep dealing until the universe provides, okay?

I cleared my throat. This was highly inappropriate for me to be listening to, as someone who was going to be giving Ryan a paycheck. I needed to turn this off and not lean forward as I waited to find out if Ryan was going to get laid. Whether she was or not was not my concern.

Besides, were there really cards that could predict sexual activity? That seemed highly dubious.

I had the vaguest understanding of tarot. They were usually cards the same size as a playing deck with brightly colored pictures of mystical things. Probably like Aladdin's flying magical carpet and such. My mother had once gone to a psychic fair and come back "renewed" but that was about the extent of my metaphysical knowledge.

Okay, pull your three. No cheating.
Bitch, I never cheat.
Liar. You cheat all the time.

More laughter. Then Luna let out a wolf whistle.

Girl, you just pulled the golden goose.

It sounded as if Ryan was rubbing her hands.

If you mean the golden cock, now we're talking.

My phone vibrated against my leg and I jolted, inadvertently pausing the show. Ryan had decided to follow up on her kill shot podcast and sent me another text.

MISS MOON:

Are you thoroughly scandalized yet? Decided to fire me before my first day?

I'm not finished.

Ryan sent a sideways smile emoji before a line of text I could barely make sense of. My brain—and other parts of me—were thoroughly addled.

MISS MOON:

Takes you a while, does it? Good to know.

Did she...

Was that...

I could not listen to more of this podcast. Unless I made it a two Scotch night and followed it up with an extra long shower afterward.

Just in case she'd forgotten the boundaries, it was time I reminded her. And reminded myself. We hadn't laid eyes on each other yet. People let down their hair and their reservations on Friday nights and then Monday morning came and regret was swift.

Even if she sounded like sex in a bottle and had a smart ass quip for every occasion.

You're my temporary assistant.

MISS MOON:

Oh, goodie. Do I get a prize? Or is the honor of being in your presence its own reward?

Your prize is your paycheck.

MISS MOON:

According to April, I'd have better luck in a Cracker Jack box. Do they still sell those?

Did I mention the smart ass quips? I should be annoyed. I was, but not at her. She couldn't make remarks if April hadn't placed these complaints in her mind.

I paid in line with other legal assistants in the area, thank you very much.

> Considering the contents of your résumé, I don't think you merit a pay raise.

MISS MOON:

> What's wrong with it?

> Not much applicable experience. Regardless, since you interrupted the podcast, what did your reading say?

MISS MOON:

> Wut?

Her misspelling of *what* made me shake my head. I truly hoped her text etiquette was a far cry from her typical grammar usage.

> Your reading on the podcast. About the golden cock.

I truly did not mean to type that. I'd never realized before that my fingers were adversely affected by my single Scotch.

MISS MOON:

> Oh, you really were listening, even past the intro. Well, far be it from me to keep you from hearing all about my sexual future. I'm touched you're curious.

> I never said that.

MISS MOON:

> No, but you asked. A question usually indicates interest.

> I thought you were too busy to talk to me.

MISS MOON:

> I finished with Ben & Jerry so figured why not?

For a second, my temples tightened with a sensation dangerously akin to jealousy. But that couldn't be possible. I did not know this woman. If she was having a ménage, good for her. Or not, as long as she showed up Monday morning.

> Ice cream?

MISS MOON:

> What else? You don't get out much, do you?

If she only knew the half. But the question reminded me I'd overstepped big time tonight, and my conscience decreed it was past time to put an end to it.

Besides, I had another reason for needing that shower now, and it wasn't just because it had been a long day. Ryan's sexy voice saying the word *cock* ranked up there with some of the hottest fantasy material I'd ever encountered.

But what she didn't know wouldn't hurt her. Besides, in person we wouldn't have this weird chemistry or whatever it was. Probably felt only by me.

Which referenced the whole *haven't been out in a very long while* thing. I couldn't even identify iconic ice cream upon first reading.

Though the ache between my legs likely had something to do with my lack of brain functioning right now. There was no other reason I'd continued this conversation.

> I'll see you Monday morning at nine sharp, Ms. Moon.

MISS MOON:

> Nine-thirty?

> Nine.

MISS MOON:

> Nine-fifteen?

> Nine.

MISS MOON:

> What if I bring you fresh donuts?

I frowned. That traitor April had revealed my weakness.

Nine-ten, donuts in hand.

MISS MOON:

You have a deal. *winky face.*

I swiped away the message and went in to take my shower. I also brought my mini stand into the bathroom so I could prop up my phone to listen to the rest of her reading.

She might not be guaranteed a golden cock, but I had one in hand by the end of it.

CHAPTER THREE

Card of The Day:
Embrace: Six of Swords | **Release:** King of Pentacles

WELL, crap.

I really hated when my cards called me out. I picked up the first card. It was a new deck that I was doing a review for. Maybe I'd read it wrong.

Sigh.

Nope. That starry and hopeful sky behind the trees and shadowed swords definitely was the six of swords. New beginnings and transitions. Most decks used a woman escaping on a boat for the imagery. Not this deck. As an artist, I appreciated the differences in interpretation for tarot.

But if this deck was talking to me, it wasn't speaking of escape. Unless I was running out of the forest. And I really didn't want to think about that right now. Especially since I'd be running to a lawyer's office and a man with a sphincter so tight he could probably create diamonds out of shit.

At least that was what I'd gotten from our email and text interactions so far.

The shadow side of the King of Pentacles could either represent my reluctance to head back into the corporate world or that I was walking into a shitstorm of a job.

Guess I'd find out.

I should be happy to have semi-positive cards as a little looksee into what was coming my way. It wasn't like I had a ton going on. I mean, I always had fifteen projects going, but nothing that couldn't be pushed back for a week to help out a friend.

April, the one person in my life who didn't have a witchy or divinatory bone in her body. If anyone was the epitome of Queen of Swords energy, it was April. All logic with a side of benevolence for those who were in her very close circle.

As far as I was concerned, it was handy to have all different types of people in my personal toolbox, and they didn't need to know that I had a significator card for most of them. It was something I'd used to learn cards back in the dark ages—when I was seventeen—to figure out how to give readings to other people.

That was also how I'd made friends in high school. Every teenage girl wanted answers from the universe, especially about her love life.

I'd become the witchy goth kid in high school to cover up for the fact that I usually had to make dodo with thrift store clothing. And it was easier to dye things black or find black items in the donation piles. Not to mention that it gave me a healthy appreciation for vintage music T-shirts. Add some cheap jewelry and black lipstick and I didn't look like a poor kid.

Weird kid was far easier to deal with. With a mother named Rainbow Moon, I didn't have far to travel down that twisty road.

Add in ten years and I hadn't really grown out of the black clothes. Now it was more of an aesthetic thing. That and it made me look damn good due to my dark hair and golden skin. I was vain enough to enjoy that part of the deal too. Plus, since I was always working with multiple mediums for my artwork, black was way better when it came to stains and the endless messes I tended to make.

I preferred wine red lips these days though. And the wine to go with it.

I lifted my *Drink Up Witches* tumbler and took a fortifying sip. I wasn't really in the mood for the merlot, but I needed to go to the store and that wasn't happening right now.

This would do.

I pushed my cards to the side of my drawing table and out of my mind. Learning and growth, my ass. It remained to be seen if my intuition was steering me into crashing waves or safety.

I scooped my hair up into a high ponytail then plopped into my drafting chair. Saturday was my day to work on my weekly web comic. I still hadn't shared it with anyone. Hoarding all the watercolor drawings in a drawer wasn't exactly what I'd had in mind when I started drawing the little fox. But I wasn't quite sure how to share her either. I'd been inspired by a rescue fox account on Facebook, but over the last six months, Sylvia had taken on more and more of my personality.

As was my ritual, I pulled my tiger's eye and citrine chain off my lamp and slipped it over my head. I needed all the help I could get when it came to my sacral chakra. Well, maybe only half of it. If I got any more of my sexuality side in alignment, I would be crawling up the walls.

Instead, I focused inward and breathed through the short meditation I used to open myself up. I focused on my hips and sinking into the chair. I flattened my feet on the floor and sat up straight, slowly picturing all of my chakras blooming.

As I meditated, I paid special attention to the moon flower I associated with my art, focusing on the silky fragile white flower slowly unfurling and allowing me to share some of its magic. I cupped my fingers around the crystals wound in silver then slowly opened my eyes and reached for a sheet of my watercolor paper.

I came alive in the evening.

I'd tried like hell to train myself to be a morning person, but it just wasn't to be. The higher the moon in the sky, the more my creativity sparked.

The longer summer days allowed me some extra daylight, like now with the last rays of the day streaming over my drawing table. I took inspiration from the pale yellow slashes and incorporated them into my drawing.

I sketched Sylvia curled into a little shrimp formation and fluffed out her tail to rest over her nose. As the rest of the room in the comic took shape, I stood to stretch out my muscles.

Ouch.

I reached around to the hand crank that changed the angle of my desk. I needed a little more height when I was standing. The heavy iron base had been a bitch to get into my studio, but I loved its antique design.

The scarred teak tabletop suited my earthy side. The antique desk had been a rusted heap headed to the landfill when I'd found it. It had taken a lot of TLC and a healthy bit of bribery for a metal worker friend of mine to get it back to working order. Even more bribes had been necessary—one of which required me to do readings at a bachelorette party for free—to get it up to the second floor of my apartment building.

My sanctuary.

I lived in a small studio in a converted Victorian just outside Kensington Square's business district on the outskirts of Syracuse, which was one more reason I'd said yes to April. I could literally walk to work.

As I drew the bit of reflection on the window beside Sylvia's sleeping form, one of the blobs sort of looked like the sleek, triangular shape of a cat's face. Before I knew what I was doing, I started enhancing the image and a gray cat came out of my damn fingertips.

I slumped back into my chair with a frown.

The comic was about the random life of Sylvia, the rescued fox, and her owner, Roz. It did not include a cat.

I reached for the eraser, but I couldn't quite pull the trigger.

My phone buzzed in my pocket.

I couldn't stop the grin as I swiped open my phone to read April's text.

APRIL:

> Thanks so much for helping out. Caramel and coconut things are bonus for bribery. Mr. Shaw has a sweet tooth. I know mornings aren't your forte so you can definitely use that for backup.

I wished I could refute that, but I could not.

I hated and also loved that April knew me so well. Between the podcast and my bookings for tarot readings, I made a good living. Not a great one, but a decent one, thanks to the advertising we'd been able to add to the podcast. Because of that, I didn't feel the need to do the nine-to-five schlock like the majority of my friends.

Yet another reason I'd said yes to April. Temping for her would give a nice boost to my not-so-cushy savings account.

ME:

> Funnily enough, I already went with the bribe for Monday morning.

APRIL:

> Is that right? You're still emailing him?

I tapped my finger along my top lip. Should I mention to April that we'd texted fast and furiously last night?

Nah.

I'd been a little too unprofessional in those texts. And maybe that clip from the podcast hadn't been the smartest move. Not that PMS was any better, texting me out of the blue on a Friday night two steps away from midnight.

I'd just change the subject for safety's sake.

> Kind of. Oh, and BTW, sending me wine is also a good bribe.

APRIL:

> Already ordered and should arrive Monday. Did I say thank you?

Yes. Perhaps the thank you should require more than just wine. This guy is a piece of work. Am I going to murder him by Friday?

I was kidding. Mostly. I'd tried to put PMS out of my head. Yeah, I'd definitely put him in my phone as that. Preston Michael Shaw, Esquire—seriously? Could you get any more pretentious? I couldn't wait to see what kind of repressed suit I'd be working for. Add in a little too much wine last night while I was editing the podcast I did with my other bestie, Luna…

Yeah, I should lock my phone down when there was alcohol involved. Things never went well.

And I'd probably given him the wrong idea about thirteen times based on my re-read of the text messages today. What had I been thinking?

I shoved up my glasses to perch on my head and went to refill my wine while I waited for April to reply. Now that I'd moved away from my desk, I realized I was hungry but not enough to go for a full meal.

The heat of the late afternoon had left me a little sweaty and always curbed my appetite.

I opened my tiny fridge in my equally tiny galley kitchen. There definitely wasn't much to go on in there. I *really* needed to go shopping. Spotting spreadable wine cheese on the top shelf, I smiled— *yes, please.*

I hip-checked the door closed and reached for the box of Triscuits in the overhead cabinet. I shook the box with a disappointed sigh and didn't bother with a plate. I'd definitely be finishing off the meager rattle of thin salty treats. I tucked my wine tumbler into the crook of my arm and padded over to the modernized Rococo couch that I'd bought from Kinleigh & August's Attic.

Kinleigh Scott and her husband, August, were good friends of mine. Since they'd hooked up, there had been a lot more interesting rehabbed furniture in their combined stores. So far, I'd added two of their pieces to my little studio, the couch being my favorite. The back and sides of the sofa were hand painted in a gorgeous lavender, gray, and blue paisley. The over the top Baroque-style leaves and scroll work were painted a deep dark plum to offset the softer colors. The velvet upholstery was a few shades lighter.

It was like the universe knew I'd needed it to go with my tapestry rug and array of framed prints that made up the corner of my apartment. Just beyond the one good window, I had a huge cubed bookcase—one of August's builds—as a room divider jammed with my collection of tarot and crystals. The other side held my bed with a special drawer the size of my full bed for storage below the frame, courtesy of Kinleigh's clever mind.

A double-door closet had been turned into my podcast recording space. My clothes made for great noise buffering.

The other half of the apartment was my art studio, meager kitchen, and child-sized bathroom with standing shower.

It wasn't much, but it suited me. When I had a hankering for television, I had a cool little projection unit that hooked up to my iPad so I could watch *The Golden Girls* on the one bare wall in my place.

I glanced at my phone—no reply yet.

While I waited, I pried the top of my cheese spread open and scooped some out. My cheese to Triscuit ratio was definitely out of whack. I shrugged and popped it in my mouth as my phone buzzed.

Instead of April's name, the distinct letters I'd plugged into my contacts glowed from the screen.

PMS.

I licked off a stray bit of cheese from my thumb and read the preview.

> PMS:
>
> I apologize for my behavior yesterday. I should not have contacted you after business hours. Nor should I have spoken to you with such familiarity.

Mercy, this dude had an iron rod shoved up his butt. I unlocked my phone and folded myself into the corner of my couch. Who the hell talked like that outside a Regency romance? I only knew because

35

that was my mom's favorite genre lately. I'd filched one of the old, scarred books with Fabio or some lookalike on the front the last time we'd had lunch.

She got them for like a dollar a bag at the library. She wouldn't miss it. Probably.

Before I could reply, another text came through.

PMS:

I hope we can clean the slate and start again.

My slate's in good shape. Takes a lot more than that to get my panties in a twist.

And there I went with the inappropriate talk. I couldn't help myself. Hopefully, he wouldn't turn out to be a troll when I got to the office on Monday.

Not that it mattered one way or the other. Maybe it would be better if he *was* a troll. Temporary boss and all that. Who needed eye candy I couldn't act on?

Either way, I'd definitely have donuts in hand.

I quickly typed off another text.

Guess I'll just have to do your cards tonight to make sure we're on the right path.

I wasn't sure what had possessed me to say that. The little chat bubbles came up and stopped, and then resumed and stopped again. Maybe I'd gone too far.

Maybe? That was basically my life motto.

I scooped out another slab of cheese for my...man, only four crackers left? *Ugh.* I wiped my hands and retrieved my review deck and went back to my couch. I shuffled as I thought about the ever-repressed Preston Shaw.

Just how would our Monday go?

I had to know.

Six of Wands reversed, Justice, and Eight of Swords reversed with a Hanged Man shadow card.

Hmm. Not exactly surprising that Justice had showed up, considering he was a lawyer. But maybe we were both a little anxious about getting things right in the workplace.

The Hanged Man definitely wasn't giving me much to go on.

I really hated to wait and see. Being patient topped the list of things I sucked at.

As I scooped up the cards, one fell to the floor.

King of Swords.

My logical and chilly boss-to-be right there in the flesh. The one who'd apparently decided to ghost me.

The cards weren't giving me much to go on. PMS definitely wasn't.

Monday would be very interesting indeed.

CHAPTER FOUR

Card of The Day:

Embrace: 6 of Swords | **Release:** The World reversed

Monday

A PURRING gray cat with golden eyes tapped my nose incessantly.

I pushed it away with a mumbled curse. The blasted nuisance came right back.

Tap-tap-tap.

Then the tapping turned to an annoying bell. Whomever put the bell on the cat's collar needed to be maimed.

By me, with pinking shears.

The bell got louder, followed by a crash of cymbals.

I jerked up my head, a sketch page stuck to my cheek. I peeled it off my face and stared down at the gray cat I hadn't been able to get out of my head all weekend.

Evidently, it had walked right into my dreams. I rolled my eyes then put it on top of the seven other sketches I'd been working on since Saturday night. "Okay, okay. I get it. You want to have a guest spot in the comic."

Of course it would be a guest spot. Not a whole change to my setup.

I stumbled out of my chair and nearly slipped on the scattered sheets in various stages of creative birthing. The cat on one of the pages even had a freaking tie.

I bent down and picked them up. "Alexa, off!" I shouted and the alarms went silent. I really hoped the alarms hadn't been going off forever. I checked my Apple Watch, but it had died sometime between Saturday and Sunday.

Sleeping at my desk was not advised, but it wasn't the first time. Nor would it be the last.

"Alexa, what time is it?"

"The time is 8:11."

"Crap." I shoved the pile of sketches on my small kitchen table and sprinted to the bathroom for a lightning quick shower. Thankfully, I'd had the foresight to pull out clothes for work the night before.

Mornings and I had a really crappy relationship. Add in a binge drawing night and it was the Mondayest Monday of all Mondays.

I didn't have time to deal with my heavy, curly hair. Instead, I twisted it into two French braids and wound the tails into a knot at the base of my neck. A few stubborn curls wouldn't be contained, and it was too blessed hot to deal with a crapton of product.

Quickly, I lined my eyes, swiped on some shadow and mascara, and called it good. "Freckles be free today."

I gave myself ten minutes to meditate while I lotioned up with my protection blend. Who knew what kind of energy I'd be walking into?

I added on all the mystical armor I could find today. I drew the delicate chains of my body jewelry over my shoulders and around my breasts to meet in the chain around my waist. Clear quartz was wound throughout the silvery metal. Along the center of my back were three chips of rainbow fluorite.

Then I put on the armor the world required.

Unfortunately, I was far too curvy to forgo a bra, especially when I had to go into an office. Luckily, it was still summer, so I didn't have to do the whole pantyhose thing. I pulled on a black maxi dress with spaghetti straps that flirted with my ankles. A celery green sweater hid all my witchy finery and turned the outfit into business casual-ish. At least as much as I was ever going to pull off. A matching pair of strappy-heeled sandals pulled it all together and gave me that little bit of confidence I needed.

I rushed back into my kitchen and flipped on my electric kettle. I definitely wasn't going to make it through the day without some tea.

I tucked some loose tea leaves into my little salamander tea infuser, and then prestuffed my kitschy sloth one for the drink I would surely need at the office. It would provide a smile later that I'd probably need. I tucked it into a reusable baggie full of loose tea and tossed it into my green bucket bag on my kitchen table.

My electric kettle was created for the perpetually late or impatient —whichever camp you wanted to sit in. Regardless, the water was ready for me in less than ninety seconds. I set my little dude in a to-go mug and let my breakfast blend steep.

I didn't have much time, but rituals were necessary for more than one reason. If I skipped them, my thoughts became chaotic, and in turn, the energy around me would follow suit.

I grabbed the deck I was using for the month and shuffled quickly.

My backup alarm filled the room with "Watermelon Sugar" by Harry Styles, my five-minute warning.

"Time to go." I flipped my daily card and pulled my shadow card from the bottom of the deck. "Could be worse. All about beginnings today." The reversed Major Arcana card gave me a little pause though.

It usually signaled big life movements.

"It's just a temp gig, Universe." I swiped up the cards and dumped them in their deck bag, and then tossed it in my purse along with a few snack items. I double-checked I had my phone and wallet—I couldn't count the number of times I'd left my apartment without them—then headed for the door.

Just before I opened it, I rushed back to my altar and snagged a few crystals. Better to be prepared for whatever came my way today.

I shut the door just as Harry finished singing about all the dirty things he was going to do to some lucky girl.

I flew down the stairs and out to the alleyway behind my building. It was a shortcut to Garden Avenue. Since I was on the verge of running late and wearing heels, I'd shave any minutes I could.

I skirted the crunch of kids playing kickball on one of the quieter side streets.

"Hey, lady!" A freckled boy with a wicked head of red curls whistled at me.

"Can't talk. Late."

"Come on. Kick the ball with us."

I turned to walk backwards. "Do I look like I'm wearing the clothes for kickball?"

"No, but you're way prettier than my friends. Come on, please?"

I grinned. Bold little charmer. "Not sure your friends would be happy to hear that."

The ginger's friend took the opportunity to whale him with the ball. "Out!"

I laughed. "See?"

"Come on, now our team needs you."

I shook my head and crossed the street. "Nope, sorry. Next time." I secured my bag over my arm and almost made it to the corner. But damn, his friend had a hell of an arm.

The thwack of the ball connecting with my ass shocked me enough that I almost turned my ankle on the cracked sidewalk.

"If I have a smudge on my ass from that ball, I'll find you tomorrow!" I picked up the ball and hurled it at his friend with the smirky, crooked mouth. I took a little joy in the fact that he ducked just in time for the ginger to take the ball in the center of his chest.

I smoothed my hand over my butt and made it to Garden Avenue. Only three blocks left to my favorite bakery. It just happened to be across from PMS's office.

"Watch it, lady."

A flash of jet black hair flew like a tangle of ribbons behind a chick with a lime green helmet. She was hunched over her bike, a matching backpack emblazoned with Lightning Messenger Service strapped to her lean frame.

The universe was literally trying to take me out today.

I glanced up at the clock in the middle of Kensington Square. "It's a miracle," I said under my breath. It was ten of nine. I might even be right on time.

The little bell over The Honey Pot's door jangled on my way in.

A tall woman with dark hair streaked liberally with scarlet highlights waved at me. "Hey, Ryan. What brings you out and about so early?" She wiped her hands on her apron and gave me a dazzling smile. Eeyore's woefully sweet face was splashed across the front of her T-shirt.

"Mornin', Dre." I dug into my bag. "I'm temping this week at a lawyer's office, if you can believe it. I was told bribing him with coconut or caramel would be a good way to make the week go smoothly."

"Preston Shaw?"

I laughed. "So, his sweet tooth is that legendary?"

"Oh, definitely. April finally took a day off?" She pulled down a bakery box. "I didn't know you two knew each other."

"Yeah, she's one of my best friends. She had a mini emergency with her grandmother."

Dre glanced up from the bakery case. "Oh, no."

I waved my hand. "Nothing serious. Well, at least not health-wise. She decided her mid-seventies was a fine time to get a divorce before the marriage."

Dre's laugh filled the room. "Good for her." She tapped her ring finger with her thumb. "I managed to give my husband the boot recently, as well."

"Oh, did you?"

"I sure did. Remember when I got that reading from you?"

I laughed. "Been a lot of readings between, girl."

Dre flushed. "Right. Sorry, made quite the impression on me at the time. You told me to watch out for a surprise arrival in the spring. I was thinking baby. Instead, it was Mark's girlfriend."

I winced. "Ouch."

"Yeah. Thank God I never put his name on the papers for this

43

place." She waved toward the room. "Him and Kimmie—with an ie because she's an infant—are going to be very happy together."

"I'm sorry that was the surprise."

She shrugged. "Better off. I thought it was my fault that the only thing rising in our marriage was my bread dough."

"Oh, girl. Never your fault. Especially with how sweet and open you are. Come see me and we'll see what kind of fall you'll have instead. Maybe some new love is on the horizon. I have a good vibe."

She rolled her eyes. "I'm done with men for a while." She tucked donuts into the box and started to shut the sliding door, and then reached toward some apple fritters that made my mouth water. "These are my new caramel apple fritters. I'm trying out a new honey glaze. Let me know how he likes it. And you." She tucked two into a pastry bag. "These are on the house."

"Aww, you don't have to do that."

"I insist." She brought the box of donuts and the bag to the register. "Fifteen-eleven."

I pulled out a twenty. "You saved my morning. Keep the change."

"Are you sure?"

"Definitely. Make sure you come see me soon." A little zing zipped up my spine when the door jangled again and a dark-haired man came in. He wasn't paying either of us any mind, his attention centered on his phone. Suddenly, his gaze lifted and bright, silvery gray eyes locked with Dre's.

Hmm.

I glanced between them. "You need to call me," I said again.

Dre blinked before clearing her throat. "Yeah, maybe I will."

I gave the hottie in the motorcycle jacket a grin then waggled my eyebrows at Dre and took my bundle. "See ya."

"Bye, Ryan." Dre cleared her throat again as she wiped her hands down her apron. "Can I help you?"

I whistled my way out the door. Love—or maybe it was just a little lust—was in the honey-scented air for sure. I was glad to see someone was getting a little whiff of happiness. I knew I sure wasn't.

I glanced back through the big picture window to see tall, dark, and silver eyes leaning against the counter, his phone forgotten.

"Watch it!" I turned to see Miss Speedy McBikerson winging her way back down Kensington.

You know when they say things happen in slow motion? Or when life flashes by your very eyes?

Lies.

The sweets-filled pink box started off in my arms and ended up pinned under my armpit when I crashed into the sidewalk in a blink.

When I opened my eyes, a bike tire spun about three inches from my nose as the biker popped up off the ground a hell of a lot faster than I did. Then again, she wasn't covered in caramel, chocolate, or some oozing cream filling.

Lime Helmet hauled up her bike. "If you broke my bike, I'll sue." She hopped back on her bike and took off.

"I'm fine, thanks for asking," I shouted as I rolled onto my hip with a wince. I didn't even want to look down. I could feel all the sugar congealing to my skin.

I peeled the box off my sweater just as Dre rushed outside.

"Are you okay?"

"Here, let me help you up." Silver Eyes hauled me off the sidewalk without even a grunt. I wasn't a small girl. Both height and curves meant I was a good handful.

"Oh, Ryan." Dre's horrified face told me all I needed to know.

A donut fell out of the box and plopped next to my shoe just as my phone shrieked from my bag. It wasn't any of my usual ringtones, which meant it had to be PMS.

"Perfect."

"Let's get you inside and cleaned up." Dre hooked a hand through my arm. "I'm not sure I have enough napkins for this."

Hot Guy glanced at his motorcycle. "I could take you home."

I sighed as my phone rang again. I gave the delicious guy—who'd now seen me at my graceful best—a weak smile. "I'm late for work."

"Think this qualifies as a get out of jail free card."

I sidestepped the delighted pigeon who was now getting a sweet treat. "You don't know my boss," I muttered. "Hell, I don't really know him either, and I know this isn't going to go over well."

Silver Eyes gave me an arched brow.

"First day."

"Ah."

I glanced at Dre. "Got a bag I could borrow?" I threw the box in the green trash bin attached to the crosswalk pole.

"Let me get you another box."

I waved her off. "It's okay. I don't have time." I used the tips of my fingers to pick up the bag that surprisingly wasn't dented too badly. "I just need to get this off."

Dre nodded and ran back into her shop.

Silver Eyes looked at me. "Can I help?"

"Not the way I envisioned asking a guy to help remove my clothes."

He laughed and lifted my mangled braids off my shoulders and skillfully tucked the ends back into my fractured bun.

I glanced over my shoulder in surprise.

"Three younger sisters. I braided a lot of hair."

Dre came back with a canvas bag. "Sorry, I only have reusable ones."

Silver Eyes smiled at her again. "That's a good thing."

Dre pinked up again. "Gotta do my part."

As much as I appreciated the romantic dance going on around me, I had to get this stupid sweater off to see just how much trouble I was in.

Dre and Silver Eyes helped me get each sleeve off. Dre gasped.

"Ugh, how bad?"

"Not bad at all," Silver Eyes muttered.

Dre gave him a quick look. He shrugged with a wolfish smile.

"That's some jewelry, Ry." Dre held out the bag for me to dump the sweater inside. It was one of my favorites. Hopefully, I could salvage it with a soak tonight.

"Oh, crap." I'd forgotten about the low back on the dress and the tiny straps. Hence the sweater. "Not exactly business casual."

Dre pressed her lips together against a laugh.

"You'll be a hit at the office," Silver Eyes said with a grin.

My phone rang again. I blew out a breath, and then shoved the fritters bag into my purse. "Thanks, Dre. Sorry about the bag."

"All good." She crossed her arms. "I wish I had something I could give you to wear. Don't think my array of aprons will work."

I laughed. "No, not really. Wish me luck." I wiped cream filling from my upper arm.

"Preston's gonna love that."

Pretty sure Dre meant to say that under her breath, but I didn't have time for another witty answer. I glanced up at the clock in the square with a groan.

"Definitely not going to make a good impression today." I crossed the street to the large building where Shaw's office was located. My phone rang again as I opened the door. "Oh, shut up." I checked the directory before I slapped the button on the elevator.

I dug out the baby wipes I kept in my bag for emergencies. I went through half the pack by the time I got to the fourth floor. Cripes, I even had frosting on my damn neck. I was debating taking off my body jewelry since it was on display now, but the door slid open and made the decision for me.

Whatever I'd been prepared for was a million years away from the man standing before me.

Dear goddess, please don't be my boss.

My gaze traveled up and up. He was all angles from his jawline to his broad shoulders to the tapered waist accentuated by the cut of his suit. Even his cheekbones were severe and hollowed out in annoyance. Dammit, he even had the little muscle flex in his upper jawline that said *danger! Danger, I'm pissed off.*

He lifted his chin and looked down his nose at me, which effectively cooled my panties.

Sort of.

I hooked my bag over my shoulder and sauntered out of the elevator. The only thing I could do at this point was try to pull off this outfit.

47

My bracelets shimmied down my arm to brush my hand. The chains of my necklace shifted under my dress and the crystals down my back felt warm. I liked to think they were doing their job to keep all my shit together, but it was probably the heat of the August day.

"Miss Moon?"

"Mr. Shaw." I just knew he was my boss. This was exactly how my day was going.

"You're egregiously late."

I pulled the crushed sack of fritters out of my bag and handed it to him as I walked by. "I'd explain the ridiculous start to my day, but it would probably bore you. Nor would you believe it."

The desk outside the glassed off corner office had to be mine. It had April's energy all over it. I set my bag down on the corner, shot the canvas bag full of sticky sugar cotton under my desk, then leaned against the side.

Mr. Shaw was still standing in front of the elevators, his jaw tight and his eyes blazing, his long fingers holding the crumpled bag away from his suit.

Like a dog's dirty business.

Panty alert again.

What was wrong with me? Had I hit my head and not realized it?

I kind of liked the heat in his gaze. And the attitude. Maybe even the sneer.

I'd assumed I would only find icy disdain from my texts and emails. And yet it was a miracle the glass around the office behind me hadn't shattered from the force of his stare.

He was a rude man, even when he wasn't saying a word. But rather than being infuriated by his annoyance, I was...eager.

Ready to get my spar on with a worthy opponent.

I crossed my legs at the ankle and gripped the side of the desk. *Fake it till you make it, girl.* "Would you like to inform me of my tasks for the day, Mr. Preston Michael Shaw, Esquire?"

CHAPTER FIVE

PRESTON

APRIL HAD INVITED the devil into my serene workplace.

To be fair, I had no knowledge of any supernatural evil at Miss Moon's command. Other than the fact that her so not business-appropriate dress had a slit up her leg to approximately just south of her panties, assuming she was wearing any.

It sure didn't look like she was wearing a bra, considering her nearly indecent top. If she *was* wearing one, I couldn't imagine what the contraption looked like.

Not that I was considering my assistant's underwear choices. I was not that sort of boss. I was merely making note of several irrefutable facts.

One, Ryan G. Moon was inexcusably late, even if she had given me a bakery bag of goods. But that gesture lost points because the bag looked as if it had been doused with grease.

Two, Ryan G. Moon was not dressed in business wear. I couldn't call her outfit casual either, since I doubted anyone wore a dress slit to *there* just to sit around the house.

Perhaps this was part of her calling it a "gig" last week. She'd forgotten what one actually did in an office, so of course she couldn't dress properly for it.

Three, Ryan G. Moon's hair was sheer black. Not dark brown. Pure, unadulterated black and escaping in endless rivulets down her nearly bare back from its messy twist.

Her back wasn't actually bare. As far as material covering it, indeed. But she also wore crisscrossing chains bisected with miniature colored rocks. Before she'd turned to face me, I'd been momentarily blinded when a chunk of rock caught the sun and refracted a rainbow of light.

Perhaps that was her plan. Render me visionless, force sweets upon me, and then I would be at her mercy. Helpless to chide her about being late or being dressed like...*that*. Incapable of even questioning her ability with a spreadsheet or if she knew how to take dictation.

Instead, I stood rooted to the spot, caught in her intoxicating floral scent, reminiscent of a garden after midnight. Surrounded by forbidden flowers I didn't dare pluck.

I really wanted to pluck.

I finally snapped out of her spell and strode into the security of my glass-walled office. And slammed the door.

The bright sunny day beckoned from beyond the wall of windows just behind my desk. Though I rarely ventured outside during the workday, I wanted to get the hell out of there before I did something...rash.

Now what?

She was still out there, waiting for instruction. That was likely a ruse too. She would wait for me to tell her to do something then she would grab one of her chains and render me mute with some witchy stone.

I dropped the bakery bag on my desk and pressed a hand to my temple. I hadn't had anything to drink today. This was likely dehydration. Not coffee—the delivery had not yet arrived, naturally— and not even water. Then again, I had a decanter of bourbon on the wet bar for clients that I'd never once touched myself.

Desperate times.

I splashed a healthy amount into a short glass. Then I tossed it back in one gulp.

It didn't make me feel better but some of the cobwebs cleared away. Just in time for my desk phone to ring, the light for April's dedicated line flashing.

I reached up to loosen my tie. Just a little. Not a full-on destruction of my perfectly composed knot, just enough to allow increased airflow.

So I didn't have to sit down and put my head between my knees.

Calmly, professionally, I took my seat and pressed the button beside the flashing light on the phone. Was it my imagination or had the light become intense since Friday?

"Yes." My tone held no inflection.

"*Yes?* Hello, I'm new here, remember? You gave me nothing to do."

Even her voice sounded like sorcery. Not that I'd forgotten it after listening to her podcast—three episodes in total, but I wasn't counting —but it seemed even worse on the other end of the line.

I'd have to end this call swiftly.

"There is a list."

I heard the obvious sounds of her making a mess on April's desk. "Where? I don't see any—" She huffed out a breath. "Unless you mean this bill from Coffee Emporium with big block letters that says 'call them.'"

"Yes. My delivery is late." And I needed it. Desperately.

"Um, not sure if you're aware, but I'm a legal assistant, not a nursemaid."

"Nursemaids do not check on delayed coffee deliveries. They provide milk."

Right. Because that was just the image I needed in my head only moments after I'd debated whether or not she was wearing a bra.

I didn't do these things. To the point that I was almost smug when it came to other men who seemed less in control of their baser instincts than I was. I liked sex, but it didn't rule me. Women and their wily charms definitely did not.

I couldn't say I'd never been led around my dick—I *was* human, after all, much to my dismay—but it had been a damn long time and not since college when Lissa Luwellan had convinced me we should have sex in the fountain in the town square in the middle of the night.

Then the cops had shown up.

I'd ridden in the back of the police car, soaked wet and frustrated. Lissa had broken up with me the next day, and my father had lectured me on upholding the law, not flagrantly breaking it.

Since then, I'd put sex in the box it belonged in. Often, I handled things myself. Such as Friday night when Ryan G. Moon's auditory porn podcast had turned out to be merely a preview of upcoming attractions.

Ryan's heavy sigh brought me back to my current predicament. "I took this position to do actual work tasks. Besides, calling a coffee place will take me, what, three minutes?"

"So you'll do it?" I couldn't disguise the hope in my question.

Mondays always went better with coffee. This Monday definitely required it.

"Since I was so *egregiously late*, I suppose I can help you out this once, because whoa, grumpy pants without your java, huh?"

I didn't appreciate her emphasis on my words. Nor did I like her calling me *grumpy pants*. But I did enjoy getting my way through whatever means possible.

"Excellent." I clicked off.

I had barely replaced the receiver when the line rang again. How was a person supposed to get any work done around here?

"Yes?"

"Do you say goodbye? Hello?"

"You don't need to say hello, I heard you just fine."

"I was asking if you say goodbye, hello, or any common pleasantries really. I mean, do you know me yet? No. You just expect me to sit down and be a faux April."

I couldn't stop my quick laughter. "Hardly."

"What's that supposed to mean? You don't think I can be as good as April?"

52

I blamed my lack of coffee, extremely long sexual drought, and general discombobulation for the picture that formed in my mind of Miss Moon on her knees beneath my desk.

I shifted in my chair. "I don't make such value judgments, and it doesn't matter in any case, as your employment here will end in," I consulted the gold clock on my desk, "four days, seven hours, and seven minutes."

"Wrong. It's nine minutes."

"Are you saying my clock is wrong?"

"I was late, but don't make it worse than it was. I risked my life to get your stupid donuts. Do you care? Doesn't seem like it. Do you have any heart at all?"

Interest piqued, I took another look at my gifted greasy bag. "You brought the donuts?"

"No. They're fritters."

I hung up on her. Rather gleefully, in fact.

She didn't call back. I wasn't disappointed.

Much.

I focused on expanding my quick hit notes from a client meeting I'd had on Friday afternoon. My tendency was to jot down first impressions then fill in the details later. I'd barely made it halfway down the page when my email dinged.

"Why are you fucking dinging," I muttered, slamming the mouse against the desk as I ignored the email in my box from Miss Moon.

Someone had altered the settings on my email—probably April, for her own amusement—and I was going to rectify it this instant. If I could figure out just how Ryan was bypassing the very clear "no notifications" toggle switch in my mail program.

Another ding sounded. And another. Then it was like a freaking ding fest, my computer nearly shaking from the endless barrage of them.

I picked up the phone and pushed the button for April's direct line.

"Good morning, thank you for calling Shaw, Shaw, and Shaw, Attorneys at Law. Rather pretentious, don't you think? You're all

Shaws here, so why name each of you separately? Were all of you unloved as children?"

"Can I help you?" I asked between gritted teeth.

"Uh, you called me?"

"I called you to avoid reading your eighteen emails." Another one came in as I was speaking. "Do you have them on automatic send or something? One word per missive?"

She ignored my questions. "I've spoken to Coffee Emporium. They regret that your coffee order is unavoidably delayed."

I growled. I simply could not help it. "Until when?"

"Tomorrow morning. However, as a gesture of good faith, they're including more of the little honey stir sticks you enjoyed so much last time. They really appreciated that review you left them."

I harrumphed.

"Hmm, I've never heard of putting honey in coffee. Is that really a thing?"

"No, I lapped it off the thighs of a woman in tech support last month."

She barely paused. "Your law firm has tech support? Why? You only have several lawyers and a few assistants, although I've yet to see anyone but me out here. Did they all quit? Can't say I blame them. The conditions here are deplorable. Have you been reported to the labor board?"

"Thank you and good day. And stop emailing me." I clicked off before she could reply.

The only salient point of her word salad was that I would have to wait until *tomorrow* for my coffee order. What was this world coming to?

Good question, since I had no business talking about honey lapping—even if it was entirely fictional—in the workplace. But what else was I supposed to say? April had already detailed my donut weakness. If I gave Ryan any more ammunition about my preferences for sweets, who knows what she would do with such information?

And she was still emailing me. Over and over. By now, I suspected she really had resorted to one word each, because there was no way she could have that much to say to a man she didn't even know.

I didn't click on her emails. Instead, I put a call into the IT department of the public relations firm on the second floor. Talking about lapping honey from Colleen had given me the idea that maybe she could fix my damn notifications. Quicker than I could, that was for sure.

"What did you break this time, Pres?" The laughter in her voice managed to tease out a smile.

"Nothing. I don't think so, anyway. I keep getting email notifications and I don't want them. You need to make them stop."

Colleen's laughter didn't grate on my nerves like Ryan's. Even in theory, her laughter pissed me off. "This is an easy one. You go into your settings, which is that gray button with the little cog wheel I showed you last time—"

"I did all that," I said impatiently. "She's still emailing me."

"*She?*" Colleen clucked her tongue. "Are you finally dating and holding out on me?"

"No. Absolutely not. Not in this life or any other."

"Well, that was rather vehement." More laughter at my expense.

That was just how this week was going, evidently.

Colleen promised to stop by before lunch, and I ended the call during another flurry of email dings. Then I settled upon a novel solution. Within a few clicks, the soothing sounds of Chopin brought a sense of calm heretofore lacking in my day.

Smiling smugly, I went back to my notes. I worked on them for a while before looking up again, when the tickle in my throat turned to a full-blown need for water. I rose to pour a glass and foolishly decided to look out the window of my office to ascertain Ryan hadn't yet burned down the place. I didn't know what she was doing to occupy herself in lieu of instructions from me, but I hoped she could at least manage to take phone calls without being told to do so, along with dealing with any foot traffic.

One glance into the outer office told me that yes, she was dealing capably with such. Even if the feet in question were hers—as in one propped on the edge of her desk while she painted her toenails and smiled far more warmly at another man than she had at me.

The man was Dexter Shaw. Also known as my little brother.

The affable asshole.

I returned to my desk and pushed the button for April's line. She took three rings to answer. "Hi there. Miss me?"

She sounded breathless and amused. I liked her voice that way too much, despite knowing who had made her smile—and it wasn't me.

"Don't let him take you to lunch."

For a moment, silence reigned on the line. I had a feeling that didn't happen often with Ryan. "Oh, your charming younger brother?" She chuckled. "Dex, were you going to ask me to lunch? PMS says I shouldn't go."

PMS? What the fuck was that all about?

It took me a few seconds to recall my unfortunate initials. No one had ever dared call me that, at least to my face. Leave it to Miss Moon.

Who was grinning up at Dexter while he raked a hand through his dark hair and grinned back. He was probably telling her I had a stick up my ass and I was jealous of him, because of course I was.

The worst of it? He was telling the truth. Everything was easy for him. He didn't have a care in the world, and sometimes it felt as if my shoulders would crack under the weight of all I carried.

"PMS? Oh, he isn't going to like that."

"He doesn't like much from what I can tell."

"Mr. Prim and Proper has never had a nickname. Not a public one, anyway. But he gave me a good idea. Do you have lunch plans, Ry?"

He had already shortened her name. Wasn't that sweet? He was just the best at inter-office relations.

"You know, I don't. I didn't even get breakfast since my fritter was in his sack."

Dex laughed. "Sounds kinky."

Listening to their banter through the phone was akin to hell. If I leaned to the right just far enough, I could catch a glimpse of Ryan painting her big toe and flashing entirely too much leg at my irritating brother. He was looking at her as if she was a tasty snack, if not the whole meal.

And suddenly, I was more than a little tired of watching Dex eat his way through a sea of women. Especially when it involved my assistant.

Temporary assistant, I reminded myself.

"You do have lunch plans, Miss Moon." I cleared my throat. "With me."

She didn't answer right away. "I think I'm busy."

"You are not."

"Says who?"

"Your boss."

"Only temporarily and I'm already counting down the hours."

I hung up.

After that, a couple of things occurred almost simultaneously.

I developed a raging headache which required a double dose of Tylenol. My brother texted me to inquire if I was cool with him "pitching to Ry," to which I did not respond. And possibly blocked his phone number.

Knowing Dex's love of sports references, that question probably hadn't been sexual. But I wasn't taking the chance.

During lunch—which I still could not believe I'd suggested—I was going to make it clear that Ryan understood the strict no fraternization policy.

So strict it just had popped into being a few minutes ago while Ryan was painting on toenail polish that matched her celery green pumps.

Shortly after that, Colleen stepped off the elevator. Since I was watching to see if Dex slunk back to Ryan's desk to try again, I caught Ryan's interaction with Colleen. I couldn't hear what was being said, but Ryan's bright smile faded as Colleen pointed at my door and shook back her efficient brown braid.

I had no reason to be pleased at Ryan's smile disappearing. Yet I was positively sunny when Colleen knocked and opened my door, poking her head in. "Have time for me now?"

"I always have time for you. You know that." If I replied a touch louder than was necessary, so what? I was allowed to express appreciation at a friend doing a favor for me.

Colleen shut the door behind her and propped her hands on her hips. "You neglected to tell me one thing about who was blowing up your email."

"Blowing up is a bit harsh."

"It's a figure of speech, Pres. You need to get out more, you know that?"

"Tell me that after I think you're having a ménage with Ben and Jerry."

That she didn't even blink as she came to my desk said plenty about how long she'd known me. She grabbed my pen and a piece of paper and block-printed a message.

I wasn't sure why Colleen had resorted to notes, but perhaps she suspected Ryan had her ear pressed to the door.

I wouldn't put it past her.

With trepidation, I read what she'd written.

She's a hottie.

I grunted.

"C'mon, you don't think so?"

"She's my assistant while April is on vacation."

"She's sitting at her desk, but not sure she's really assisting you. She's reading *Cosmopolitan*."

I waved it off. "Whatever keeps her busy and not bothering me."

Frowning, she leaned over the desk and touched my forehead as if she was checking for fever. "You okay?"

At that instant, a knock sounded at the door.

It opened before I had a chance of answering in the affirmative.

Not that I would have. I was much safer when Ryan stayed on the other side of the threshold.

Now she was glaring daggers at me as Colleen leaned precipitously across my desk and pulled her hand away from my face.

One part of my brain logged Ryan's reaction as fascinating. The rest of me decided the better part of valor was to dig deeper into my metaphorical hole.

"I'm okay as long as you're here," I said to Colleen, who was not moved by my shenanigans. Then I cocked my head and acknowledged Ryan. "Can I help you, Miss Moon?"

"You sure can, boss." She sailed in and gave Colleen a thin smile before she snatched the bakery bag off my desk. "I know we have lunch soon, but I'm just famished. And you took my fritter."

I was about to tell her to take the bag and go, but she didn't want the bag itself. No, she just withdrew one plump pastry, positively dripping with glaze and caramel. And proceeded to bite in, sending a spray of crumbs into the vee of her dress like roadmap leading to a not-so-buried treasure.

She might as well have said *checkmate*.

Damn, she was beautiful. With her flashing blue eyes, smirk around her mouthful of pastry, and sex dungeon scent, she was dangerous in more ways than I could count.

Probably because watching her eat had sucked all skill at mathematics—and everything else—out of my head.

"Lunch soon." Colleen blinked innocently. "I should hurry up and fix that pesky issue with your computer then. You know, why you called me down here."

I grunted again. I wasn't one to outright lie, especially when I had no clue what the hell I was doing right now.

"I'll just get back to work." Ryan's smile was as close to a non-verbal *fuck you* as I'd ever seen.

It was obscenely hot.

"April needs to come back from vacation," I said as soon as Ryan vacated my office. Which was not fast enough to suit the stiff column in my trousers.

59

I hid it by walking over to my mini bar while Colleen tinkered with my desktop. I had another half glass of bourbon since it was there, and my head was about to explode.

It was up for debate which head of the two would combust first.

"She's been gone, what, half a day? You're in deep."

"This is only my second glass, and a half at that."

"I wasn't referring to your alcohol consumption, although that says plenty." Colleen spun around in the chair to face me. But I didn't do the same, since I was currently willing the pole in my pants not to embarrass me. "Why can't you just ask her out?"

"What?" I sputtered and tried to swallow. "Why would I do a thing like that?"

"Other than you swallowing your tongue as soon as she walked in here, you mean? She sent you so many nice emails too. My favorite was 'your brother is cuter than you.'"

"She did not say that."

"Okay, that's true. She said your brother was sexy. Didn't mention you at all."

Since my cock was now fully deflated, I turned back and glimpsed the twinkle in Colleen's green eyes. "You're not the least bit funny."

"Sure I am. You're just too twisted up to appreciate it right now." Colleen rose and sauntered to the door. "Computer's fixed by the way. You'd toggled the notifications back on just for mail somehow. Should be good now. Catch you later. And good luck with your hottie." At least she lowered her voice for the last part.

As soon as she left, I returned to my client notes. It wasn't long before a knock sounded at the door once more.

Shockingly, Ryan did not wait for my approval to enter.

"Is she your girlfriend?"

Deliberately, I didn't look up from my notes. Between phone calls and texts and emails—including ones not from Ryan, imagine that—I'd thus far gotten approximately no work done today. This was the last Monday I should be jetting off for lunch with a woman I'd yet to spend more than three minutes with in the flesh. But fuck, I was hungry. The smell of that fritter coming from the bakery bag was making me lightheaded.

Or it was those damn night-blooming florals wafting from Ryan's skin. Probably both.

Dammit, she was poking at the bag yet again, toying with the fritter she'd purportedly gotten for *me.*

"Well, you're not eating it," she said when I pinned her with a look.

"I've been busy. Unlike you. See anything good in *Cosmopolitan?*"

She gasped. "Why that traitor. She broke the code of the sisterhood."

I snorted. I couldn't help it. Then I stuck out my hand. "Give me some of that."

She held the bag against her chest. I almost warned her about grease transfer before shrugging it off. At least I couldn't see her cleavage that way. "You don't really want it."

I arched a brow. "Do you want me to beg?"

Ryan eased a hip on the corner of my desk, the one with the mile-high slit. "Do you ever? Seems improbable."

"If I were to start, I doubt it would be over an apple fritter."

"It's really good." Almost gleefully, she took a large bite, and apple filling spilled across her lip. I wanted to lean in and lick it off. See what she tasted like mixed with the fruit. Would she be tart or sweet?

All over.

But I already knew. She would taste like a Granny Smith green apple. A quick tang followed by that delicious finish that made you crave even more.

She was still nibbling and shamelessly licking her fingers, openly enjoying the pastry she'd proffered for me and stolen away. Almost daring me to grab it out of her hand.

Instead, I sat back in my chair and crossed my ankles, watching her without restraint. "Going to leave me a crumb?" The question was lazy, as if I wasn't the slightest bit invested in the outcome.

"Well, you don't want to spoil your appetite."

"No danger of that happening."

She edged her painted nail over a flaky section of crust. "You never answered. Is she your girlfriend?"

"Who?" I was so consumed with watching her fondle that fritter that I truly had no recollection.

"The pretty brunette. Her hair is a shade away from cinnamon."

"Is she pretty?"

"Are you blind?"

"No. I see you quite well. Give me that."

Committing the most unwise act in the history of off-limits office gestures, I rose and leaned forward, planting my hands on the desk. And rather than snagging that purloined bit of pastry with my fingers, I grabbed it with my teeth.

Stunned, she stared at me while I chewed, our heads entirely too close for workplace propriety.

She had a crystal lodged in her belly button. Or freaking close, because yes, her summery dress dipped nearly that low.

The stone was clear. Shimmery. An icy chip against her bronze skin.

"Good?" That husky question made me think many thoughts, and not one of them was about the fritter I'd just swallowed with a damn near orgasmic groan.

"It's buttery," I managed.

"Mmm-hmm."

"Flaky."

"Definitely."

"Just the right amount of caramel coating the apples."

"Moist apples," she agreed, delicately licking the corner of her mouth.

"The moistest." Was that even a word?

Were we still talking about apples? I suspected not. But it had been so long since I'd done this particular dance that my moves were rusty.

What wasn't rusty was my eager cock, threatening to split a seam in my Hugo Boss trousers if she so much as commented on sticky juice.

"Since you've waited so patiently," she licked her lips, "you can have the last bite."

I started to argue. Foolishly, since I really wanted that fritter. It was surprisingly good and would have been even better if I'd been able to eat it off her thighs.

Apparently, that was the body part I was fixated on today.

But she shut me up before I even got going by dangling that last piece over my mouth then sliding it between my lips. Slowly. Like nothing had ever been slid into my mouth before.

At least that I could remember, which wasn't saying much considering I was pretty sure my name was now John Doe.

"What do you think?" She placed her hand close enough to mine on the desktop that our pinkies touched. "Should I pass along your appreciation to Dre?"

I chewed and swallowed. "I'm definitely appreciating."

I had no clue who Dre was. Did not care.

Ryan's eyes were the exact shade of aquamarine, surrounded by the densest darkest lashes. Inky black like her hair. Her dress.

My supposed cold, dead heart that was now practically a glowing ember in my frigging chest.

Her eyelids lowered a fraction. "So...lunch. Where are you taking me?"

To bed.

The thought arrived unbidden into my mind. And then the followup.

Why wait for a bed when we have so many convenient walls? And this handy desk...

Without warning, her eyes popped wide. She slid off the corner of the desk so fast that she tripped and would've landed on her ass if I hadn't grabbed her wrist—and nearly suffered a contact burn from the fiery bolt that traveled up my arm.

What the hell?

"Are you okay?" I hoped I didn't sound as dazed as I felt.

"Fine. Dandy. I just need mouthwash. My dentist freaks if I don't spit—I mean, gargle after sweets. I had cavities as a kid, so I have to

63

listen to him. Sorry. Bye." She ran out of the office, practically limping, and slammed the door with the same gusto I had after meeting her in the flesh approximately two hours and twenty-nine minutes ago.

I sagged into my desk chair. I was breathing hard, my pulse chaotic. The honeyed sweetness on my lips tasted so delicious that pressing them together made my dick throb.

My fucking fingers were still tingling. Who was that woman? Had she put some kind of sex hex on me? Was that a thing?

I pulled up Google and was typing in those very words when my email dinged.

Bypassing the other fifty emails from her, I opened the latest.

We can't go to lunch. I mean it this time. I'm not hungry. Too much fritter.

For probably the first time all day, I smiled. Slowly, like a shark scenting blood. I sent back a reply.

We're going to lunch. You need some protein to balance all that sugar.

With her usual speed, she responded.

Actually, I'm allergic to protein.

I volleyed back.

To salt too?

I received her quickest answer yet.

Unfortunately, yes. All I eat is apples and whitefish. Sorry.

Whitefish it is. Be ready to go at precisely 12:45. I'll make reservations.

And I knew just the place that was far enough from town we would never be spotted by curious onlookers.

Not that we were doing anything untoward. Of course not. This was a business lunch.

I brought up a fresh Word document. Said lunch would start with this To Do list for my brand new temporary assistant.

If she wanted to be told what to do, I would abide.

CHAPTER SIX

PRESTON

WE WALKED into The Longshoreman seafood restaurant at nearly one-thirty, a full half hour past our reservation.

Silly me, I'd forgotten one of us could never be on time. I just didn't realize that didn't only apply to arriving in a timely fashion for gainful employment.

"You're still glowering," Ryan hissed somewhere near my shoulder.

She was the perfect height for me, a rarity among the women I'd dated. A fact that was neither here nor there.

"This is just my face. My apologies if you don't like it."

"Well, my apologies if you got pissy because I was late due to the heel on one of my *favorite* shoes snapping on your stupid uneven floor."

"My floor is not uneven. Perhaps you shouldn't wear such high heels if you aren't able to walk in them."

"I can walk in them just fine. Getting your stupid sweets this morning probably weakened them structurally. When I was almost flattened by the bike messenger, you unfeeling toad."

Her ire was still as blatant as it had been on the fifteen-minute drive from my office building in Kensington Square to the opposite side of Crescent Cove. The ride had been chock full of tense silence punctuated by frustrated sighs. Mostly hers. Along with the occasional comment about my choice of vehicle.

Apparently, she didn't like beige as a color option, so I was tempted to buy a beige suit just to annoy her. Even if it violated my personal preferences.

Irritating Miss Moon would be worth it.

"Perhaps you'll be able to speak in coherent sentences once we get some food into you." And into me, since my stomach was roaring loudly enough for the other patrons to hear.

"I'm not hungry."

"Suit yourself. Watch me eat." I put my hand on the small of her back and nudged her forward to speak to the maître d' when it was finally our turn. "I've already done that once today myself."

"You weren't watching me eat. You were just watching me."

The sleek redheaded maître d' cocked a brow. "Mr. Shaw, how lovely to see you…and your companion."

"My assistant, Tanya. I have a reservation. We're regrettably late."

"Egregiously." Ryan tapped her nails on her huge green bag and flashed me a wholly insincere smile.

"Ah, yes. We reserved your table. In fact, I was about to phone you. You're never late." Tanya shot Ryan a look.

"He got the dregs from the temp pool." Ryan smiled again. "But considering what he's paying me, can't really be too surprised."

"You don't even know what I'm paying you." I gazed at the side of her stupidly beautiful face. "But I can still pay you less, so keep it up," I added against her ear.

It required me not breathing in her sex scent, but I was devoted to the cause.

She stared straight ahead. "I don't need your money, Fancy Pants."

Tanya cleared her throat and grabbed a pair of menus. "Lee, can you see Mr. Shaw and his assistant to the free table near the fireplace?" Her lips curved. "Mr. Shaw always likes to sit near the fire."

Lee stepped forward and aimed a devastating smile at me. "Mr. Shaw, this way, please."

"Do I exist? Do I still have a corporeal form?" Ryan patted her sides and slapped at her arms as if she was fighting off a bug infestation.

I fought a grin as I nudged her forward on her unsteady heels. "Don't worry, Miss Moon, I see you quite fine," I said in an undertone.

The glare she sent my way made my grin widen.

Then I looked up, and the person I saw wasn't Ryan. Wasn't anyone I wanted to see, especially in that scenario.

My father was seated in a cozy booth on the other side of the fireplace. And he wasn't alone. A gorgeous blond who looked young enough to be his daughter—young enough to be my sister—was feeding him shrimp. The smile he had for her was one he hadn't given my mother in ages, if ever.

Wait.

Not just any blond.

She threw her head back with a throaty laugh. A very put on one that she never used in the office. My father's administrative assistant, Courtney, was smoothing her fingers down the lapel of his suit in a far too familiar way.

Lee said something as she brought us to our table. I didn't hear her. Didn't hear Ryan though her lips moved as I unbuttoned my suit jacket and took the seat opposite her.

My head was full of white noise.

"Are you listening to me? Preston." I glanced up as she leaned over to place her hand on my arm. "Are you all right?"

Same white-hot electric reaction as earlier, I noted dully.

I had to tell my mother.

She couldn't live with a lie. I couldn't be complicit in it.

"Preston," Ryan said gently, curling her fingers around my rock-hard forearm. It felt as if all my muscles were locked for battle. "Look at me for a second."

I looked. I didn't know the source of the power she held over me, but the glow of it radiated from her jeweled eyes. Somehow she eased my stampeding heartbeat and cooled the sweat that had already pooled at the base of my spine.

All at once, I was steady. And back to idiotic.

"Did you put a sex hex on me? I didn't finish Googling."

For a long moment, she just stared back. Then the corners of her lips twitched.

"No. I don't know what exactly that is, although it sounds intriguing."

"I may have made it up. I just want you to know I don't act like… this."

I wasn't the same as my father, coming on to my employees. I didn't take advantage of my position.

I wouldn't.

More twitching. *"This?"*

"I don't banter. I don't eat pastry out of strange women's hands. And I normally wouldn't try to pretend my father isn't with a woman who is *not* my mother eating shrimp and probably figuring I can handle his divorce, because hey, that's my specialty, right?" I let out a bitter laugh and spread my napkin over my lap as our server returned. I couldn't seem to add the appalling bonus level slight of a clandestine workplace romance.

Much to my shock, Ryan took a cursory look at the menu and ordered for both of us. Worse? The orange chicken she chose for me was my favorite dish here. And she did not order whitefish, but a medium rare steak.

The last thing she asked for was a bottle of Riesling from a local winery, Apothecary Wines. I would've protested that business lunches didn't include alcohol, if I didn't currently have bigger issues in my life.

Like my happy childhood going up in flames.

I refused to look past Ryan's shoulder in their general direction. I wouldn't give him the satisfaction, the faithless bastard.

"Stop looking prune-faced. I didn't steal your balls and offer them up as garnish. I just ordered for us because you needed a minute. Don't fret." She patted the back of my hand. "You're still the alpha cock, darling."

Stuck between a laugh and a grimace, I pointed at her. "You're never to say that word in my presence."

She caught her tongue between her teeth. "Which?"

"You know which. Bad enough you said it on that podcast."

"Oh, yeah? You listened to all of my golden cock reading?"

I glanced around then decided I didn't give a shit if some of these upper crust-types heard us discussing dicks with our lunch. Apparently, my give a damn had busted upon seeing my sneaky father. "I listened. It said you were going to get lucky. Has that happened yet?"

"Not the lucky part yet, but I'm beginning to wonder," she muttered. "Gotta say it doesn't look the way I figured it would."

The server returned with our Riesling and a couple of glasses. Once she'd poured and left again, I took a long sip and decided the sweet apple and pear finish was just what this meal needed. And quite possibly, my sanity. "I normally have one glass of bourbon a week."

"Oh, no." She smacked her cheek. "A rule broken in the big book of them?"

"I had a glass and a half this morning. Wonder why?"

She pressed her lips together. "Your perfect little world blown apart by a hex kitten?"

I shouldn't laugh at her. It was only encouraging bad behavior. Problem was, I was cruising hard to be very bad indeed.

"I never had these problems with April."

"No?" Ryan picked up her glass and peered at me over the rim. "Why do you think that is?"

Because I don't have a visceral response to her words on a computer screen. And her voice. And her...everything.

I rubbed my temples as my headache warned of a reappearance. "She's an altogether different sort of woman."

"She definitely is," Ryan said cheerfully. "She said you were staid."

I wasn't going to rise to her bait.

I simply was not.

"Trust me, some of the thoughts I've had today were the furthest thing from that."

Ryan took a long sip and then set down her glass. Rather than touch me, she just placed her hand close to mine. "Tell me exactly what happened between the foyer and when we sat down. Keep in mind I don't know any of the players."

My first instinct was to *deny, deny, deny.* My second was to *not* lie, since I didn't want to be like my father in any way.

I could have misconstrued what I saw. Maybe they were having a work lunch just like we were. Perhaps he was checking the shrimp for doneness. Maybe they were doing a taste test. Or he'd sprained all his fingers, and she was helping him.

Right.

"Seated behind you on the opposite side of the fireplace is a distinguished older man with salt and pepper hair and a young blond female. She was feeding him shrimp."

His assistant.

When I berated myself for workplace impropriety, I had no clue that it was most assuredly something I would have to look into for the entire firm.

Like father like son?

My gut twisted into foul knots.

"Okay."

"The older man is my father. In case you didn't realize my age, the young blond is definitely not my mother."

Ryan pursed her lips before immediately knocking her silverware to the floor. "Oops!" She bent over to retrieve it and spent a moment checking out the couple at the other table as she straightened. "He's definitely hitting it to her." She shook her head. "Watch them and tell me when she goes to the bathroom."

"What? Why?"

"I'm going to have words with her." She propped her chin on her fist. "Which do you think is better? 'I'm curious if his STD results have come in' or 'how is he acclimating after that prison stint?'"

I didn't expect to laugh. Then again, I'd been caught between annoyance, laughter, and lust since the first time her name appeared in my inbox. Had it only been a week?

The blond walked away from her booth. Had she overheard us talking about bathroom breaks?

Ryan popped up from her seat.

"No. Don't. Ryan." I lurched over the table and grabbed her hip when she started to take a step.

My fingers tingled as I upped the pressure. Heat flashed up my wrist. At this point, I wasn't even surprised.

Touching Ryan was an electrical event every damn time.

She gazed down at me through her darkly lashed eyes. "If you wanted to touch, you just had to ask."

I didn't let go. If anything, I gripped that soft handful of flesh harder. Possibly leaving marks she'd remember later. Maybe even burns.

Surely I couldn't be the only one who felt that incredible warmth every time we touched? I didn't dare ask, but from the way she trembled faintly in my hold, she had to be feeling *something.*

Her throat moved and she slicked her tongue over her lips. "Don't like the STD question? I could pretend to be an ex of his and slap her and call her nasty names. That'd probably work too."

"Sit. Please."

"You going to unhand me first?"

I did, reluctantly. I took my seat again as she sat in hers, and then let out a long breath. "I appreciate the gesture. Truly. But he's your boss too."

"Temporarily. And if he's a sea cretin, maybe I don't want to work for him. That ever occur to you?"

"No, because I didn't know you had an aversion to sea cretins."

"I do. They give me hives." She shuddered. "Easy enough to tell someone you're not feeling it anymore and you need to go."

I picked up the napkin that had fallen off my lap and spread it over my trousers. "Yes, when there isn't a million-dollar fortune at risk. That makes it harder."

She didn't even blink. "Are you excusing what he's doing? You didn't look like you were cool with it when you sat down. Or is that the bro code kicking in?"

"Bro code? He's my father. The woman he's hurting is my mother."

"Then?" She snapped out her napkin over her lap.

"He's a divorce lawyer. I'm not going to say we become immune to endings, but we definitely see how transient relationships can be." I jerked a shoulder. "People aren't forever, but money lasts a good long while."

"Nothing is forever. Especially not money. You can't take it with you. Unless someone forgot to tell you that."

"No, but you can't take supposed love with you either."

"Supposed, huh?" She shook her head, but not as if she disapproved of what I was saying. More like she was disappointed in me.

Hot on the heels of my father's deception, that stung.

"Let's just say I'm not a believer in Valentine's Day. This is not helping my outlook."

"You sound jaded as hell."

I had been privy to far too many broken relationships, many of which ended due to tawdry extramarital affairs, frequently with staff. No wonder I took work boundaries so seriously.

I smoothed my hand over my napkin. "Yeah, well, do my job for as long as I have and see how you feel."

"So don't do it anymore. If it doesn't feed your soul, let it go."

The laugh that cracked out of my chest was loud enough to make the couple beside us look our way. For all I knew, my father had heard me too.

I didn't care. I wasn't the one who should be hiding, even if I'd traveled to the other side of Crescent Cove in case anyone saw me lunching with my brand new assistant and assumed things they shouldn't.

Guess the joke was on me.

"If you're able to construct your life that way, you're lucky. I'm not. A role was waiting for me when I was born, and I stepped into it."

The compassion that softened her expression made my shoulder blades itch. "Your brother must have too. But he enjoys his work."

"Oh, you know that much about him already, hmm?"

She gave a dainty shrug, and her spaghetti straps slipped a fraction lower on her shoulders. "We chatted for a few minutes."

"Before he asked you out."

"Actually, you asked me out before he did." She smiled serenely as our server rolled a covered cart to our table. "To lunch," she added while I stared at her.

I waited to speak until the server set down our lunches and left. "This isn't a date. It's a working lunch."

"Right."

"It is," I insisted.

"Silly me. Here I thought you were staking your claim, in deed if not words. You know, pissing on my tree before your brother could."

I didn't know what part of that to unpack first. "Absolutely not. Fraternization is vigorously frowned upon at Shaw, Shaw, and Shaw, Attorneys at Law."

Hypocrite. The voice in my head was even louder than the drowning waves of lust this unusual woman inspired in me.

"It's frowned upon in marriages too, I believe, and I know of one Shaw who likes to bend the rules there."

"One too many rules. The blond in question is also his admin."

Her exotically arched eyebrow spiked higher. "Not only did he go for another cookie jar, but he has doubly sticky fingers. And you thought you were a bad boy."

I didn't know how to respond. I hadn't done anything as out of character as my behavior today since college, and look where that had gotten me?

She took a bite of her steak and let out an orgasmic moan.

"Good?" I asked in a strangled voice.

It went well with my equally strangled cock being imprinted by the angry teeth of my fly. My ardor should have cooled thanks to this ugly situation I'd found myself in, and yet…no. Nothing had cooled at all.

"Delicious." She batted her ridiculously gorgeous eyes at me. "When does the work start?"

Instead of digging into my lunch, I withdrew a long sheaf of folded papers from the inside pocket of my suit jacket. Wordlessly, I passed them across the table.

Her eyebrow did that artful arch again as she began paging through the hefty document.

Granted, only the first page or so consisted of genuine tasks I expected her to complete this week. The last two pages had been borrowed from a free legal resource I'd found online with tips to make your law office work smarter, not harder. One suggestion was to use a white board and Post-It notes to visually shift tasks from the to do column to the done column as things were completed. That seemed like something she'd like.

Especially since they recommended including notes with inspirational woo-woo phrases among the work ones. Pithy quotes such as, "when life gets tough, turn your lemons into lemonade and add a garnish."

How terribly helpful. But we were all just trying to set our souls free. Or some such bullshit.

"I'm only your assistant for a week."

"I know and there are so many issues of *Cosmopolitan* to read. And all ten toes with nails to repaint." I took a bite of my orange chicken and nearly let out a moan of my own before going back for more.

"You're the one who flounced this morning before giving me actual work to do. Although it took some time to craft this, didn't it?" She shook her head. "Make sure the water carafe in the waiting lounge is replenished twice daily? Seriously? I thought you'd mention something about that godawful filing system. I don't know how you find anything in that records room. Dusty boxes of old client information going back to when, 1975? Those people could be dead."

"My father started the firm in 1992. And those files are confidential. Did you sign an NDA?"

"Did you give me one?"

I could answer that in the negative. Upon first sight of her, my system had gone into lockdown.

Potential lust override. Abort!

"You'll be signing one as soon as we get back." I started plowing through my baby peas, since my chicken was now merely a puddle of orange glaze.

If I'd been alone, I just might have licked the plate. Since I couldn't lick her and still face myself in the morning, why not?

"Oh, goody. My excitement is palpable. Can you tell?" She pushed aside the sheaf of documents and went back to her steak, eating with a gusto I had to appreciate.

I less appreciated how she downed two glasses of wine in short order, but perhaps her soul felt trapped. I didn't see how since her dress was so...airy, but I was determined not to notice.

Even if I caught quite a few men checking her out. I may or may not have incinerated them with the power of my mind as they ambled past our table.

"Do you have a suggestion about improving the filing system?"

I didn't think she'd have an answer. Or that she'd be so animated in sharing it that the sparkling crystals on her many necklaces would move with her body, catching and refracting little bursts of light. I was mesmerized by those shifting hues against the warmth of her skin.

Couldn't help imagining wrapping her wrists in thin, fragile chains laced with those stones and pulling on them as I drove into her from behind.

"Are you staring at my tits?" she demanded, breaking the spell. "I'm not saying I mind, but if we've reached dessert, I'd appreciate more eye candy than your red tie."

The cleared throat beside us was my warning someone had approached us—and not from the direction I'd anticipated. My father was staring at me with clear disapproval.

Me. As if *I* was out to lunch with my girlfriend while stepping out on my wife.

"Good afternoon. I didn't expect to see you here, Preston."

"I just bet," I muttered.

My father extended a hand toward Ryan. "And you are?"

"Ryan Moon." She didn't hold out her hand, just glowered in his direction. "I know all about you."

"Oh, is that so? I know about you too. You're my son's assistant."

"Temporary," we said in unison.

"Even so, lines exist for a reason."

I couldn't say I was struck speechless by his hypocrisy—okay, yes, I was struck speechless by his hypocrisy.

Ryan, however, had no such issue.

"Why, you pig. You're cheating on your wife with your assistant, and you have the balls to accuse your son of impropriety?" She jerked to her feet and pulled out a large, gleaming hunk of rock that she held in front of her as if she was warding off evil spirits. "I'm getting out of here. This room is filled with bad energy."

She dug into her purse and tossed a wad of bills on the table before doing exactly what she'd accused me of this morning.

She flounced.

CHAPTER SEVEN

I SHOULDERED MY DOOR OPEN, juggling two bottles of wine as I shoved in the case waiting on my doorstep with my foot. I'd forgotten about April's promised wine delivery, but I didn't think I'd have trouble finishing them all. Then I would attach myself to the nearest rehab clinic to recover from both the booze and my new boss.

My purse slid down my arm and thudded to the floor. I flung my emergency pair of ballet flats into my living room—my stupid heels had been beyond repair—then headed straight for the cabinet for my wine cup. Obviously, glasses were not a good idea today.

"Not even gonna feel guilty." I grabbed some ice and it clunked against the thermal sides of my sparkly purple cup. I kicked the box of wine closer to my fridge before wrestling it open. I loaded two bottles to chill and cracked open the one I'd bought on my way home.

"I can't believe him," I muttered. It was a miracle I wasn't shouting.

The day had been chaos from start to finish. Dust coated me from my braids to the tops of my feet, courtesy of the boxes of files I'd attacked post-lunch.

Screw his NDA. He hadn't asked me to sign it yet, and I certainly hadn't reminded him. He was lucky I hadn't quit on the spot at the restaurant.

I'd stormed out of the restaurant on my wobbly heels, hopped an Uber back to the office, and proceeded to lock myself in the file room. Cataloging 1992 hadn't exactly been in my packet—dude, seriously, a packet—of duties, but I'd needed something to take my mind off the shitshow that was lunch.

How was I supposed to look Isaac Shaw in the face after knowing he'd been literally cheating on his wife across from us?

With his assistant.

I'd doubted Preston could clench his ass any tighter, but he'd proved me wrong after discovering his father's indiscretion. That was an extra slap with all the energy humming between us.

Ugh. Now we were an *us.* I didn't want to be the united front with Preston against the senior Shaw, but PMS's eyes had been so...

Nope. Not going to think about that right now.

I sloshed wine in my cup and took a long swig before refilling and putting everything away.

Before I did anything else, I needed to rid myself of this day. A total cleansing, spiritual and actual.

I took my wine into the shower with me and rinsed off the dust. It was even in my hair. I hated washing my hair more than twice a week, let alone twice a day. I tucked a towel around me and grabbed one for my crazy mop then sighed.

My dress and jewelry stared at me from where I'd left them on the floor as I stepped out of the stall. It was tempting to leave it all there, but my desire to keep my small space tidy won out over my mini-tantrum.

Gently, I detangled the chains of my rainbow fluorite, even though it had failed me spectacularly today. Not that it was its fault. Actually, I wondered how much worse the day would have been without it.

I padded across my apartment to my altar and set it onto the jewelry tree in the window for a little sunshine recharging. I made a pitstop in the kitchen to refill my wine again—the tumbler was small, dammit—and ate three pieces of cheese. That was totally enough for dinner.

Sure.

When I was dry enough, I put on yoga pants and one of my loosest shirts. I quickly braided my hair as I paced up and down the main living space.

The shower should have washed off my mood. This was my sacred space. It usually soothed me immediately and not just because of the specific network of crystals and diffusers I'd created with a bonus bit of sage work. I usually made sure to kick this kind of energy off me before I entered.

Now the vibe in my sanctuary was all off because my nerves were a jangling mess of lust, anger, and something else. The lust part was very annoying.

Usually in this situation—not that I'd ever been *quite* in this situation before—I'd just bang it out with the dude. Sometimes an energy exchange was all it was.

With PMS, it was a damn fireball and I wasn't looking to get burned, thank you very much.

I grabbed my yoga mat and sat down in the pale stripe of sun at the center of my apartment. I needed to meditate.

Desperately.

I drew in a long, slow breath and let it out. Another one as I visualized myself sinking into my mat, connecting with the ground as each of my chakras opened like a flower. I filled myself with calm, expelling the anger.

My phone rang.

I opened one eye. "Seriously?"

I lifted my shoulders and sat up straight, closing my eyes once more. "Just ignore it. Orange flower, Ryan." Another deep breath.

Luna's text tone went off.

She could wait. She'd understand.

Another message.

I dropped onto my back with a groan then rolled to my knees. I didn't even have the strength to stand up. "Pathetic."

Another text came through as I crawled across the room to my purse by the door. This time, it was PMS.

"Ignore." I stabbed the screen. I was tempted to turn the whole damn thing off, but it rang as I stared at it. Luna's sweet face and blond curls filled the screen.

"Hello?"

"What the hell, girl? Aren't we meeting tonight?"

I'd totally spaced out about recording tonight. Crap. "I'm sorry, Lu. I got home from work later than I thought I would."

"Oh, right." Her voice went sly. "Working for sexy texter guy. Is April's boss hot? I can't believe we've never bugged her at work and met this guy."

"His texts weren't hot."

A little unprofessional maybe, but not that hot.

Okay, maybe a tiny bit.

"Hmm. So, is *he* hot?"

I staggered to my feet and rescued my cup for one more refill. "If you think a repressed suited-up dude in need of a surgical scale removal of the stick up his ass is cute, sure."

"Hmm."

"Stop with the hmm. There is no hmm."

"Is he tall, dark, and yummy?"

"He's tall."

"Well, that's already giving him some points. Can you stare him in the eye or do you have to look up?"

I gnawed on the corner of my bottom lip. "Look up."

"With heels?"

"Yes, with heels."

"What did you wear?"

"Why do you care?"

"Because I want to know if you went all witchy tarot girl on him or played nice."

Curling up on the couch, I pulled a pillow onto my lap and rested my chin on top. "I started off very professional. He would have had absolutely no idea I was wearing my chakra chains down my back if it hadn't been for that stupid bike chick and the donuts."

"Okay, back it up. Donuts?"

"Yes. I was running late—"

"Shocker."

"Shut up. Do you want to hear this or not?"

"I'm sorry. Go on."

"I went to The Honey Pot."

"Oh, you really must have been late. Or you were trying to impress him…"

"Can I continue?"

Luna cleared her throat, which suspiciously sounded like a laugh. "Oh, yes, please."

I hugged the pillow tighter as I slumped on the couch. "You know those movies where you see the girl flipping a box of pastries in the air, and everything goes *splat?*"

Luna snorted. "Only on Hallmark movies."

"Yeah, well, reality is much squishier and messier. Though there *was* a hot guy to help me up."

"That doesn't sound so bad."

"Yeah, but he's already into Dre. Could practically scent the pheromones in the air. He was ready to try out *her* honey pot."

"Is that so?" Luna hummed in appreciation. "Dre could use it."

"Truth. The whole thing was rather adorable. Something was different about him."

"Bad vibes?"

"No, just…different. Anyway, this maniac bike messenger tried to take me out."

"Those are still a thing?"

"Evidently." I punched the pillow and tried to get comfortable. "I appreciate your concern."

Her musical laugh came across the airwaves as I put her on speaker. "I'm sorry. You okay?"

"Just my pride and maybe my hip." I rubbed at it absently. It was a little sore. "Luckily, there's plenty of padding there."

"Girl, we all wish we were as lush and beautiful as you are."

"Don't try to butter me up now." I picked at the fringe on the pillow. "So my respectable business wear was toast."

"Did you say you were wearing your body chain thing? Dude, that is super hot."

"It's to balance—"

"Whatever. You know that's hot as fuck. You sure you didn't wear that to toy with him?"

I sat up. "It was armor, dammit. I had to go into that stuffy law office. Besides, it was under my sweater. He would never have known it was there."

"Except that it drapes in the front too. It's literally a network of chains that go around your boobs."

"Okay, so it was a little sexy, but it was mostly hidden. And I wore it for myself, not him."

"Hmm."

I curled my arms around my middle. "Stop *hmming* me."

"You're awfully pouty." I heard shuffling happening.

"No, I'm not. What are you doing?"

"Pulling cards."

"You don't have to do that." I popped up from the couch and snatched my AirPods from the little charging nook on my end table. I tucked them in my ears so I could pace as I talked.

"Obviously, we need to do a little card therapy."

"No, we really don't."

"Then I definitely do since you're so wound up."

"No, it's not that. I just don't think I need it."

"Whenever you think you don't, you really do."

I nibbled on the corner of my thumbnail. "We have podcast stuff."

"It can wait." Luna was a bridge shuffler so all I could hear was the snap and riffle of cards as she did her usual routine. I could see her in my head. Sitting cross-legged on her massive pink floor pillow, her short table in front of her.

The *snap-snap-snap* of cards came through my earbuds as she laid them out.

"What spread are you doing?"

"A love spread."

The way she emphasized *love* in a singsong voice made my thighs clench. "We are not involved that way."

"Not yet."

Damn these super good AirPods. I could hear every card she set down. How big was the stupid spread? "Not ever. He's my boss."

"Yeah, for a week."

"And then I'll never see him again."

"Best time to get that *boom-chica-wow-wow* out of your system."

"No one says that."

"Doesn't matter, you get the reason behind it. Besides, this spread says *woowee* on fire, girl."

I reached for my wine and took a fortifying sip. "What? Why?"

I heard rustling. "Okay, I'm coming over. This is just too much to do here on the phone."

"You don't have to do that." I tapped my AirPod. "Luna?" I went over to my phone, and yep, she was gone.

My stomach rumbled its displeasure from no food. I'd gotten a few bites of my steak lunch before Pig Shaw came over and ruined my appetite, and the few bites of cheese I'd had upon arriving home hadn't done much.

Foraging in my fridge was close to fruitless. In the end, I went with more wine and a pair of Pop Tarts with a bag of Boom Chicka Pop for when Luna arrived.

I dumped a bunch of the sea salt caramel popcorn in one of my reusable bags and downed my Pop Tarts like a starving woman using wine as a chaser. There was a knock just as I was wiping down my table.

"Since when don't you just walk in?" I opened the door to find Luna with two huge bags in her arms and her crossbody boho bag stuffed to the gills. "My day wasn't *that* bad." I grabbed one of the bags.

"Cards say otherwise. And your freaking glowing aura. Girl, you are in trouble."

"Isn't it *'you're in danger, girl'*?" I parroted the way Whoopi Goldberg said it in *Ghost*.

"I don't think spirits are coming for your soul." She gave me a once-over. "I hope."

"Oh, stop."

Luna smiled hugely and put down her bags before enveloping me in one of her bear hugs, which pretty much put her face in my boobs. "Goddess, you smell good."

"Thanks." I'd doused myself in one of my essential oil blends to try to get myself out of my funk. It wasn't working. Even my chunky amethyst pendant couldn't get rid of this bitchy mood. Maybe I should invest in a black tourmaline suit.

She slung her huge bag off her back and unearthed a few pouches of crystals along with her wand. Then she pulled out her decks and a bottle of wine.

"I have wine."

She shrugged. "I wanted to try this new one. It's a witchy wine maker from Luna Falls. I mean, the town has my name. I had to try it." She lifted the bottle. *Apothecary Wines* was in a hand-drawn font scrawled over the front with an ink drawing of a pretty cove and waterfall with a full moon above it. She tipped the bottle upside down. "It has amethyst and clear quartz blown into the glass."

"Wow."

"I know, right? I'm pretty much in love with the little pop up they had in town. The winery was more on the fringes of the town." She righted the bottle and set it on the table. "We'll have to take a trip. There's a really cool crystal shop down the street."

I grabbed the bottle. "Kinda crazy that you brought it over. I just ordered some of this for lunch."

Her arms jangled as she reached into her bag for more treasures. "For lunch? That's my kind of meal."

I laughed. "No, for PMS and I when we were talking work."

She glanced at me. "Work and wine on your first day? Hmm."

"Do not start that again."

Shrugging, she gestured to all the pouches on the table. "I have many pretties for you."

"You don't have to buy me stuff, Lu." I plopped into the chair and pulled my foot up against my butt to rest my chin on my knee.

"So says the Debbie Downer." She pulled out another huge bubble-wrapped piece and tore into the tape. "I knew I'd gotten this for you for a reason. Just didn't know it at the time." She spun the wrapped piece out until a blue and white skull was revealed. "Meet George."

I laughed and cupped the dome of the sodalite skull. I could feel the calming influence already. Most of the crystals I had were gifts from Lu, other than the few I picked out myself. She had a knack. "Nice to meet you, George. You will look very pretty on my altar."

"Right? I knew it would be perfect to pair with Julia."

I shook my head, my mood already brightening from her presence. How could it not? She was pure sunshine.

Her short blond hair was in spiky space buns wrapped in magenta old school bubblegum-sized ball hair ties. Her lips were a matching pink and sparkles winked on her eyelids. A pair of denim cutoffs brushed the tops of her thighs, short enough that the pockets peeked from the bottoms. Three layers of tank tops and five layers of chains and crystals made up the rest of her outfit. A lacy see-thru shirt tied around her waist added to the retro 90's ensemble. Magenta Doc Martens and cute lacy-topped white socks peeking from the top of her tall boots completed the look.

I picked up George and put him beside Julia, the amethyst skull I'd bought when I wanted to boost my intuition enough to open a virtual practice. I'd been doing parties and fairs here and there, but when I finally became serious about reading cards for people, I'd had to do a lot of work to believe I was worthy to do it.

Reading cards for teenagers to fit in was one thing, but to actually heed the call to do it as a spiritual practice was very different. It wasn't just about me anymore.

I murmured a few words and set some incense burning to welcome him to my home. By the time I got back to Luna, she had a crystal circle set up, wine poured, and the spread laid out.

"You weren't kidding about this one." I tapped the Ace of Wands, the center card of her wide diamond-shaped spread.

She slapped my hand away. "No reading my cards. You know the rules."

I lifted the mason jar she'd filled for me with the new wine. No regular wine glasses for us. "Sorry."

"Reading for tarot readers like you is the worst."

"It is not." I took a drink and licked my lips. "Mmm. I had something different from them today. Riesling. That was good, but this is delicious."

"Right? New favorite wine." She took a sip of her own and shifted my chair until I was cocked her way. "Normally, I'd do this on the podcast, but these cards are a little crazy."

"Definitely not announcing any of this shit on our podcast."

I didn't mention PMS had listened to at least part of an episode, which was entirely my fault. I had invited him into our world, but I hadn't expected he might want to hang out there.

"Announcing? Our listeners are our family."

"Maybe so, but kooky Aunt Edna doesn't need to hear about my... stuff."

"You have an Aunt Edna? Why didn't I know this? Is she a fan?" Luna was already whipping out her phone. "I'll send her a Tramp pack. What's her address?"

I rolled my eyes. "Metaphorically speaking. I don't have an Aunt Edna."

"Oh. Bummer."

"Secondly, I am not interested in getting involved with PMS."

Her musical laugh filled my kitchen. "That really is such a great nickname. And it fits his cards." She ignored my declaration and tapped a short, sparkly nail on the uppermost card. "All this Queen of Swords energy for both of you? You might as well each be wearing a forcefield of emotions. It's gonna be a rocky one, but lots of orgasms."

"Luna!"

"What? There's lot of orgasms in this little setup here. Wands for all the bang time stuff." She took another sip of her wine. "You know, physically speaking. But wow, there is so much mental energy. Then again, not surprising since you're all wand and sword energy to begin with. Impulsive girl with a lockbox on her heart."

She tapped the Three of Swords. "But this is complicated. See, actually, you both have lockboxes. That should be interesting."

I leaned forward, clutching my glass. "What's the placement?"

"Differences between you."

I gave a sharp laugh. "Fits. He doesn't believe in love at all. Divorce lawyer."

"You are thinking about a relationship! I knew it."

"No, it's just an observation."

"Hmm."

"Would you cut that out?"

She reached for the popcorn. "Girl, it's obvious he's got you twisted up. I don't need the cards to tell me that."

"It's more that I have to work for a man who is definitely repressed as hell."

"Yeah, Justice card is right there for all his tightwad vibes. But I don't know. You guys have a lot of stuff going on. And your aura is usually a pretty steady violet and right now, you're a neon red. He's got you all juicy, doesn't he?"

"Gross."

She shrugged. "I didn't mean that. Though I bet you won't need that little drawer of bonus lube to get your rocks off with him."

"Hello? No one is getting any rocks off."

"Hmm."

"You say *hmm* one more time and I'm going to jam your wand up your nose."

"So red." She gathered the cards and started throwing more.

I got up from the table and the room spun a little. I definitely needed real food. "How about we order some Chinese?" I dug through my menu drawer.

"Veggie Lo Mein for me."

I glanced back at her. "Since when are you a veg?"

"Just trying it out."

I frowned at her.

"Okay, so my shorts are a little tight."

I laughed and snagged the correct menu and hip-checked the door closed. "*Ow.* I really hit the pavement hard." I rubbed my hip and tried to ignore the embedded soreness. Almost like a burn.

"Yeah?" She dug into her bag, "I have some CBD oil balm that helps. Let me see."

"I can put it on myself, thanks."

"Well, let me see if it needs more than the balm, silly."

I rolled my eyes and lifted my shirt.

"Um, are those finger marks?"

I glanced down. "Of course not." I tugged my yoga pants to the side and gasped. "What the hell is that?"

"I'd say love bruises, but you'd be in a better mood if they were."

"Thanks."

Lu shrugged. "I speak truth."

I held my hand out for the balm.

She handed it over, still eyeing the faint fingerprints on my hip. He hadn't touched me that roughly, but it was almost as if he'd branded me. "Hmm."

"I'll kick you out and steal your wine."

"Testy, testy." She stood and plucked the menu out of my hands. "Go chill out. I'll order for us."

Guilt clawed at me. "I'm sorry."

She waved me away. "You're just in denial and cranky with it. As soon as you get a few orgasms under your belt, it'll clear you right up."

"It's not like I have a disease." But I sat back down and held my wine against me. Would it be too much to get a straw?

"Your usual?"

I stood up and grabbed one of my silicone straws. Fuck it. "Yes, please."

While Luna called for food, I flicked open my phone.

PMS:

I regret our unfortunate lunch interruption. I hope you'll be returning tomorrow. On time.

I propped my head on my hand. Only PMS would put a reprimand into an apology.

> Do I get any bonus points (bucks) for dealing with a douchey dad?

PMS:

> My father is the head of this law firm. He's not a... All right, perhaps his lapse in judgment would be considered ill-advised.

I blew raspberries at my phone. That was an understatement.

"You wouldn't be blowing raspberries at me, would you?" Lu tossed her phone on the table.

"No."

Her eyebrow winged up and her blue eyes sparkled.

I slurped the last of my wine out of my cup. "If you must know, it's PMS."

"Oh? Texting after hours?" She picked up her deck again.

"Would you quit it?"

"Did I mention glowing red aura?"

I refilled my cup. "I'll admit to a teensy bit of attraction, but again, he's my boss. That's a no fly zone. I might be out of the loop when it comes to office politics, but even I know that much."

She shrugged. "Only for a week. Bang it out when the week is over."

I toyed with the end of my straw. "Tempting."

What was I saying? It was *not* tempting. The idea was abhorrent. Even if certain parts of me didn't seem to get the correct message.

That part of me was a horny cow.

"I don't want to suck up all that prissy stuck-up suit energy though," I added.

"Then don't blow him."

"Luna."

"What? Just sayin'."

"Stop being obtuse." I stood up and crossed to my desk where that blasted cat was staring up from my tablet. I flipped it over. "You know

91

how energy exchange works. You're the one who practically takes on the personality of the person you're sleeping with."

"I can't help if my empath abilities get heightened with sex."

I wasn't that bad, but it definitely could adjust my mood post sex sometimes. The way my system pinged and zinged around Preston, I wouldn't be surprised if our aftermath was pure insanity.

I really didn't need any more insanity.

It didn't stop me from going back to my phone when his text chime rang.

> PMS:
>
> I shouldn't have brought you into personal business in any case, and for that, I apologize. It was a rare moment of weakness.

After a moment, another text came through.

> PMS:
>
> I hadn't had anything to eat yet, and my coffee was delayed.

Unbelievable. This dude was blaming being hangry and missing his coffee as the explanation for a genuine moment of vulnerability.

I chucked my phone onto the couch and went back to Lu.

"Draw me some new cards. How is my week going to go?"

Luna scooped up the cards she'd been throwing. "Podcast?"

"I might be a little drunk for that."

Luna popped up and ran for my bedroom area. "Best time then."

I leaned forward and rested my forehead on the table. "I say stupid shit when I'm drunk."

She came back and set the microphone in the middle of the table. "Yes, but those are our best podcasts. Now where's your laptop?"

I refilled my cup and pointed to the end table.

"Excellent."

She set up everything along with my little recording board. And because she was Luna, she circled the mic with her crystals and lit candles.

Guess we were going all in.

"Heyyyyy. Welcome to Tarot Tramps, we are your cardslinging hosts, Luna and…"

I dragged my chair to the other side of the microphone so I would sound semi-professional. "And Ryan."

"Don't mind Ry. She's a little down in the dumps. We're going to do a reading for her to cheer her up. And maybe pour some water into her to combat the bottle—or two—of wine."

"Really good wine. Really shitty day."

"And what happened today, Ry?"

"If you don't take that Carol Brady tone out of your voice, I'm going to stab you with your wand."

"Stop threatening my wand."

"Then why did you bring it?"

"Because I knew we needed a little extra today before I even came over. You see, dear listeners, Ryan has a wee little problem with her love life."

I tried giving her all the signals for cut and hell no, but she ignored them. I slurped more wine. "I don't have a love life."

"Which is your problem."

"Bottom drawer boyfriend begs to differ. We can take care of ourselves, right, ladies?"

"And gentlemen."

"And non-binary," I added helpfully.

"Either way, we all know we can take care of business, but it doesn't make up for that delicious weight on top of you. Or you can be the weight." Luna's voice went smoky and low.

"I do prefer to be on top."

"See. Now we just have to get you—"

I gave her a hard stare.

She cleared her throat. "A man to play with. Shall we throw some cards?"

"Can we look in the Tramp Box instead? I'm sure there's listeners that have much bigger and better problems than mine."

"Nope. Special episode. Let's see what we can do with Ryan's troubles. I already did her love spread with a certain someone and it came up full of fire. She just doesn't want to face it—or him."

"We're not talking about that."

"Ry, you need someone to pin those long legs behind your ears and do you good."

I was in the middle of taking another sip of my wine and choked. "What did you say?"

Luna shrugged. "Don't sound so surprised. There's nothing wrong with needing a good di—"

I held up my hand. "Got it."

"Do you though? Do you really?" She threw down three cards and picked up the middle one. "Look at that Ace of Wands coming up again. Fire, girl. All the fire is coming your way."

"What if I don't want to get burned?"

Luna reached over the table and covered my hand. "But what if it's a beautiful bit of amazing in the ashes?"

"What if it's just ashes?"

Luna sighed. "We have so much work to do."

CHAPTER EIGHT

Card Of The Day:
Embrace: Two of Swords (rev) | **Release:** The Moon

Tuesday

GETTING ready for work at five in the morning seemed a little excessive. Especially when I'd spent the evening with Luna tearing my life apart.

Okay, that was an exaggeration.

I had faceplanted at nine o'clock since I'd started drinking immediately when I walked in the door just after five. Things had gotten a bit fuzzy before Luna put me to bed.

In the end, there was one thing I remembered.

Wands.

Lots and lots of freaking wands.

Normally, I was excited to see them in readings. They described me in a nutshell. A little wild, a lot of fire, and brimming with ideas. But fire *and* PMS? Yeah, that wasn't what I wanted to hear.

Or more, what I didn't want to face.

Wands also could burn.

I'd put myself in the shower before my eyeballs were all the way open and went right to my drafting table to settle myself down. I'd been dreaming of that blasted cat and my little fox all night. This was one thing I didn't have to fight. Art was always my solace.

A little rejuvenating tea to get the toxins out and my pencils and paint would get me right. Then I could deal with Preston.

Maybe.

I dabbed my brush in the fresh glass of water and watched the water bloom with crimson. The gray cat had snuck into the drawings again. I followed my intuition and let him do his thing.

Sylvia was just as pissed as I was about the intrusion. She chased him around the apartment, creating chaos.

I stayed bent over my table for so long, my back screamed for mercy, but I still kept working. I drew panel after panel of the silver fox trying to urge the cat back out the open window. Instead of reacting, the cat simply sat there cleaning himself, ignoring Sylvia's antics.

"Watermelon Sugar" blasted into my subconscious and I swore.

For once, I'd been up early enough to be on time for work, and here I was, still in my damn towel.

I stabbed my paintbrush into the glass jar and got most of the paint off, rolling it into a damp cotton towel to clean later. I slammed my watercolor tins shut then sprinted for the closet.

Luckily, since most of my wardrobe was black, it was easy to pull out something to wear. I went with a black sundress with a smattering of daisy appliqués on it, nude heeled sandals that wrapped up my calves, and a short black jacket that fell right below my bra strap.

Black lace and cotton for my underwear since my little apartment was already hot. Today was going to be a scorcher.

Hopefully, not personally. That fire energy needed a bucket of cold water right about now.

I snatched my watch off the charger, glad that Luna had so considerately peeled it off my arm before she put me to bed.

"Five minutes. Crap." I ran across the room to my altar and

snagged a few citron and silver chains and my heavy amethyst pendant.

I had a feeling I'd need all the help I could get walking into that office this morning.

Hair and makeup was going to have to wait. My thick ebony waves were going to be too hot later, but that was what messy buns were for.

I stopped at my kitchen table and found a note leaning against my favorite crocheted bag.

I figured you would need a little help with the morning.

Xoxo,

Lu

Inside my huge black bag were my glasses, emergency bag, deck of tarot cards, and snacks. As well as my favorite sloth tea diffuser and three baggies of tea. There were two more pouches on the bottom of the bag, but I didn't have time to look closer.

"Bless you, Lu."

Taking no chances, I folded up my backup ballet flats and tucked them away in my purse. Then I grabbed the bag and flew out the door. Driving would take longer than walking with morning traffic. Never mind trying to find a damn parking spot in Kensington Square.

I cut through the shortcut and was glad to see the kids weren't outside playing today. The sun was too hot for blacktop kickball. They were probably down at the community pool.

I faltered as the bakery came into sight.

Bribe?

Nope. No way was I testing the gods again there.

I crossed the street to the Shaws' office building and hurried inside, my heels clicking on the tiled floor of the lobby.

Dread filled my belly as I took the elevator to their floor. Seventeen after the hour.

Late again.

I glanced down at my hands and groaned. I was still covered in paint and ink. "Way to go, Ry," I muttered just as the doors opened.

The elder Shaw was waiting for me. Or the elevator. But he got me. Ugh.

"Miss Moon, you are late."

"Aware."

The older man—who looked far too much like PMS in a slimy, slick, distrustful way—arched a brow at me. "No excuse?"

I flipped my heavy fall of hair over my shoulder. "Would you believe it if I had one?"

His chin lifted. "I understand you're only a temp, but two days in a row is unprofessional."

"How do you know I was late yesterday? I don't punch a time clock."

He said nothing.

PMS had ratted me out. Good to know.

"Not the only way you've been unprofessional," he added as if I'd not questioned him at all.

I could literally feel every one of my vertebrae locking into place as I stood up straighter. "Is that right?"

"April is an exemplary employee, and my son took her word that you would be a good fit. She was clearly mistaken."

Isaac Shaw was not as tall as his son, and I could stare him directly in the eye. "I'm doing a favor for both of you. And believe me, the fact that April is one of my very best friends is the only reason I walked in these doors at all."

"Then perhaps you should turn around and walk right out. You aren't responsible enough to show up on time, and you've already shown your propensity for public displays. Who knows what else you might do to besmirch our firm?"

"*My* propensity?" I took a step closer until I was definitely far too close for comfort, but my temper always got me into trouble. "Oh, honey, I think you're doing the besmirching all on your own."

Crimson raced up his neck. "How dare you."

"I don't need you, darlin'. You need me. There's a difference when there's that kind of power exchange. Then again, you probably don't understand those kind of roles since you and Admin Barbie had to sneak off and feed each other shrimp by the fire on the other side of town so your wife wouldn't find out."

Elder Shaw had the same jaw tic as his son, but I didn't find it at all intriguing.

Nope.

Now I just wondered how much shit I had to shovel to make him break. I *really* wanted to see him break.

Preston's door crashed open, bouncing off the hinges. "What is going on out here?"

I took a leisurely step back and readjusted my purse on my shoulder. "I was just quitting."

"What? Why?" Preston crossed the room. "You can't. I need you this week."

"You'll make do." His father smoothed a hand down his tie, as if I was some lint to be brushed away.

Preston raked his fingers through his hair. "I will not. We had an agreement."

"Things change. I don't like the atmosphere."

That was an understatement.

Preston turned to his father. "Having this sort of conversation in the foyer is a bad idea. What if I had a client in my office?" He glanced from me to his father and back again. "And you are late, Miss Moon."

"Even later now that Pops decided to give me a dressing down."

Crimson was heading toward five-alarm-fire red. Now the flush was overtaking his cheeks too. "I—Preston, you need to take care of this immediately. This…this *woman* is not fit for this law firm."

"Ah, but it's okay for you to be the oldest cliché in the book? That's fine. Again, I don't need to be here. I was doing Preston and April a favor."

"She's the one in the wrong here. I will not stand for this." Isaac turned on his heel and started across the room.

"Dad? Please stop. We need to discuss this. You can't talk to my employee like that."

"*Me?* She's the one who verbally accosted me. Twice!"

"I feel like I verbally accosted him more than that." I crossed my arms. "He will not belittle my accomplishments."

PMS adjusted his tie, then smoothed it down much as his father had before dipping his hand into his pocket. "First of all, Miss Moon is not your employee to fire. You have your own admin to take care of your," *hello, pregnant pause,* "personal business. You both need to calm down and think rationally."

"Calm down?" My purse slid down my arm to thud onto the floor beside me. "I didn't start it. I realize I'm late, and I apologize."

Huh, who knew I had an apology in me right then? The things you learn.

"I was working—yes, working," I added with a sneer when Isaac gave me a withering glance. "I have a business of my own."

"And what is it that you do?" Isaac crossed his arms.

My smile was slow and wide. "I'm a professional tarot card reader and artist."

Isaac's gaze slid down my dress and crystals then drifted over my handmade bag. "I see." Disdain dripped from his voice.

I tipped my head, my dark hair tumbling forward as I picked up the chunky amethyst that was hiding inside my dress and pulled it out. "Oh, and I'm a witch."

Sort of. More of a kitchen witch, but he didn't need to know that.

"Dear God. *This* is who you hire?" Issac glared at his son. "Are you insane?"

To Preston's credit, he didn't break his father's stare. "Dad, you cannot judge anyone for their religion or their profession. You should know better. That is not what this law firm is about."

My eyebrows rose. Did Preston just defend me?

Whatever. Too little, too late. Working here was obviously a mistake.

One that I was about to rectify.

I stalked to my desk and took the crystals I'd brought in from the little stone pedestal along with the tea diffuser I'd left behind.

"I don't have time for this nonsense. I expect her gone, Preston."

PMS clenched his hands at his sides as his father strode off to his lair. "My office, Miss Moon," he said through gritted teeth.

"We don't need to discuss anything. I'm out of here." I jammed the very few items I had into my bag and headed for the elevator.

Preston grabbed my arm.

My chin tipped up to meet his dark stare. "Take your hands off me."

His hand slipped away, and the unfathomable warmth that came with it receded. "We need to talk before you go. I don't want you leaving like this."

I crossed my arms against my instantaneous—and very annoying—response to his touch. "Who cares? You barely know me. Let's just chalk this up as April's crazy idea. Just don't take it out on her too much. Her gram means a lot to her, and she's worried about her."

His shoulders squared. "I would never do that. She's an—"

"I know, I know, an exemplary employee. Everything I'm not."

He jammed his hands into his pockets. My gaze dipped down and then instantly bounced back to his face. What the hell was I doing? I didn't need to know about any of that action.

It was bad enough I had my own…problems. Why hadn't I worn my padded bra today? Thank the goddess I wore black. Maybe he wouldn't notice the headlight flash going on.

"I wouldn't say that. I took a look at my file room this morning, since you closeted yourself in there for the whole afternoon yesterday."

I huffed out a breath. "I know that wasn't on your bulleted list, but I just couldn't…"

Ignore a problem waiting to be solved.

Deal with anything that put me in your sphere.

Share the same air with you and not by turns want to throttle you and kiss you brainless.

A, B, and C were all equally true.

Obviously, I was the brainless one. This man was not the evolved, equitable sex god I'd been looking for.

Even if he had defended me. Even if our heights were perfectly in sync, which meant horizontally everything would line up just right. Even if I hadn't been looking for any action in his pants, but I had damn sure found some.

I cleared my throat and told the biggest lie of my life thus far. "I couldn't ignore what was right in front of me."

He reached a hand out to me then swiftly hid it in his pocket again. "I understand this is a difficult situation."

"Difficult? I was blissfully unaware of your family drama, but you dragged me into it and now I can't *un*-know it."

He tipped back his head. "Dammit, I know that. Do you think I love knowing…what I know about my own father and that this dirty laundry has been aired to a virtual stranger?"

That hurt. It shouldn't have, but it did. It was no more than I'd just said a moment ago, but still, it felt different. All because my emotions and this ridiculous bit of lust were tangled.

I was a live and let live sort about most things. Except adultery. That was a hard *no* in my book.

Not after all the things I'd seen in my life.

"Please, Miss—Ryan."

I huffed out a breath and sailed across the room to his office. "Five minutes."

He caught up with me and blocked the door. "I believe you owe me at least twenty."

"Is that right?" I pushed him out of the way and rushed into his inner sanctum with him right behind me. Too close for comfort. "Shove your twenty minutes up that tight ass of yours. The meter is running."

"Sit down, Ryan. And calm down."

I whirled to face him as the door thudded shut at his back. "I don't want to calm down."

There was too much energy between us. The space was too small. I wanted to peel my damn skin off or…

What the hell. I was leaving anyway.

I grabbed his face and dragged him in, slanting my mouth across his. He went as still as stone and then those crazy-powerful arms locked around me. He hauled me up onto my toes and took the kiss from quick and annoyed to dark, carnal craving.

Every hair on my body lifted and buzzed as he owned my mouth. One of his arms anchored along my lower back as he fisted my curls with his other hand. He tipped my head back and literally *plundered*.

I'd read about it. But the actuality of it?

Beyond my wildest fantasy.

Flames didn't begin to cover it. We were a conflagration of lit wands lighting up the night sky. My arm hooked around his muscled shoulders. What the hell was he hiding under his suits?

There was no air between us. The flames had sucked it all up. Oxygen was at a premium, and I couldn't comprehend why I needed it. I just wanted more of *this*. More of this light filling me up enough that it seemed like it was going to burst out of my pores.

Finally, he ripped his mouth from mine and went right for my neck. His teeth scraped down my shoulder as he pushed at my lightweight jacket.

"Preston."

We had to stop.

Nope, wait, maybe after...*mercy.* How did he know how to do that with his tongue? I definitely had slotted him as lights out missionary sex.

Wait.

"Preston."

"Ryan." He pushed aside the strap of my sundress and nibbled his way along my shoulder. "Your skin is like the finest silk. And I have no idea what your scent is, but I want it inside me."

It was getting harder to remember why this was a bad idea. I was leaving. Who cared if I walked away with some truly excellent desk sex as my exit package, right?

"What a way to get fired." I slipped my fingers into his thick dark hair.

"Fired?" He lifted his head and met my gaze. His eyes were a little lost, a lot blurry. I kinda liked him this way. All mussed up and letting loose.

I licked my tingling lips. "Yeah." I undid his suit jacket and slipped my hand inside and around to his back. I absorbed all the warmth pulsing from beneath his dress shirt, and then I inched down to grab his truly excellent ass. Tight in all the best ways right now. I groaned at the very impressive length of his cock trying to break out of his Brooks Brothers pants against my belly. "Best exit interview ever."

"What?" He pulled back.

I grabbed his belt loops and dragged him back against me. "You didn't think I was going to stay after all...*that* went down outside the elevator."

"I don't even fully know what happened. I was on the phone—"

"Whatever. Just kiss me." I went on my toes and lined up our mouths.

He dragged his teeth over my lower lip before he delved inside, his fingers gripping my hips until everything buzzed and burned once more. He did this rocking thing against me that would have made my eyes cross if they were open.

But they were not. They were closed, and there was a sexy, mesmerizing little light show going off behind my eyelids. I'd only had this happen one other time in my life. When I was so in tune with another person that I actually saw colors.

Pure energy.

I wanted more of it. I had a feeling I'd get addicted, but it would only be this one time.

I could handle one time.

The energy started to dissipate, and I hummed out my displeasure. I was losing him again.

"Preston, what's the problem?" I sighed and opened my eyes, already knowing what I was going to see.

He was deliciously disheveled, with his hair sticking up in all directions and his mouth bruised from mine. But his dark eyes were full of turbulence. Not the fun kind.

The kind that said this was stopping.

"I can't do this week without you. I have three depositions this afternoon and four more tomorrow."

"Divorce is big business."

He clenched his jaw. "I can't dispute that statement."

I sighed. "I already quit. You really don't have a choice."

"Please reconsider." His gaze dropped to my mouth again, and he brushed his thumb along my lower lip.

"Is this supposed to be my perk?"

He frowned again and dragged his gaze up to mine. "What?"

"To work here?"

"What? No. Of course not. What sort of man do you take me for?"

"Oh, I don't know. A man who was two minutes and a ready condom away from taking me on that desk?" I didn't add that I'd be taking him too, since his mind was already blown enough.

I didn't want to kill the guy. Not until I'd used him for my personal aims anyway.

"Two minutes? You give me little credit. I do know the word foreplay."

I did not want to smile right now. Next thing I knew I'd like the guy, and that was not happening.

When I didn't reply, he cursed under his breath and took a step back, immediately straightening his tie. "I forgot myself for a moment. It's you. I don't know what it is about you that makes me so nuts."

"Sorry. I'll get out of your hair."

He moved in front of the door. "No. Ryan, please." His gaze dropped to my breasts and then immediately rose to sync with mine. "We can be professional."

I drew a lazy, winding line down his tie with my forefinger. "Not really interested in that. I was sorta hoping we could just bang this out of our systems and then go our separate ways."

"*Bang it out?* That's ridiculous," he sputtered.

"You've never had a wild fling? It's really good for you."

"No. I don't have those types of relationships anymore."

My eyebrow winged up. "Anymore, hmm?" I purred.

Damn Luna and her *hmm*-ing.

His jaw tightened. "No. I don't do that."

"You mean to tell me you haven't gone on a business trip or to a conference and had a crazy fling with another lawyer or paralegal or bar fly...whatever."

"No. Of course not."

"Well, you're missing out. And missing out on *this* because my lady boner is definitely deflating." I evaded him once more and dropped into the chair across from his desk, barely resisting the urge to fan my skirt.

He cleared his throat and walked around his desk to sit down. "I've never heard that particular description but I can infer."

"Infer away." I waved my hand and hauled my bag onto my lap. I wasn't sure how I'd managed to hold onto it during our kiss.

Kisses, plural.

I pulled out my compact and winced at the image. My already full lips were bright red and bruised with a bonus bit of beard rash along my neck. Great.

I snapped my compact shut and stuffed it in my bag. "Look, I appreciate how stubborn you are about wanting some help around this place. Obviously, your dad is super tight-assed like you."

"I resent that assessment."

"Yeah, well, I resent we're not naked. We all have our issues." Taking pity on him, I sighed. "Don't you have a temp agency you can tap? Surely April has taken some time off over the years."

"No."

"Can you elaborate?"

"She wasn't supposed to take vacations."

I laughed. "Are you serious right now?"

"Deadly." Strain lines crinkled around his eyes. He looked tired and stressed and rumpled in a way that made me want to bite him.

Could that sex hex work both ways? I was beginning to wonder.

"People take vacations. They have to. Since, you know, people have lives outside the office."

His bland stare didn't inspire confidence that he did. I didn't want to feel compassion for him any more than I wanted to like him. Add in his asshole father and Preston's genuine hurt the day before at his father's behavior and...

I was softening in his direction. A bit. In ways that had nothing to do with how he kissed like a damn stud and was built like an Italian race car.

If they had big packages. Which probably wouldn't help their aerodynamics.

At his silence, I rubbed my forehead. "I'm a disaster as you and your father have pointed out."

He sat forward, his fingers steepled. "Actually, that's not true. I was going to try to find middle ground before we were...distracted."

"Ha."

He pressed his lips together. "It was a very nice distraction."

I rolled my eyes. "Please move on before I use that stapler on your forehead."

He cleared his throat again. "Right. It was inexcusable that I—"

"Oh, put a sock in it." I rummaged through my purse. I was operating on no caffeine. No wonder my pistons were misfiring all over the place. "Can I make some of my tea?"

"Uh, sure."

I stood and went over to the small bar in his office. There was an electric tea kettle pushed to the back. Perfect. I filled it and pressed the button to start it up. "You're a tea drinker?"

"No. But my mom is. She stops by now and then."

There was no missing the tension in his tone.

Not that I empathized with him. Of course not.

I hated him. I was almost sure. Not including his mouth—at least when it was on mine.

I turned back to him and cocked my hip against the bar. "Did your coffee come in?"

"Not yet. I have one last pod." He grimaced. "I was saving it for an emergency."

Today qualified on all levels.

Without him even having to ask, I retrieved a clean mug and put it on the Keurig pour tray. Then I reached into the sad, empty coffee pod basket and found one last caramel-coconut shivering under a neatly folded napkin. He'd even hidden it from view not to be tempted.

I put it in and started the machine. "I'll call about it again on my way out as a parting gift." I tapped the mug. "And look, I'm even making you coffee before I go."

"You can't go."

"I can and I will."

"Hear me out. As I was trying to explain to you, the filing system you started is inspired. It's efficient and makes it easy to find files. It's even a perfect way to do digitals so we have backups."

"I know."

He frowned. "You know?"

I nodded. "Look, I used to work in an office much like this. It was insurance instead of law, but the basic principles apply when it comes to documentation. I set them up for digital filing as well."

He smiled. Actually smiled.

That he hadn't even looked that pleased after kissing me was something I was not going to examine.

"See, this is perfect. I'm prepared to give you a very nice bonus to do April's standard duties, which isn't much this week since she prepped most of the clients. It will mostly just be manning the phones and greeting my clients. Maybe some light transcription."

"What about the list of doom?"

He waved his hand. "You can shred it. Well, at least the last few pages. The first is made up of perfectly valid tasks."

"If you say so." I narrowed my eyes. "Did you say bonus?"

He stood and came toward me. "Yes. A sizable bonus."

"Does it come with orgasms?"

He halted in his tracks. "April returns next Monday."

"That wasn't a yes."

"April returns next Monday," he repeated as if that weighty sentence was the answer to all the world's problems.

Or at least ours. And maybe he was right.

We could handle dealing with each other for four more days. Slightly less than that because we were already into Tuesday. Surely we could manage that much.

Possibly.

I gave his tie a lengthy stroke before I walked to the door and delivered one last parting shot on my way out. "The best way to get rid of temptation is to give into it, Preston."

CHAPTER NINE

PRESTON

"THE BEST WAY TO get rid of temptation is to give into it, Preston."

One sentence should not have held my dick in a vise, but that was the power of Ryan G. Moon.

The vixen April had set upon me for reasons unknown.

To rub salt in the wound, I received a postcard from my assistant—the real one. The one who didn't make me sit like a fourteen-year-old boy trying to hide my half-mast.

Anyway, it was digital taunting, of course, because no mail moved that fast. But the email contained several beachy shots of palm fronds waving in the breeze and rolling turquoise waves and April in a bikini frolicking in the surf.

I envied her frolic.

Having the best time. Hope all is well. See you soon (not too soon!)

I sent a pithy reply and clicked the email closed. Couldn't be soon enough, since it was already too late.

Or it would have been if I wasn't exceptional at blocking my own impulses. My skill at ignoring my own desires was the only reason I was still a divorce lawyer.

Otherwise, I'd be doing some other specialty. Like…family law, maybe, or something that did some good. Making sure kids were protected seemed so much more worthwhile than ensuring Betty Studebaker got all the good china and the cabin in Tahoe.

But that wasn't the road in front of me right now. All I wanted to do was survive this week without fucking Ryan on my desk—or her desk, that actually belonged to April—so that I could still look at myself in the mirror.

It wasn't as if she was my permanent assistant. She was just a temp. But with my father's exploits still fresh, I couldn't let that breach happen. If I didn't follow my own standards, how could I criticize his?

Short answer: I couldn't.

Since I had no better options at the moment, I locked myself in my office. I didn't inquire about the digital indexing Ryan had mentioned or concern myself with my missing coffee. It would come when it came.

In the meantime, I finished my last cup of my beloved caramel-coconut. Then I resorted to drinking soda by the gallon while wondering when I'd turned to compulsive behaviors to avoid my assistant.

Not just her. I was also avoiding my father. There were hard conversations that were needed to be had, and I wasn't ready. Once I pulled that trigger, the next step would need to be taken.

Telling my mother what I'd seen.

The front blinds were pulled as tight as possible. Not even a shaft of light could escape, just in case Ryan wanted to peek in. Or in case my brother wanted to taunt me by flirting with her as if I was a lion behind the glass. Consigned to always look but not touch.

Except I had touched her, and she'd touched me.

It hadn't been nearly enough.

I worked for as long as I could, forcing myself again and again to refocus on the paperwork in front of me. I left my computer on standby. That way I couldn't hear the email dinging. As for the phone, it couldn't interrupt you when it was disconnected.

Who knew?

After awhile, I needed a break, so I pulled out the hunter green folder I'd received last night from Kitten Around. I'd left after promising to review the materials and to offer my support if it was a good fit. Since my part usually just required money, I was fairly certain it would be.

I had to admit the idea was intriguing. They'd come up with the idea to do a kind of speed dating event—except matching kittens and critical care cats with pet parents. They'd included the forms participants would fill out to be part of the program, and damn if it didn't look like one from a dating app.

Not that I knew what those looked like. Because of course I'd never considered turning to one of those sites after the long, lonely nights got to be too much.

All right, so maybe I had once a few years ago. I hadn't gone through with it, because—

I didn't know why.

Liar.

Deep down, I'd harbored a belief much like Ryan's. If it was meant to happen, it would, and I wouldn't need to pay for the privilege.

Guess I was more of a sap than I realized.

A knock sounded at my door when I was pouring my third glass of Coke. I hadn't had this much soda since college. Maybe high school. At least it wasn't bourbon.

I debated not answering. I knew it was cowardly. At this point, I didn't care.

My only hope for this week was to get through it intact.

Harm none.

I frowned and rubbed my blurry eyes. Now I was thinking in Wiccan tenets, which was my own fault for doing some research past midnight when I couldn't sleep. I'd started with tarot cards and stumbled into witchy stuff, an interesting coincidence considering what Ryan had told my father this morning.

Whether or not she was truly a witch, Ryan's world was surprisingly fascinating. I had a feeling I'd only scratched the surface.

Of her too.

Another knock sounded and I pushed to my feet. I'd face her standing and send her back where she'd come from the same way. "Yes?"

That should've been my clue it wasn't Ryan. She didn't wait to be invited in. She just blazed through my world like a tornado.

"Sweetheart." My mom strolled in. "Are you busy? Of course you are, you never stop."

I'd heard the phrase *my heart sunk* before, but I had never lived it. Shit, this was the last thing I needed today.

Then again, when was the right time to tell the mother you adored that her husband was cheating on her?

That the man in question was my father didn't lessen my anger.

I shook my head. "I always have time for you. Shut the door. Please," I tacked on when she shot me a look.

She did as I asked, but as she turned, I caught a glimpse of Ryan at her desk. Sitting ramrod straight, her hair long and loose. Typing away like the assistant of my fucking dreams.

The last part was true too. I was definitely having fucking dreams about her. And today's tongue swordplay would not help on that score.

I pressed a finger to my temple and sank into my chair.

My mother came around the desk and leaned down to hug me as she always did, smelling of Chanel and freshly overturned dirt. An odd combination, but that was my mother in a nutshell. She wore a pristine pink pants suit with a plaid shirt more fitting for a gardener. She'd styled her hair in a flawless brown wave with tucked under ends, and pearls shone at her ears. Her perfect makeup was marred only by a muddy streak she'd overlooked on her cheek.

I swiped it away for her and eased back. "Been pruning again?"

"Oh, did I miss a spot?" She held her hand against her face and laughed. "I didn't pay much mind to my makeup after I finished getting the garden ready for fall planting. Fifi was running around in circles. She tried to get a squirrel today. Can you imagine? Blasted thing was almost as big as she is."

Fifi was her purse-sized chihuahua who thought she was the size of a wolf and possessed the same hunting prowess. She was wrong.

"She figures she can do anything, and you'll be happy about it."

"She's not entirely wrong, minus squirrel killing. What's wrong with you?"

"What? Nothing. Why?"

"A mother knows."

I gulped my drink. I used to handle things directly. No beating around the bush. No hiding. If something was unpleasant, I dealt with it with a modicum of fuss and got the job done.

Now avoiding women I didn't want to have difficult conversations with seemed to be my MO.

Not only women. I didn't want to talk to my father either. Or my brother for that matter, who was probably just waiting for me to give him a sign to descend on Ryan. He wasn't good enough for her.

For that matter, neither was I. She deserved someone who was all in. Totally committed to riding that magic carpet wherever it would go.

My only commitment was to my job. It was a pledge I'd made years ago to my father. My family's legacy was this firm, and for the last few years, I'd been the one doing the bulk of the work. As my dad neared retirement, I was poised to take over. And I couldn't do that at this level and have a relationship.

Or a life.

"Preston?" My mom snapped her fingers to get my attention. "I won't disappear if you don't answer me."

"I'm swamped." It was an easy lie, and reaching for one was yet another thing I didn't do before this week.

"You always are. But you don't usually have that look in your eyes." She didn't move away as she usually did to take one of the chairs opposite my desk. "What is it?"

When I didn't respond, she brushed my hair back from my forehead as she had when I was a child. And for the first time in more years than I could remember, I wanted nothing more than to lay my head on her chest and pretend everything was all right. That the world was predictable and safe and my parents would never let anything hurt me.

That they wouldn't be the ones doing the hurting.

"I bet I know." She angled her head to examine my face. "Your new assistant is one of a kind."

I laughed. I wasn't even sure why. She'd nailed Ryan succinctly. "Temporary."

"Oh, she was quick to tell me that too. She's a friend of April's, she said."

"Yes."

"Is she the reason you're barricaded in here?"

"Who says I am?"

"Your door is shut, your blinds closed all the way. You're not answering phone calls, personal or business." She walked around my desk to pick up the pulled out phone cord. "This explains it."

I rose to go to the wall of windows at my back. When I first moved into this office seven years ago, I'd been drawn to them many times throughout the day. Instead of looking down at the cars chugging along the city streets below, I'd always looked upward. The sun and sky were my touchstones.

It wouldn't stay dark forever. It never did.

Now I rarely remembered to look out. To look up and watch the shifting sunlight as it emerged from behind the clouds.

Work was more important. I was always racing for an invisible finish line I would never quite reach.

I glanced at my watch. Almost noon. "Mom, I have an appointment at one with a client. I appreciate the visit, but—"

"You don't have time." She was already making herself tea, so she had no intention of leaving me in peace anytime soon.

Nudging her along had been a knee-jerk reaction. Her weekly visits for lunch were a bright spot in a hell of a lot of hectic mornings and long afternoons. My mother was quirky and a little kooky and frequently made me crazy. She also made me laugh.

Much like someone else I knew. I didn't know her at all really, but I wanted to.

I wanted far too much.

"I really wish I did."

"You know, you have choices."

"What?"

She shook her head and returned with her hot cup of water and teabag to sit across from my desk. "You're thirty-four years old, Preston. Thirty-five soon enough."

I clamped a hand on the back of my neck. Tight, throbbing muscles were a mainstay for me, and today was no exception. "Thanks for the reminder."

"You have no social life. You don't date. Don't have pets. For God's sake, you don't even have a plant."

"It died," I said shortly.

"I know, since I was the one to give you that tomato plant. I gave you a card with instructions, and still, it was brown and withered within weeks."

"I'm too busy to—"

"Live," she said quietly. "You're not living, baby, and I don't want that for you. Anything but that."

I turned back to the window. There was a crow—raven?—perched on a high branch of a tree across the street, staring at me. Judging me with its beady little eyes.

Everyone was judging. Worse, they had every right to.

Okay, probably not the bird. He didn't know my struggle.

"Did you think I need a lecture today?"

"Yes. I've thought you needed one for a while. And it's not a lecture. It's advice from someone who loves you and doesn't want you to waste the beauty inside you."

I couldn't even laugh. I tried to, but the sound got stuck somewhere between my chest and my throat.

Her cup rattled in the saucer as she set them down on my desk. A moment later, she stepped up beside me and laid her hand on my lower back, rubbing gently. "She was reading your tarot cards when I arrived."

"Mine?"

"Yes. She said you were full of tower energy."

"What the hell does that mean?"

"You're on the edge, Preston. A step forward can take you into the abyss. Or you can fly."

Leave it to me to have a mother who liked to attend psychic fairs. She probably saw Ryan as a kindred spirit.

Hell, maybe she was.

"That sounds like a bunch of crap."

"Definitely tower energy," she affirmed. "Change is all around you. You were never meant to live in stasis. If you won't make the choice, the universe will make it for you."

"I'm supposed to believe she told you all this within a moment of meeting you?"

"Oh, no," my mother said cheerfully, returning to the desk to retrieve her tea. "We chatted for a good hour."

If I'd been drinking something, I would have sputtered it out. "During work hours?"

"Spiritual work is far more important than piddly tasks." She waved her ringed fingers before lifting her tea for a sip. "This rose hibiscus is very good."

"I didn't put that there."

"No, Ryan did. She said she replenished the tea because it was running low. She's quite a find, isn't she?"

I grunted. I could sense where this was going, and I did not like it one bit.

"She's also single," my mother continued. "And quite lovely."

"And?"

"You're not arguing."

"I have eyes, don't I?"

"The lovers card came up while she was doing your reading. Are you avoiding her before or after?"

"Before or after what, exactly?"

She lifted her eyebrows and sipped again.

"She is my assistant," I said through gritted teeth. "I know what is right and proper doesn't matter to anyone else around here, but it does to me."

My mother rolled over that point as if it was insignificant. "So you *are* interested."

"I'm interested in her doing some work during the time she is in my employ. I can be a very generous boss," I swore I heard my mother snort, "and I'm willing to compensate more than fairly, but I need to know she cares enough to try."

For God's sake, was that the source of my irritation with her? Not counting misplaced lust, of course. I didn't want to do this job, but I tried my hardest. Ryan sometimes behaved as if it wasn't worth her time. As if *I* wasn't.

I massaged my forehead. Psychobabble was taking over my brain.

My mother sighed. "She cares. She's organizing your Rolodex into active and inactive clients, cross-referencing the log of their respective cases. Why April never thought to do that, I don't know."

I did not respond.

"And she was considerate enough to replenish the tea with her favored blends. There's a new assortment in the waiting room for clients as well."

"Along with a fresh stack of copies of *Cosmo*?"

"She's so personable. I don't doubt she will make your clients feel more comfortable at a very difficult time in their lives. Not that April isn't more than capable, but she isn't as warm and friendly."

My mom singing Ryan's praises didn't exactly kill my annoyance. I'd just begged her to stay this morning. Obviously, I grasped her potential. But having potential didn't mean she would use it, other than when it suited her.

I'd promised her a bonus either way, because she'd made inroads into the chaos of the records room. If she didn't do much else this week, that would be worth it.

Not that I intended to tell her that.

My mother was still talking, although I'd clearly missed some of what she was saying. "I don't worry about your brother, because he enjoys everything."

"Too much."

"How can you enjoy life too much?" My mom shook her head. "I married young, and sometimes I wonder what I missed. But then I look at you boys and take stock of my life, and I realized I have everything I could ever want." She smiled and the frown lines creasing her forehead vanished. "Besides, I have plenty of time. As do you. When you look back at your life, always make sure there's something to see."

I swallowed hard. I should tell her. Soon.

But how? The last thing I wanted to do was to cause her pain. It wasn't even my secret to tell.

But my father wouldn't. That meant I'd have to.

"Why did you and Dad get married?"

She didn't seem surprised by the question. "We were going in the same direction." One corner of her mouth lifted then she drank more tea. "Then."

I frowned. "What about now?"

"Why are you asking about marriage?" she asked in lieu of an answer.

"I'm not. I'm asking about yours. I want to understand what makes someone take a leap of faith like that."

And why it goes wrong.

"Leaping with a net isn't leaping at all. The jump is the destination." She returned her tea cup to the wet bar and then moved to the door. "Sorry I can't stay longer, but I'm meeting the girls to go shopping." She paused with her hand on the knob. "You'll think about what I said?"

I didn't have much choice. What she'd said—and what she hadn't—was spinning in my mind. Mixed in were flashes of memory of Ryan's mouth, hot and hungry against mine.

She wasn't one to leap with a net, that was for damn sure.

"I will. Have fun with the girls." I paused. "Mom, you're happy, right?"

It wasn't a fair question. She didn't have all the information. But I needed to know she was.

Even just for now.

Her smile answered for her. "I'm happy. I want that for you too. You deserve it."

She closed the door behind her, and I resisted trying to get a glimpse of Ryan. Instead, I went to my desk and picked up the phone.

After I plugged it back in.

When the call connected, I took a deep breath. "Hi. I want to set up a date."

CHAPTER TEN

PRESTON

Wednesday

My mother's heart-to-heart talk had hit home.

Sort of.

I'd listened to her thoughtful words of advice, promised to give them some thought, and made a hasty decision I was even now reconsidering, a full day later.

There were reasons I did not move fast. One of them was so I never had to reverse course. I still could, but it would be sticky.

I didn't like sticky.

I also didn't like avoiding my assistant.

Today had been better. She'd come in almost on time. Ten minutes past nine was practically perfect for her. I'd mentioned some calls I needed her to make, and she'd even taken dictation on a letter I needed her to send Judge Tremont. She'd doodled smiley-faced daisies in the margins of her pad while I collected my thoughts, but I didn't care as long as the letter sounded coherent.

After that, we'd behaved mostly like boss and employee. I'd been in the courthouse part of the day, but when I was in-house, she kept her finger perpetually on the button for my line. Half the time she asked me stuff just to be annoying. And she definitely still sent me too many emails.

Isn't Esquire just a pompous word for attorney?

Don't you think putting a large red X next to the line where people need to sign is overkill?

Are you a super brainiac to get through law school in two-and-a-half years?

Some of her more salient questions I answered. The rest went into my circular file.

Her missives still dinged every damn time they hit my inbox. I was convinced my computer was hexed too.

I glanced at the time. I'd almost made it through. Soon, the day would be over, and I could follow-through on that questionable decision I'd made.

There was yet another item on my docket to contend with first.

I walked up the hallway in time to witness Ryan crouching outside my office, balancing on her heels and craning her neck to peer through the gap in the blinds. Pity I'd opened them marginally today. "This angle sucks. His desk is too high. I can't see him."

Lifting a brow, I tucked my hands in my pockets to watch the show. My last client meeting of the day was in a few minutes, so I'd gone to the conference room to make sure it was prepped.

To my utter shock, it was. Carafes of water and coffee—not mine, oh no, that was still purportedly en route—and a fruit plate were in the center of the table, along with a vase of fresh flowers. They were nice touches, especially since I suspected Stacey would need those small comforts.

When she'd called to make the appointment, she was crying. Never a good sign.

Just in case, I'd stopped by the supply closet to get a box of tissues for the conference room. Better to be prepared.

Now it seemed as if I'd get some free entertainment before what promised to be a challenging meeting.

"You act like it's easy. I'm telling you I can't see him." Ryan blew her loose curls out of her face. She'd pulled her hair on top of her head, and strands escaped to rain down onto her back. Not bare today, thank God, but I remembered.

I remembered far too much.

"Do you think I have time for this? It's almost quitting time, and I have to get back to digitally indexing—no, I can't do just anything because I kissed the guy. I didn't blow him."

I reached up to loosen my tie. She just had to insert that image in my head. And who the hell was she telling she'd kissed me?

So much for discretion. I really should've made her sign that NDA. Not that unexpected tongue battles would have been a line item, but obviously, they should've been.

As much as I wanted to hear the rest of this conversation, I was an officer of the court who'd already fallen upon boggy moral ground yesterday morning. I didn't need eavesdropping on my conscience too.

"No, that was the thing. He's packing. Seriously."

I straightened my shoulders and tried not to grin. Maybe I'd just listen a moment longer.

"I know, can you believe it? But honestly, I'm not even sure he can seal the deal. You know what happens in the sack when a guy hasn't had any relief for a while." She made an unflattering finger gesture that I assumed was a quickly faltering erection.

Ha. She didn't have the slightest clue. Since listening to her infernal podcast last Friday, I could've hung a flag off my cock and saluted our nation.

"To whom are you speaking?"

She went stock still, which made her lean precipitously to one side since she'd been mid-creep toward another gap in the blinds.

"Gotta go," she whispered and deposited her phone somewhere she assumed I couldn't see.

Such as down her shirt.

"Hmm?" she asked with false cheer, appearing to buff the window with the side of her fist, thereby smearing the clear glass. "Just found a spot. I figured you'd want this clean."

I crossed my arms. "Now you do windows? Also, I've heard glass cleaner does wonders for that. Here, let me get the bottle for you."

She stood. "No thanks, the spot is—"

I was already halfway down the hall to the supply closet. When I returned, she was seated behind her desk with a pile of rocks stacked high on the blotter. She appeared to be chanting to herself with her eyes closed.

"Are you actually a witch?"

Her eyes flew open, and she knocked some of her rocks to the floor. I set down the window cleaner and bent to help her gather them. Naturally, our heads nearly collided. We avoided that disaster, but when we readjusted, our mouths were entirely too close.

Her aquamarine eyes were like a cat's. Sly, wary, and stunningly beautiful.

"Who were you telling about my...package?" Sounded like something I'd neglected to retrieve from UPS.

A heavy rock landed on my shoe.

We both looked down, but when I picked up the big golden hunk, she gasped and grabbed it back. "Don't mix your energy with mine. It'll fuck everything up."

"Just like my efforts at lovemaking?" I mimicked her limp finger gesture and had the satisfaction of watching her golden skin flush.

Only problem was, she was even more gorgeous when she was blushing.

"I can't believe you eavesdropped on me."

"I can't believe you told people you laid your lips on mine."

Her brow arched. "I believe that's called a kiss in most societies."

I made a show of looking around, although I knew for a fact that my father had left hours ago, and his admin Courtney had followed shortly thereafter.

Gee, I wondered why.

I wasn't sure Dex had even come in today, and his assistant had been out sick. Therefore, we were very much alone in the office.

But she didn't need to know that—unless she already did.

"That is hardly appropriate office conversation. But just so you know, being discreet and discriminating does not indicate lack of skill." I cleared my throat. "Also? I would never discuss you so crassly with another male."

She swallowed deeply, looking down at her lap. "You're right. I'm sorry. And it wasn't actually a person. Just my best friend. She wanted to see what you looked like after I mentioned you. "

"Your best friend isn't human? Figures."

"I mean, she's not just anybody. Lu's a vault when it comes to intel. She would never spread shit."

"Lu being la-la-Luna from the podcast?"

"Her name is Luna. No la-la."

"She said it that way, not me."

"Yeah, well, I say my middle name is Goddess. We do what we want."

I rocked back on my heels, unwilling to move away from her just yet. We were crouching behind her desk, and I liked being in her space. Even if her witchy night floral scent was making me lightheaded. "Regardless of either of your names, the size of my physical blessings is no one's business."

She snorted. "Not even mine, since you put the kibosh on anything right quick."

"Shut up or I'll touch your rock again."

She cocked her head. "It's rather fascinating how you make that sound like porn."

"You'd be surprised all the things I can do, Miss Moon."

With a sigh, she rose from her crouching position and sat on the edge of her chair. Then she picked up a small chunk of pink rock and held it out to me. "Wrap your hands around this."

I frowned. "What is it?"

"Rose quartz. A kind of crystal," she said slowly, as if I was new to learning the English language. "Crystals are used for channeling energy and protection and different kinds of spellwork."

"In your witch practice."

"Sure."

"Sure? That sounds like a pat answer meant to shut me up."

"Shut up and wrap your hands around the ro—I mean, crystal. Crap, you're annoying."

I managed to control my smile and did as she asked. In a manner of speaking.

Instead of wrapping my hands around the rock, I wrapped them around hers holding it.

Instant flooding warmth. The heat rapidly rose as we stared at each other. We were caught in a vortex that felt so much bigger than we were, yet somehow was more about us than anything I'd ever experienced. The pink stone seemed to subtly glow, pulsing with faint energy as I tightened my hold on Ryan. It was as if she was being pulled from me, and only by sheer will could I hold on.

I dropped my hands away. The stone was merely a faceted pink rock once again. Not glowing or pulsing or anything else.

"Wow," she murmured.

"Is that…" I didn't even know what I wanted to ask.

"Part of the sex hex?" She didn't laugh. "I don't know."

"Is this a witch thing?" I sounded choked, as if I'd lost all my air. "Something you usually do."

"I've never done anything like this." Swallowing hard, she moved the rock from hand to hand. "I'll discuss it with Luna. She should know."

"Is she going to ask for a picture of my unmentionables too or is your word enough?"

Her gaze dropped and lingered on my groin. I couldn't say I minded either. "I don't have nearly enough words about them." Her voice was low and smoky and made my blood hum.

"Give me your phone."

"What?"

I held out my hand.

"I have your number already."

"Miss Moon."

She did me the great disservice of peeling down the front of her dress just enough to pry out her phone. Then she handed it over. "If you destroy it, I will do a binding spell on your unmentionables."

I didn't know what that meant, but it sounded unpleasant. Besides, I had a brand new fixation.

Her phone was warm from her body. All those delicious curves had been snuggled up against this plastic.

I'd never been jealous of an inanimate object before.

"Are you okay?"

I wasn't at all sure, but I nodded and let out an exasperated breath. "You have to unlock it first. I don't have your face."

"You are truly the king of the obvious." She did the honors for me before setting it in my hand again.

I scrolled through her contacts in her message app. Luna was on top—labeled Best Bish—but half a dozen down was an entry labeled Big Dick Energy.

"Who is this?" I stabbed her phone.

"I can't see it when your big finger is blocking the screen. Stop flailing about and let me see." She batted my hand away and smiled slowly. "Oh. Him. He's no one."

"That's why you reference his dick in his contact information? Or is that just standard operating procedure for you to reduce men to their most base level?"

"Turnabout is fair play. But if you must know, he's our yoga teacher."

"I want to petition for a nickname change," I muttered as I went back to her phone.

"You certainly make his look small."

I was not above preening as I did something I had never done in my life. I pulled up Luna's chat window, hit the camera icon and reversed the direction, and then cocked my head and hoped for the best as I pressed the button. I hit send without looking at it.

"Did you just take a selfie?" She snatched back her phone and started to laugh. "Oh my God." She doubled over with her hand over her mouth as she giggled at my expense.

When I pulled back the phone and saw what I'd sent, somehow I started laughing too.

I'd messaged a stranger a picture of the top right corner of my head, and the one eye in the picture looked cock-eyed and droopy. That was surely going to satisfy Luna's requirements for a photo.

"That's the best. Wow."

"It was my first one." I straightened my tie.

"Ever?"

"Yes."

Ryan sobered quickly. "But you wanted to send her one for me."

I shrugged.

"Come here."

"What? I have a client due to arrive in approximately—"

She yanked me toward her by the tie before angling my face toward the camera she held away from us. Then she pressed her cheek to mine.

"Smile, PMS."

I didn't know what expression I managed in that one second before I gave into temptation and turned my face into her neck. Dimly, I heard the shutter go off as I nibbled her earlobe. "Jesus, you smell good."

"Not exactly the picture I was going for," she said as as she tilted her neck to give me more access.

Which I took, greedily and without shame.

I kissed my way down her throat, scraping my teeth over her skin. She hummed in her throat, and my dick hardened in a nanosecond.

I'd probably give up everything just to spend an hour in this woman's bed.

Even her desk would do.

"But I think I like it. Keep going," she said breathlessly as I licked my way across her throat to the pulse hammering wildly under her jaw.

"Oh, I will." The proximity to her lips was making me mad. "I have to kiss you."

"For fuck's sake, don't ask. Just do it."

"Not the only place I want to kiss you." I slanted my mouth across hers and absorbed her groan like oxygen.

All at once, it was overwhelming. Just like yesterday. Wildly wandering hands competed with the desperation of my lips racing against hers. I couldn't taste her enough. I knew I was being rough, and hell if I could stop it.

She tasted like cinnamon. Fiery and unforgettable.

I cupped her jaw to direct her where I needed her. She opened up to me freely, lifting one of her legs to wrap around me. I was still kneeling on the floor and she was sitting on her chair, and I couldn't keep from rocking into her, grasping for any part I could touch. The chair tried to roll away and I scrambled after her, holding on fiercely as our mouths warred with each other.

In a minute, I'd pull her down onto my lap. Finish this insanity once and for all.

The elevator dinged. It might as well have been miles away for all the attention I paid to it. Same for the sudden flurry of chimes from Ryan's phone.

I was too preoccupied with Ryan's lips, all luscious and wet. And her body, sensuously wrapping around mine.

Sex hex be damned. I think I loved that curse.

Then I heard a loud sniffle. And another.

"I'm sorry. I'm sorry. Is this—are you—oh, God, are you cheating on your wife too?"

My head whipped around. My new client—at least I assumed— was sobbing into a too small tissue that allowed approximately a gallon of tears to leak onto her pale pink top.

With her hair askew and her lips swollen, Ryan rocketed back in her chair. "Oh, honey, what's wrong?"

I was still kneeling, dizzy and half crazed, when my assistant somehow got her bearings and hurried around the desk to scoop Stacey into a hug.

"That's okay. That's a girl. Just let it all out. Men are pigs, aren't they? Yes, they are."

I cleared my throat, but no one seemed to notice me and the unattended club between my legs.

On second thought, that was a good thing when it came to Stacey. I didn't need a lawsuit on my hands.

"I'm sorry I interrupted." Stacey pinned me with a slightly accusing stare out of streaming eyes. "But it was just like my husband. He was screwing his secretary. Oldest cliché in the book, right?"

"She's not my secretary." I cleared my throat. "We aren't...having intercourse."

"Oh, sure, right."

Had I ever heard a less sincere agreement? I had to say no.

Ryan didn't seem to mind Stacey was calling our character into doubt. No, she was too busy steering her to the small sofa in the client waiting area. "Clichés exist for a reason. They happen all the time. As awful as it is, you aren't alone, Mrs.—"

"Franklin. Well, soon to be Platt. I'm divorcing that dirty cheat. Do you know he gave her my brownies? I teach elementary school, and I stayed up after grading papers to make them for his lunch. I hope she enjoyed them, the hussy." She dashed at her tears while I tried to read the sudden slew of messages flashing on Ryan's phone screen.

> LU:
>
> OMG, he's kissing you. Or...licking you?
>
> LU:
>
> Fuck, that's hot.
>
> LU:
>
> He's hot.

And then something about a big dick, which could either be about me or the yoga teacher, but no matter how I stabbed the phone, I did not have Ryan's face. Also, my dick was not visible in that picture.

Was it?

"How low did you aim that selfie?" I demanded.

Both Stacey and Ryan glared at me.

"Never mind."

"He didn't deserve your brownies," Ryan said soothingly, rubbing Stacey's back while she sobbed.

I set down Ryan's phone and decided I'd assume I was the well-endowed one Luna was referencing. Ryan's commentary had indicated such.

The extent of their conversation I probably didn't want to know.

My own phone vibrated in my pocket. I dug it out and saw an unknown number with an interesting text.

UNKNOWN:

What happened to no cookies in the office?

I frowned.

Excuse me?

UNKNOWN:

Don't play dum. Are you conning her? She has a legion of spirit sisters behind her.

I looked up just as Stacey burst into a round of fresh sobs while Ryan poured water into a paper cup. "He told me he was taking me to Bimini for our anniversary. I found the tickets. Then I realized he was planning to take *her.*"

I needed to usher Stacey into the conference room if I had any hope of getting out of here anytime soon. And I had to, due to my followup appointment from yesterday's impulsive move. Whatever happened, it had to make more sense than the chaos my life had recently become.

Forget sex hex. A life hex might be more accurate.

Another text appeared.

UNKNOWN:

I realize you've been in a drought—or is that a lie too?

Finally, the mad texter had revealed herself. La-la-Luna. It had to be.

I quickly responded.

> What do you mean too, as if there is more than one lie? You don't know that I've lied. How did you get this number?

UNKNOWN:

> How do you think I got it? I borrowed Ryan's phone when she was drunk dozing.

My frown deepened. When had Ryan been drunk? Obviously, in the recent past, since she'd only had my number for a matter of days.

I quickly added her to my contacts and tapped out an irritated response.

> And you accuse me of lying when you are a thief?

LUNA:

> Hello, I am her best friend. All her stuff is mine & vice versa.

> Thank you for educating me. Now if you'll excuse me from this inane conversation, I have work to do.

My client was now dramatically reclining on the sofa while Ryan slid a pillow under her head and cooed softly to her. I didn't know how we could possibly have a meeting while she was prone. This was not a therapist's couch. I didn't deal with people who weren't upright for the conversation.

But thank God Ryan was here. She was handling all...*that*. I'd had a few crying clients in the past—and screaming, swearing, and occasionally physically violent ones, though usually at their soon-to-be ex-spouse, not me. But Stacey Franklin seemed particularly full of woe.

"It was just yesterday that he told me about Bimini. I was so excited. Then I came to pick him up after work because his car was in the shop, and his penis was in her mouth!"

I shut my eyes. Was it too late for me to consider a new career? Right now, anything sounded good.

And la-la-Luna was still texting.

> **LUNA:**
>
> You know what's inane? Claiming to be so righteous then dropping drawers in like, a sec.

She had a point, even if I'd not claimed righteousness nor stripped down. But I could agree my message had been inconsistent with my behavior. I didn't accept all the blame, however. Some could be laid at the green-tipped toes of one Ryan G. Moon.

But Luna had more to add.

> **LUNA:**
>
> Also, I didn't accuse you. I asked if you'd lied. I do not tolerate the XY chromosome messing with my best friend.

"What are you doing?" Ryan asked.

I put my phone in my pocket rather than telling Ryan her best bish was interrogating me. Luna's behavior was actually admirable. She was stepping up to make sure I had honorable intentions toward Ryan.

How many people were willing to put themselves out there for a friend? My closest friend Bishop would go to bat for me, but he was rare.

As was la-la-Luna. I didn't want to get her in trouble for being annoyingly decent.

Emphasis on annoying.

"Nothing." I swiveled my chair to face Ryan, and then just as quickly turned again to make sure Stacey was no longer in the waiting room. "What did you do with her?"

"She booked it to the ladies' room. Texting, huh?"

"No."

Ryan placed her hands on the arms of the chair and loomed over me, putting her ample cleavage entirely too close to my face. "You should be thanking me."

In a feat of Herculean proportions, I kept my gaze on her face. Mostly. I wasn't a saint. She had a purple wand necklace dangling between her breasts. I wanted to pull it between my teeth as arousal flared in her eyes then work my way under her dress to see what sort of lingerie she wore.

If she wore any at all.

"Hmm?"

"So much *hmming* going around. I really earned that bonus now. While you were over here being furtive, I convinced Mrs. Franklin that you were helping me with my contact and there are no issues with propriety in this office."

"Did you swallow your contact?"

"Huh?"

"I can't see how I could have been helping you with it unless I was attempting to retrieve it from your throat with my tongue."

She smirked. "There's an image. Besides, now she knows it's not like her situation. You're not secretly married, right?"

"Of course not."

Why did everyone seem to think I was lying about everything? Was it because I was a lawyer, or did I somehow give off an air of distrustfulness?

Everyone trusted my brother, and he lied as easily as he breathed.

She straightened with a proud smile. "So, yeah, I really can do this assistant thing. Stacey's washing her face, and then she'll be ready for the meeting. I did that. I mean, *she* did it. She's stronger than she gives herself credit for, but I helped her realize men are—"

"Pond scum?" I guessed.

"Close. But actually, I told her if a guy does something like that, he's not the one for you." She ran the edge of her nail along her crystal necklace. "If he's the one for you, nothing and no one can keep you apart."

"Is that so?"

"You know it is."

Looking into her eyes, I knew with one hundred percent certainty that she was right.

Which meant I needed to break her hold on me. *Now.*

I didn't want to, but I didn't trust myself around her. Yesterday morning had proved I was out of control, as had the last few minutes. The only way I could be certain we could stick to our respective corners was through distance.

And possibly a sex hex destroyer. I wondered where I could find one of those.

Regardless, Luna's texts had reminded me this wasn't a game. I couldn't let my dick lead me into perdition because real people got hurt when these kind of things went wrong. I knew that better than most.

Ryan might annoy me more than any human on this planet ever had, but hurting her was the last thing I ever wanted to do.

I made a show of looking at my watch as I stood. "I'll have to keep the meeting brief because I have something to get to."

"Oh, really?" She didn't ask what, but I could hear the interest in her tone.

Deliberately, I didn't tell her more. Maybe that made me a bastard, but I was doing the best thing for both of us.

"Mrs. Franklin," I said smoothly as the other woman emerged from the short hallway off the waiting room. "We're all set up in the conference room. This way, please."

"Stacey," she corrected, holding out a hand. "I'm sorry about before."

"No problem."

After we shook, she smiled warmly at Ryan. "Your assistant is worth her weight in gold. I hope you pay her very handsomely."

It took everything I possessed not to look toward Ryan. I could feel her pleasure at Stacey's words, and she deserved them. Clearly, I hadn't given her a fair shake when she'd taken this job, even if she did have some questionable personal traits and an inability to be on time.

But that didn't mean I intended to throw all caution to the wind.

She would finish her work here on Friday, and we would go our separate ways.

Thank God Luna had been the cold water I needed before it was too late.

I forced a smile. "She's worth more than I could ever give."

CHAPTER ELEVEN

Card of The Day:

Embrace: Page of Swords | **Release:** Five of Swords

BETWEEN BEING CAUGHT TRYING to take a photo of Preston, my crystal going haywire, him kissing the hades out of me, and then being interrupted by Stacey, I'd had entirely too much stimulation for an afternoon.

Never mind the secret plans he wouldn't tell me about. Which should not matter, except he'd just had his tongue in my mouth—again—and I guess I'd liked it.

Fine, no guessing required.

Since my energy levels were near the basement, I took a quick trip downstairs to suck in some sunshine and walk around the park across from Preston's office. I slipped off my heels and let the grass and the earth seep into my skin.

I wasn't an empath, but any woman would need a little recharge after that much emotional turmoil. Add in my own chaotic energy thanks to being in PMS's vicinity, and yeah, I needed a break.

"Whatcha doing?"

I blinked out of my minor cleansing bubble and looked down at the little girl. She couldn't have been more than six years old. "Hey there. Where's your mom? Or dad? Or…" I glanced around.

The girl's dark hair was scraped back into a messy tail, and she had a smudge of some kind of fruit on her face. She craned her neck up to meet my gaze. "Can I try?"

Desperately, I looked around for someone who belonged to her. "What?"

"The thing with your toes. Does it feel good?" She plopped on her butt and pulled off her sandals.

I clenched my toes into the grass. "Um, yeah, sure."

"Just watch for doggie doo. Sometimes people don't pick up after their dogs." The little girl's voice was matter of fact. "I always remember though. Even if it's gross, my dad says you gotta take responsa-reponsa—"

"Responsibility?"

"Yeah, that's the one. Responsibility for yourself and that includes your doggies. I have a doggie. His name is Bosco."

Do you have a daddy? That was the part I needed to know.

I crouched down to meet the girl on her level. "Are Bosco and maybe your dad around?"

"Oh, yeah." She pointed to a man chasing a multi-colored mutt of unknown origin with its leash dragging behind. "I got tired of chasing Bosco. He gets away a lot." She stood up and put her hands on her hips. "My dad is a mess. Grass feels nice though."

I stood back up and held out my hand to the girl. "Let's go help him."

She looked back at her shoes.

"They'll be fine with mine. We'll just mind the dog bombs."

She laughed then took my hand. "You're kinda funny."

"I've heard that many times. What's your name, kiddo?"

"Penelope, but my dad calls me Poppy." She smiled. "I secretly like it, but tell him I don't."

"Gotta say I enjoy Poppy. It's one of my favorite flowers."

"Me too!"

"You don't say." I laughed.

A dog's bark pierced the air. He—based on name, of course—went low on his front paws then cornered like he was on an opposite track and darted left while the tall man went right and tripped on his own feet and did a rather spectacular tuck and roll then bounded back up on his feet.

"Whoa."

"Yeah, my dad is weird."

"I can't roll like that."

"Oh, you should see him in his Judo class. He tosses people around like rag dolls."

I grinned down at Poppy. "You guys get more intriguing by the minute."

"Bosco!" Poppy giggled as the dog headed our way full steam ahead.

"Oh, crap." I braced myself for impact and went down hard. A lapful of dog and a very exuberant tongue was my reward. There were worse things. "Get down, you crazy mutt."

Bosco's eyes were a piercing Husky blue in a mottled calico-colored face. Another tongue lick took off half my makeup then he bounded off again.

"Dad!"

"Shit—shoot!" The guy winced and crouched down in front of me. "Are you okay?" His attention was still on the dog, but I could tell he was torn.

I gave him my most responsible smile. "Your kid is safe with me—go get the dog."

He pushed his overlong feathery hair out of his eyes. "You look okay. More than okay." He gave me a quick grin, and his accent gave me a little shiver.

I rolled my eyes. "I work in the building across the street. I'm harmless."

"Anything but harmless, love." A dimple dented his cheek. "But I'll be right back." He glanced at Poppy. "Good?"

Poppy nodded and gave him a thumbs up.

I laughed and crossed my legs under my long graphic sundress then prepared to enjoy the entertainment.

Super Judo Dad took off. Poppy plopped herself in the grass next to me and we both giggled at the antics.

"Bosco should be in agility training."

"What's agility training?"

"You know those dog shows you see on TV sometimes? Where the dogs do the obstacle course?"

"Oh, right!" She clapped when Bosco zipped around a tree. "Not sure he'd follow directions enough." She slapped her hands over her eyes as Bosco took out a picnic basket lunch and swiped a sandwich.

"Sorry!" Judo Dad yelled as he upped his speed.

The dog stopped long enough to wolf down the sandwich and that was his mistake. Poppy's dad dove on the leash. Then again, the dog didn't seem inclined to run now that he was happily killing a perfectly good foot-long sub, wrapper included.

He stopped at the picnic blanket and tried to apologize. He even went for his wallet but they just waved him off and gave the dopey dog a good scratch. The dad took out a business card, and the couple grinned, taking it and thanking him.

Hot dad and the dog came running back to us. The man collapsed in a heap on the grass in front of us. He was barely winded, but he was sweaty. It didn't take away the hot factor. In fact, his perspiration just curled his feathery hair even more.

The dog shoved his head under Hot Dad's arm and laid his huge head in his lap. The man ruffled his fur and there was no censure in his touch. "Dumb dog." He sighed. "I'm really sorry. Thanks for watching Poppy."

I wouldn't mind being called Poppy the way he said it either. "No problem." I held out my hand. "Ryan."

"Grant."

Hot Judo Dad had a hot name too. Figured. I was hoping for a zing when I shook his hand, but alas no.

Apparently, all my zings were reserved for one particular sexy, suited pain in the ass.

Grant had a warm, manly handshake that didn't crush, but he didn't treat me like I was a weak and helpless sort either. "I'd be happy to treat you to an ice cream as thanks." He moved back.

"And have Bosco steal it?"

Bosco lifted his head and his spotted tongue lolled out.

"Considering Bosco isn't supposed to eat bread, I probably shouldn't add ice cream to his list of offenses, I guess."

I grinned. "I have to get back to work anyway."

"We took off our shoes and smushed our toes into the grass, Dad."

"You did, hey?" He glanced down at my toes. "Should I ask why?"

"A little grounding exercise. Rough day at work."

"Ah. I never thought of it that way. But I do the same, I suppose. When I have a rough day, I go for a walk."

"See?" I rolled to my knees and stood up, shaking the grass out of my skirt. Another reason I wore black most of the time. Stains didn't show so much.

"Can I go get our shoes, Dad?"

"Stay where I can see you."

She darted off, her little feet kicking up in that carefree way kids had of running.

"Sorry about that whole thing. I do keep track of my daughter when I'm with her, I promise."

"I won't report you to CPS, don't worry."

"And why would you know those initials, fair Ryan?"

I hadn't meant to blurt that out. There had been many a time I actually did worry about someone calling Child Protective Services on my mom. Not that she didn't try her best, but not everyone understood Rainbow Moon's version of parenting. "I work for a lawyer."

"Ah." He frowned a little, but Poppy came racing back before he could say anything else.

She held up my wraparound sandals. "Here you go."

"Thanks."

Grant's eyes went hooded and he swallowed. "You work for a lawyer, you say?"

143

"I'm a temp."

"Explains a little. You don't look like any paralegal I ever knew."

"Lowly admin, I'm afraid."

"Never lowly." His dimple flashed again. "My admin would de-ball me if I said such things."

I laughed. "You sound like my friend Luna."

"Sounds like I'd like Luna. We should all go for coffee." He frowned. "Wait, that didn't come out right." He grabbed the back of his neck. "I mean, we should go out for coffee but if you're more comfortable in a crowd—man, I'm out of practice."

I laughed. "That's sweet." My pocket vibrated and I sighed. "I gotta get back."

"Right. Sure." He gave me a rueful smile. "Thanks, fair Ryan."

Poppy slid her hand into her dad's. "Thanks, Ryan. I liked squishing my feet with you."

"And I liked squishing my feet in the grass with you too." I waved and padded to the edge of the grass then put my heels back on.

I checked my phone, and sure enough, PMS was looking for me. Considering I hadn't taken a real lunch today, he could hold his very nice ass. And I ignored the immediate flutter at seeing his name.

Why, oh why, couldn't that have happened with the hot single dad with the accent?

When I drew that Page of Swords that morning, I had no idea I'd literally have a child flying into my life. The Universe had a damn sense of humor. Sighing, I crossed to Preston's building. As I got into the elevator, my phone buzzed again. I checked the readout and typed back that I was on my way.

By the time the doors opened, half the lights in the office were shut off.

"PMS?"

"You do realize that using my unfortunate nickname isn't professional."

I rolled my eyes. "Do you see anyone here?"

"You were not here, so a client could have been in my office."

"Don't get your boxers in a twist. You said you had an

appointment." He was standing by my desk, a folder in hand. "Do you have anything you need me to do while you're out?"

"No, you've done enough today. Try to be on time tomorrow. I have an important deposition at ten."

I narrowed my eyes. "You mean you have one at eleven and are telling me an hour earlier?" I knew since I kept his schedule for him.

"It was just moved ahead. If you weren't out galavanting, you'd have gotten the email notification."

"Look, I skipped lunch thanks to prepping for your last client. Give me a break."

He crossed his arms, his file tucked against his chest. "Is there a problem? You seem a little surlier than usual."

"And how would you know that?" I was trying to rein it in, but he was right.

"We usually enjoy a sort of banter."

"Enjoy?"

He dropped his hands to his sides. "Okay, now I know something's wrong. I know for a fact you enjoy needling me."

"It's just a little residual energy from Stacey. I'll be fine once I have a shower."

"You didn't shower this morning?" He frowned. "I—" He cleared his throat. "I'd have to say that was a definite yes from our…situation earlier."

"Situation? Oh. The neck thing." And the kissing thing. And the so many inappropriate tingles thing.

No big deal.

He frowned. "You forgot? Are there so many men in the same spot that you've forgotten?"

"What's it to you? You're the one with all the rules, not me. I'm a free agent."

Yet annoyingly, that freaking delicious vet had done nothing for me. Sure, I was free as a damn bird.

Preston stiffened and a sheet of paper slipped from the folder and floated onto my shoe. He lunged for it, but I was quicker. My stomach bottomed out and every ounce of moisture dried in my mouth.

Dating profile.

Needs.

Likes.

Dislikes.

He snatched the page out of my hands. "That's none of your business."

No, it really wasn't my business. He was so very right about that. "Nice to see that you don't want to actually enter a monastery, PMS." I arched my brow and loosened my muscles until it seemed as if I really didn't give two craps.

Even if I literally wanted to rip out his tongue and slap him with it. Goddamn him.

"I'm not a monk. I'm just careful with my sexual partners."

"Oh, right? You work all the time and won't dip your wick in the office ink. So what does that leave you with but a dating service? Not shocking really."

He so didn't seem the type. Then again, Mr. Logic probably loved the idea of a computer shitting out his perfect match.

Blond, petite, unassuming.

Not me.

Of course.

He crowded into me. "Is that right? You think I need a dating service?"

It was unnerving that he was taller than me. Most men were not. I hadn't gotten used to it yet. Maybe I never would.

I tipped my chin up to meet his gaze, and then I slid my knee between his legs. "You aren't willing to seal the deal with me, so it's not surprising you need a hand."

Shock hadn't let me really comprehend what I'd been reading other than the profile part. I dragged my finger across his lower lip. "So what gets that big...brain of yours hot? A sweet little blond with a soft voice? Deferential, polite. *Punctual.*" I said the last word with a hint of bite.

"Why don't you come with me and find out?"

"Excuse me?" My spine snapped straight, and I took a step back.

"Pretty sure your date wouldn't be into a threesome." My neck heated. "Or do I have you pegged wrong? Emphasis on the peg."

"What? No. Peg?" He shook his head. "I don't want to know. Your mind is startling. The tracks it takes are absurd and astounding." He turned to the briefcase sitting on my desk and slid the folder inside. "No, it's a speed dating appointment."

"I thought you said you didn't like to do everything fast. Guess that was just you being boastful."

It was his turn to arch his brow. "Are you frightened? Don't think you can survive a speed round, Miss Moon?"

"Oh, honey. You don't know what I can survive."

He snapped the locks and lifted the black leather briefcase. "I dare you to come."

"I'm not interested."

"Afraid you won't procure yourself a date?"

Me and my grass stained skirt could out-date his repressed suit with my hands tied. "You really want me to show you up in front of all those people, PMS?"

He smiled. "I'm game if you are."

CHAPTER TWELVE

HOW I FOUND myself in his car and not walking back to my own damn apartment, I really didn't know. Pretty sure it was the red haze of annoyance and jealousy that put my ass in his beige car.

Beige. So him and yet so not.

The energy and colors vibrated out of him when our lips locked, but then like a switch, his aura became the equivalent of flat ecru wall paint. I wasn't sure how he did it. Were his shields that good?

Did he even know he had them?

Why did I care?

I tapped my fingers on my thigh to the music playing on low. It was some watery, mid-tempo type song that I would listen to while I was sketching. Not exactly the stuff I'd listen to in the car. The car was for loud music—pop, singalong hair metal, classic rock—anything but sleepy chill out stuff.

Then again, he was driving a Grandpa car.

Why was this the guy who got my libido to sit up and take notice? Was it just because I'd been in a drought? Not on purpose or anything. I just had been happily in my own lane for work and enjoying spending time with friends instead of looking for someone to get horizontal with.

"So, how much is this going to cost me?"

"I'll cover your entry fee."

"I can handle my own finances, thanks."

His lips twitched. "Two hundred."

"What? Are we meeting billionaires or something?"

"For two hundred dollars?"

"Fair." I crossed my arms. I could afford it, but damn, that was steep. "I suppose that gets rid of the players."

"One would think."

Then again, he'd had his lips on mine a short time before he put himself out there for the next twenty or so eligible bachelorettes. Guys were pigs. Even the supposed good ones.

I'd learned that growing up with a free spirit for a mother. She'd gotten hurt so many times I lost count. Men promising she was the one, if only that pesky wife wasn't in the picture. And yet, the wife was never *out* of the picture.

Preston took a left, away from the eateries, cafés, and shopping district of Kensington Square and headed into the heart of Syracuse. The maze of byways and highways took us deeper into the flat grays and industrial flavor of the city.

"Where is this place?"

"Not far."

I dug my phone out of my bag. "What's the name of it?"

He was silent for a beat too long. Enough that I gave him some serious side eye. His finger tapped on the steering wheel. "It's new. There's no site."

"Don't be ridiculous. Everything has a site. That's how you market these days. Especially for startups."

"Patience, Miss Moon."

I huffed out a growl and scrolled through my messages, but unfortunately, there wasn't anything pressing or interesting to reply to. Luna had a group session tonight at her new apartment building. A few of the tenants had been interested in learning about tarot.

Not that I wanted to tell her I was going to some random speed dating event tonight—especially if I didn't ask her to come. She'd kill me.

Hell, she *would* kill me when she found out. She always knew.

I straightened in my seat as Preston pulled into…a clinic? I turned to him. "What the hell are you into, PMS?"

He didn't answer me, just got out and came around to open my door. I was so flabbergasted I didn't even try to open my own door. He held his hand out for me, and I couldn't think of a good reason not to take it. Especially when his eyes dared me to say no.

The hum and near burn of contact darkened my mood even further. I quickly snatched my hand out of his, swung my bag over my shoulder, and stalked for the door.

A huge window took up most of the front of the building. It was decorated with hearts and flowers in colorful window paint. Balloons decorated the door and were also tied to one of those chalkboard sandwich boards. A rather realistic drawing of a kitten peeked from the corner with an invitation to come inside for the speed dating event.

I could feel him looming behind me, so I glanced back. "I suppose it's only natural they need to use animals to help humans hook up."

Preston's eyebrow lifted, but he just gave me an amused look. And again, he managed to get around me to open the door, dammit.

The little clinic was bustling with people. The air was a bit antiseptic with a soothing overlay of lavender. As a mystical sort, I approved of the soothing use of essential oils, especially for something as nerve-inducing as meet and greets.

Secondary approval for the fact that lavender was one of the few essential oils safe for cats. It was amazing how many people could poison their animals with the essential oils craze that had taken over the world.

A short line of people were waiting to be checked in, and little pens were set up with blankets and toys for the supposed meet and greet areas. Before I could open my mouth and ask more questions, PMS took my hand and we wove around to another desk lined with pamphlets, fancy cat food adverts, and various medicines that I'd never heard of.

"I'd like to check in, and I've got a plus one."

The woman behind the desk gave him a wide smile and fluttered her astoundingly fake lashes at him. Her friendly factor dimmed a few notches when she noticed me.

"Of course, Mr. Shaw." Her fingers flew over her keyboard.

They knew him here? Just how many times had he done this kind of thing?

"I am not your plus one. How does that even work with speed dating—" I stopped short.

No way would he be into that... Or would he? How well did I know him, after all?

I swallowed and refused to assess the quick prick of sweat forming between my boobs. "Look, I'm open-minded, but I'm not really into the poly thing."

The woman glanced up from her computer, her mouth dropping open.

Preston cleared his throat. "Do you have another application, Tracy?"

"Yes, of course."

He handed her his sheet and the card he'd somehow whipped out when I wasn't paying attention. "You can put both on my card."

I lifted my chin. "I told you I can pay my own way."

"It's fine. My treat."

I elbowed him out of the way as I dug into my bag. "I don't need you to."

He blocked me with a clipboard. "Fill that out."

Seething, I grabbed the board and automatically filled in my details. It was a pretty clever questionnaire, to be honest. "Wait, what does this mean, 'are you willing to take on a special needs kitten?'"

He snatched the board out of my hand and scribbled something on it in that slashing way he had. He smiled at Tracy and took my hand again. "We'll just wait over there for things to start."

"Right." Her huge, overdone eyes kept darting between us and narrowed at our joined fingers.

I almost shook him off, but something wouldn't let me. I didn't have time to psychoanalyze my reaction before he hustled me to the side of the room near the windows. Now that I wasn't huffing across the parking lot, I noticed cats of all different types and ages were climbing, playing, and sleeping in the little atrium. The most elaborate cat tree I'd ever seen filled the entire room.

"Pretty amazing, aren't they?" His arm slid along my back as he braced himself behind me.

I looked up automatically. Preston's face was too close, but there wasn't much room since everyone in the room practically had their noses pressed to the glass. Our height difference yet again had my stupid hormones doing the samba. And the stupid ocean-tinged scent he wore was distracting as hell.

And why was he getting all up in my business anyway? He was the one who wanted us to strictly remain in our boss-employee roles. At least I thought it was mostly his idea. Okay, and I guess it had been mine too.

Except we kept kissing, and that was not entirely my fault. Then he dragged me here to this damn dating thing, and now he was definitely encroaching on my freaking personal space.

I tried to push back against him, and my ass slid across the front placket of his suit pants. *Careful*. I didn't want to feel anything that would contribute to my personal failings later on.

Too late there.

I closed my eyes and drew in a calming breath. His resulting exhalation brushed the tendrils of curls near my ear.

"I made a few calls and convinced Piper Lockwood to donate one of her famous cat trees to the clinic."

He just kept chatting along like he wasn't half hard against my butt. "Famous?"

"Well, in cat circles anyway. She has a cat café in California that went viral, thanks in part to how clever she is and her famous rockstar husband. She only does special orders."

I forced myself to focus on my surroundings. There were little shelves and ramps bolted to the carpeted wall. A dozen pillars in varying heights were scattered around the space, offering a dizzying array of levels for cats to perch, play, or sleep on. The room was a proverbial princess playground for cats. "So, she makes up cat trees?"

"Does that look like a typical cat tree?"

I tipped my head to study his face. "You sure know a lot about cats."

He swallowed, his gaze bouncing from my lips to my eyes and back again. "I donate a lot to this place. The cats they take on deserve so much more than the universe gives them." He straightened up and moved away from me. "The least I can do is help out monetarily."

I grabbed his tie before he could totally escape me. This was something that was important to him. There was a passion in his voice that I'd never heard before. "This isn't a dating thing, huh?"

He gently pulled his tie out of my fingers. "No. This is a way to raise money for the treatment of these sweet animals that people forget about. And an adoption clinic for those who are ready to go to regular homes."

"And you're adopting a cat?"

"No—well, yes." He folded his arms. "I usually just donate. I don't know why I got the stupid urge to adopt one. I don't have time for a cat."

"Sure you do." I patted his lapel. "You make time. It can even be a mascot cat for the law office. You know, like some have a dog. Helps to have a support animal, right?"

He frowned. "That's not very professional."

I shrugged. "Screw professional."

"That may be your take on things, Miss Moon, but that's not how I treat my business."

"Maybe you should."

Before he could answer me, a woman with a jaunty ponytail clapped her hands. "Attention, everyone! We're going to start out with our first speed round. Now it won't be super fast like the ones some of you may have been part of in the past." Her voice was friendly and perky like Elle Woods from the *Legally Blond* movies. "But we want you to meet as many amazing kittens and cats as possible and hopefully, bring one home!"

She quickly told us how to line up and gave us little buzzers like people used at restaurants.

"When this goes off, you move to the next playpen. And don't worry if you don't find your perfect *purrmate* today. The entry fee will go to helping all of our special needs kittens and cats here at Kitten Around, and we truly appreciate it."

Since I had my own buzzer, Preston and I wouldn't be seeing the same kittens. However, I couldn't stop myself from watching his reactions to each cat or kitten. The tentative and patient way he had with the frightened ones, and the overwhelmed delight he couldn't disguise at the playful ones.

Okay, my ovaries were in serious peril here.

Ignoring the warmth in my belly, I focused on my own tiny bundle of fluff. The initial rounds had gone quickly, and we were now in round four. I was thoroughly covered in kitten fur, but the energy of the room had boosted my mood.

I sat crosslegged in one of the larger pens. This was a special case with a bonded pair. The sweet white kitten with a heart-shaped spot to the left of her nose was freaking adorable. But her protective, jet black brother was a bit thornier.

I let my hands rest in my lap and didn't make any sudden movements, allowing them to come to me. Eventually, the white one climbed up my sleeve to get to my shoulder while the black one gave me some serious side-eye.

A minute later, the little white one was purring from her perch in my curls.

Oh, crap. I had not been entertaining the thought of actually getting a cat today. Let alone a troublesome pair of pre-teens. They weren't itty bitty kittens, but according to their paperwork, they'd been returned twice because of problematic behavior.

"You do not need this in your life, Ryan."

Maybe if I said the intention aloud…

Then the black kitten jumped into my lap and I was sunk. He tucked himself against my hip, under the light sweater I was wearing over my black linen sundress.

I looked up and met PMS's gaze. He smirked at my predicament as he was lightly stroking the top of an elderly cat's head. His or her ear was torn, but it only made the cat more beautiful.

The buzzer went off in my sweater pocket.

It was now or never.

I huffed out a sigh and tucked my flag into the top of the gate to let them know I was interested in taking these kittens.

I almost took my flag back when the black cat took a swipe at my ribs when I had to move him. I lifted him gently so I could look him in the eyes. "Feisty, aren't you?"

He yowled and leaped away.

Okay, then.

He continued to meow and yell at me until I detangled the white kitten from my hair and set her back down with him.

"All right, that's enough. I didn't steal her."

He hissed at me, and I stuck my tongue out at him before I lifted my skirt to climb out of the pen.

"You want me to take away my flag?"

He flounced to the blankets heaped in the corner and settled down to stare at me.

"Look, the kitten has your temperament."

I knew that voice. I dreamed of that damn voice.

When I elbowed Preston, he chuckled. "Planted your flag?"

"Maybe." Both the buzzer and flag were caged in his long fingers. "I see you have not."

"Haven't quite met my match." His gaze drifted to my lips then back to meet my eyes. "I'm very particular."

I swallowed. I just bet he was. Stuffy, pent up, repressed suit that he was. Of course he'd be picky about every little thing.

He'd be very thorough.

And I needed to put that thought in a box, thank you very much.

Before I could articulate a response, Elle Woods rang her little bell for us to move to the next station. "Happy hunting."

He stepped into the pen I'd just been visiting. "Let's see if this little devil likes me or not."

"Good luck." I took a page from the kitten's playbook and flounced.

The next few rounds included perfectly sweet cats, but none of them seemed to be especially 'mine'.

Finally, most of the cats had been homed, and another flag was stuck beside mine for the bonded pair. Elle—aka Beverly—clapped again to get our attention.

"Thank you so much for making this such a success. Most of our lovely cats and kittens have been requested, and now we'll just make sure everyone is a perfect fit. We have a bonus round of our more special needs cats if you'd like to stick around for that. But first, we'll have our amazing volunteer vet come out and talk to us about what it means to be a special needs cat owner. Dr. Thorn?"

"Thanks, Beverly."

My heart gave a little kick when I recognized my hot dad from the park. His flyaway hair was in a little more semblance of order, but those sharp cheekbones and that lilting accent were definitely the same.

Preston came up beside me while the vet discussed the things to be aware of when choosing a special needs cat. After a moment, PMS laid a proprietary hand on my lower back.

My skin did not sizzle. I couldn't decide if I was relieved or disappointed.

"I'm not here to dissuade you from taking on a geriatric cat who needs a little more medication, or one of our more serious cases. I'm just here to answer any questions if you are of a mind to take on an animal who may need just a bit more love. We appreciate all of you for coming today. I'll be walking around while you're on your dates." Dr. Thorn gave us a wide, dimpled smile and handed the mic back to Beverly.

This round of the speed dating would be slower in deference to the animals who required a little more care.

The vet caught sight of me and crossed the room. "Ryan, it's lovely to see you again."

"You know him?" Preston blurted.

I ignored him. "Hi, Grant. And look at you, this time you're not even sweaty."

"Excuse me?"

I swallowed the smile, but I was still annoyed at the hand-on-my-back thing. Hot then cold, in my business then pushing me away—PMS needed to figure out that I wasn't his plaything. "I ran into Grant in the park today. He was chasing his dog that got loose."

"And the fair Ryan was sweet enough to watch my daughter while Bosco sent me on a merry chase."

"Daughter...oh, so you're married?" Preston sounded positively giddy. For him anyway.

Grant slid his gaze to Preston. "'Fraid not, mate. Just a dad."

"Oh."

"Are you interested in one of our special cases? I'm sorry, I didn't get your name." Grant held out his hand.

"Preston Shaw."

Their shake was firm and possibly a little overdone. I rolled my eyes and hip-checked PMS. "He hasn't found his perfect cat yet. But he's definitely interested. Especially if one would be good for an office space as well as a home."

PMS gaped at me. "The animal doesn't need to come to work with me."

"But it would be a plus. Especially if they're good with people."

Grant looked from me to PMS and back. "Well, we do have a three-year-old cat who may just fit that bill." He nodded to a gray cat who had just been released from a carrier. "We just transferred the cat from a kill shelter in Chicago so he's had a bit of a rough start. But he's healthy and good-natured."

We followed the veterinarian to the pen.

A small face popped out of the carrier with a red collar and a shiny silver bell.

"You have got to be kidding me."

Preston gave me a sidelong look. "What?"

The cat buzzed the side of his head along the wires of the carrier before scampering out on three legs.

Well, that wasn't quite like the cat who had been climbing in and out of my dreams, but he was damn close. Instead of a red tie, he had a collar, but dear goddess. He was a sleek and complete gray without any other patches of color save for a tiny white patch on his remaining front paw and another on the tip of his opposite ear.

"We don't have a name for him," Grant went on. "We've tried a few, but he doesn't seem to be interested in any of them. So, you'd have your choice of names. And as you can see, the three legs thing doesn't really hold him back."

The cat did a feat of acrobatics around an arched…was that like a mobile for a child? Then he perched nimbly on top of it and started washing his chest.

Delighted, Grant rocked on his heels. "As you can see, not much holds him back."

Preston had his arms crossed and he was nearly shouting with his closed off vibes, but he couldn't keep his eyes off the cat.

"Miss Moon?"

I turned to the voice at my left. Tracy from the front desk was twisting her fingers nervously. "Could I talk to you for a moment?"

I nodded and followed her, looking briefly over my shoulder at the two men—so completely different and yet equally attractive. My gaze drifted from the wilder, freer Grant Thorn, whom I should have been instantly drawn to, to the taller, stiff, frequently grumpy Preston. I could tell he was practically aching to go meet the cat in the pen.

Yet he held himself back. Of course.

"Dammit," I muttered under my breath.

"Excuse me?" Tracy's comedically thick lashes waved at me.

"Nothing. Pretty sure my boss is about to get a cat."

"And that's a bad thing?" She frowned.

I pasted a smile on my face. "Nope. Serves him right." I waved her off when she opened her mouth to ask for more details. "He's just going to blame me for getting a cat, that's all."

"Did you say *boss*?"

I nodded. "Yep."

She seemed relieved. "Oh, that was nice of you to come and keep him company." She grabbed a clipboard from the slot with my flag's number.

"Yeah, I'm a real gem."

"He just always seems so lonely. He comes in a few times a month and then donates a ridiculous sum of money, but he never even asks to visit with the cats."

Well, that tracked. Preston Shaw lived to be in a repressed state. What I could do if I got a hold of his...chakras.

She pointed proudly at the golden name plate. "We even built on the kitten hospital wing due to his generosity. Allie's Wing is named after one of our tiny babies we lost. She was a very special case. Mr. Shaw was very invested in her care."

My eyes pricked. Well, hell. Damn him for being so thoughtful. Now I was the one with the fluttering lashes so I didn't freaking cry. I cleared my throat. "You needed me for something?"

"Oh, yes. We were going through the applications for the bonded kittens."

My stomach dropped. "Oh, right. I saw that there was more than one flag on their little enclosure."

"Yes." She tapped her pen against the clipboard. "You put on here that you have a small apartment."

"I do, yes."

"We weren't sure you'd have enough room for two very active kittens? Do you think you could care for them?"

I opened my mouth to quickly agree, but I followed her gaze to a young couple waiting in the wings.

"You were the first to put your flag in for the kittens. We'd be happy to—"

I held up my finger. "Are they looking to adopt them too?" I nodded to the couple.

Tracy sealed her lips and nodded.

I laced my fingers and set them on the counter. "Can I talk to them?"

She blinked at me. "You want to talk to them?"

I nodded.

"Um, I think that would be all right."

Disappointment hit me the closer I got to the couple. The two little kittens had wormed their way inside me already, but I could tell they weren't mine to have.

The young woman, barely old enough to drink, tucked her long, springy red hair around her ear. A lanky man with a spotty beard, wearing clothes that were two sizes too big, stood next to her, sweetly rubbing her back.

Yep, those cats *so* weren't mine.

"Ili, I'm Ryan."

The girl toyed with the fringe on her bag. "I'm Melody, and this is Lonny."

"You guys are interested in the two kittens?"

The young woman nodded and tucked her hair again, an obvious nervous habit. "They're so sweet. Lonny and I just moved in together last month, and we've been hoping to add to our family." Her voice was soft and uncertain. "We saved up to donate here. Dr. Thorn was so sweet to me when I had to put my cat down this past winter."

Well, shit.

I reached out and covered her trembling fingers. "They're yours. I couldn't possibly keep them from you."

I pushed a little soothing energy into her to ease her mind. She was clearly a sweet soul. I didn't read auras as easily as Luna did, but I knew good people when I saw them.

After digging into my bag, I pulled out a card. "If you're one of those people who takes a zillion photos of your babies for social media, do you think you could send me the link?"

Her eyes widened. "How did you know?" She looked down at my card. "Oh, you're a psychic?"

"More of a tarot cards and divination kinda gal. But I had a feeling."

"I'm a photographer." She leaned against Lonny. "We both are."

"Then I expect all the photos of those two crazy kittens. Careful of the black one."

"Oh, we've already named him Lucifer," Lonny said with a smile.

"See, they were meant to be yours. That's exactly the name I was thinking of when he took a swipe at me."

We all laughed.

We said our goodbyes, and I stopped in to let Tracy know I'd deferred to the couple for the adoption. She looked relieved and pushed a pamphlet on me for the next event.

By the time I made it back to Preston, Grant had moved on to answer questions about another cat. PMS was sitting with the gray cat in his lap, and he was purring loud enough for me to hear it from ten feet away.

The cat, not PMS, but it was a close thing.

"Got yourself a cat, hey?"

Preston frowned, but he couldn't stop stroking those long fingers down the cat's head and neck. "I shouldn't."

I crouched outside the pen and hung my arm over the side to pet the cat. My fingers tangled with Preston's, and the cat's bright green eyes widened before his purring intensified.

Quickly, I pulled away my hand and stood. "Well, let's get you two home."

And *me* home, preferably into an ice cold shower.

CHAPTER THIRTEEN

PRESTON

I WAS GOING HOME with a cat.

And my assistant. I wasn't sure which was more troubling.

In truth, my assistant wasn't coming to my house. I was just driving her home. That should've been a safe endeavor.

At least in theory.

The problem was we had entirely too many hormones bouncing around between us. On top of that, I had never given April rides home or anywhere else. I also hadn't invited her to a "working lunch" the first day of her employment. We had never kissed or fondled glowing hunks of rock or attended speed dating events. That Ryan and I weren't being matched with each other hardly seemed to matter.

I couldn't keep my hands off her. And it didn't even matter if that overly smiley vet Thorn was lurking around. My hand seemed to be magnetically drawn to the small of her back.

Before the speed dating event, Luna had reminded me I had no business entertaining the possibility of anything with Ryan. Too bad I couldn't seem to remember that when we were alone.

Or even when we weren't.

She was like oxygen, and I'd been starving for air for far too long.

Now we were walking out to the parking lot, my hand between us carting the carrier holding my new charge, and I could feel her gaze lingering on me. She made an attempt at light conversation, commenting on different things about the event, but the weight of her stare was a physical thing.

Being alone with her in my car was not a smart plan.

I smiled as an idea took form. I would take proactive steps to protect her virtue.

Luna would probably approve.

Before Ryan could stop me, I rushed around the car to open her door.

One black brow winged up. "What's with this new chivalrous side?"

"What do you mean, new? When have I ever been anything but a gentleman?"

"When you groped me every time you saw Dr. Thorn."

"I hardly groped you."

"You touched me in a way to indicate possession."

I reached up to run a finger under my suddenly too tight collar. "You are my temp. That indicates a kind of...employment possession." Even I knew that was ridiculous.

She rolled her eyes and got into the car. Then she stuck out her fingers to touch the cat in the carrier. "You're such a good boy. Just sitting there quietly while your daddy says nonsense."

"It's not nonsense," I muttered. Then I frowned. "Daddy? Me?"

"It does seem like a biological impossibility, but that sweet cat doesn't know the difference."

I stepped back as she pulled the door shut. Then I rounded the vehicle and opened my door before leaning in to try to fit the carrier on the console area between us.

"What the hell are you doing?"

I grunted as I tried to make the carrier fit between the seats. The cat let out a sound between a growl and a meow at the violent rocking. I couldn't say I blamed him.

"If you're this bad at fitting everything, you just made my decision a lot easier. Give me that." She tugged the carrier away from me and climbed out of the passenger side.

What decision was she talking about?

She opened the back door and set the carrier on the floor in the back before returning to the front.

"Maybe you should drive," I heard myself suggesting as I reluctantly slid behind the wheel and shut the door. "I'll sit back there with the cat."

"Do you have some fantasy about being driven around by a lowly peon? Sorry. I don't drive beige grandpa cars."

"Grandpa? I'll have you know this car has plenty of horsepower."

"Horsepower only gets you so far." She clicked her belt into place. "You need to know how to use it."

I put on my own seatbelt. "Trust me, I've never had any complaints."

"Oh, I'm sure. I bet the society types you take out to socially approved events get a thrill from your...torque."

"Not sure if you've forgotten, but I told you it's been awhile for me." I put the car in drive and reversed out of the space too fast. It was nearing sunset, and the sun was like a spotlight through the trees as I drove away from the shelter.

"Been awhile for a relationship is one thing. Surely you date. Maybe have the occasional long lunch—"

"Don't." My voice whipped out.

"I didn't mean that," she said after a moment, sounding chagrined. "I was just going to make a rude nooner comment, but not about that. I wouldn't."

"Why wouldn't you? You think I'm just like my father, don't you?"

"I do believe you aren't married."

I let out a frustrated noise and signaled to get onto the highway. "That's all that you see that separates us?"

"No. I doubt your father would do all you've done for those sweet cats." She shot me a quick glance. "Or look at them the way you do when you think no one is paying attention."

I swallowed uncomfortably. "I'm no hero. I don't help to get praise."

"No, and that's why you deserve it."

I merged onto the highway and grabbed my sunglasses, sliding them on. "I thought we were talking about my dating life."

"Why would we talk about that? I can't see any reason." Slowly, she crossed and recrossed her legs. "Can you?"

"It's a point of fact."

"And not my concern, unless you've forgotten your unbreakable rules regarding employees."

I tightened my fingers around the wheel. "I have a photo on my phone that indicates my rules can bend."

"You mean on *my* phone."

Ah, dammit, it was on her phone. I'd wanted to keep the picture, so I could stare at it when I was alone. So I could imagine what it would be like to live like that all the time. To just think of the pleasure of the moment. To take what I craved and give back so much more in return.

"And yes, your rules can bend. But you never make the choice freely. You're always led by the woman cursing you for unknown reasons with a sex hex."

"Probably just for the amusement of seeing me at your mercy."

"Oh, Mr. Shaw," her voice dropped to a purr, "if I had you at my mercy, I guarantee neither of us would be laughing."

Neither of us spoke for the rest of the ride to her apartment, other than a few short directions from Ryan. The cat was mostly quiet, but she twisted around a couple of times to slide her fingers into his cage. Each time, she was rewarded with some action that made her murmur softly to him.

I'd never been jealous of a cat before.

Once I pulled into the small parking lot, I drove into the far back, near an alley partially blocked off with a chain link fence. A canopy of trees overhead provided some privacy, and no cars were parked close by.

That was intentional.

She frowned and took off her belt, turning toward me on her seat. "What are you doing? There were spots near the building."

I took off my own belt and undid the button on my jacket before shifting toward her. "Making a choice," I said softly, cupping her soft cheek in my palm.

The pulse just beneath her jaw fluttered wildly against my finger. "Of your own free will."

"Yes, but I can't make any other choice right now. Not because of a sex hex," I acknowledged as the cutest wrinkle formed between her brows, "but because you're the most maddeningly intoxicating woman I've ever known. Now shut up so I can kiss you."

She smiled when our lips met, but that was the last lighthearted moment between us. I slipped my arms around her under her sweater and somehow lifted her into my lap with a minimum of banged knees and flailing arms, and she straddled my legs as if she'd been meant to fit in that very spot, steering wheel in her back and all. She coiled her arms around my neck and our lips refitted together on a long groan, one I was pretty sure we shared.

I couldn't stop sucking on her tongue, and she kept driving her fingers through my hair, tugging on my scalp with every twist. Her full breasts were mashed against my chest, her nipples hard and tight, and she tasted like a mix of sin, moonshine—the actual moon, not the alcohol—and the peppermint tea she'd had at work.

I wanted to drown in her. To thrust between her legs with every bit of the savage gentleness with which I was attacking her sweet, sexy mouth.

And most especially, to forget a world existed outside what we were like together.

She scraped her nails down the back of my neck and swiveled against me, grinding her cleft against my very insistent cock. The purr of satisfaction she made in her throat gratified me in ways I couldn't explain.

"You came to play ball." She nipped my lower lip, her lashes flickering over her sultry eyes. "Sir."

That single word made me grip her jaw that much more forcefully, my other hand lowering to her breast. It flowed into my palm, full and perfect, and she gasped into the kiss, her mouth battling mine for supremacy. I twisted her nipple and drew on her tongue as she rocked against me, testing us both.

I had to have more of her.

Breathing hard, I pulled back long enough for our gazes to connect. Then I lowered my head and sucked on her nipple like I had her tongue, hating the layers of fabric between us. Lightly, she scratched the back of my neck again, adding those little frissons of pain that made my shaft jerk every damn time. As if she loved pushing me to the very boundaries of my control.

Getting some of my own back, I peeled down her jersey dress and swallowed a groan at the sight of her lacy low-cut red bra. Of course it was sexy. Everything about her was. I nudged that out of my way too and her hard brown nipple was there for the taking.

Using my lips and tongue and teeth, I pulled hard enough to make her pant and squirm against me.

"Fuck, we're outside." But she wasn't pushing me away. If anything, she was clutching me closer, her fingers drawing alluring circles on the back of my neck as I licked and nipped her taut little tip.

"Are you asking to fuck outside? Because we absolutely could. You taste like fucking peaches."

"So much swearing from such a normally repressed male."

Her rich, throaty laughter jogged something loose inside me. "You think I'm repressed?" I couldn't decide if I was insulted or if she was challenging me.

Daring me to prove her wrong.

"Right now? Now I think you're lust-drunk."

"And I think you talk too much."

I slanted my lips over hers, kissing her long and slow before capturing her nipple between my teeth once again. The last rays of the sun sparkled on her crystal necklace, dangling so erotically between her breasts. One of which I hadn't given any attention yet. I freed the other and swallowed at its sheer perfection before I took her nipple into my mouth.

Her hands returned to my hair as I devoted myself to my task. I was *very* good at focusing. And from her quickened breathing, she didn't mind one bit.

Distantly, I heard a meow. Then another. Concern pricked at the edges of my consciousness, but Ryan was moaning now, her nails rough against my scalp as she rode my cock through my trousers.

"I want to taste the rest of you." She had no idea how close I was to begging.

How close to just pushing back my seat all the way and taking her right here, possible witnesses and potential public embarrassment be damned.

I was burning up for her. My clothes felt too tight. I needed to get out of this tie, this jacket, these freaking torture device pants.

And I needed to get *in* her. So deep that neither of us could think straight.

Not that we were now.

"Mmm. I think we can arrange—" She turned her head and gasped out a laugh.

Panting, half crosseyed, I turned my head and discovered my new cat sitting on the passenger seat, watching us unrepentantly.

"What the hell?" I tried to catch my breath, to resist her shiny nipple gleaming up at me. My lips were humming from just the feel of her.

Ryan tipped her head against mine. "Did you forget to latch the carrier?"

"No?"

"That doesn't sound very certain. Did you head bonk your way out, Smoky?" Her hand shook a little as she held it out to the cat, who rubbed his head against her in a clearly adoring manner.

One I fully identified with, especially when she was seated on my lap. My damn zipper was about to bust.

"Smoky is a great name. Do you like it?" I asked the cat, and then I frowned and pretended I hadn't.

Ryan's laughter rumbled in her throat. "He's probably hungry. Or has to pee."

"We all have needs."

"Don't we just?" She arched a brow, clearly amused at me. She was recovering much faster than I was. "You have a setup at home?"

"What kind of setup? I have bathroom and kitchen facilities like everyone else." As her mouth curved, I leaned back against the headrest and took another moment to look my fill at her breasts before covering them back up. The last thing I wanted was anyone to wander by and get a glimpse of her like this. "I blame blood loss."

"You mean blood rerouting." She rubbed against my painfully aroused cock. "So, about that fitting conversation..."

I grunted. "I need a damn litter box. And cat food. I wasn't thinking. I've never been a parent before. Pet parent," I added belatedly, but it was too late.

"You always surprise me, PMS." Her expression softened beautifully in the fading sunlight. Her skin had the sexiest flush from the rasp of my whiskers, and her lips were puffy from mine. Her nipples were too.

Just the way I wanted them.

I brushed my thumb over her mouth. "I like seeing you swollen from me."

She nipped the pad of my finger before she slid a glance down my body to where my erection was still doing a mighty fine job of trying to escape my trousers. "Same goes."

Before I could say the words circling in my brain—*how about we fuck like people who don't work together*—she let out a long sigh. "Let's go to the pet store."

"Really?"

"You have a better idea?"

"Define better."

Her throat rose and fell on a quick swallow. "That was hot, but…"

"But?"

How was there still a *but* between us? All the many, many logical reasons aside.

Ones I was not considering at all. Not until I'd handled the situation that was causing my precipitous drop in IQ points.

She dropped back her head, exposing the long line of her throat. "I'm not looking to be your morning-after mistake."

"I made a choice," I reminded her. "I kissed you with almost all my faculties intact."

"With a dick that hard, I doubt it. Impressive, by the way." She climbed off my lap and managed to land in the passenger seat without flashing more than a forbidden glimpse of her thigh or crushing the cat.

"C'mon, Smoky." She scooped him up. "Let's get you back in that carrier and go get you some toys and goodies."

I reached down to refasten my jacket and adjusted myself with a wince as she got out to settle Smoky in his carrier. I briefly worried about his potential to flee, but he didn't seem to be a flight risk while she was holding him.

Who could blame him?

"Do you have pets?" I asked as she latched the carrier.

She got back in her seat and clicked her belt back into place as I did the same. She looked seductively mussed with her lipstick partially worn off and her dress askew, and I couldn't stop staring at her.

"I have my hands full with plants." She grinned, studying me. "Your hair is a wreck."

I flipped down my visor mirror and discovered she wasn't lying. I tried to get it back into a semblance of order, and she huffed out a sigh before grabbing her purse. "Come here."

I came.

She did some magic with her hair brush and some spray I didn't question yet probably should have. "Have you ever tried guyliner? You have the eyes for it. That panty-melting golden brown."

"Not sure it's the proper image for a law office," I said dryly once she moved back.

Luckily, she hadn't added a pink stripe or God knows what to my hair. I just looked put together again.

I had no reason at all to be disappointed.

Smoky let out a plaintive meow, which was my cue to slip the car into Drive.

We arrived at Pet-O-Rama a few minutes later. I wasn't back to normal, but I was no longer prepared to take her in the front seat. Although I could be ready in an instant, should the situation warrant it.

I had a feeling it wouldn't.

As I parked, Ryan quickly fixed her lipstick and rearranged her hair, ensuring that no one in the world would ever guess we'd behaved highly inappropriately. My biggest regret was that we'd been interrupted.

"I had sex in a fountain once," I announced as she was about to get out of the car.

She glanced back. "Drinking or ornamental?"

I had to laugh. "Ornamental. It ended with us in the back of a police car."

"Ouch." She grimaced. "But did you get an orgasm first?"

I frowned. "I can't quite remember."

"I'm gonna go with no then. Pro tip—always make sure you have the orgasm first. C'mon, Smoky," she said into the back. "We're going in to get you all kinds of stuff. Daddy's got a platinum card." She climbed out to open the back door and free the cat from his prison.

I was still smiling when it fully clicked in what she was doing. "You can't bring a wild animal into a retail establishment."

She snorted as she nestled the cat against her chest. "Watch me, PMS."

She shut the door on my astonished expression.

I joined them at the double doors and she tapped the sign that said *pets welcome* before we walked inside.

We were immediately confronted with a leashed Saint Bernard who lifted his head and licked my likely terrified cat with a pink tongue the size of a chaise lounge.

I expected the cat to hiss and jump down before running away to hide in the bowels of Pet-O-Rama, never to be seen again.

Instead, Smoky turned his head and began to wash his face.

"I thought cats hated dogs," I said when my voice returned and we'd turned down an aisle with many fish tanks.

"Don't believe the hype."

"Hmm."

"All animals are as different as all humans are. Take you and me."

"You always get the orgasm first?"

It took a father hurrying his young daughter down the aisle away from us for me to fully grasp I was not using my indoor voice.

Ryan buried her face in the cat's fur to stifle her laughter. Then she glanced up and gave me a sly look. "I'm going to say no. Because you definitely left me hanging in the car."

"Don't blame me for that," I said under my breath and nodded to the cat.

She scratched his neck. "Don't listen to him, Smoky."

I followed her down the maze of aisles after accepting the basket she thrust at me, vowing not to speak again unless I was spoken to—at least not before I'd had an opportunity to relieve myself properly in the shower.

Obviously, I wasn't capable of rational, voice-modulated discourse beforehand.

We wandered through the store, filling the basket. Cats needed a lot of items, apparently, although they themselves were quite small. Things such as dishes for dry and wet food and for water. At least that was what I believed, but she shoved a fancy fountain thing at me and told me fresh was best.

Next up were treats. Soft ones. Hard ones. She offered them along with a lecture about not overfeeding, which seemed counterintuitive since she was the one suggesting I offer my cat all manner of junk food.

When the basket overflowed, I traded it for a cart, and Ryan put Smoky into the extra large bright pink litter pan she had selected. I expected the cat to jump out, but he seemed quite content to be pushed around while we loaded up on jumbo bags of cat litter—how much did one animal go?—and dry food containers and cans of food.

Throughout, Smoky observed all, silently and without judgment. Well, without *much* judgment.

It helped that she found a large catnip snake for him to amuse himself with. Half the filling had spilled out and was smeared all over his chin and cheeks by the time we made it to the checkout line. I blamed my distraction with the destroyed toy for how Ryan was able to sneak a cat harness into our purchases.

Also bright pink.

Worst of all, it had a pouch-like add-on called a Pussy Papa. Or maybe that was what they thought you'd be called if any of your neighbors saw you wearing one.

"I'm not putting this on," I said once we were in the parking lot, and Ryan was loading Smoky into the carrier. I held the ensemble up by its two pink straps. "Not in this life or any other."

She shut the back door before yanking the contraption out of my hand and tucking it into a bag with some paw-shaped lights she'd added to the cart when I wasn't looking. I had no idea what I was supposed to do with those either.

"Being secure in your masculinity is sexy," she informed me before closing the trunk.

"My masculinity isn't in question. What makes you think Smoky wants to ride around in that? We got him a leash, which again, he's a cat not a dog. If he wants to go outside, I have a backyard. Fenced, I might add."

"Right, and all it takes is one errant wild dog to leap the fence and take him out. And you know they can climb, right?"

"Oh, but he's going to be safe strapped to my chest?"

"Well, of course." She reached up to pinch my biceps, fluttering her lashes. "Why, you could protect a little defenseless feline without even breaking a sweat."

"I can still fire you even if you're a temporary worker."

She leaned up against me and whispered in my ear. "So you can get my breasts in your mouth again? You don't need to fire me for that, *obviously.*"

The part of me that cared obsessively about rules bristled. What we were doing—what *I* was doing—wasn't proper in any way. Then she turned around and sauntered back to the passenger seat, putting a swivel in her walk that could've drawn me straight to the gates of hell.

And I didn't care about wrong or right.

I got behind the wheel and glanced into the back. Smoky was sleeping head down, the partially destroyed catnip snake mashed beneath his face.

Clearly, I wasn't the only one getting high on my own supply.

I put on my belt and started the car. For all of ten seconds, I contemplated going back home. I thought of my empty house, waiting in the dark for me. Lights burning to give me the illusion I wasn't all alone.

"You hungry?"

She didn't hesitate as she clicked on her belt. "Yeah."

Already my mind was wheeling. "We could go to The Stadler House. It's private and remote and—"

"How about Denny's?"

I frowned. "I haven't been to Denny's since college."

"Were you sober?"

"Definitely not. Does anyone eat at Denny's when they are?"

"I do." Her amusement came through loud and clear. "I can introduce you to a few things that will blow your mind."

"Are we still talking about Denny's?"

She laughed, low and rich. "Feed me and see."

CHAPTER FOURTEEN

PRESTON

"What do you think?"

I didn't set down my sandwich long enough to answer, just nodded.

"Good, right?"

I gave her a thumbs up and kept eating. Who knew toasted bread, cheese, scrambled eggs, and ham could be so delicious? This was definitely hitting the spot.

My dinner companion brightened the table considerably. Just sitting across from me in our corner booth, Ryan sparkled. More than once, I noticed a guy checking her out, usually after she laughed that sexy, throaty laugh of hers.

It wasn't an exaggeration to say I thought about maiming each and every one of those men.

I didn't blame them. How could I? With her flowing jet black hair and armful of jingling bracelets and that smile that could kill a man dead, she drew the eye every bit as much as that bewitching crystal hanging between her breasts. Now that I knew what she looked like beneath her dress—at least above the waist—I found it even harder to keep my eyes where they should be.

"And you made fun of me for ordering this." She popped a gooey piece of cheese in her mouth, chewing slowly. Then she tore off another piece and slipped it into the carrier at her side.

Smoky snatched it through the bars.

She'd told the server with all sincerity that the cat was her emotional support pet. I half expected her to go get that pussy papa contraption and put it on while she ate.

But no, that ensemble was evidently reserved for me.

"You're setting him up to be miserable." I finished my sandwich and wiped my greasy hands on my napkin.

Good thing I enjoyed the punishment of a ten mile run.

"Hmm, yeah, I probably shouldn't be feeding him table scraps. You're right. He'll never leave you alone at the table." She made a face and went back to her sandwich. "Sorry. Wasn't thinking. See why I don't have pets?"

"I didn't mean that. I mean, he's going to miss you when he's stuck at home with me." He wasn't the only one who would miss her.

Who already dreaded taking her home.

My self-protective jokes about sex hexes aside, I just...liked her. It didn't make sense. We didn't line up on any level. She was pure sunshine with that witchy hint of pleasures I couldn't even begin to dream about. Free in a way I wouldn't ever be.

I didn't like admitting it, but I was probably repressed.

Okay, I definitely was. By necessity. If I didn't keep my urges on lockdown, who knew what would happen?

This would happen.

It *was* happening, and I couldn't make myself stop it. Not anymore. Not that I'd put up much of a fight since the first obnoxious email she'd sent my way.

"We can FaceTime." She was utterly serious, her big beautiful eyes trained on me as I poked at my hash browns.

"You and the cat?" My lips curved. "Are you sure he knows technology?"

"He can learn. Anyone can, if they want to bad enough. You have to want it, Preston."

I glanced up, my throat going surprisingly tight. Her expression

178

was so earnest that I knew she wasn't talking in the abstract or making jokes.

Somehow she meant me. She got something about my situation I'd only begun to articulate and was opening a door.

I'd never even tried to look for a window. I'd just settled for the closed-in dark.

"I do want it." My jaw locked. "But I don't let myself just do—"

"Anything. Even getting a cat was a big decision for you."

"Shouldn't it be?"

"Sure, if you're not in the place for one. But you are. You have a stable life. Too stable."

"How can you be too stable?"

"When all the joy is gone."

I poked at my potatoes. I didn't want them. They had no flavor.

"You can't live like that forever." Her hand slid over mine around my fork and the warmth of her skin made me grip the cool metal that much tighter. "You keep pushing everything that makes you happy down, soon enough nothing will."

"Dinner and therapy?" I asked lightly, but it took everything in me not to toss aside our plates and drag her up on the table.

That would spark some damn joy, in me if not in the other patrons.

"Dinner and friendship. Contrary to popular belief, being attracted to someone doesn't mean you can't be friends too." She scraped her nail lightly over the back of my hand, tumbling me right back to our heated moments in the front seat of my car.

"Are we friends?" I frowned. "Do you actually like me?"

"No. I hate you. Why I climbed in your lap in the first place." She rolled her eyes and would've pulled back if I hadn't seized hold of her wrist.

"There's never been anyone else like you for me." Her lips trembled as our gazes connected. "You'll never believe me but—"

"I believe you."

"I'm not my father." I let her go although I wanted to do anything but.

She rubbed her wrist and I regretted possibly hurting her—I didn't want that either—but she lowered her arm into her lap before I could ask. "Do you think I'd be here if I thought you were?"

Silence fell over the table, the only sound the chirping meows of the cat who'd just realized our conversation was keeping him from getting more cheese.

"Do you have siblings?"

She blinked, her heavy fringe of dark lashes hiding her expression for an instant. "No. You just have the one?"

"One is plenty." I tried the potatoes again before setting down my fork.

"You're not eating them right. Watch and learn." She grabbed the bottle of ketchup and saturated her potatoes. I could barely tell there were any under the puddle of red. Then she leaned over to do the same to mine.

"I don't eat that much ketchup." It was more ketchup with a side of potatoes than the other way around.

"Try it," she insisted.

I stared at it dubiously before forking up some. It wasn't the best thing I'd ever tasted but it was an improvement over the bland potatoes.

"Well?"

"Better." I kept eating them.

"Why don't you like your brother?"

I immediately started to correct her then went with the truth. "It's not that I don't like him. I don't like that he doesn't understand his obligations."

"Why should he? You understand enough for both of you."

"Do you make a habit of being unnaturally perceptive or do I bring out something unusual in you?"

She forked up her potatoes with gusto and smiled after she chewed and swallowed. "Little of both."

"Did you go to college?"

"Did you see one on my resumé?"

"No. But maybe you didn't graduate. Or didn't have a good experience."

"I didn't go. I barely got out of high school." She rested her chin on her palm. "I'm not qualified to work for you."

"Says who?"

"You before you wanted in my panties." She sounded teasing, but she looked down at her plate quickly.

Too quickly.

"That's not true."

"You don't want in my panties?"

"I wish you never wore panties, ever."

"Hmm, sounds like a lawyerly deflection."

"Ryan." I reached for her hand and circled my thumb over the center of her palm. She watched me touch her, saying nothing. "You were so good with Mrs. Franklin. You helped her in a way I couldn't. I wouldn't have had any clue how."

"I just reacted. It's not like—"

"And the records room. Already it's so much better than it was before. Because of you. You have talents you don't give yourself credit for."

She sniffed. "Hardly. I know exactly what I'm worth."

"You don't know what you're worth to me." I pressed my thumb harder into her soft flesh, and she gasped before her fingers wrapped tight around my finger.

Neither of us spoke for a moment before I shifted my hold and laced our fingers together on the table. We were in Syracuse, not near Kensington Square, but I wouldn't have cared if we were. I wanted to hold on to her.

Had to. And I wanted her to hold on to me.

"You mentioned art," I said suddenly.

"I did?"

"In passing, I think. Tell me about it."

"Why?" She seemed genuinely perplexed, but she didn't try to draw away. She even started eating with her other hand in deference to our position.

"I want to get to know you. It's not just about your panties."

Her lips twitched as she shot me a glance. "The ones you wish I wasn't wearing?"

"Tell me. Please."

She jerked a shoulder. "I've just always drawn. It's a hobby and an escape. A way to process my chaotic life."

"What was chaotic about it?"

"You can't possibly care."

"I care, Ryan." I went back to eating to give her the space to speak.

She frowned, an expression that almost seemed foreign on her face. Her relaxed features were meant to reflect happiness and pleasure and clever humor. "I was the odd kid. The weird goth chick. Kind of the opposite of my mom. Her name's Rainbow."

"Rainbow?" I cleared my throat. "Rainbow Moon."

The corner of her mouth ticked up. "Yeah. She loved me, but she had a million and one things to keep her busy. Especially her rich men."

It took effort for me not to tighten my grip. An emotion that felt disturbingly like shame made me take a deep breath. Right then, the last thing I wanted was to be wealthy.

"Where was your dad?"

"Absent. Classic story. We moved around a lot in our van, and things weren't real stable financially. You know, lonely only kid growing up by her wits, doing what she could to get by."

I rubbed my thumb against the side of her hand. "Were you safe?"

"No one hurt me." She let out an unsteady laugh. "Nothing that lasted anyway. I did stupid stuff, but I didn't land in jail. I didn't get in serious trouble."

I needed to do something to lighten the heaviness I'd invited into our meal. That was the last thing I wanted. I just craved to know more about her than the information in her resumé.

"So, you never got taken to the station for public lewdness?"

Her laughter rolled through me, loosening the muscles in my shoulders that had gone stiff. "Definitely not." She smirked. "Though if I keep hanging around with my new crowd, it could happen."

"Crowd of one?"

She inclined her chin toward the carrier. "Two."

"How did you get into tarot?"

"Oh, boy, you're really fishing, huh? Scared I was serious when I told your daddy I was a witch?"

"No. I find it fascinating. Witchcraft has so many different facets, and the connection to nature is—" I stopped when her fingers clamped down hard on mine, hard enough to hurt. "What?"

"Don't."

"Don't what?"

"Don't do that. Don't pretend to give a shit about things that matter to me to soothe your conscience about wanting me. It doesn't have to be that deep."

"So, I'm supposed to find my joy as long as I don't get too close? Don't step on your toes and dent your protective shield? Or are these therapy sessions supposed to be one-sided?"

"I don't need therapy. And I don't need a man to fill me up. I'm happy alone."

"Do you think I want to change that?" I gentled my grip on her. "You intrigue me, not because you're a curiosity, but because you're brave. You live authentically." Part of being brave was honesty. Another thing I wasn't familiar with anymore. "And I don't."

"You can. Anytime you want to. You can make the choice."

"I'm figuring that out. In the meantime, I want to do what feels good."

She took another bite of her potatoes. They had to be cold by now. "You wouldn't be a man if you didn't."

"I don't mean just sex. I don't see you like that. I wish you didn't either."

"Right."

"Would I be sitting here with you if that was all I wanted?"

"You tell me."

"There are hotels all over. Places we could stop and fuck and no one would be the wiser."

"Your pinstriped soul would know. By the way, I'm surprised you haven't shown up in a suit like that. Or a three-piece one. Vest included." She caught the tip of her tongue between her teeth. "All buttoned up so someone could imagine stripping off the layers to see what's beneath."

"I haven't been intimate with a woman in over two years." Saying it felt like I was baring my soul. I wasn't a virgin—far from it—but somehow even this admission to a woman as free and open as Ryan made me feel like the next thing to it. "Sex doesn't rule me."

"Maybe it should. Nothing wrong with needing a release valve."

"No," I agreed. "There isn't. And maybe you shouldn't think the worst when someone with a penis wants to hear about what you like. Not all men think with their dicks."

"And not all women want to be peeled open like a banana to reveal all their secrets."

"Tit for tat." I cocked my head when Smoky let out a sound that sounded suspiciously like a sigh. "I won't ask you for more than I'm willing to give. How's that sound?"

"Like a lawyer's negotiation."

I shrugged and ate some of my own cold potatoes. They really were better with ketchup.

"Fine," she said after a minute. "Have it your way. I got into tarot because I wanted to make friends in high school. People like to hear about themselves. Especially young women."

"Not only young women," I said drily. "I meet plenty of men who can't get enough of talking about themselves."

"Well, lawyers. You know how they are. Pompous windbags." She waved a hand then rubbed her thumb over my hand to soften the joke.

"You should read my cards."

Her laughter was loud, quick, and unprompted. "I know I have nice tits, but wow."

"Not arguing there."

"Imagine if you'd seen the rest of me?" she asked silkily, her thumb still on the move against my skin. "I'd probably have the keys to your house by now."

"I'm serious. I'm curious what you'd see."

"It's not all fun and games. The cards intuit things we don't always want known. Allowing someone to read your cards can be as intimate as sex."

"Then I definitely want you to read mine." It wasn't like I was going to get lucky tonight. That barn door had closed.

Slammed shut might have been a more accurate description. But blue balls aside, I liked this new direction we were headed in.

Tomorrow, I'd wake up and think I was losing it. But right now? I liked holding her hand and watching her stunning eyes narrow at me as she tried to figure me out.

Good luck there. I hadn't managed to figure myself out yet, and I had more than thirty years practice.

"You think you do," she said after a moment. "But if the cards see something you're not ready to face…"

"I'll take my chances. I'm making the choice to trust you," I added. "You could try trusting me back."

She didn't answer. And she didn't laugh again as we finished the meal and paid—separate checks of course, despite my disagreement—or on the ride back to her place. Smoky was thoroughly tired of the carrier and meowed the whole way, but he saved the loudest one for when Ryan climbed out of my car.

I exhaled as I waited while she went inside. "I don't like it any better than you do, Smoky."

Returning to my house seemed even more hollow after having Ryan's energy around me for so much of the day.

"Energy," I muttered as I drove up the long driveway and parked. "Now who's going woo woo?"

I collected Smoky's many, many items from the trunk and grabbed his carrier for the trek inside. His meowing had turned into full-blown yowls now.

Either he was hungry or he was disgusted I was his new owner instead of Ryan.

I couldn't even say I blamed him on the second point.

It took two trips to gather everything we'd bought him. Rather than letting him loose inside my place when I wasn't there to supervise, I set the carrier on the floor while I toted in the rest. Then I stalled a little more, setting out his new fountain along with a bowl of wet food and one with dry kibble, both high-end brands I'd seen workers using at the shelter.

After some debate, I put his litter box in the laundry room and filled it up with litter to the very brim. Okay, so I overflowed it, but that was what the handheld vacuum was for. After vacuuming up the mess, I went to set the cat free, only to find him plastered to the back of his carrier, his eyes the size of saucers.

I opened the door and he didn't come out, just stayed adhered to the back. I frowned. Was he mad at being caged for so long? Going to dinner with Ryan instead of taking him home right away hadn't been ideal.

"Already I'm a failure as a pet parent. And it's been what, a few hours?" I glanced at my watch. "Good sign, Shaw."

At a loss, I picked up the carrier and tried to gently shake him out. He did not budge. Even with only three legs, he was hanging on for dear life. I'd have to remember to mind his claws if he became annoyed, because he clearly knew how to use them.

I set the carrier down and went to get his food dish. It probably wasn't healthy to be bribing him on night one, and he was probably not as hungry due to his goodies from Ryan.

And I wasn't thinking about any of her goodies anymore tonight.

I put the small dish outside Smoky's open door. I waited five minutes, but he did not come out to investigate.

Okay, then. I had other things I could do with my time. Smoky would come out when he chose. If I was him, I'd need a while to process that Ryan wasn't my new owner too.

Or something comparable to the plight of a horny human male.

Apparently, one of the things I had to do was to call my brother. It was hard to say which of us was more surprised.

"Pres, what's wrong?"

I forced myself to relax in my leather wingback chair and studied the carrier on the floor. From the way Smoky had affixed himself to the back, you couldn't even tell there was a cat inside. Considering his size, that was a feat. "Nothing. Why do you ask?"

"Oh, I don't know, maybe because you haven't called me since the last presidential term? Possibly before that. You usually act as if a text is imposition enough."

I didn't have an answer for that.

"Not to mention, it's past ten. Aren't you usually in bed by now? Early riser and all that. Up before dawn to make your mogul millions." He laughed at his own joke, but I didn't.

"I'm not that predictable."

"Since when?"

Since a certain someone made me wonder if I shouldn't be.

"Being predictable is overrated."

"I've always thought so. What's up? Need advice on women? I knew she had you all twisted up."

I nearly denied. Or deflected. Both at the same time wasn't out of the question. But Dexter had a way with women I would never have.

"I don't like being a remedial student." I gripped the arm of my chair until my knuckles were bone-white.

I expected Dexter's quick bark of laughter. When it didn't come, I waited.

"You're kidding me, right?" His voice was surprisingly soft. "The great Preston Shaw, needing help at anything? You aced every class. Dated all the most desirable girls, until you moved on to the next. Now you're one of the most successful divorce attorneys in New York. You collect fat retainers like candy."

I was struck speechless. He couldn't see me that way. I certainly did not.

"You're the best, Pres. You always have been."

I searched for my voice. "It takes all my time. I don't know how to do anything else but work. It's like I'm Dad's machine. He pointed me in the direction he wanted me to go and I just...went."

"He pointed you because he knew you wouldn't let him down. He never even considered asking me." Dex's laughter was too sharp.

"Good thing I never minded being in your shadow, because God knows I'm not destined to step out of it."

"What are you talking about? Women flock to you. Your little black book is a phone book with extra pages stapled in."

"Right. Because you can't get dates if you really wanted them." He chuckled. "Come off it, man. You give off an air of being too important for us mere mortals. Don't blame people for noticing and giving you your space."

When I didn't reply, his voice dropped an octave. "Getting a little lonely up there in all that rarefied air you breathe in your house high on the mountain?"

"It's not a mountain. Just a hill."

"It's a goddamn metaphor for all the rest and you know it."

"No, I really don't."

He laughed again. "I live right in the center of the square."

"You think I don't know that?"

"Ah, there's the irritation. You held out longer than I would've given you credit for." He paused. "I need people around me. Especially women. I enjoy them. You always made fun of me for that. Actually, no, correction, you never spoke enough to insult me. Just gave me that famous cold-eyed sneer that is so effective in a courtroom."

I put my phone on speaker and set it on the side table so I could lean forward and drop my head into my hands. My tie tightened around my throat so I dragged it off and let an article of clothing drop to the floor for the first time in my life.

Fuck Ralph Lauren.

Just fuck all of it.

"I didn't want any of this," I said when I could speak again. "I wanted to go to LA and live on the beach and represent drunken rockstars against their tyrannical record companies."

"I suppose that sounds wild to you, but you know, most people want to *be* a rockstar, not their attorney of record."

I had to laugh as I loosened the top few buttons on my shirt. The air against my still too hot skin made me think about kissing Ryan, wishing she'd seen more of me—and that I'd definitely seen more of her. I was wishing entirely too much tonight.

"You know, Pres, you can have that. You can just quit tomorrow. Get a place out there. Start a new firm and hang out your shingle, if that's really what you want. Live, man. You only get one life, but you get a hundred chances to do it over." He exhaled. "As for Dad, just fuck him. He never gave you the option. Repay the favor. It's his fucking firm. Not yours. You don't owe him shit. And if you ever did, you paid off that debt years ago."

"I don't want that old dream anymore. I don't," I repeated when he made a derisive sound. "But I do want something else. I need it." I pinched the bridge of my nose. "My buddy Jared from college needed help with a paternity case last year. He found out he had a little girl with a woman he'd had a fling with, and now she's his legally. A happy ending, you know?"

"Yeah, I get it."

"But in my line of work, I hold a blowtorch for people to raze everything around them."

"Still could make for a happy ending," Dex argued. "Staying in a bad marriage is worse than walking away."

"It is. Not every divorce I help litigate is worthy of a reality TV show. But far too many are. I need to walk. Especially now that Dad is having a fucking affair."

Once the words were out, I braced my hand against my forehead. My brother had gone deathly silent.

"I'm sorry," I said finally. "I didn't mean to spring that on you."

"You didn't. I knew."

"You *knew?*" The question exploded out of me as I glanced at the carrier. I didn't see anything. Either Smoky was still Velcro-ed to the back or he'd slunk away when I wasn't looking.

The food dish was empty though. Hmm. Well, hopefully, he would find his way to the litter box on his own.

Cats didn't make a habit of going to the bathroom just anywhere. I hoped.

Dex sighed. "It's not the first. Mom knows. She's known for a while."

"I don't believe that."

"You should. I confronted him about it over a year ago, and he was unrepentant. He told me to go ahead and tell Mom, that she'd just tell me to mind my business."

"I don't believe it," I said again. "He could've been bluffing. How did you find out? And why didn't you tell me?"

"Why *would* I tell you? How often do we talk?" He let out a bitter laugh. "Imagine if we didn't work in the same damn office? I wouldn't have a clue what was going on with you. Hell, I barely do now. And you barely know what's going on with anything beyond your briefs."

"Hey—"

"Legal, son. Not the ones you wear. If you focused more on those, you'd probably be a hell of a lot happier. But then again, that's what has you all messed up, huh? She's a fucking knockout."

"She's my assist—" I swore and cut myself off. "If you breathe a word about this to anyone, I will carve your nuts off and feed them to my new cat. Not that he'd want them."

"Whoa, new pussy? You?" I could hear the smirk in his tone. "New pussy on a couple fronts, I'm guessing."

"Watch it. And no. We haven't slept together. You're my fucking brother. Isn't there like an honorary oath that you have to be the keeper of my confidences?"

"No, and you've told me nothing in confidence."

"Getting there." I rubbed my jaw. "Tell me it's not wrong to do this."

"I can only surmise what 'this' is, but she's not going to be your assistant for much longer. And hey, if you quit, two birds, one stone."

I knew he was kidding. Of course he was. Ryan was supposed to work for me for just two more days and then April would be back. If we broke any rules now, they wouldn't matter in the span of a weekend.

Besides, a lot of these so-called rules were artificial constructs. Outside her very limited time engagement at the law firm, I knew our relationship wouldn't influence her employment. Other than the fact she was already proving herself to be indispensable to me—both in and out of the office.

But then I started to smile. No, I started to fucking grin.

"You know what? You're right. Thank you. I'm sorry I ever called you a manwhore."

"You didn't. At least to my face. Wait," he said when I would've clicked off to go find my cat. "What the hell are you doing, Pres?"

I took a deep breath. "Making a choice."

CHAPTER FIFTEEN

Card of The Day:

Embrace: King of Swords & 3 of Cups | **Release:** Death

Thursday

"Balls."

I stared at the cards on my kitchen table next to my super-sized mug of Morning Mojo tea. Sleep had been elusive. I was still wound up from seeing a new side of Preston yesterday. The guy behind the suit who had an affinity for animals in need. Who also had a sense of loneliness in his eyes that made me ache.

I didn't have time for that nonsense.

But that didn't seem to matter to my hormones or sleeping habits. My bed was all tangled sheets, and two of my pillows had ended up on the floor by the time I'd finally given up on pretending to sleep. And now I had all that King of Swords energy waiting for me today.

It could be for me, since I was locking shit down. But I'd bet that freaking card was for Preston.

"Two more days. You can do this." I tapped the Three of Cups.

Maybe I'd get together with the girls this weekend and decompress. Some wine and Luna would do me some good.

The Death card was my real worry. Majors weren't just little pats on the ass. They were a slap to the back of the head and usually meant something major—duh, Major Arcana—but I was tired of all these major life hits. I had two days left and then I could get back to my life.

I glanced at the drawing on my desk, with the little cat face peering in the window.

The one I hadn't touched in two days.

The one I'd been avoiding. I'd only drawn it eleven times now.

I swooped up the cards and set them on my altar. I tucked the death card behind my skull. "Keep me from doing anything super dumb today, huh, George?"

I finished packing my bag. The temperatures were supposed to soar today, and I'd dressed in an unusually short dress. Nothing indecent, but the air laid heavy on me and I'd been tempted to take another shower before leaving for work.

"Enough waffling, Moon." I reached for one of my lighter crystals off the jewelry tree in the window. I chose rose quartz and citrine to settle my crazy mind and a few obsidian and silver rings for protection.

Protection from what, I so wasn't going to say out loud.

Even to myself.

I had enough time to stop into The Honey Pot and got a sugar-charged six-pack of donuts. My phone chimed that a delivery was waiting for me at work.

My lips twitched. Preston's coffee had finally come in.

"Need anything else, Ryan?"

I glanced up at Dre, the owner of the shop. Behind her was an obnoxious mug with a closeup of a llama with *no drama* scrawled on the inside lip. "I'll take that too."

Dre turned. "The llama?"

"Yes, definitely."

She rang it up and quickly wrapped it in newsprint, then tucked it into a white handled bag. I handed her my card and smiled.

"That smile seems a little sinister."

"Maybe."

Dre shook her head. "Preston is a good guy, you know."

I gripped my wallet more tightly. "How do you know it's for him?"

"You've glanced over at his building three times."

"I have?" I frowned and looked again.

"See?"

"I'm just seeing if I beat him to work for once. I wanted to do it at least once. Since I'm usually late."

"Sure. Early." She handed me the bag and my card.

I glanced outside to make sure there wasn't another speeding biker in my future, then stopped at the door. "Oh, did you ever see that hot guy that came in last time I was here? I felt...something."

Dre blushed. "He's been in a few more times."

"Talk to him." I pointed at her. "I have a good feeling."

She waved me off. "Have a good one, Ryan."

"Don't forget to call me for a reading."

"I won't."

I hustled out and across the street. I was a good thirty minutes early for once, which had never happened to me in my life. I was either on time or five minutes late for pretty much everything. Early wasn't my style.

It wasn't as if I was eager...much.

I stopped in at the mail drop and sure enough there was a box from PMS's fancy coffee place. I tucked it under my arm and headed for the elevator. In between juggling my parcels and not paying attention to my surroundings, I bumped into the senior Shaw at the threshold of the elevator.

He moved back and straightened his suit jacket. Even in this wilting heat, he was crisp and buttoned up. "Miss Moon, watch yourself."

I readjusted my purse on my shoulder and forced myself not to stiffen. I really didn't like this guy, or the way he reminded me of all the men who came in and out of my life. Suits and oily smiles with no backbone. I shouldered past him and slapped the button.

"I am one of your superiors, you know."

I gave him a tight smile. "When hell freezes over," I said just as the door started to close.

He gave me an icy glare and stormed off.

I dared him to try to pull rank on me. I was pretty sure Preston would stand up to him about it, simply because he *really* didn't want to be without an assistant.

Sure, that was the reason.

I ignored that little voice and stalked off the elevator. The lights were on and Dexter was on the phone at my desk. I set my things down.

"What are you doing over here?" I asked as he hung up.

"Solicitor calls started coming through. I'm not sure who actually says yes to these robo-calls about an extended warranty on your car."

I snorted. "Yeah, I have at least one of those a day. Did you turn on the phones early?" I took a peek at my phone and saw that I was still very early.

Dex sat on the corner of my desk. "Yeah, good ol' Dad's assistant did. Evidently, her qualifications don't include actually handling the phones."

I sat down and kicked the box of K-cups under my desk as the elevator opened again and Preston's long-legged stride ate up the waiting area.

"Miss Moon?" He checked his watch. "It's nice to see you on time this morning."

I swallowed my gasp and managed to smile. How he was wearing a three piece suit in this heat, I had no idea, but it was ridiculously fitted and made him look taller and broader somehow at the same time. I cleared my throat. "I even brought gifts." I unearthed the box of pastries and took a moment to collect myself.

Dexter snatched it out of my hands. "Oh, Honey Pot? You are a goddess."

I leaned back in my chair and crossed my legs, feigning a relaxed vibe even as my pulse boomed in my ears. "You both finally realized this when it's almost my last day."

Preston's gaze flicked down my legs and he swallowed, then met my gaze. His dark eyes were intense and far too focused for my liking. "Did you happen to find my coffee pods on your way up?"

I shook my head. "Nope."

Dex shot a look at me with a raised brow, then went back to the box and plucked a Boston Cream from the bunch. "Thanks for the morning sugar, Sugar."

I rolled my eyes. "Enjoy."

Preston watched his brother walk away. "Did he want something?"

I stood and let my dress float around my hips. "Have a Honey Glazed, PMS. He was just handling the phones."

"Oh." He tapped his fingers on the corner of my desk. "I shouldn't."

"You should. I'll see if I can find your coffee."

"Oh, would you?" His face brightened. "I'm getting tired of the ones you found for me in the supply closet. They're good, and I appreciate it, but..."

"They're not what you like." I nudged the box farther under my desk.

His gaze drifted to my mouth. "No. Not what I like."

I did a cursory scan of the room to make sure we were alone, then leaned forward to slide my fingers down the buttons of his vest. "A little warm for this, isn't it?"

His tongue flicked out to wet his lips. "It's a summer blend."

"Is this because of what we talked about yesterday?"

"It's simply the next suit in my closet."

"Sure."

He gave me a wolfish smile, then took a donut. "Meet me in my office, Miss Moon. I have some correspondence you need to attend to."

"Shall I bring my steno book?" I called after him.

He didn't reply, just shut his door behind him.

The fact that he assumed I would follow him like a docile little kitten annoyed me enough that I pulled out a pod of his coffee and stuck it in my pocket. Knowing it was so close to him and yet so far made me hum a happy little tune.

I took the llama mug out of the bag and washed it before turning on my electric kettle at the small kitchen station in the break room. Would serve him right to have tea today.

I took out one of my tea infusers, also a llama and filled the little belly with loose leaves, then set it in the mug and poured hot water over it. I brought it back to my desk with me and while I waited for it to steep, I had a fritter.

The blinds were opened in his office and he kept looking up at me as I ate.

Very, very slowly.

He gave me a hard stare, but I didn't budge until it was officially nine o'clock.

I licked my middle finger and gave him a wide smile before picking up his mug and the legal pad I used to scribble things on during the day. I went to his door and gave it a sharp rap with my knuckle.

"You know very well I'm waiting for you, Miss Moon."

I opened the door. "Yes, Mr. Shaw," I answered with a saccharine smile.

Miss Moon was better than Moonbeam, I supposed. Marginally.

His eyes narrowed at my mug. "What is that?"

"Oh, just a little something to get you through until I can track down that pesky box." I set it down in the middle of his leather blotter, making sure the llama stared right at him. "How's Smoky?"

His mouth opened, but no words came out. He frowned. "What?"

"The very active three-legged cat you adopted last night?"

"Oh, right. He's getting acclimated."

"In other words, he's hiding?"

Preston stared hard at the mug. "Yes. I mean, no, he's only hiding occasionally. He's eating and his litter pan definitely got used, so he must be okay so far. Have to say that whole cleaning it out thing was a rather unpleasant start to my day."

"That's good to hear."

His eyebrow winged up. "That my morning started unpleasantly?"

"I meant about Smoky doing all right. The unpleasantness is just a side benefit."

He grunted, still examining the mug as if it contained toxic waste.

I sat down across from him and smoothed out the skirt of my dress, closing my knees and tucking one ankle behind the other in the primmest of poses. I took my pen out of the twist of my hair. "Now what letter did you need me to take care of?"

He was still staring at the llama.

I pressed my lips together. "Mr. Shaw, you needed something?"

See, I could do this whole professional thing. Sort of. And there was only a small amount of sarcasm in my tone.

He touched the mug with a fingertip. "I need to know precisely what this is if you expect me to drink it."

Oh, for goddess's sake.

"It's a mug of tea. Highly caffeinated tea, to be exact. It's actually better for you than coffee. I picked a blend that is infused with vanilla for sweetness. Though not to your usual level, I imagine."

"Yes, but what is that?" He pointed at the metal figurine standing in the middle of his mug.

I looked down at my pad and desperately tried not to laugh. "It's an infuser."

He peered down at it. "It has a face."

"It's a llama. The little neck and head makes it easier for you to take it out of the mug."

"There's a llama urinating tea in my mug."

I barely stopped the snort of laughter. The K-cup burned a hole in my thigh with every laugh I suppressed. "I suppose you could see it that way. Now you have a deposition at eleven and—"

"I know my schedule, Miss Moon." He sounded exceptionally pissy.

I shouldn't take such pleasure in bringing it out in him. Obviously, there was something wrong with me. Luckily, tomorrow was my last day, and I wouldn't have to worry any longer about why I so enjoyed tormenting him.

And kissing him senseless.

"Right." I had my pen at the ready. "So, how can I assist you?"

He lifted the mug and set it at the edge of his desk like it was contaminated and pulled his keyboard forward. "You're sure you can't find the coffee box?"

I heard the hope in his voice and almost reached in my pocket. "Sorry. Not yet."

He huffed out a near growl. "Fine. I'll just have to make do. I don't have time to go to the bakery on my way across town."

I barely resisted rolling my eyes. Only PMS could make missing coffee pods seem like a calamity.

That they weren't really missing was neither here nor there.

"You have plenty of time to stop."

"I still have to revise a few things before I leave." His fingers flew over his keyboard, those very intelligent eyes skimming the screen even as he rattled off things for me to do while he was gone.

I stuck my hand in my pocket and rolled the little cup around. I felt a bit bad for holding his caffeine from him on a busy day. Maybe I should hand it over.

I'd had my fun.

He frowned at me briefly before resuming his mad typing. "That's enough for now. You can go, Miss Moon."

I nodded briefly and stood. He wasn't getting it with that attitude. The dude brought a whole new meaning to the words *hot and cold*.

Last night, he'd made out with me in his car and pretended he wanted to know everything about me down to my favorite color. Now he was back to all business. Or maybe he didn't like that I'd been chatting with his brother.

Who even knew?

I shrugged it off. If he wanted to keep things strictly professional in the office, I could handle that. And then after tomorrow, he was officially back to being April's problem.

"Miss Moon, don't you think that skirt is a little...brief?" He sounded strangled.

My fingers curled around the doorknob. "It's perfectly

respectable." Okay, maybe a little less so since I was almost six feet tall with my heels on. "I've seen a far shorter skirt on your father's admin."

It was a low blow and I knew he was sensitive about the whole situation with his dad. But right now, I wasn't above taking shots where I could.

Not when he left me edgy and wondering what the hell his game was. If anything.

I could practically hear his jaw grinding. "She's irrelevant."

"And I'm only a temporary assistant, and it's almost ninety-seven degrees today." I opened the door and let it slam behind me.

Go ahead and fire me, PMS.

It was probably the best thing he could do for both of us.

CHAPTER SIXTEEN

I DIDN'T SPEAK to him for the rest of the morning. He'd left the office promptly thirty minutes before his appointment and barely looked at me on his way by.

I finished his To Do list in record time, mostly because I was fueled by anger and a touch of guilt. Acclimating Smoky to his new home had probably killed some of his sleeping. But his general stick-up-the-assery was enough to keep me from feeling too bad about it.

There were no other clients due in the office until late afternoon so I escaped to the records room with my earbuds to play rage rock while I chipped my way through the 2000's.

I was well into the L names before I flipped off my heels and ended up cross-legged on one of the executive chairs PMS had put in the room for me.

I'd moved on from my rage playlist to true crime. I was mentally knee deep in the horrific story of Willie Pickton when something white and gold landed in the center of the Lyle folder.

It rolled onto its side until the label for Preston's caramel confection K-cup stared at me.

I looked up to find him looming over me, his knuckles resting on the table. His muscular forearms were tight with annoyance, the white sleeves of his dress shirt were rolled up to his elbows, and he'd lost his suit coat—leaving him only in that damn vest.

My nipples instantly tightened.

Damn traitors.

I flicked out my earbuds and the ladies from the *Morbid* podcast stopped talking.

He tipped his head, his dark eyes glittering. "What is that?"

I picked up the K-cup. "Columbian Coconut-Caramel blend," I read aloud then set it in front of him.

"And why is it not at my coffee station?"

I laced my fingers on top of the file. "Not sure. I only had one in my pocket."

"In your—"

I unearthed the warmer one that was still in the pocket of my dress. I'd actually forgot about it while I was working. "Look at that, now you have two. Okay, forty-eight if you want to get technical." I gave him a brief smile.

He straightened and crossed his arms over his chest, making his arms bulge with all those muscles that just didn't compute for such a desk jockey.

"Maybe you should have one now, and it will put you in a better mood." I frowned. "The box is under my desk—how did you get this one?"

"My brother chucked one at my head when we were arguing about who was going to take the Donnelly case."

I winced. Mary Donnelly had been particularly vicious when she'd come in earlier in the week. "Your brother shouldn't have been under my desk."

Preston's jaw flexed, and I was pretty sure he was going to crush his molars. "That is not the point. And why exactly aren't you manning the phones?"

"Because I'm manning all this." I gestured to the stacks of files before tapping the K-cup from my pocket. "Look, it was just a little fun. You were being all rude and PMS-y."

"Would you cease and desist with that name?"

"It's your name."

"It is not." He brushed the pods to the side and leaned over my table, his long fingers curling over the lip right in front of me. "Preston. Say it."

My heartbeat thundered between my ears. Or was it my thighs?

His gaze never wavered even though I was pretty sure I was the definition of having heaving bosoms at the moment. I'd been perfectly comfortable ten minutes ago in the air conditioned room, and now my skin was dotted with a light sheen of sweat.

I swallowed and couldn't stop myself from leaning forward. What was it about the alpha side of this man that made me all...stupid? There was no other word for it.

Our lips were an inch apart. "No."

He shoved the table out of the way and I gasped. He stepped into the empty space and hauled me up into his arms.

Startled, I grabbed at his shoulders. God, he was so damn hot under the fine cotton and silk blend.

He swung me around and set me on the table. It didn't put us on an even playing field. If anything, I was even more trapped. He stepped between my thighs, drawing his fingers gently under my knee to lift it up and around his hip.

"I'll find a way to get you to say it."

"I've used your name before." I was pretty sure I didn't always use his initials. But right now, my brain was a fog of lust and white noise.

He tipped me back a little so he had the upper hand. The placket of his trousers rubbed over the cotton panties I was wearing in deference to the inferno of heat outside. At this point, it was inside too.

So, we'd apparently reached the *hot* portion of the day's agenda.

His fingers dug into my thigh as he widened my legs a little more to fit his hard shaft against the center of me. "You're so fucking irritating," he said against my lips.

I smiled. "You like it." My gaze dropped to his mouth. The puff of cinnamon on his breath made my lips tingle. I braced myself on the table and didn't touch him. I was certain if I did, I wouldn't stop. "We're at work, PMS."

Poke the lion much, Ry?

Well, *something* was poking back. And I wanted it inside me, dammit.

"I don't fucking care." He slanted his lips over mine, his other hand at my lower back, dragging me closer until we were nearly conjoined.

His finery to my muslin.

His muscles to my softness.

His former resolution obliterating mine.

I hooked my knee higher on his hip, bringing the other one up to hold on for good measure. My fingers fumbled for his red tie and the buttons on his vest, but I couldn't seem to get anything to work.

Finally, he leaned back and took care of both.

I couldn't stop staring as his impressive shoulders seemed even larger as he dropped his tie into my chair and stripped off his vest.

My inertia dissolved at the first glimpse of his throat, then a sliver of toned belly as he jerked the tails of his shirt out of his pants. I tunneled my fingers under the fabric, my nails scraping his skin on the way up until I found his nipple.

He hissed and jerked at the tiny buttons on the front of my dress. "You have the most magnificent breasts on this planet."

I laughed. "Let's not go that far, pal."

He pushed the material aside and cupped one with his long fingers, his thumb brushing over the tip that was trying to tear its way out of my lacy demi-cup. And those deliciously long fingers didn't waste any time. He tugged down the half cup and then covered my nipple with his mouth.

I arched back and wished to hell this room was soundproofed. I'd been so damn wound up for so long that I didn't know if I could keep quiet.

He sucked strongly on my nipple, letting it pop free only to blow on it and flick his tongue along the aching tip. He smiled at me, but it wasn't a reassuring smile.

It was...wolfish.

I was prey.

And I wasn't quite sure I was ready for any of this.

The urge to push him away and escape overwhelmed the pleasure for a moment. There was no going back after this.

No way that I could say it was just a fluke between us.

But maybe if we got this out of the way here, I could end the week and put all of this behind me. Put *him* behind me.

Because while it felt amazing right now, we didn't fit. He'd probably go back to treating me like his pesky assistant as soon as the sweat dried.

Too bad I didn't care.

His mouth raced over my skin as he peeled my dress apart. His nose pushed aside my amethyst crystal until the chain looped over my other breast. His teeth scraped down my belly to the elastic at the top of my panties.

He pulled it away and let it snap back, making me gasp from the quick bite of pain as he straightened.

I was literally splayed out over his files, my dress completely unbuttoned at this point. He undid his shirt and hauled it off, sending it flying.

Mercy. I dragged in a breath as I took him in.

I'd had my hands on him, but always over clothes. I'd never seen what was hiding under those proper suits and dress shirts. He was smooth save for a light bit of fur over his pecs and a line of hair above his belt.

He was endless golden skin with the kind of lean muscles that came from running or one of those home gym kinds of things. Honed from years of discipline. Because this man was nothing if not disciplined in every aspect of his life.

From his work ethic, to his responsibilities, I was pretty sure he'd never taken a lazy day on the couch to watch trash television and eat a pint of ice cream.

He stepped closer to me and pulled up my foot to rest on his chest as he lightly trailed his fingertips over my ankle bracelet. "Where did you go?"

I shook my head. "I was just thinking your responsible side is going to freak out right after we're done here."

"This is only the start, Miss Moon." He used his foot to drag the chair up behind him as he sat down. He drew my ankle higher to his shoulder. "I love how tall you are." He kissed his way down my inner thigh, opening me as he got closer. "How you smell."

I fell back on my elbows. "This isn't a good idea."

He scooted forward and stretched me open. "Isn't that my line?"

"Yes, why I'm trying to remind you...fuck."

He tugged my panties aside and lightly licked over the skin just beside my slit. "Oh, yes. We'll get to that, but first, we'll have to see if I can get you to say my name."

I dropped my head back. "Don't bet on it."

Then his mouth did all the talking for him as well as those very, very disciplined fingers. I stared at the ceiling tiles above us and tried to hold out.

I'd meditated away my fear through a tornado in Kansas when my mother left me in our van. I'd made it through that, I could make it through this.

He wouldn't break me.

I let myself open to the pleasure. Relaxing my body by degrees and put the future in a box and shoved it at the back of my mind. Embrace the now.

Embrace the moment.

I arched off the table as he slipped two of those long fingers inside of me, stretching me and drinking from me. I squeezed my eyes shut. I didn't want to see what he was doing.

If I didn't let him in, I'd be okay.

"Ryan. Look at me."

His deep, rough voice broke down the walls, obliterated the box. He stared up at me as he sealed his mouth around me, his tongue lightly pulsing against my clit as he thrust into me with his fingers.

I needed more than that.

I needed him.

But my body detonated anyway. I reached down and raked my

fingers through his thick hair to hold him there. I bucked up against him and his name was a burn on my tongue.

We stared each other down.

Tears raced down my temples and I bowed up as the orgasm razed me like a forest fire. My whole body was ash and destruction for that single moment.

Then he was gone.

A second later, I was being pulled up and found myself face to face with wild brown eyes that held determination and the strain of something else. Something I couldn't—wouldn't—name.

He tugged me down on his lap and the tip of his latex-covered cock scraped along my swollen slit. Damn, he felt delicious against me. He curled his fingers around the back of my neck and held me up completely straight as he slowly lowered me onto him.

My mouth opened on a soundless cry as he invaded me until there was nothing but our bodies making way for one another. Me, opened wide, and him swallowed whole in one greedy thrust.

I held onto his shoulders, my nails biting into flesh as I rocked against him. The friction and overwhelming fullness and my sensitivity from my first orgasm fuzzed my brain.

He nipped my bottom lip and I tasted myself. I leaned in for more and our tastes mingled until heat and cinnamon dominated as he sucked on my tongue.

His hips lifted to match every one of my fluid rocking motions. The chair wasn't really built for this kind of action and groaned in reaction.

But we didn't care. There was only now.

Only the chase of pleasure.

I wrapped my arm around his neck and threw my head back. His mouth found my breast and drew sharply on the one that was bared and then the other through the cotton and lace. And he never let up on me. Driving into me over and over until there was no way to tell where he started and I stopped.

He flipped my dress out of the way so his could get his hands on my ass, nudging my panties aside so he could slide his fingers along my cleft from the back.

There was nowhere to hide. Both of us were still half clothed, and still, he wanted to touch and invade all of me.

He used one hand on the arm of the chair to give himself more leverage as he thrust into me until my teeth rattled. My name was a groan as he buried his face in my neck and his teeth seared into my shoulder.

He was close.

I knew he was holding on for me.

I rolled my hips and bore down on him and conceded to the battlefield of our first time together.

Probably only time.

"Preston."

He lifted his head and cupped my face, locking his eyes on mine as I shook around him. My release was a tremor, then a storm as I had no recourse but to hold on to him.

He waited for me.

Surged into me even as I clamped down on him and everything tightened, then softened like water. I took everything he offered. Even with the protection between us, I knew all the energy he had inside of him for this moment was mine.

The sun-bright shimmer of pleasure flowed from him into me and his name tumbled out of my lips again and again.

He covered my mouth with his and swallowed my cries and the chain reaction of his orgasm triggered another for me, even more incredible than the first.

I collapsed on him, my cheek falling to his shoulder as my bones went from solid to liquid gold.

"Holy shit."

I laughed as I tried to make my fingers work, but they just fell against the chair like a fish flopping out of water.

He wound his arms around my waist and settled me against him. "I didn't intend to do that here."

I nipped his shoulder. He was still semi-hard inside me and I wasn't in a huge hurry to have him leave. "Rule-breaker. Are you freaking out already?" I sighed.

"It's not that. We were a foregone conclusion—you know that as much as I do. I just mean I wanted you on a bed the first time. Or at least near a bed." He trailed little circles along the base of my spine. "I may not have made it to my bedroom with you. Or any bedroom."

I snorted. "We almost fucked in your car just last night."

"I know. I'm not sure what you do to me."

"You're not blaming the sex hex again."

"No. This is all us." He dragged his thumb down my lip to my chin. "It's always been all about us. I'm not sure why, but I don't want to let it go."

I stiffened.

"Don't." He cupped my cheeks with both hands. "Don't do that."

"You can talk. Who was cold as ice this morning?"

He looked away and let out a breath. "I had a difficult conversation with a client that set my day off on the wrong foot. I regret it if I seemed cold." He gave me that cool-eyed expression he'd perfected. "Although you did secrete my coffee, Miss Moon. Perhaps I should… reprimand you."

The rattle of the doorknob and an older version of PMS's voice came from the other side. "Open this door immediately."

"Oh, shit." I scrambled off him and hissed as he slipped out of me. He still hadn't fully softened yet even after all we'd done to one another.

Probably because he was halfway to wanting me again with all his reprimanding talk. I suppressed a shiver.

He swore then looked down at himself. The condom was mangled from my quick dismount. We both looked around desperately for a way to clean up, but there was nothing but files and white banker boxes in this room.

I spotted a tissue box and ran over to get it, then threw it at him. I jostled my underwear and underwire bra into place before quickly buttoning my dress. Dammit, I was missing a button.

"Who is in there? Preston?"

"Jesus," he muttered as he tried to tidy up and get his boxers and pants back into position.

I found his shirt and tossed it at him.

The door rattled again.

Preston bunched his fists at his sides before he picked up his tie and shoved it in his pocket. As he looked around helplessly, I crossed to him and grabbed his hand, jerking him forward to the door.

"Just go," I mouthed at him, flattening myself against the wall behind the door.

"I'll be back," he mouthed to me.

I shook my head. I couldn't think about what would come next. If I started analyzing what happened, I'd be fucked.

And I already had been spectacularly.

He gave me a hot, annoyed look. "Just a moment," he called out.

I waved him away and he managed to slip out without showing the detonation of the room—and me. I sagged against the wall. Goddess, what a clusterfuck.

Then I put the room back to rights.

When I finally girded my loins enough to peek out into the office, I was relieved to see the main waiting room was empty. Preston's door was open, but he didn't seem to be in his office.

I ran for my desk, grabbed my purse, and made a quick delivery. Then I flew toward the elevators like the coward I was.

As the numbers descended downward over the doors, I smiled. At least PMS was guaranteed to have a good afternoon now.

CHAPTER SEVENTEEN

PRESTON

I'D NEVER SEEN my father fire-breathing mad before.

Annoyed, often. Bad-tempered, sure. But flames practically shooting out of his eyes with enough force to scald me where I stood opposite his desk? This was a first.

This day was destined to have many of them apparently, and it was only—

I glanced at my watch. Past three already. Guess fucking my assistant on the conference table had taken longer than I'd realized. Pity it hadn't taken even longer. I could've spent years lost in her luscious body. And I probably would have—at least for a second round—if not for my father deciding to epically cock-block me.

"Was this necessary?" I asked in a brutally low voice, searching for calm.

"I assume you mean interrupting your...work." His smirk as he sat back in his desk chair set off a pulse at the base of my skull. "You have a bed at home. Use it."

"I have no idea what you're talking about."

"Sure you don't. Interesting that your sharp-tongued new assistant isn't at her desk right now, isn't it?" He crossed his arms, straining the shoulders of his crisp gray jacket. It didn't have a single wrinkle, unlike mine, I was certain. "Have to say I'm surprised at you, Preston, considering your attitude in other ways. But I've found out plenty of things about you today that surprised me. That you've taken up with some witchy floozy barely rates."

"You are not speak of her like that ever again. Do you understand me?" I made a fist and barely resisted slamming it on his desk. "My mistake was not taking you to task the last time you dared to open your mouth about her."

"Taking me to task?" he thundered, his face blanching as he rose to his feet. "Have you forgotten who started this law firm? Who can fire *you* at any time?" Before I could respond, he smiled thinly and leaned forward, bracing his hands on his desk. "Or is that what you're hoping I'll do, so you don't have to make the decision to walk?"

I almost didn't hear the question, because the way he was looming toward me, deliberately trying to intimidate me, reminded me how I'd done the same move to Ryan over a damn coffee pod.

I was my father's son, in far too many ways to count. So, how did I have the right to question his behavior? I didn't have an explanation for mine, except ones that cleared my guilty conscience.

"How do you feel about Courtney?" I asked suddenly.

If he'd been any more surprised by my change in direction, he would've toppled over. As it was, his dark eyes narrowed as the color slowly returned to his cheeks. "What?"

I repeated the question.

"What business is that of yours?"

"I'm your son," I said tightly. "I might not be particularly proud of that fact right now, but I am. If you have feelings for her, it's not an excuse, but it's not as bad as if you're just using her. Just using Mom."

Almost as if it had never existed, his anger drained out of him and he sank into his chair, looking years more exhausted than he had when we entered his office. "Did it ever occur to you they're using me just as much?"

I refused to believe it. "No. Mom isn't using you. She loves you."

"We love each other as friends do, Preston."

I yanked on the knot in my hastily redone tie. "Explain."

"This isn't really appropriate for us to discuss."

"Right, because it's appropriate for you to take cheap shots at a woman who's done nothing to you just because she means something to me."

"What does she mean? Besides a convenient—"

"Don't," I interrupted, shoving my fists into my pockets. It took everything I possessed not to use them. "Don't even say it. Don't even think it. Because not only will I quit this godforsaken firm, I'll walk out the door and never speak to you again."

He inhaled deeply through his nose. "You don't even know her."

"I feel like I do. I feel… Jesus, far too much."

And I'd never even gotten a chance to ask if she was all right afterward. She'd seemed fine for those brief moments we'd spoken, but maybe I'd missed a cue. I didn't want her to be alone right now, shoring up her walls to shut me out.

She probably figured I was doing the same.

"Be careful, son." His voice gentled. "I know we're at odds right now, but contrary to what you obviously believe, I've never wanted anything but the best for you. I don't want to see you hurt."

"Then don't look at me, because I've been fucking miserable for years." When he started to reply, I held up a hand. "I'm not asking for a violin accompaniment, okay? I know I'm lucky that I've had this job, that my lifestyle is beyond comfortable. You gave me opportunities my whole life that so many others haven't had."

Ryan, riding around in a van with her mother, hadn't had them. She'd struggled. She hadn't even told me all the ways she had, but I could see some of what she'd gone through in her eyes. Her bravado draped around her like a cloak. Keeping her safe from those who would make judgments.

Making friends through tarot. Wearing black so she didn't attract too much attention, although that was impossible. Quietly helping others while claiming she didn't need any herself.

My first instinct upon learning about her work history had been to look down at her. None of the jobs she'd held were important. She wasn't suitable for an attorney of my caliber.

What a crock of shit. She'd hugged a woman she didn't even know, because she was crying and broken-hearted. Her first instinct was to heal, not harm.

And *she* was the unsuitable one? No, that was me, with my rigid rules and my need for order above all else. Meanwhile, the life was being constricted out of me, day by day.

"Yet you aren't happy." My father phrased that as a statement, not a question.

"No."

"You want to do something other than divorce law."

"Yes." I didn't know how he knew this all of a sudden, but I had to assume Dex was involved. "I want to help people instead of helping them be awful to each other."

I didn't expect him to laugh out loud. Or that I could smile too.

Until I thought of him cheating on my mother—and denigrating Ryan. Neither of those things could stand. My silence might as well have been agreement.

"When did you stop loving Mom?" I asked quietly.

"I didn't," he said after a long moment. "We love each other, son. We just aren't in love. I don't know if we ever were." He let out another short laugh, this one far darker. "What is love anyway? Some romantic notion in the books. It's not real. It's not worth ruining your life."

I swallowed hard, thinking of the feel of Ryan's skin under my fingertips. So soft and vulnerable, with that strength beneath that was both enviable and scary as hell. "It's everything."

"We're happy enough," my father went on as if I'd never spoken. "She lives her life, I live mine. I take care of her very well. She wants for nothing."

"Except your love and fidelity."

"If you asked her, she'd tell you she was happy," he insisted.

Since I knew she'd done that very thing, I said nothing. How could she be happy when her husband wasn't faithful to her? Money was a poor substitute for a true companion who adored you as much as you adored them.

Not that I knew what that was like. I didn't. My longest relationship had lasted perhaps half a year. We hadn't been in love, just serious like. She'd dumped me when she fell for her polo instructor, a fact I'd found mystifying. The falling in love part, not that she'd developed a particular fondness for polo.

But over the past couple of weeks, I'd started to question things. To wonder if maybe I could have that too.

If I even had any choice in the matter.

A sex hex wasn't to blame, but something much more elemental. I'd never believed in love at first…email before, but I had to say, I was beginning to. And being with Ryan had only sharpened my hunger for her.

Would that still be the case next week, next month, next year? Hell, sixty years from now? Once, I would've said of course not. Now everything was in flux.

Especially me.

I sagged into the chair opposite my father's desk. "Are you happy?" I asked finally when the silence between us grew too deep.

He didn't answer for a long time. "Why does it matter?"

I simply shut my eyes.

My father let out a frustrated breath. "What the hell is going on with you? This isn't you. You don't behave like this." Then after a moment, he made a sound that verged on a growl. "Let me guess."

"Don't."

But he was on a tear. "Not since you were caught in that fountain with that ridiculous girl have you acted so erratically."

"Yeah, and that was probably the last time I was truly happy." What a sobering realization that was.

"So what? Do you think we all dance through life every day? No. We handle our responsibilities and take advantage of the perks we're offered—"

"Like your secretary, right? Was she one of your perks?"

"I could ask you the same question."

"No. She's not a goddamn perk. I wouldn't be surprised if she never let me touch her again, and you know what? She's probably

217

right. I'm not worthy of her. I haven't lived the way I truly want to for so long that I don't even know what it would look like. It's a fucking miracle my dick still works."

At my father's shocked expression, I gritted my teeth. So, I probably could've stopped before saying that. Honesty didn't mean a need for family therapy sessions.

But we did need one. All of us. Probably even Mr. Happy Go Lucky Dexter, though he was seeming wiser all the time. He understood he couldn't put his real life on pause, because the world didn't stop. I didn't want to look back and realize my best years had passed me by and for what? I had enough money.

What I didn't have was fun. And pleasure. And freedom.

And if I was truly being honest, love. A home with someone I could build a life with. I hated coming home alone, but maybe I didn't have to.

Not anymore.

I kind of hated that Dexter was turning out to be the smart brother. Not that I'd ever tell him that. A man had to have some secrets.

My father gripped the back of his neck and stared over my shoulder. "You never told me any of this. It took Dexter coming to me today to clue me into the fact that I was ruining your life."

I would've laughed at the melodramatic turn of phrase if it hadn't been so true. Well, partially. "Someone is ruining my life, but it's not you. It's me." I ran my fingertip over a slash of red on my wrist, rising like a welt. Ryan must've marked me. Would it be too much to get a tattoo right there?

Huh, I could get a tattoo. I'd never done that before. She had a tattoo right in the same spot. A crescent moon and a scatter of stars. A good reminder to always look up.

I'd forgotten that for too long.

"This is starting to sound like a support group." My father rose. "Do you want to step back?"

"I do. All the way back." I took a deep breath. "I'm giving my notice. I'll stay on for as long as needed to close out my cases, but I'm done. Officially."

My father continued on as if I'd never spoken. "Dexter indicated he can take on more, and we can always bring in someone to help you after I retire. You can help with that selection. What about Bishop?"

"Did you hear me? I just said I'm leaving. I have to go." I shoved my fingers through my hair. "But yeah, I can talk to Bishop. I need to anyway. I won't leave you in the lurch."

"You can't leave. You handle everything here. Without you, this law firm will become a shadow of what it used to be. What about my legacy?"

"Your legacy is your own. It's not my responsibility." Saying that—and finally truly believing it—was like dropping a burden I'd carried for far too long. "You just said Dex can help more. I'll call Bishop. He's been having some growing pains of his own, so maybe he'll want to throw his lot in here. Maybe not. If he doesn't, I can put out some feelers."

"You owe me," my father said in a low voice, a muscle jumping visibly under his jaw. "After all I've sacrificed for you, that's it? You'd just walk away and let this law firm crumble? And for what, Preston? If this is about your temp, hell, keep fucking her. See if I care."

"So happy you're offering your approval." I dragged off the tie I'd only just put back on before coming in here, punishing the fabric between my hands to keep from strangling my father.

I never would've said I had a violent streak, but lately, the man was testing me.

"As of tomorrow, she won't be working here anymore, and April will return." He adjusted his cuff links. "Maybe then everything can go back to normal."

"No, it can't. I'm done. You know me well enough to know I don't make idle threats. I never threatened to go before because I wasn't ready."

"Oh, and now you are?"

"So ready." I pocketed my tie and moved to the door. "You can count on me to finish things out, as I said. I won't leave until my clients are satisfied they are in good hands. But I *will* be leaving. And if you talk to Dex before I do, please pass along my thanks." I flashed my dad a thin smile as I turned the knob. "As usual, he ran his mouth before I could, but in this case, I appreciate it."

I stepped out into the hall and shut the door behind me. And I grinned, already palming my phone in my pocket.

I was free.

Finally, I was fucking free.

Oh, it wasn't that simple. I'd likely be tying things up for months. But it didn't matter. There was a light at the end of my metaphorical tunnel, and this time, it wasn't a train bearing down on me. I could imagine making it through to the other side.

Even if I wasn't entirely sure what my life would look like yet.

It wasn't as if I was going to chuck my law degree to become a professional surfer or something. Never mind that a job like that was impossible in central New York. I wasn't going to relocate either.

I rubbed the mark on my wrist. I had a very good reason to stay exactly where I was.

But I also loved my house. I loved my family, regardless of the fact that one of them was shortsighted, pigheaded, and a damn fool. I didn't want to go somewhere else. More than enough existed for me right here.

It was past time I figured out how much more I could have.

Walking down the hall to my temporary office—oh, yeah, I was already moving out in my mind—I pressed the speed dial for my best friend. It had been far too long since we'd spoken, but it looked like I was suddenly going to have a lot more free time.

He took a few rings to answer. Once he did, I could barely hear him.

"Where are you? You sound like you're in a wind tunnel."

He replied again, not that I could make it out in the rush of noise. I distinctly heard a feminine laugh and then there came the sounds of movement before the line quieted.

"Sorry about that. How the hell are you, Pres?"

"Where are you?"

"On a beach loving life. You could use one of those."

So, my buddy was on the same track as I was. Summertime and the living was easy. Well, it was almost fall, and my life wasn't easy yet, but I was getting there.

"Which beach? I can meet you."

"Before five on a Thursday? Who are you, and what have you done with my best friend?"

"Try me."

His laughter was loud and rich. "Pretty sure you can't meet me, bud. I'm in the South Pacific."

"What? Are you serious?"

"Sure am. I told you I needed some time off. Well, I took it. Now I'm not sure I'm coming back." He laughed again.

I frowned. He was kidding. Of course he was. People didn't go on vacation and just…stay there. Did they?

Then again, most people probably didn't sleep with a woman one time and rip apart their whole life. Was insanity catching?

Possibly.

The truth of it was that I'd been considering deconstructing my life even before I'd touched Ryan. She'd just helped accelerate things.

"When you say you need a vacation, you're not kidding around." I went into my office and eased a hip on the edge of my desk as I fingered the tie in my pocket. I wouldn't mind not wearing those annoying things every minute of my day, that was for sure.

Besides, who said I had to? Of course I would when I went into court, but there was nothing wrong with trousers and a button-down shirt. My clients would probably expire if they saw me in anything but a full suit, but hey, maybe they needed to be shook up too.

"Nope, I'm tired of the grind, man. It wears at you. Especially in our line of work." Bishop released a long sigh. "My last client before I hopped on the plane cried on my shoulder, thanking me for saving her family's compound on Maui from her evil ex. I might've felt like Superman, if I didn't suspect she was just as sketchy as her awful husband."

I laughed. That was a scenario I knew too well. "I hear you. How long have you been there?"

"Just a few days. Not long enough. Especially since I've found an especially interesting distraction to occupy my time." I could practically hear him waggling his brows.

I chuckled. "You sound like you're on the prowl."

"No need. I saw her my first day here. Damn, Shaw, I think I'm in love."

My laughter sounded a little crazed. "You too?"

Immediately, I sobered. What the hell was I saying? It was one thing to acknowledge I could want love, and that the possibility of love was more likely than it had been, say, three weeks ago. But to think I was actually in love already?

Nah.

Not possible.

I went to work on the top few buttons of my shirt. For fuck's sake, I couldn't be.

Bishop coughed. "Okay, now I think I've entered into another dimension. Never mind my own crazy situation, but you? *The* Preston Michael Shaw, king of all he touches and with no concern for any human emotion ever? I mean, dude, how long has it been since you've even hooked up?"

Though I wasn't one to kiss and tell, considering my recent past I couldn't help feeling smug. "About an hour ago."

Static filled the line, and then Bishop let out a laugh. "No way. Same goes. Who is she?"

"Who is yours?" I countered, not wanting to go there yet.

As close as Bishop and I were, too much was in chaos right now. I didn't want to say too much about Ryan. It seemed wrong somehow. It should be private, at least for a bit. Personal.

Just ours.

Too much of it had already been up for my father's consumption due to his interruption. I wasn't about to gossip to Bishop.

He sighed and the sound was decidedly misty for my normally non-emotional best friend. He'd certainly had his share of pain in his past, which he rarely liked to talk about. That included not getting too involved in his personal relationships. In a lot of ways, he was like my brother. He was more discriminating than Dex, but he never stayed lonely for long.

I understood all too well why he didn't want to be, after what he'd dealt with.

"She's amazing. Seriously amazing. We've been wrapped up in each other for days. We barely break to eat. Unless it's off each other. I put slices of pineapple on her—"

I held up a hand, but he obviously couldn't see me. "I get the picture. And normally, I'd say I was jealous, but I'm pretty pleased with my own situation right now. Mine is also local."

"Yeah. That is a problem." He paused. "I'm thinking of asking her to come back with me."

My eyes widened. Something was definitely in the air, even on the other side of the world. "To live with you?"

"Well, she doesn't have to move in right away, but she could. Why not, right? I like this feeling. Hell, I *love* this feeling. She's incredible, Pres. Just the sound of her laughter makes me grin like an idiot."

"You know, you're on a tropical island. I think the hotels pump drugs into the air conditioning system so you spend all your money. Falling for some pretty girl in a lei is just the next step."

His laughter was quick. "Not in Hawaii, son. No leis. But she wears the fuck out of a bikini. Like I can't even tell you."

For a moment, I let myself imagine Ryan in a bikini. Hot pink, to offset her dark hair, jewel eyes, and olive skin.

I shifted on the edge of my desk at my definite discomfort down south. Would she like to go to the South Pacific? I should ask.

And hey, look at that, my schedule was opening up.

"You'll have to connect me with your travel agent."

"Oh, is that so? Thinking of finally taking a vacation in oh, 2024 or so?" Bishop teased.

"I'll have more time on my hands much sooner than that, coincidentally enough."

Not that I wouldn't be working. I couldn't *not* work. It was in my

DNA. I'd just be taking more time to play, especially if I could figure out how to convince Ryan to play with me.

Innuendo absolutely intended.

"Why is that? Your dad's retiring anytime now, isn't he?"

"Yes. And so am I. Well, not retiring. But I gave my notice."

"Notice of what?"

My lips twitched around a smile. "Has too much sex dulled your hearing?"

"Dude, maybe. I'm not sure half my senses are still working. But what a damn way to go. Now what exactly are you talking about? Use small words. I'm exhausted."

"My heart breaks for you." I had to grin. "I quit. I'm no longer a partner of Shaw, Shaw, and Shaw. Guess they're going to have to change that name, huh?"

We would've had to anyway once my father officially retired, but now the firm wouldn't only be made up of Shaws. It would be Shaw and Stone, assuming Bishop didn't run off with his cabana girl and never returned to Kensington Square.

Such a thing would've seemed impossible just a short time ago, just like my giving my notice.

Just like either of us—hell, both of us—falling for some mystery woman. Not that Ryan was a secret to me. I knew there was so much more left for me to learn about her, but I was committed to the prospect.

I would leave no stone unturned, starting with how many times I could make her come back to back. So far we were at two, but I'd always been an overachiever.

"You're going to have to do some serious backtracking, man." Someone spoke over Bishop's shoulder, and he laughed in a way I'd never heard from him before. Free and easy and unburdened. "Look, I've gotta go but I want to hear the full story when I'm back in a few days. Drinks at Lonegan's on me?"

"Absolutely, but they'll be on me since part of the story involves you. Have a good time. Do everything I wouldn't do and then give me some tips." I hung up to the sound of my buddy's laughter.

It was a great sound, one I hoped to hear a lot more often.

I smiled as I walked around my desk and found the box of my coffee pods sitting on my chair with a lipstick kiss on the box.

Ryan Goddess Moon was a godsend in more ways than one.

While I popped one of them into the brewer, I called my car dealership and made a few subtle inquiries. I was interested in a new vehicle. Something less…beige.

My account representative got very excited indeed and invited me to come by for a test drive in an hour. I started to say no, since it was only late afternoon and I still had a stack of paperwork waiting for me —and apparently, my assistant had taken her leave early.

Hard for me to get too mad there. Emphasis on hard. Especially since I intended to see her again this evening.

Wouldn't this car make a statement when I did?

I agreed to meet for the test drive and hung up to take my first sip of my beloved. I sat behind my desk and let the sweet warmth slide through my system, prodding my already overstimulated nerve endings. In no time, I'd finished the cup and went back for a second. The substandard kind from the supply closet was no comparison to this.

Now that I was fully caffeinated, I glanced down at myself. I couldn't go to the dealership like this. I needed a shower. Desperately.

I took one glance at my pile of files and grabbed my briefcase to sweep them inside. On the way to the door, I grabbed my phone again and texted Dex.

> What's the name of your tattoo parlor?

> DEX:
>
> Dude, don't do it. Not if you're going to tat something like ESQ on your ass.

I snorted.

> Did Ryan tell you about her fascination with that word?

DEX:

No, but I know she has a fascination with you.

My typical response would be to change the subject. But since I had it on good authority she did have a fascination with me, I only sent back a quick reply.

And vice versa.

DEX:

Finally he admits it! Is she the reason for the tattoo inquiry? Not that your last tat choice wasn't inspired.

I winced and wiggled the toes on my left foot in my shoe.

I've done questionable things while drunk in college. But I'm not drunk now.

DEX:

Sure about that? And why do you say that? Tattooing big beneath your big toe seems logical 2 me.

I rode the elevator downstairs and headed out to my car. The sunny afternoon was sweltering, and my shirt clung to my skin within a moment of stepping outside. I was already looking forward to that ice-cold shower.

It seemed smart at the time. Tattoo place, please? I'm about to drive.

Dex rattled off the address before sending over a followup question.

DEX:

Seriously, I know you don't have much of a social life lately, but no matter how good the pussy is, do not put her name on you. Do not do it. I implore you. You're begging to hate her by Tuesday.

I laughed as I unlocked my car and slipped inside. The interior was like the surface of the freaking sun. I turned on the car and blasted the AC. My new possible purchase was seeming smarter all the time.

> No names, I promise. And you really shouldn't be so crass.

DEX:

> But you didn't deny it. Go big or go home, right? Even your toe knows that.

I smiled as I replied.

> Thanks. Later.

I quickly called the tattoo place and asked to make an appointment, which struck the guy on the other end of the line as odd. He told me to come in two hours from now and that was that.

All at once, I had a packed schedule this evening. Now I could just hope my last stop of the night appreciated all these changes.

And if she didn't, well, I would.

Go big toe or go home.

CHAPTER EIGHTEEN

I UNFOLDED myself from my cross-legged position. My back—and other tender things—reminded me that drawing on my bed was stupid. But I hadn't been able to settle since I left work.

More than a bit early, to be honest, but I didn't care. My level of overwhelm was in the red-line zone. Drawing was usually the only way for me to handle it. Yet even my little fox couldn't lure me in like she usually did.

Roz, my human character, was even snarkier than usual.

I tossed my iPad and iPencil on my twisted sheets before heading into my kitchen for something cold. I'd tried to call Luna, but she had clients until late evening. I really didn't want to have to explain my jangling nerves to my best friend. She was far too astute.

It was just sex.

And okay, it had been more than a few months since I'd gotten naked—or partially naked—with a guy. I stayed in my own lane most of the time. Between work and the web comic, I just didn't have the mental space to date.

It was also too damn hot to think about getting naked with people.

Didn't stop you from doing it in the records room, chick.

I rubbed my hands over my face. I'd taken a shower as soon as I got home and stripped down to the basics, choosing a long, shapeless dress that was super light, and I'd let my hair air-dry into its natural waves.

But even my ancient dress felt like too much. My skin was still buzzing from PMS's touch and it had been hours ago.

Usually, a shower reset me. It was how I ended my work day and switched to my creative brain side. Right now, I was drowning in flashbacks from the records room.

His mouth.

His fingers.

The way he held me like I was breakable one moment, then proved to me I was invincible the next.

But then I'd left and he hadn't texted me, not even after finding my present. Which actually he'd bought for himself, but whatever. It was the thought that counted, right?

Unless he was already regretting what we'd done…

"Stop it," I ordered myself as I swung open the refrigerator door. I pulled out a pitcher of ice water loaded with citrus slices and filled a thermal cup. I had a million things to do and none of them included Preston Michael Shaw.

I sat at my kitchen table and opened my laptop. My email was mocking me with that ugly number of unread messages. I shook my hair back. I could answer some emails.

"Alexa, play work playlist."

The heavy bass of a Daughtry song filled the room. I spent the next twenty minutes hacking away at spam and parceling out requests for readings for the following week.

When my life got back to normal.

One more day of working for PMS and I was free.

I rubbed the knot sitting in my chest. Free, dammit. It was only supposed to be a week. No, it *was* only a week. Period.

When I opened a third email for a love reading, I snapped the laptop shut. I didn't want to think about love readings or relationships. I pushed my chair back and grabbed my favorite kickass tarot deck.

This wasn't the one I asked about intimate stuff. This was the deck that told me the ugly unvarnished truth.

I went back to my bed and folded myself back into a Lotus pose. I hissed out a breath as my body reminded me what I'd done just a few hours ago.

As if I could forget.

A notification popped on my iPad, blinking the screen to life. My background was my favorite drawing of Roz and Sylvia. That was what I should be focused on.

I closed my eyes and shuffled my deck. "Should I post a photo of my comic?"

The cards heated and tingled under my touch. It didn't always happen that way. I was mostly an intuitive reader. Luna was the one who got more of a jolt from her gifts. I just usually instinctively knew it was time to stop shuffling and throw cards.

Not this time. They practically popped from the deck.

I threw three cards.

Desire, obstacle, solution.

The Fool, Three of Swords reversed, Six of Cups.

"Dammit."

I swiped up the cards.

I knew I shouldn't have asked. As if I didn't know the true answer.

It was time to begin. Stop blocking the freaking pain of putting myself out there. I'd never be able to move forward if I didn't grab that courage I used to have. Back when I flung myself into any creative venture without looking back.

When the hell had I lost my fucking wings?

I set my deck aside and pulled my iPad into my lap. I'd just post a little something to my stories on Instagram. They only lasted for twenty-four hours.

No one would even see it probably.

It was totally safe.

Before I could overthink it, I picked one with the little white fox curled up on Roz's shoulder, her tiny face buried in her human's wild red curls. Rain splashed the windowpane behind the cozy scene of

Roz reading with a patchwork blanket in her lap and oversized glasses balanced on the tip of her upturned nose.

Serenity.

Safe enough.

Before I could second guess myself and delete my post, a horn bleated out my window, and a text buzzed from my phone in the kitchen as well as my flashing on my iPad.

> PMS:
>
> Come outside.

Before I replied to him, I went to my jewelry tree and selected a pair of smoky quartz earrings. I definitely needed some energy purification. All the stress and chaos in my mind needed an outlet, so I would release them. The crystal would help me to find my sense of calm. Time to let go of anything that was holding me back.

I would stay in the present moment and look for the good.

Another text came through.

> PMS:
>
> I'm coming up.

My eyes widened as I whirled around and took in the state of my apartment. It wasn't in awful shape, but there was stuff everywhere. Books, tarot decks, hunks of crystal, sketchbooks, and random articles of clothing covered many of the surfaces, including the sofa.

Fuck.

> I don't think that's a good idea.

He was already at the door, knocking with heavy thumps of his knuckles. Rude. He didn't even give me time to say if I was busy.

But when it came to PMS, that was surprising, how?

I hurried over to stuff the items on the couch underneath, so at least he had a place to sit. I hadn't invited him over, so he got what he got. But yeah, I needed a maid. Or to spend an afternoon tidying up.

Probably more likely than the maid.

I flung open the door. "How did you get my—"

He pushed up his dark sunglasses and dragged me to him, cupping my jaw and silencing my irritated question with his firm, persuasive lips. He didn't hesitate before sweeping his tongue inside and rendering me mute with slow, teasing flicks of heat that made flames scorch the base of my spine.

Literally, since his other hand rested there and I couldn't breathe from the lack of space between our bodies.

He finally moved back and rested his forehead against mine. We were both breathless. "You were saying?"

"Who are you again?"

His laughter was a deep rumble that made me grin in response before I caught myself. I was annoyed.

Right.

"My resumé was not meant for you to use to make surprise visits."

He was already nudging me aside to enter my apartment, continuing the whole uninvited theme.

I tried not to see my place as he would. I had people over all the time. Usually, I cleaned up a little better than this, but I'd been distracted this week.

That was a good word for it.

He went right to the sofa and bent over to pick up a dark piece of material sticking out from beneath the piece of furniture. That was when I noticed he was not wearing a suit. In fact, he wasn't even wearing pants.

"Whoa, you own shorts?"

Damn, he had a nice ass too. Who'd've guessed? Well, every part of the man was fine, so I shouldn't have been surprised.

He turned toward me and held up the item he'd found, a black T-shirt that proclaimed Witches Make Better Lovers. It had stress lines around the chest area because I'd had the shirt forever and it had never fit quite right.

"I can say this is a true statement. Put it on."

My nipples immediately hardened so I crossed my arms over them. "Excuse you? I'm already dressed."

He stepped toward me. "So, get undressed."

Nope, nuh uh, I wasn't doing that again. Repeats were dangerous.

"Uh, not sure if you realize, but we aren't at work right now. You don't get to boss me around here."

His voice dropped to a level guaranteed to disintegrate my panties. "Would you be more likely to comply if I say please?"

It was a lot harder to maintain my stiff backbone when my thighs were trembling. "No?"

The corner of his sinful mouth lifted. "I hear a question mark."

My eyes zeroed in on his bandaged wrist. "What happened to you? That wasn't there earlier when we..."

"Turning shy on me, Miss Moon?" He tucked a curl behind my ear. "I love your hair all wild. I want to feel it falling around us when I slide into you."

Ignore him. He's just horny.

Ignore yourself while you're at it.

Why were we both in heat? It was really freaking annoying.

And inconvenient.

I cleared my throat. I'd just not answer him. That should work.

"What happened to your wrist?"

He tossed the shirt on the sofa and offered his arm for my inspection. Gently, I touched the base of his palm. Right below it, a red angry-looking scratch sat just above the narrow gauze bandage.

"Did I do that?"

"The scratch? Either you did it or my secret mystery lover. So secret I don't even remember her."

I bit my lip and touched the scratch. "Sorry. Didn't realize I got so enthusiastic."

"You're apologizing for that? Hell, I wanted to get it tattooed there but the guy didn't think that was wise with possible infection."

My gaze lifted to his as I continued to stroke his wrist. It was almost instinctual, the need to draw out discomfort and take it into myself. Especially his.

Which didn't make any sense at all.

"Take a look," he said when I didn't move to uncover the tattoo.

I peeled off the bandage and swallowed at the combination symbol of a moon and sun in virtually the same place I had a crescent moon and scattered stars on my own inner wrist. His was on the right, mine the left.

"Dex told me not to tattoo your name on me no matter how good the pussy was." He jerked a shoulder when my gaze shot up to his. "It was spectacular, but I didn't tell him that."

I couldn't decide whether I wanted to laugh—or cry. "Moon, huh, ace?"

"Goddess Moon." He pushed back that same errant curl. "Also, a reminder that there is more contained in the earth and sky than you can imagine, Horatio. Or something like that."

Now I did laugh. "Quite possibly the worst mangling of that line ever."

"Yet you recognized it."

"I did." I covered the reddened tattoo and made myself take a definite step back. "So, what made you decide to invade my privacy and stop over for a visit?"

"Not the only thing I invaded today."

I raised a brow.

He tucked his hands in his pockets. He had on a blindingly white T-shirt that showed off his golden tan. How did a lawyer lizard get such a glow?

"I figured we could take a ride to my place, eat under the stars."

It moved me more than it should have. This guy liked his romantic gestures. "We screwed on a conference table. Don't think we need a followup date."

He didn't acknowledge me. "I debated bringing Smoky along, but he's touchy after today's litter box mess. He's afraid of the vacuum. Can you imagine?" He walked in front of my bedroom divider, examining all the shelves and crevices and the many items contained there. Thoughtfully, he trailed his fingers over a large hunk of citrine. "What does this one do?"

"Do?"

"You know, aid in. What is it used for?"

"It energizes and encourages self-confidence, and it also attracts success and wealth. Don't touch it too much. You already have enough money. Leave some for the rest of us."

He moved on to my collection of tarot decks. "What if I wanted you to pull cards for a particular question I have? Would you do it? Or should I find another reader?"

"Ask Luna," I said immediately.

"You said card reading can be as intimate as sex, but yet you want to send me to your best friend." He glanced over his shoulder, still strolling and examining my possessions. "Interesting."

"You aren't Luna's type."

"But I'm yours?"

"Absolutely not."

"Your orgasms seemed to indicate otherwise. What about this?" I assumed he would pick up one of the velvet tarot bags on his eye level, which was personal enough. But he diverted to one of the uppermost shelves almost out of my reach and picked up a purple glass moon-topped cylinder.

A very special one.

"And this?" He turned toward me, running his blunt-tipped finger over the tapered end, offset with small ripples in the glass. "A beautiful piece. What is it used for?"

That cultured voice did unspeakable things to questions he should not be asking.

I gave a nonchalant shrug. "It's decorative."

"Is that so? But it's built so...specifically." He rubbed his fingers along the glass bubbles while his heated gaze roamed over my face. "These smaller ripples right here almost make me think of—"

"Never mind." I grabbed the moon cylinder and gave him a light shove.

Right toward my drawing table, bathed in a shaft of sunlight. One that shone right on my scattered drawings.

Goddess, no.

He'd taken a single step when I grabbed him from behind and

forced the glass back into his hand. The damn thing was burning up from his touch anyway. "It's a sex toy. Rippled for my pleasure."

His fingers closed around mine on the shaft's graduated tip. "If you think I didn't know that, you must've been impressed I managed to put the condom."

I couldn't help laughing as I tried to slip back—not that he allowed it.

He spun me around and dragged the glass shaft up my thigh, right between my legs. He pulsed it against me there, holding the warmth against my clit through my dress and my panties. His mouth came down hard on mine as he rubbed tiny circles against my already throbbing flesh.

Then he drew back to lift the glass to his lips, sucking slowly while I fought to maintain eye contact. Knowing he knew what I'd done with it in the past—it'd been a while—only made me hotter. Wetter.

Which he realized as soon as he rolled up my dress and nudged aside my panties to tease me directly.

"Fuck, Ryan," he groaned against my ear.

At the moment, I had no complaints about that idea.

His thumb rolled over my swollen clit before he drew the glass tip over me again and again, catching the sounds I made with his lips against mine.

Then he tossed the glass toy toward the sofa. "My fingers and tongue and cock will be what gets you off, not that."

CHAPTER NINETEEN

PRESTON PICKED me up so fast that I slapped a hand against his shoulder for balance. He swung his gaze around, and for a second, I imagined him taking me on my drawing table.

Would it hold our weights? And would coming my brains out literally on top of my sketches provide some creative...juice?

Not that I wanted him anywhere near my sketches, so I'd tried to distract him with sex toy 101.

Turned out he excelled at distraction himself.

"Finally," he said under his breath, spotting my bed on the other side of the shelf divider. He juggled me while I flailed at him, but he still managed to sweep aside my laptop—though not the papers that crunched beneath my body as he set me down.

My eyes popped wide. More sketches. Dammit, why was I so cursed?

He reared back to haul off his shirt from behind his head, and I forgot anything except his toned chest and abs and that buffet of shifting muscles as he ranged over me to kiss me again.

His lips bruised mine as he fought with the many buttons on my dress. When he finally got it open, he swallowed a sound of pain at my lack of a bra, his gorgeous eyes devouring every inch of me.

"I love these." He trailed kisses between my breasts, cupping them in his wide hands. His teeth scraped my nipple, and I jolted upward on the bed, trying to discreetly slide my sketches out from under me.

The problem was that I was also very turned on, and now his mouth was skating downward, heading toward that place he'd already primed. My panties went soaring, and I didn't even see where they ended up.

"Love this even more," he murmured, lowering his mouth to my pussy.

His gaze zeroed in on my face while he licked me. His focus was erotic as hell and I forgot all about my sketches and everything else as his long fingers slipped inside me and stretched me open. I was still a little sore from earlier, but he wasn't being gentle with me. I didn't think he could be right now. His touches were rough, but somehow exactly what I needed as he sealed his lips over my aching clit. He rubbed over a certain spot inside me that had me digging my toes into the bed, and then I was arching and grasping his hair as I came apart for him.

I cried out, dragging on his thick hair to keep him right where he was.

He didn't even pause, just kept fingering and tonguing me until I flew into another orgasm, even more powerful than the first.

I rolled on my side to try to breathe, to try to hear beyond the pounding of blood in my ears. I felt him at my back, pulling up my dress that he still hadn't fully removed and pushing his thick cock inside me while I was still convulsing.

He retreated an inch. "Shit. Fuck. Dammit. I forgot a condom."

I giggled breathlessly into my bent arm. "I'm covered."

"Are you?" He nosed my hair away from my ear. "Can I? I never have before. And God, I want to."

I nearly teased him. It was our way after all. But I glanced back and saw the deep lines of tension bracketing his eyes and decided he really needed an orgasm.

Fresh off my pair of them, I was feeling generous. And I was curious too.

"I haven't either," I admitted. "Do it."

He thrust into me so deeply that I swore he hit the end of me in one pass. His teeth sliced into my shoulder, and he banded his arm around my belly to pull me back into him. The juxtaposition between how he was holding me so tightly and driving into me so desperately made me claw at his tensed forearm. His hand came up to clasp my bare breast through my open dress and I pushed back against him, grinding into him as if I'd never come at all.

His hot, hard length grew even more inside me, and I couldn't stifle my moans as he stroked into me over and over. Then he dropped his hand between my legs and frantically rubbed my clit, holding his cock inside me at just the perfect angle while I clutched him and let go one more time.

And this time when I fell, he fell with me, burying his face in my hair, his body shaking against mine as he emptied himself into me.

Nothing between us but skin.

His breath fluttered against my neck, already slowing into an easy rhythm. Lulling my heartbeat to match the beat of his.

Synced up entirely.

I wasn't one to fall asleep after sex, especially when I was squeezed into my too small bed with a huge, overwhelmingly warm man who hadn't even bothered to lose all of his clothing—again. But apparently, coming oh, five times since lunch tended to wear a girl out.

When I woke, my face was smushed into a piece of paper, and I was half on top of my laptop with the keys mashed under my thigh. I felt decidedly achy between my legs, and a quick check of my breasts confirmed they were reddened from Preston's stubble.

Oh, and my thighs were wet, but not just from my deluge of orgasms. I was pretty sure he'd cleaned me off while I'd been in a fucking coma.

Literally.

I reared up, remembering my sketches. Oh my goddess. Were they all still here? I got on my hands and knees to grab every one of them, tossing the laptop to the side to pluck up the last paper beneath it.

Which was how Preston found me when he entered the room, amiably chatting on the phone.

"I'm so sorry, Mary. I know I agreed to be there to sign the papers this afternoon with my notary. Yes, my assistant was unavoidably called away. Oh, she had a very good reason. A personal emergency, if you will. Surely you understand."

With my bare ass in the air and my open dress falling forward over my head, I clutched my sketches to my chest and prayed to disappear.

Maybe I'd be beamed up into outer space by a more intelligent life form than a woman who fucked her boss multiple times in one day.

Without a condom, no less. I was practically a walking billboard for questionable decisions.

And PMS was still on the phone, chatting away as if he had all the time in the world.

I glanced over my shoulder, only to discover he was listening to the other end of the line while studying my ass equally intently. His head was even cocked. When he realized I was watching him, he grinned and pretended to look out the window.

He was not cute. I shouldn't grin at him as if he was. But I couldn't help myself.

This was probably due to some biological imperative. If a guy made you come enough times in rapid succession, your body figured he was a decent sort so weird things started occurring all on their own. Like my smiling at him dopily while I tried to tuck my papers under my dress as I backed off the bed.

Luckily, he decided to return to the living room, so I shoved my sketches into a drawer and decided I'd take a quick shower.

Escaping into my bathroom also bought me some time to prepare myself to deal with him. Conversations after sex could be a minefield, and we didn't know each other that well.

Even if certain parts of me were getting *very* acquainted with parts of him.

I moaned out loud when the cold water hit my oversensitized body. I'd gotten more action in one day than I'd gotten all year.

When I couldn't stall any longer, I finished up and toweled off before slipping back into my dress sans panties, since they were currently missing. The whisker burn on my chest was still vivid, so I lathered up with some of the honey rose cream I'd picked up from the apothecary in Luna Falls. My bestie liked to claim the town was made for her, so we'd gone a few times.

My fingers lingered on my breast for an extra moment, imagining Preston's intense dark eyes lasered on mine while he sucked on my nipple. I had to appreciate his dedication in some areas.

And I seriously needed to get a grip. Fawning over PMS's skills in the sack—even in my own head—was not on the agenda.

I tied my crazy hair on top of my head as I walked into my bedroom, coming to a halt at the sight of my boss stretched out on my bed.

He was still on the phone. What the heck could Mary Donnelly have to say?

"She just covered herself in some kind of witchy potion that smells like a bakery. Do you women all just know what to mix up to make men beg?"

I blinked as he laughed, sounding far more cheerful than I was used to. Then again, great sex had that effect on most males.

"Right. I know. Actually, there's something else in it too." Eyes closed, he lifted his face as if he was scenting the air. "Floral. Usually, she smells like a garden blooming at night. This is fresher, sweeter. Almost innocent."

"Who is that?" I hissed.

If he was talking about my scents with a client, I was probably going to kill him. And he'd thank me tomorrow once the afterglow faded and he came to his senses.

Why hadn't it faded yet anyway? I wasn't sure how long I'd slept, but the shadows in the room were longer and sunset wasn't far away.

"Hang on. She's annoyed again." He laughed at whatever the person on the other end of the line said, then held out the phone to me. "It's your best bish, as she called herself."

As a rule, I wasn't someone who blushed. My coloring made that more difficult, for one, and I also didn't get embarrassed that easily.

Score one for PMS that he managed to make me flush from my hairline to my coral-painted toes with one sentence.

I took the phone and closed my eyes as I moved into the living room.

"Don't say it," I said in an undertone.

"Say what? That your boss is all cozied up in your place?"

I'd just ignore her question. "I thought you had a full slate tonight."

"I had a cancellation. So, guess I'm not the only one playing my cards close to the vest, hmm?"

"I'm not playing any cards—what? What cards are you playing?"

"How good was it?"

"Amazing," I said before her laughter told me I'd spoken without thinking. But hey, it had been. "PMS, you better not be eavesdropping," I called over my shoulder without looking in his direction.

I so didn't want to know.

He hummed a little tune. "Nope. Just looking at the *amazing* view."

Luna must've heard the ass because she was laughing again. And so was I.

Then I realized I was talking to my best friend on Preston's phone, not my own. "Wait a second, why did you call him? *How* did you call him?"

"He called me."

"What?" I whirled to stare at him, but he was conveniently facing toward the window, hands clasped innocently behind his back. "Why?"

"We, ah, actually texted a bit yesterday. My doing," she said hastily. "I gave him a hard time. You know, protective bestie. But he called me tonight to ask what kind of date you'd like. Gotta say, Ry, he sounds like the total package."

Warmth spread through my midsection, and I wrapped an arm around my belly. I was not going to be swayed by him. "He's a package of something, all right."

His tune increased in volume.

"And obviously, he's got some skills, since you've got O voice."

"I do not."

"You so do. And the first time can be awkward, so that's a very good sign."

"Try second," I whispered.

PMS and his bat hearing heard me just the same, since he added a swivel of his hips to his song.

"Really?" Luna's screech broke the sound barrier. "You know you're going to share after your date, right? You better."

I wasn't going on any date. I didn't think.

My stomach growled. Then again, I could eat. If he wanted dinner, we could just eat in the same place.

Not a date. Just like Denny's hadn't been a date. Just mutual food consumption.

"You too. I can't believe you've been holding out on me."

"It wasn't a thing. Then it maybe could might be." She let out a breezy laugh. "We'll see. Just focus on you. Have a good time, okay? Don't overthink it."

"Thanks, but too late there."

I clicked off and returned his phone to him after smacking his upper arm with it. "Why were you texting with my best friend yesterday?"

"She texted me after you sent her that photo of us. I need a copy of that."

"Uh huh. Texted you about what?"

"She was worried about you." He pocketed his phone without looking at it. "I tried to abide by her wishes."

"Which were what?" I asked uneasily.

I did not like people in my life talking with other people in my life without my knowledge. Besides, how could anyone know what was best for me when I didn't have a clue myself right now?

He skated his thumb over my lower lip. "She cares about you. I tried to stay away."

I glanced at the tangled sheets on my bed. "So, this is you showing restraint?"

"Actually, yes. If I hadn't shown restraint, we would've been on that conference room table by Monday afternoon."

I narrowed my eyes. "Yet now you're asking my best friend about what kind of dates I like."

He shrugged and dipped his hand into his pocket. "Well, I had an idea in mind. But if she knew something you loved, I'm not averse to suggestions."

I studied him for a long moment, taking in his handsome features highlighted by the sun. His dark hair messy from my hands, his surprisingly full mouth, the black slash of his eyebrows and carved line of his jaw all added up to a hell of an attractive picture. Beneath his austere surface, he had hidden slices of sweetness that came out at unexpected times.

And every time, they rocked me.

"You were asking for her approval," I said once I could speak around the lump in my throat. "She'd warned you off, but you had no intention of going."

"I tried." He shifted toward me. "But I can't seem to stay away from you."

I wanted to be flippant. The last thing I wanted to do was to behave as if this made any sense. Lust at first sight—or at first type—was one thing. Chemical reactions couldn't be explained easily. But this wasn't that. Or not only that.

I didn't know what the hell *this* was, and that scared me to death.

When I looked away, he cupped my cheek and brought my gaze back front and center. "Will you come over to my house?"

"Why?"

"Because I want you to." He covered my lips with his fingertip. "Let's just spend some time together."

The same question sprung to my tongue but I forced it down. Tomorrow was my last day at work. I hadn't been on a date in a long time. Not that this was one.

Ugh, I was sick of my brain.

"Okay," I said finally.

His grin was quick and entirely too charming as he nudged me out of the room with his hand on my lower back. "Great. I have food waiting at home."

"I thought you wanted to ask Luna what I liked?"

"Well, yes, but I had a contingency plan."

"Of course you did, PMS."

He pinched my ass as I grabbed my sunglasses and my purse, making me laugh as I evaded him. While he was taking out his key fob, I slipped on my sandals and discreetly tucked a mini-sized tarot deck into my bag.

We'd see if he warranted a reading tonight. The jury was still out.

We walked down to the street, talking about the Donnelly case and how he'd rescheduled the signing with the notary for early tomorrow. He said it as if he didn't expect me to be punctual, which I took offense to considering I'd been early today.

Of course I'd also left early, but I still felt like it was a moral victory. His penis was directly responsible for my unintended absence in any case.

I came to a halt beside an eye-searing red convertible with black leather seats and every amenity known to man. "Look at that. Someone's showing off their money. Probably a dick compensation toy. Jeez, donate to the homeless or something, why don't you?"

Preston lifted his wrist to do something on his smart watch, and the convertible purred to life. It took me a second to realize he hadn't just wanted to check the temperature.

He'd started the car with his watch. The dick toy.

"Think so?" His tone was mild as he took my elbow and guided me toward the vehicle. "You might want to reconsider that assessment."

"And I might not. What the hell? Where did you get this?"

His brow arched as if I was a cranky child. "From the dealership. I didn't steal it, Miss Moon."

"But what about your grandpa car?"

"Careful, you'll make my head swell with all this praise. Assuming it even can."

"Is that a sex joke?"

"Is it?" He circled the hood without bothering to open my door.

After my diatribe, he'd probably decided manners were overrated. I wasn't entirely sure he was wrong.

I slid into the car and tried not to moan at the buttery feel of the leather against my legs. It was hot as Hades out, so it shouldn't have felt so sinful. I couldn't help looking at all the dials and gauges and popping open the glove compartment to *ooh* and *aah* over the space.

What didn't have a lot of space was the backseat.

"Barely even enough room for a carrier back there." I clicked on my belt as he signaled into traffic.

He didn't respond, but his acceleration to the next light was a little...excessive. As was his cornering and the force of his braking.

I shoved my sunglasses higher on my nose and tried not to wiggle into the bucket seats. This car had some serious power, and it was evident even on the city streets. The warm wind felt like heaven blowing back my hair, and I couldn't help fiddling with the incredible sound system. The bass was intense. He wasn't playing with it, so why shouldn't I?

To be an ass, I put it on the heavy metal station. He didn't so much as flicker a long dark eyelash.

His silence was like a cushion of disapproval. The hot curves of the car, sexy leather seats, and great music pumping from the truly magnificent speakers couldn't dent it.

He still didn't speak as he pulled into a long driveway a little while later. The house came into view slowly, surrounded by trees and dappled by the oncoming sunset. I glimpsed a lot of fenced-in space in back and a wide wraparound porch on at least three sides. The second level had a couple of small porches too. Light reflected off the many panes of glass, almost blinding in the late day sunshine.

The car rolled to a stop at the end of the drive, and I realized I was clutching my purse as he turned off the ignition.

"I'm sorry."

"For what?"

"You're entitled to spend your money however you choose." I shoved back a piece of hair the wind had tumbled into my face. "You work hard, and hey, I'm all for trading in your grandpa car for this sweet little ride."

"Glad to hear you approve." He climbed out of the car and walked around the back.

I shut my eyes and wanted to bind my own tongue to the roof of my mouth. Maybe then I wouldn't say such thoughtless things anymore.

Then again, probably not.

He waited for me on the walk, one hand tucked in his pocket. He didn't reach for me as we ascended the steps to the porch. Nor did he speak as he unlocked the front door and let us into a large, sunlit foyer with an old, expensive-looking rug over gleaming hardwood. A stained glass window on the stairs leading to the second level shot colorful rays in all directions, adding a soft, diffuse light to the space.

"You have a lovely home. A home for a family."

"Why do you sound accusatory when you say that?" He dropped his keys in a crystal dish on a café style table with inlaid stained glass tiles.

"I didn't mean to. Just this is a lot of house for a single guy."

"Still wondering if I have a wife stashed away somewhere? Maybe a couple of kids?"

"Can you blame me for wondering how a catch like you isn't taken?"

"Probably because I'm trying desperately to make up for my perceived inadequacies. Come on." He headed down a couple of steps into a huge sunken living room with more walls of windows and a fireplace with a carved mantlepiece meant for hanging Christmas stockings.

I took a minute to get myself back in line. PMS unnerved me, and when I was off-balance, I tended to say snarky things. But I couldn't help considering why a man who'd been single for so long would buy a large house created with a family in mind.

Unless that was what his end game was. Work himself to death now, settle down with two-point-five kids later.

And a tripod cat, who was currently nowhere in sight.

I reached up to grip one of my dangling smoky quartz earrings. They would start me on the path to grounding myself, but I clearly should've stacked on my armor. Bracelets, necklace, possibly a giant She-Ra style belt made of fluorite.

A blur of gray shot down the stairs and into the foyer. Was I seeing spooks? Then I realized what I'd witnessed wasn't a ghost.

"Hiya Smoky."

He pranced over with his three-legged grace to sit on my sandal. I rubbed his head. "I was wondering where you'd sequestered yourself."

"Probably one of the closets." PMS turned around in the living room to look at us. "He's been enjoying exploring. This morning, I found him on top of the curtain rod."

I laughed and picked up the cat, tucking him against my chest. To my surprise, he decided to settle himself over my shoulder, so I turned around to let him face PMS.

"That cat loves you." He sounded resigned. "Are you sure he wasn't meant to be yours instead?"

"No, he was meant to be—"

Ours. The sentence formed in my head without conscious thought. But conscious thought was sure as hell keeping me from saying it.

"Cat got your tongue?"

"Haha. Funny." I tipped my head against Smoky. "Let's take a tour so you can feed me. I hope you're well stocked. I had a microwave meal for lunch so I'm famished."

"Yeah, well, I ate half a sandwich outside the judge's chambers this afternoon. I think we're equally hungry."

Somehow when his voice dipped, I wasn't thinking of food.

I cupped Smoky against me more securely as we roamed through the house, but he seemed perfectly happy with his new perch. And I liked having him to hold on to.

Together, we examined the place. Gleaming dark wood was offset by neutral colors that created a serene oasis, sheltered from the outside world while still bringing it inside through the myriad windows. There were a couple of fireplaces and I even spotted a windowseat in the den, piled with cream-colored pillows that looked like they'd never been used. There was a wall of bookshelves filled with colorful leather bound books, and I yearned to roll over the library-style ladder to explore.

But instead of focusing on most of Preston's beautiful home, I was far too aware of how often his elbow bumped against mine or the feel of his broad palm low on my back as we climbed the stairs to the next floor. His warm breath fluttering against my ear while he pointed out the view from the master bedroom made me think of things that had nothing to do with the glittering curve of Crescent Lake in the distance. I wanted to check out the view from the telescope on the balcony but I was clutching the cat for all I was worth. Something about the gigantic bed with its pale blue, obviously high thread count sheets intimidated me and I couldn't stop staring at it.

"Tired?" He stroked the cat, his gaze locked on my face. "You didn't sleep long earlier."

"I'm not in the habit of sleeping at dinner time, so no, I'm fine."

"Maybe you're thinking of other reasons one might use a bed..."

"No," I said too quickly, and he laughed as he led me down the hall to yet more bedrooms, all with high ceilings and massive windows that let in the maximum amount of light. Night had fallen now, so he turned on lamps as he went.

Making my throat ache with every step, even if I had no clue why.

"Are you planning on having a baseball team? I can't see any reason for so many rooms."

"It's an investment."

"Hmm." My best friend was with me in the form of her favorite dubious expression even when she wasn't. "I could fit my whole apartment in here like six times over. Your hall closet is bigger than my bathroom."

"Your point?"

"Doesn't this strike you as weird?" I motioned between us, but he didn't seem to have any interest in looking my way.

"That we're still talking when we're both hungry, and I have a refrigerator full of food? Absolutely. I'll go get things ready." He disappeared down the stairs before I had a chance to follow.

Maybe he needed a moment too. Goddess knew I needed about a hundred of them.

I had friends from all walks of life. But I didn't know anyone with this level of wealth. I'd gone to the bathroom midway through the house tour and looked up the model of his new car on my phone.

The thing cost *six-freaking-figures.* And he'd never mentioned having another car when I teased him about his grandpa-mobile, so that meant it was probably new. Plus, this model was the latest one on the market. So, not only was it expensive as hell, it was also trendy.

That wasn't me at all.

Now I was probably going to go down there to discover he'd set the fancy dining room table with Irish linen and heavy cut crystal candlesticks that could kill a man dead. The ornate armoire beside the table held enough china—probably some family heirlooms—to fill that long table and then some. Our dinner would probably be the finest cut of salmon or filet mignon and lobster tails with new potatoes in a delicate herbed sauce.

I was a Moons Over My Hammy sort of girl.

"I'm wigging out," I whispered to the cat, digging my toes into the thick, expensive Aubusson rug beneath my feet.

One of my mother's "boyfriends" had bought her one in this style a million years ago, and she'd gushed over it for weeks. Then he'd cheated on her with the neighbor and demanded we move out by morning.

Fancy things meant our van would have a Tiffany lamp crammed against the back window before we had to pawn it for rent money for the in-between times.

I held Smoky tighter, and he made a little squeak. Or that could've been me. "I don't know if I can do this."

The cat stared up at me, his unblinking green eyes steady on mine. He didn't fight to get down, just bumped his head against my chin in silent solidarity.

There was no reason at all tears should've sprung to my eyes. It was just sex and dinner. Dinner and sex. Easy, enjoyable stuff. I'd been dating since I was thirteen, for pity's sake.

I was making this way too hard.

But that didn't stop me from sitting on the edge of the neatly made guest room bed with its plush dark green comforter to give myself another minute. Smoky decided to jump down and do a big stretch before coiling into a perfect circle in the center of the mattress.

"Are you allowed on the beds?"

Unshockingly, he didn't answer.

I sighed and did a quick centering spell using the smoky quartz at my ears as my crystals to focus on. Then I took out my mini tarot deck and did a fast throw of the cards.

"What will happen with this?" I asked into the silence, feeling a bit like a kid waiting for her mom to walk in and catch her with her hand in her panties.

No one walked in, and the two cards I drew didn't quiet my nerves.

The Tower and the Star.

All the changes, but ultimately, they would be good ones. Upheaval could be positive in the end, but that didn't mean it didn't hurt in the middle.

I really liked my life as it was. Sure, I wished some things would improve. Like I wanted to make a real go of it with my art.

But even there, that pesky cat kept sneaking in. I wasn't in control. I could keep fighting it, or I could let events unfold as they would.

If this was my Tower moment, I had to trust I would make the right choices. Part of that included really being present tonight.

No distractions.

I shut off my phone and made myself smile at Smoky, who was watching me with one slitted green eye. And maybe I could even have a few more orgasms along the way.

CHAPTER TWENTY

PRESTON

I WASN'T SURE HOW, but I was fairly certain I'd scared off Ryan.

I puzzled over it as I took containers out of the bags in the refrigerator. I didn't know if she'd think I was strange for grabbing this stuff for our dinner. Not to mention I did not know how to properly reheat egg sandwiches.

Typically, if I wanted to charm a woman with a meal, I would've made reservations at my usual seafood restaurant. Or if it was a nice night, we could've gone to Sherman Inn, a place across from the water in Crescent Cove. But neither of those options felt like Ryan, and besides, I wanted her to see my house.

To see me, when it came right down to it.

I finished unbagging then faced down my loaded kitchen table. I didn't know how to properly prepare our dinner, but she wasn't coming down in a hurry anyway.

Maybe she was still tired despite her assertions to the contrary. One thing I had was plenty of comfortable beds. All unused, waiting for my supposed baseball team.

As if I was ready for a family.

I mean, someday, sure. I'd never thought of it in depth, but I'd hoped one day that I would have something in my life besides work. Whether that was a wife and kids or not...well, I wasn't set on that precise outcome, but it wasn't an unpleasant thought.

More and more, I liked the idea of a house filled with noise and life. Man couldn't survive on NPR and The Wall Street Journal alone.

Even if admitting that to Ryan would probably be tantamount to saying I was into sacrificing flamingoes or something in my backyard.

A fruitless search on my phone didn't give me the details on how to reheat this stuff for maximum palatability. Even if I'd been able to stumble through, I didn't want to have to reheat it twice if she'd fallen asleep or something upstairs.

Or if she was fashioning a rope of bedsheets to escape with minimum fuss.

I moved to the counter and started hacking at the plastic packaging of the next item on my list. If she wasn't going to come down on her own, then she could just stay up there. Or climb out the window. Or send out for help from her best bish.

I had these attractive paw-shaped lights to put down in the backyard for reasons I'd yet to fathom.

Fifteen minutes later, I'd finished placing the lights in a meandering fashion on a path in the backyard to the rarely used picnic table. Since I'd neglected to consider ahead of time that they were solar and therefore needed to charge, the paws looked like scattered little bubbles due to running off their weak battery backup.

Hey, I'd tried, and Ryan was still nowhere in sight.

So, I took my cold food outside and also brought along a couple of old Coleman lanterns I still had from my camping days. Within a few minutes, I was wishing I'd worn Citronella cologne thanks to the swarm of mosquitoes, but good enough.

Cold Moons Over My Hammy wasn't really that bad. Who knew?

I'd eaten my sandwich and moved on to hers—*you snooze, you lose* was an edict applicable to business and life—when a dark figure finally appeared in the doorway, backlit by the kitchen light.

"PMS?"

I didn't answer. That was not my name.

She tried again. "Yoohoo, PMS?"

I took an exceptionally big bite of her sandwich and chewed it with relish.

She eventually decided to cross the deck and head down the side steps to the backyard. A flash of skin beneath her dress alerted me she'd taken off her shoes. I wondered if she still had on her anklet. I'd forgotten to check when I was fucking her from behind on her painfully small bed.

"Are you even Irish?" she demanded upon seeing me eating at the picnic table.

"Not the question I was expecting." I patted the bench beside me, but she bypassed my chosen spot for her to sit across from me and frown at all of the styrofoam boxes.

"What is all of this?"

"I'm a quarter Irish. A quarter English. I believe almost half Scot, with a small amount of Norwegian and Scandinavian—what are you doing? Hey, that's mine."

She grabbed several containers, after having peered inside them with obvious disgust. "Cold Denny's is the absolute worst." She pried the hunk of sandwich out of my hand and dumped it in one of the containers. "And I believe that is mine, thank you very much."

"You took forever. I'm hungry." I licked my lips as she leaned over and the bodice of her dress dipped just enough for me to see the side of her unencumbered breast, cloaked in shadows. "Extremely so."

"You're eating my sandwich after clearly eating your own and—" She noticed the probably glazed expression on my face and set down the boxes with an altogether disturbing smile. "Oh, is *that* why?" She undid a few buttons while I tried to swallow over the sudden grit in my throat. "And here I'm so hot..."

I was five seconds away from undoing my shorts for necessary breathing room. "You certainly are."

Her smile grew as she stacked the boxes again and glided across the lawn. I stared after her like a lustsick puppy.

Rather than waiting for her to come back, I followed. I walked through the path of her honey and floral scent and breathed in deeply, knowing I would never forget how she smelled mixed with the scent of lush greenery in high summer.

I swallowed again for a much different reason as bittersweet longing twisted inside me. Not the kind that came from anticipation, but loss. As if I already knew she was a fever dream, and I was on the verge of waking up.

But if that was the case, I was going to focus on where we were right now.

I opened the back door and couldn't help but grin at how she looked in my kitchen. Her curls hellbent on escaping their loose topknot, the gap in her dress revealing enough skin to make me grip the door, and her clear annoyance as she turned dials on the oven and pushed buttons on the microwave like a pro.

My grin faltered. Like she lived here.

Like she belonged. Not just for a night, but a lifetime.

Instead of that thought making fire ants crawl over my skin, I leaned against the door jamb and let myself pretend that we were a couple for real. Maybe we'd gotten home late after a long day at the office, and she was irritated at me because I burned dinner. If that was the case, I probably wouldn't be smiling and undressing her mentally.

But hey, it was my fantasy. I could do whatever I wanted.

"Why are you smiling?" She didn't look up, just kept moving about efficiently.

"Why did you ask me if I was Irish?"

"The Irish linen. The tiny shamrocks on the china." She gestured impatiently as she took down a pan from the ceiling holder above the island. "The Irish prayer banner thingy in the bathroom."

"It's a crocheted scroll made by my Grandma Doyle."

"It's pretty. I got a little nervous thinking it was a Catholic prayer until I looked closer. You know, since I follow a loose form of Wicca."

I snorted. "If you knew my grandmother, you'd realize how ridiculous that possibility is. She's a chain-smoking, rollerblading, kickass poker player who thinks the main reason churches form is for organized thievery."

"Oh, I think I'd like your grandmother."

"I think so too. My father hates her, and the feeling is mutual. Dex said it's like a rite of passage. If the in-laws like you, it's not meant to be." I scratched my stubble. I hadn't bothered to tidy up this evening, and my whiskers were already intense. "My mom loves you though."

I expected Ryan to screech about the association I'd made with in-laws, but it was her turn to snort. "Your father covers the hatred bases for both of them. He wishes he could scorch the place where I'm standing with the power of his mind." She shoved a pan of hash browns under the broiler and closed the oven door. "Speaking of him, what happened after he almost saw me naked?"

I shut my eyes and held up a hand. "Uncomfortable imagery."

"Seeing me naked?"

"Hardly. Him seeing you naked." I walked fully into the kitchen and let the door slap shut behind me. "Now where were we?"

She stuck the sandwiches in the microwave. Guess she'd found the extra sandwich I had gotten for us to share. "Did he ream you?"

"Your word choice leaves something to be desired."

"So, in short, yes." She hit a button and turned to look at the clock. "No wonder I'm starving."

"You took forever in here. Did you take a nap?"

"I already slept once this evening, remember? Do you think I have narcolepsy?"

"Did you go through my drawers?"

"You wish, buddy."

So, she wasn't going to tell me what she'd been up to. I shouldn't have been surprised.

"Actually, I would wish more to go through yours."

"You had your chance while I was asleep."

I couldn't stay away from her any longer. It was physically impossible. "I wouldn't violate your privacy like that."

"Oh, right, Mr. Morality." She tucked her tongue in her cheek. "What're you doing with me, hmm?"

I ignored her question as I steadily came closer, boxing her in on the other side of the island. "Also, if I looked, I'd have to keep stuff."

"Like my panties and bras? Or maybe my red string teddy?" She ran her fingertips up and down the partially open placket on her dress.

"All of them. You'd be forced to go to work bare beneath your clothes."

"And sleep naked?" She looked up at me, bracing her hands on the island behind her as I loomed over her. "I sleep in that teddy."

I knew she was bullshitting me. It was basically her number one skill. That witch T-shirt I'd seen today was more her idea of sleepwear, not candy-colored butt floss meant to torment men.

"Yes. You would have to join a nudist camp, and I would join just to become the camp leader so I could spend my time worshipping your gorgeous tits." The word made her sexy eyes flash as I slid my hand under her dress and grasped her breast.

She pressed up against me and reached up to feather her fingers through my hair. I wanted to turn my face into her hand. "Mr. Shaw, I'm scandalized by such filthy talk."

"Just wait until we get down to more filthy action." I gripped her hips and brought them flush against mine as I lowered my head to kiss her.

Her moan at my very obvious erection spilled into my mouth, and I boosted her up onto the island, ready to take her right here and now.

She broke away, breathing hard. "You have impressive stamina for an *esquire.*"

I laughed and pressed my face into the very alluring curve of her neck. "Only for you would that be an insult."

She undid a couple more buttons on her dress. Now it was open all the way to her navel. Next stop was her pussy, and by the gleam in her eyes, she knew I was all too ready to get another glimpse.

"I'm unique. Now what do you say if I finish undressing and—" The microwave dinged and she hopped down, neatly evading my greedy hands. "Oops, saved by the bell. I'm dying of hunger, aren't you, PMS?" She opened the microwave and pulled out the sandwiches. "Oh, that's right. You already ate...mine."

"And I'm going to eat it again. For hours. Until you beg me to stop, and you know what I'll do then?"

"Call 9-1-1 and request oxygen?" she asked innocently as she turned to slide the sandwiches into the pan under the broiler.

Once she closed the oven door, I reached for her wrist and spun her back into my arms, our bodies colliding in a way that felt entirely too right.

"Hey Alexa, play 'Jailhouse Rock' by Elvis."

Ryan grinned and reached up to loop her arms around my neck. "You dance?"

"Not exactly."

I spun her around a few times anyway, just for the enjoyment of drawing her back against me. Then I added some flourishes and dips, combining every dance move I knew into a terrible mishmash. But she was laughing, and I was laughing, and by the end of it, we were both breathless and flushed and more than a little sweaty.

The song ended too soon. I tugged her arms behind her back and held them there with one hand, using the other to tuck her hair behind her ear.

And then we weren't laughing anymore.

"The food," she said as our lips hovered a hairsbreadth apart.

"The food," I agreed, searching her eyes. Needing to see in their blue depths even a hint of the chaotic emotions rocketing through me.

She was right there with me. I was sure of it.

I rubbed my thumb over her silken cheek. "It doesn't happen anymore." I couldn't keep the disappointment out of my tone.

"What?" Then the side of her mouth lifted. "You mean the fire."

"Oh, the fire still happens." Lightly, I ground into the apex of her thighs.

There was no denying that the temperature between us was hot enough to leave only destruction in its wake. And I wanted more.

Wanted everything with her.

"The spark when we touch," she amended. "I couldn't really shield myself at first with you. I didn't expect anything like that."

I frowned. "You're shielding yourself now? Whatever that means?"

She flexed her wrists in my hold. "Sometimes. It's also kind of like static electricity. Your body gets used to the charge. But opening yourself up to it changes the intensity." She looked up at me under her thick dark lashes, as if she knew what I was going to ask.

Steeling herself for it.

"Will you open yourself up to me?"

"You don't know what you're asking."

"So, show me. Teach me."

Her breath caught. "You can't control something like that. Once you open the door, anything can happen. It's not something you can turn on and off."

"You don't have to hide yourself with me." I dropped my forehead to hers and let her feel the weight of my words against her trembling lips. "You can trust me, Ryan. I swear."

For a second, her eyes were too bright. Then she arched up on her tiptoes to capture my lower lip between her teeth. "You don't want me unshielded until I eat, PMS. Trust me on that."

"Okay. How much longer?"

"Not much."

"So, we'll dance."

I told Alexa to play more Elvis, and we danced next to the oven in my kitchen. The memories of her easy laughter as I whirled her around and around would probably fuel me for a lifetime.

Or so I told myself when that longing feeling swept over me again while we were eating by lantern light outside in the dark. The breeze kicked up, slightly lessening the oppressive humidity, and she told me about her mom while she fed me gooey bits of egg and cheese and ham with her fingers. I only nibbled her fingertips every other time or so.

"She always shows up in the summer. Usually, without warning. Blows in like a summer storm to tell me all about her fabulous new adventures. Her van is an Airstream now." She shook her head and nibbled on a crust. "She always asks why I stay by myself when the world is full of so many hot, wealthy men."

I didn't know what to say to that, especially when she looked down at her plate as if it was a crystal ball. What she was seeing there I was almost afraid to ask.

"Will you tell her about me?"

CHAPTER TWENTY-ONE

PRESTON

HER DEPTHLESS EYES flashed up to mine, somehow gleaming blue even in the low light. Or maybe that was my newly found fanciful side talking.

"Tell her what, PMS?"

I jerked a shoulder, feeling like a class-A jerk.

"You want me to tell my mom I'm fucking an esquire?"

"You just can't quit that, can you?" I scooped up ketchup-laden hash browns—and man, did she have a way with the broiler—and shoved the fork between her lips. "Here. Keep your mouth busy."

She laughed and chewed, swallowing it down with a mouthful of iced tea. I'd bought her a jug of the stuff, intending to keep some in my fridge for her.

Not that I hoped she'd keep coming over. That would be foolish.

Tomorrow was her last day of work.

Tomorrow already.

"She won't get it." She set down her glass. "How it is with us."

My heart started beating way too fast. I wanted her to say more, but this was Ryan. I should be grateful she'd even said that much. And with a mother like the one she was describing, how could I blame her? It wasn't as if she'd had a good example of healthy relationships.

Nor had I, but I hadn't known that fact until this week. Until a week ago, I'd believed for over thirty years that my parents were happy and in love and faithful. They'd never argued, not even over petty stuff like who was going to drive that day. Everything between them was seamless—and loveless, apparently.

Whereas Ryan and I fought over even the smallest things. I had no doubt that would continue to be true.

"What direction is your toilet paper?"

She tilted her head as if I was an unknown life form. "Did I run out at home? I didn't have to go before we left."

"No. I mean, the direction. Do you tear off from the top or bottom?"

"I don't look, dude. I just use it how it hangs." She didn't add *weirdo,* but she might as well have.

I leaned across the table to cup her cheeks. "Thank God for you."

"Goddess," she corrected, turning her head to nip my fingers.

We finished the rest of the food, and Ryan went in to the bathroom while I checked on the cat. He was sleeping on the pillows in the guest room bedroom, stretched out like a king. I didn't have the heart to move him.

Any future guests would just have to deal with cat hair on the sheets.

I found Ryan walking barefoot over the dim paw lights outside, stepping over them as if she was playing hopscotch.

"They don't work properly yet."

"No kidding, Obvious One. The sun tomorrow will charge them. But they're so cute, right?"

I grunted noncommittally.

"They go with the solar lights over there." She gestured to the neatly manicured bushes and ornamental trees. "Your yard is so pretty."

"Thanks. True Green Home appreciates your praise. They're the ones who did all that stuff."

"Oh. I should've known Mister Grumpy Pants wouldn't have time to dig in the dirt."

266

"I wouldn't know what to do."

"You can learn."

"Or you could come over and commune with the dirt whatever you want." I came up behind her and gathered her long, loose waves in my hands. "I love when you take your hair down. I'm going to hide all your rubber bands."

"You are such a male, PMS. I don't use rubber bands."

I took her hand. "I want to show you something."

"I've already seen it. Very nice."

I squeezed her fingers, leading her into the deepest part of the yard. "Anyone ever tell you you're a smart ass?"

"Me? No way. Where are we—oh." She picked up the pace to reach the hidden gate in the back that led to the secondary yard behind the garage. "I didn't even see this here. You have so much space."

"For the baseball team," I reminded her, opening the gate and nudging her ahead of me.

We walked behind the garage and emerged on the other side where a small fountain bubbled merrily. Beside it was a pair of cushioned wicker chairs.

"This is such a beautiful spot. Secluded. Probably gets a lot of sun?" She looked up at the break in the canopy of trees overhead. The moon shined down like a spotlight. "Wow." Her voice was reverent.

I came up behind her and nudged her dress off her shoulder to kiss her fragrant skin. "You're not going to comment on the fountain?"

"I figure it's kind of a theme with you."

"I like the sound of water. I don't get out here nearly enough, but when I do, it relaxes me. Someday I'll put in a pond maybe."

"With koi fish?"

I wasn't exactly sure what those were, but if she liked them, I was onboard. "Sure. Why not?"

"You're so easy." She shot me a heavy-lidded look over her shoulder. "At least outside of work."

"Mmm. How do you feel about being naked outdoors?" I was already undoing the rest of the buttons on her dress.

"I'm okay with it. I've done a couple rituals skyclad on Beltane and Litha and Lammas."

"Skyclad?"

"Nude."

"With other people?"

"I'm more a solitary witch."

I kept undoing her buttons from behind, moving into a crouch as I reached the bottom. "What kind of rituals?"

"Spellwork and candle magic for the most part. Releasing intentions into the universe. Utilizing smoke and fire to—" She let out a low laugh. "Are you going to get me entirely naked while you stay dressed? That seems to be a habit with you."

I rose to pull the dress off her shoulders and searched for my voice as the moonlight cast her curves in pure white light. "You are magnificent."

"You're good for my ego." She hooked her hand around my neck as I cupped her breasts from behind. Her nipples pebbled in the breeze as I sucked on the soft skin next to her ear. "You're going to be naked too this time."

I released one breast to slide my hand down her belly to the small smattering of hair on her mound. She drew in a quick breath at the brush of my fingertips over her clit. Slow glides meant to tease at first, then I slipped a finger into her and her head dropped back against my shoulder. I could just hear her low moan over the burbling water while I played with her, using her body for my enjoyment as much as hers. Feeling the trust that she was giving me without question like a steady hum between us.

Her breathing sped up as one finger became two. My thumb flicked over her swollen clit while I rolled her nipple between my fingers and kissed the side of her neck.

She was so responsive, and she seemed even more so out here. Her honeyed scent mixed with the hint of flowers and fresh earth drifting on the warm breeze made me almost lightheaded. I needed more of her.

I pulled my hand up and slid it up between her breasts so I could taste my fingers before I offered them to her. She didn't hesitate, gripping my hand and shifting her head to meet my eyes in the darkness.

Her pupils were so deep and dark as she erotically licked my skin. Almost as if she was holding me with her gaze, she turned toward me and ran her hands down my chest to the belt of my shorts. Slowly, she pulled it open and drew the leather through the loops as she knelt before me, her hair tumbling over her back.

She never fumbled, reaching her hand inside my shorts and boxers to scoop me out where I was like stone against my stomach. Her tongue darted over the swollen head, and I grasped handfuls of her hair, the silken darkness flowing over my skin like water.

Like ink, branding me every bit as much as the tattoo I'd gotten for her. For me too, as a reminder to never forget the world beyond work. To always keep my eyes on the sky.

But most of all, the moon and the sun were the dichotomy of Ryan. That touch of wickedness inexorably enmeshed with sunshine.

She took me into her mouth, slicking her warm lips and tongue over my flesh in a deep, easy pass. Her gaze remained riveted on mine in an unbreakable connection as I started to breathe faster. I wasn't aware of her nudging me toward the chair but then she was pushing me down, rising up against my legs to suck on me so deeply that my hands turned into fists in her hair. Cool fingertips stroked my sac while she led me to my destruction, and she dragged the taut tips of her breasts over my lap with every pull.

One more torment in a night of them.

I wanted to haul her back. Every time I tried, she withstood my efforts. I was panting now, half bent over her, but she wouldn't stop, hollowing her cheeks with every suck. Her eyes glittered in the shadows, and her nails nicked my skin with an arousing warning.

"Do I need to tie you up?" She cocked a brow, inching back just enough to catch her breath. Her mouth was puffy from her ministrations, and her hair was wild from my hands.

I was so near to detonating that I couldn't answer. She took my silence as a yes, yanking my belt free and shoving my shorts and boxers off faster than I could process. Fluidly, she wrapped the belt not around my wrists but around the base of my cock, constricting it until the intensity was just this side of pain.

I'd never been harder in my life. Even the air against my dick made my balls throb.

"Christ, really?" In a second, I was going to wheeze.

"If you want me to free you…"

"No. You can make me your sex slave forever."

She had no clue how true that statement was. It was probably better for both of us that she didn't.

She flipped back her hair and licked her lips to dive down for round two. The belt helped prolong the pleasure, nudging me to the precipice and keeping me there while she alternated licking my rigid shaft with taking it deep into her throat. I couldn't keep my hands out of her hair and lifted my hips, crazed for her to take all of me.

She complied, again and again. Pushing me to the very limit.

Even her makeshift cock ring wasn't enough to stave off my impending orgasm. And the temptress knew it, reaching up to loosen the belt just enough that even that minor assistance in holding back was gone.

"Come," she whispered into the night.

I couldn't resist her. Not now, not ever.

I groaned as she sealed her lips around my shaft one last time, helpless to keep from spurting into her mouth while she caressed me with her moonlit-soaked gaze.

She gave me mere moments to gulp in air. Then she rose to brace her hands on the arms of my chair and slipped her tongue between my lips, transferring my intimate taste. I reached for her, knotting my hands in her hair as I dragged her onto my lap, not even fully aware if I was hard yet. It felt like I'd barely even come, and it had been the best climax of my damn life.

My want for her had no bottom. There was just more.

She settled over me, grinding her wet slit against my cock. No problem with getting hard again. Not with her. I pushed two fingers into her and she threw back her head, releasing a sound that almost befit the moonlight silvering her from her cascading hair to the tight tips of her breasts to her swollen pussy, spreading open around my fingers.

We didn't speak, just kissed like the world was ending and her body was mine to use as I saw fit. Just as she'd done with mine.

I rubbed her clit until she was crying out, only stopping to grip her jaw with damp fingers. "Watch me."

She watched, her gaze zeroed in on the sight of me thrusting into her body. Bare. Without anything between us but shadows and desperation.

The need spiraled higher and higher. I couldn't temper my strokes into her, and she rode me with her knees jabbing into my hips as she anchored herself on my shoulders. Hair flying back, breasts bouncing, my name on her lips.

Mine.

I bit her nipple, nearly manic to see her covered with my marks. I rubbed my scruff against her delicate skin, knowing from her keening moans she enjoyed the extra sensation. And I fucked her like I would never fuck her again.

This was forever, contained in the span of one moment in the dark.

She wrapped her hand around the back of my neck as she stared into me, linking with me in a way that transcended anything I'd ever known. For a second, the sweet agony was almost unbearable. A flash of heat streaked over my shoulder as she drew back her hand, and then she touched her own lips.

The instant she removed her touch, the burn cooled. But the ache remained.

She tightened around me and finally let go, drowning me in her pleasure. Breaking around me and going limp so that I could cradle her against me and fasten my mouth to her throat while I joined her.

Pouring into her felt like dying and being reborn. I'd been stripped down to my most elemental state.

We didn't move for the longest time. I stroked her hair when I could lift my arm, and she snuggled into me, boneless and replete. Her weight in my arms felt so right.

Perfect.

There was no teasing. No words at all. I'd never felt such... harmony. It was a strange description, but it fit. We were in total sync, from our heartbeats to our breathing.

I didn't want to lessen the moment with something inconsequential, and everything felt inconsequential after this.

We stayed so long in that same spot that the moon rose to its peak in the shifting clouds overhead before beginning its descent. The heat of the day cooled until the breeze turned cooler. And Ryan stayed watchful, her fingers curled against my chest as if she was in no more of a hurry to move on than I was.

I didn't know what time it was when I finally admitted defeat.

"I need to use the facilities."

She giggled against my chest, probably the best sound in the universe. "You can just say pee. You can squash your prim and proper side outside of work, you know. I mean, you can squash it there too, but I don't want to blow your mind."

"Too late there, Miss Moon."

"Gotta say I rather enjoyed it."

"Rather?" I tugged on her hair. "My dick probably has a belt imprint."

"I can kiss it better."

I had to laugh. "Give me a couple hours."

"You underestimate yourself." She gave a testing wiggle against my lap. "After earlier, I have no doubts you could get up to anything you put your mind to."

"That wasn't my mind."

She looked up under the fringe of her lashes. "No indeed."

I nearly broke our quiet spell with my necessary truth.

Hey, guess what? I quit today.

It would be so easy to tell her what I'd done. Especially out here where work seemed so far away and not at all related to the heart of us.

272

Then she shifted against me to stretch her arms far above her head, and I forgot all about things that didn't matter right now in favor of sucking on her pretty nipples.

A guy had to have priorities.

Eventually, we dressed again and shambled inside like drunks, leaning against each other every few feet when walking seemed too complicated. She stumbled over something on the path and I picked her up, savoring her laughter as I tried to summon enough coordination to get us both inside in one piece.

The cat eyed us as we made it into the master bedroom. He'd changed his location to the pillows we needed to sleep on, most likely so he could be a peeping Smoky while Ryan undressed for bed.

Not that she was exactly comfortable with the prospect.

"I can go home. I should go home." She stood in her bare feet, tugging on the dress she'd buttoned entirely incorrectly so that the slightest shift revealed a hint of nipple. I didn't mind, although I'd prefer the full naked picture.

I propped my head on my hand where I was stretched out on the mattress, already dressed in my silk sleep pants. "If you want to, I'll drive you home."

"Oh, no, you're already undressed. I can catch an Uber. Or call Luna. Or Luna can get an Uber and come get me."

I was tempted to ask why she needed best bish accompaniment on her ride home, but she probably intended to rate my skills in the sack —or in the wicker chair. I wasn't sure why that couldn't be done via text, but far be it from me to question such things.

But there was one thing I definitely needed to ask.

"Why are you afraid of my bed?"

CHAPTER TWENTY-TWO

PRESTON

"Wʜᴀᴛ?" Ryan gave a light laugh. "That's silly. I love beds." She smirked. "I love chairs outside even more. What about you?"

"Come here." I sat up and patted the bed beside me.

She sat reluctantly on the edge.

From his pillow perch, Smoky started to wash as if he had no interest in the proceedings, but I could tell he was a giant faker.

I cupped her cheek and lifted her face toward the light, gently stroking the corner of her lip with my thumb. The place she'd touched herself earlier after our connection had singed my shoulder.

"*Ow.* What are you doing?"

"It burned. You really did lower your shields with me."

She swallowed audibly and caressed my shoulder as I suppressed a wince. "Matching war wounds. It's not always like that," she said quickly. "Energy exchange rarely manifests physically."

"Rarely? You've had this happen before?"

Silently, she shook her head, her expression begging me not to ask more.

I didn't. As unreal as tonight had been, I felt hollowed out and raw and like I could sleep for a month. I couldn't remember when I'd been so exhausted.

Maybe the weight of all the changes were finally crashing down on me, sparked by a back-to-back orgasm chaser.

"Let's just sleep." I brushed a kiss over her forehead. "I want to hold you. Will you let me?"

Instead of answering, she drew away to shed her dress before reaching over to turn out the light. She crawled into my arms, settling there with a sigh I echoed.

Until I yawned and glimpsed glowing green eyes fixated on us in the dark.

I jumped and Ryan laughed, bumping my chin with her head. "You knew he was there."

"Yeah, but his stare is intense. He's a total creeper."

"Silly." She reached up to lift the cat down between us, a furry cockblock. Not that my cock could do anything at the moment.

I'd already perpetrated blood-defying feats tonight. There was no way I was getting it up again before I had a solid eight.

Make that ten, because we woke just before noon.

Ryan's arms and legs were wrapped around me, and her soft breast was against my mouth. And my dick had suddenly found the will to survive for another day.

Even if Smoky was stretched out on Ryan's hip and watching me balefully.

Try it, buddy. She's mine now.

I leaned up to check out the strangely silent clock on the bedside. I had three alarms. None of them had registered in my sex coma.

Since I'd technically quit yesterday, I couldn't really find it in myself to care—until I remembered Mrs. Donnelly's irate phone call and her rescheduled appointment for this morning.

Absently, I rubbed my shoulder and tried to tell my dick to simmer down. This wasn't the time. I had to get my ass into the shower and—

Shit, she really had branded me the night before. I craned my neck to look at the definite wound on my shoulder. So much for it fading overnight.

We had rocked each other's worlds in more ways than one.

"Can't go again," she mumbled into my shoulder. "Unless you do all the work this time. You get on top."

I grinned and separated the tangle of dense dark hair over her face. A sleepy blue eye peered out at me as I kissed her nose. "Can I now? How about doggy style and every other possible position I can come up with?"

"I'm game." She shook back her hair and rolled over, sending the unsuspecting cat flying with a thud. "Whoops! Oh, no. Baby, are you okay? Do you need help?"

I grabbed her hand and dragged it to my cock. "This baby of yours does."

She made a noise as she yanked her hand free. "Come here, Smoky. I'm sorry. I didn't realize." She flashed her stupendous ass as she crawled off the bed and onto the floor.

A moment later, she emerged victorious with the cat cradled in her arms. He was nestled against her chest where I had been just a short time ago.

I wasn't terribly bitter.

"Sorry, sweetheart. Daddy didn't tell me you were on top of me."

"Daddy was too consumed with getting on top of you himself."

"Daddy is a pervert," she told Smoky, who head bumped her in agreement. "And we don't have time to—oh my God, it's noon."

I propped my head on my hand and grinned. "Yeah. I've never played hooky from work before. It feels bad."

"Bad unpleasant?"

"No, like *I'm* being bad. It feels good."

She shook her head and set the cat on the bed, giving his rump a little push. "Head bonk some sense into him, Smoky."

The cat promptly rerouted to lean adoringly against her thigh as she climbed back on the bed. I couldn't fault his logic.

I also couldn't just not tell Ryan forever that I'd quit. But if she thought I was crazy for willingly being late, telling her I'd given my notice would be akin to shaving my head and joining her coven.

"Do you have a coven?"

"Solitary witch, remember? And where are you getting your terms? Some witch show on TV?"

"No." I tried manfully not to flush. "A supernatural glossary site. I ordered the paperback. It will be here in two weeks."

She rolled her eyes skyward. "You're a nerd."

"It's not my fault you haven't allowed me any hands-on research yet. I have so many questions I could ask Miss Cleo."

"Who?"

"That TV psychic from a million years ago."

"I'm not psychic and reading tarot cards isn't a game. It doesn't have to be deadly serious either, but a tool for harnessing your intuition should never be treated dismissively."

Great. Now I'd insulted her. The last thing I wanted to do.

"I didn't mean to do that. I promise. I just made a stupid joke pre-coffee."

"Would you use lack of coffee as an excuse for justifiable homicide?"

"Obviously not, as I didn't attack you when you hid mine." I gave her a quick, hard kiss, and she grimaced before she could school her features.

"Either my morning breath is exceptional today or you're hurting."

"I just need some balm from home. It'll be fine."

I reached out to touch the slightly puckered corner of her lip. "You touched yourself to take the burn from me."

"You didn't know what you were asking for. Actually, I wasn't sure either." Her laughter was unsteady. "New territory for me too."

"That was the most amazing night of my life. Actually, the whole damn day was stellar."

She smiled faintly. "So, you went out and bought a car that costs 100 grand to celebrate amazing sex?"

I didn't tell her I hadn't bought it yet. I was probably going to take it back and select a more cat carrier-friendly SUV. Something that felt more me. Or at least a bridge from old uptight Preston to the new edgier model.

There was no reason to go completely hogwild with this whole 'living my life exactly as I wished' thing. I'd already quit my job and gotten a new—albeit very small—tattoo and was having otherworldly sex with a witch.

Not like I'd gone in with half-measures thus far.

"It's time to get rid of the grandpa car. I want something more fun to drive when I get away from my damn desk. Which I intend to do a lot more often." I reached over to scratch between Smoky's ears. "How do you feel about hiking?"

"I don't."

Her swift denial made me laugh. "How come?"

"I prefer walking on nice trails that don't require me to bring a tank of oxygen rather than on ones that seem like training for the next Olympics."

"Pretty sure there's not an Olympic hiking event."

"You know, it's possible to meander too. Not everything has to be a race. You don't always have to be testing yourself."

She did have a point. Changing my mindset would not be a simple process.

"Okay, how do you feel about wandering by the lake?"

She grinned. "Very positively."

I leaned over the cat to kiss her, mindful of her sore lip. "Kayaking can be slow too," I said between gentle, playful kisses. Those were surprisingly enjoyable too.

She caught her tongue between her teeth. "I do like some fast things."

"Do you now?"

"My dad has a power boat. We used to spend a lot of time on the lake. My mom gets seasick, but she always tried to make do."

"Seems like she does that a lot."

I blew out a breath. "I never saw it. I don't know how I didn't. I just figured they were comfortable together. Instead, it seems like they both settled. Her more than him, since he's having all his cake and pie too."

"Do you know she doesn't?"

I did a doubletake. "You think my mom is cheating too?"

"Maybe. Maybe not. Do you think she knows about his affair?"

"I didn't," I said at length.

"But now you do?"

"My brother clued me in that he'd confronted our father sometime ago. Dad claims she knows. That they have a happy life."

Ryan shook her head, her lips twisting into a smile. "He surely does. Why not, when he gets the best of both worlds?"

"You think that's what that is? That being with one person is somehow less?"

"No. No," she repeated softly, her changeable eyes drifting over my face. "I think if it's the right person, there is nothing better than a bond of fidelity."

I covered her hand with mine. "I agree. Which is part of why I want to do something different. I'm tired of listening to people who claim they once loved each other rip each other apart. Even worse is when *things* matter more than human beings."

"Says the man with a six-figure crotch rocket." She scraped her nail over the center of my palm, letting me know she was teasing.

But she wasn't, not deep down. At the very least, she didn't trust people with money. From her comments, her mother had questionable taste at the very least, and she'd probably known some real doozies.

"I didn't have much else before. Making financial goals and pleasing my clients were my only benchmarks."

"Sounds stimulating."

"It wasn't. At all. Why I need a change. I don't want to turn into my father, rationalizing shitty behavior."

She remained silent and let me get the rest out.

"I definitely don't want to forget what it's like to help people. To me, that's the only good reason to be a lawyer. And helping Mary Donnelly sock it to her husband by taking him for everything he's worth plus the toy poodle isn't at all what I had in mind."

"You actually care about people," she said slowly, as if she could scarcely believe it.

I tugged at the tie on my sleep pants. "I know that's considered a liability in my line of work, but yeah, I do. So many people don't have a way to get excellent representation. I can do that for them. I don't need the fucking money."

Her smile unfurled warmth through my chest. "And you're the best."

I didn't preen. Much. "I'm very good. And it matters to me."

"No one is more thorough than you. I know that without a doubt." She curled her fingers around mine. "Your files are scarily in-depth. I'm pretty sure you know all about your clients down to their shoe sizes."

"A good lawyer finds out everything he or she can about a case. Surprises mean potential future obstacles. If I know what could trip us up later, I can put together a strategy."

"PMS is never without a plan."

My ears heated. "Fail to plan, plan to fail."

Smoky stood up and bumped my hand—the one cupping Ryan's. I thought he was looking for me to pet him until he showed me his rump and arched up to rub his head against Ryan's neck.

I laughed. "Possessive sod."

"Can you blame him?" She snuggled him against her chest.

"Considering where he's hanging out right now? Nope."

She shook her head. "Incorrigible."

I scrubbed my hands through my hair. "I have to get moving. *We* have to get moving. First, we need a shower."

"Do we now?" She lounged against my pillows in a patch of sunlight with the cat in her arms, completely at ease with her nudity. "Anything else you think I need, *sir?*"

A block wedged in my throat. I was the one who needed a hell of a lot.

More and more with each passing moment.

"Yes. You need me to wash your back."

Her dark eyebrow spiked. "So, you're planning on taking the rest of the day off entirely, hmm? Don't think you won't have to remit my paycheck if you keep me away from my desk through dubious means."

I pressed a kiss to her bare shoulder while Smoky shifted to try to displace me. He'd probably hiss at me soon. "Oh, I know exactly what I owe you. Starting with a full slate of orgasms the next time I get you anywhere near this bed."

"But there's that handy dandy conference table…"

"You deserve a raise." I grinned as I made myself roll out of bed.

If I stayed with her a moment longer, I was going to say the hell with work and anything else.

I hummed through my shower and through putting out Smoky's food and dealing with his litter box, though the indolent feline didn't deign to stop lazing around with Ryan long enough to come investigate.

When I returned to the bedroom still dripping in my towel, she was on the deck checking out my telescope and talking to Smoky while he pranced along the railing. Spotting me, she let out a screech and ran into the bedroom with the cat right behind her.

"No, let me pick."

I had no clue what she was referring to until she went to my walk-in closet, muttering to herself as she sorted through and discarded suits. After a minute, she chose a deep gray one with a thin pinstripe and a heather gray tie.

"Pinstriped? Where's the matching vest?"

"Is there one?"

I pressed a button and a panel slid open, revealing more accessories. Her mouth dropped a little before she reached in and plucked out a deep gray vest.

"I figured you'd go for black like you." I gestured to her dress.

"I'm not wearing my sex clothes to work. Talk about tawdry."

"Sex clothes? Do you have a whole wardrobe for boudoir activities?"

She ignored me, as she so often did. "You can drop me off at home, and I'll shower and change then head back."

"I'll wait for you."

"No, you'll go to work. You're impossibly late."

"And I'm the boss. Who's going to yell at me?"

Not technically true. It was my father's firm until he finally walked away, but I wasn't concerned with getting a demerit.

At least not from my dad. Mrs. Donnelly, however, was another story.

"Me." She stepped up to me and arched onto her tiptoes to kiss my freshly shaven jaw then nuzzle her lips along my neck. "You smell really fucking good. Like a badass captain of financial industry."

I laughed and took the clothes she was holding. "And you smell like sex."

"Literally. I haven't showered yet."

"I have a shower you can use, you know."

She waved a hand. "I need fresh clothes. Besides, this will get you to work faster. Here, let me do that," she added after I shrugged on my shirt and reached for my tie.

I'd been doing my own ties for a long time, but there was something about the way her nimble fingers tugged and arranged the silky fabric. I couldn't help kissing the little wrinkle in her forehead as she fussed with it.

Her phone buzzed and she darted back to check it, pursing her lips.

"Problem?"

"You can handle the rest." She bent to collect the cat and left the room before I could figure out what the heck had just happened. Maybe she had to speak to someone.

I finished dressing. Good luck on her ever telling me voluntarily.

We left a short while later. Smoky wasn't enthused about Ryan going. He didn't seem to care much about me.

Definitely a stunning turn of events.

I glanced back before I got into the car and he was basically Velcro'd to the window with a woebegone expression on his tiny furry face.

At least I understood his thought process. As for Ryan's? Dream on.

I got behind the wheel and neither of us spoke as I headed toward the heart of Kensington Square.

As I took an unexpected left, Ryan shot up in her seat. "This isn't the way to the office."

"Nope. You should call your emergency contact. I'm absconding with you."

She gripped her seatbelt as if she really believed me. "Whatever you have in mind, don't do it. Isn't this car enough crazy for one week?"

"You forgot the tattoo and getting naked with you."

"That tattoo is the size of a ladybug."

I flicked a glance at my still bandaged wrist. It was a miracle I'd remembered to put on the cream the tattoo guy had given me this morning. "At least a cockroach."

"Where are you taking me? I know Jiu-Jitsu."

"You do? Really?" I slanted her a look. "That's incredibly hot."

"I'm not telling. If you're a predator, I need to keep you on your toes."

"No worries there. If I was tiptoeing any more, I'd be on a highwire."

I went down another couple of streets then turned at the corner and double-parked.

"You need sugar and caffeine. Girl caffeine," I amended. "They have your tea, right?"

"Plenty of males drink tea, PMS. Enlightened ones, so that leaves you out." She looked out the window toward The Honey Pot.

Oddly enough, she probably would've been more at ease if I'd kidnapped her and taken her to a cabin in the forest. Why, I had no clue.

"I'm going to tie you up and take you to my underground lair. Be very afraid."

She didn't blink. "I'm not going in there."

"Did you just hear me say I was going to abduct you and spirit you away for dastardly reasons you can't even begin to fathom?"

She yanked off her belt. "Right, because real criminals say dastardly. Come on already then. Let's get this over with."

Not exactly the enthusiasm I'd hoped for from her when greeted with the possibility of donuts, but I'd take it. Our last day working together should be special.

I swallowed hard. But this wasn't a real ending.

Of course it wasn't.

She glared at the vehicle as I met her on the sidewalk. "You can't leave that car there."

"We'll be in and out in a minute." I grabbed her hand and towed her into the shop with me.

The purple-haired woman behind the counter gave me a wide smile and chatted about the many selections in between slanting looks at the surly, silent Ryan. She answered her friend almost coolly, though it was clear the other woman was used to joking around with her.

When the woman—Dre—turned to box up my order, Ryan drew away from me and crossed the shop to look at her phone. She was texting frantically, her thumbs blurring.

Tension throbbed in my shoulders. She was probably telling Luna I'd forced her to get donuts against her will.

We didn't spend long in the shop. The scent of the donuts filled my head, but the prospect of them wasn't nearly as enticing when Ryan was acting so strangely. She couldn't be *that* annoyed that I'd wanted her to come in with me.

Then again, she was stubborn as hell. And how well did I know her really?

Dre called after Ryan as I opened the door to usher her out. "You better call me. I need that reading asap."

Ryan didn't even wave, just marched over to where I'd double-parked the car and slipped inside without a word.

I circled around to my side and noticed she was back on her phone. Lovely. I was about to get in when I noticed a telltale slip on the windshield.

My incredible morning was devolving into utter bullshit.

She didn't even ask about the ticket when I got in and set the bakery box on the floor on her side. Whatever held her attention on her phone was far more important than dealing with me.

"I'm taking you home?"

"Yeah. Thanks." She never glanced up.

A couple moments later, I pulled into her lot. She thanked me absently once more before climbing out and hurrying around the side of the building.

I drummed my thumbs on the steering wheel. Okay, then.

At a loss, I turned on the phone I'd silenced last night and had no fewer than thirty-seven voicemails and texts waiting.

The last from my father.

DAD:

Where the hell are you? What are you doing?

CHAPTER TWENTY-THREE

THAT COULDN'T BE RIGHT.

I frowned as I scrolled through my Instagram. It couldn't be right. No way, no how.

My DMs were bulging. The red number in the corner of the app was in the triple digits. What the hell had happened?

I scrolled and saw the expired story in every single one of the replies.

More?

What's this? What are their names? I need more!

So cute!

Is that a fox? *insert pterodactyl screech* I NEED MORE!

A screenshot of my work was reshared by Penn Masterson, the famous graphic artist. *The* Penn Masterson who could write his ticket at DC Entertainment or Dark Horse. I wasn't a huge comic girl, but I followed his stuff. It was epic shit and his was one of the first indie comics to really blow up.

And he'd shared my Roz and Sylvia to his seventeen million followers.

My heart raced and my stomach pitched. I bent at the waist near the side of my building as the gravel went sparkly. Panic and shock layered one on top of the other.

I'd only posted the story with the sketch so the universe would show me that it was nothing.

And okay, maybe a little tiny part of me thought it would get a few nice replies from people who followed my tarot posts. Tarot Tramps, my podcast with Luna, also had a decent following. But not like this.

My phone kept buzzing in my hand as more notifications rolled in.

I gulped in huge lungfuls of oxygen, trying to calm the panic threatening to drop me on my ass.

You can do this.

You will not pass out right outside your apartment building like a chick with the vapors.

I forced slow breaths in through my nose and out through my mouth until the world stopped tilting.

Finally, my chest eased enough for me to stand up straight—and then I noticed a silver Airstream parked on the side of my building.

I glanced up at the sky. "Are you kidding me?"

Maybe it was another Airstream. Retro was trendy these days, right?

The tail end of the rust-pocked vehicle was partially obscured by trees, but an airbrushed rainbow-colored peace sign with the initials RM drawn in bubble letters was like a neon arrow.

Of all the days for my mother to come into town.

Would she notice me sneaking inside? Maybe I could pretend I wasn't home.

I crept up the stairs, only to find the door unlocked and my hide-a-key missing. I sighed as I slipped inside. My shower was running, and my mother's off-key singing floated out into my apartment.

A massive sack of laundry sat in the middle of my kitchen, half of the contents spilling out in front of my oven. A plethora of tie-dye shirts and yoga pants could not be contained.

Rainbow Moon had arrived.

She'd had me when she was barely eighteen. Her music of choice was the hair metal channel with a side of nineties grunge to make her a little more well-rounded. She also loved traveling around to music festivals.

My mother, the perpetual groupie. At least when she was between boyfriends.

I was actually shocked she hadn't leaned into the rockstar thing, but she always said opposites attracted her the most.

Maybe I was more like her than I thought.

I touched the burn on my lip. I'd literally been burned for thinking PMS and I were a good idea. Was that the universe having another laugh at my expense?

Or was it a warning?

I collapsed into my chair at my kitchen table. The residual energy from having PMS in my space made everything feel... different. The room divider that closed off my bedroom area was see-through enough that I could just glimpse the twisted sheets of my bed.

My whole body was still humming from yesterday. I had a healthy relationship with sex. I liked it, embraced it even. I'd had a few lovers over the years, and while it was rare for me to let them in my personal space, it wasn't completely out of the ordinary.

Preston Shaw was not ordinary.

He was pushy and overwhelming and rigid, but at the same time, he was the most giving lover I'd ever been with. He didn't make sense.

We didn't make sense.

It was better if I just cut things off now before either of us got too invested.

And if I'd wanted to believe otherwise, even for a second, here came Rainbow Moon to remind me that opening up meant I'd better prepare for a crash landing.

I was just about to call the office to tell him I wouldn't be in when my mother came out of the bathroom.

She jumped, slapping her hand over her chest. "Ryan Genevieve Moon, you scared me half to death."

I winced at the middle name usage. "A little breaking and entering to start your visit, Rainbow?"

She waved me off. "That hiding spot for your key is ridiculous. Anyone could find it."

I rolled my eyes and made a mental note to find a better hiding place. I thought I'd been pretty clever by using one of the carvings in the door frame. Guess not.

She bustled into the kitchen, dripping water on the floor. She was short where I was fairly tall, light to my dark in all ways from hair to skin. Biology had not given us much in common. Personality wise we were legions apart as well. In fact, when I *had* managed to go to school, the teachers hadn't believed she was my mother.

Me either, to be truthful.

"Do you have a washer?"

"A small stackable unit in my closet."

"Perfect." She toed over her bag to me. "Be a love."

I pressed my lips together against a pithy reply about her taking it down to the laundromat. It was just easier to do a load for her.

Shoving the clothes back into the bag, I hefted it and headed over to my bedroom area. "How long are you in town?"

"Actually, I was heading to the Adirondacks and wondered if you might want to come with me. It's been a long time since we've hung out."

"Need money again?" I called.

"No—well, okay, maybe a little."

Of course she did. The only time she came to see me was when her bank account was low. Not that she ever had much to add to it. I had just made her get one, so I didn't have to worry about her being stranded somewhere.

And I added to the balance monthly because I was an idiot.

She followed me and tugged a black dress out of my closet. "Oh, Ryan. Don't you have anything with color?"

"My style is all black. You know this."

She dropped her towel. "I don't look good in black."

I focused on stuffing her clothes in my washer and not on the fact that my mother just flashed all of her wares at me. "Well, it is my closet."

She sighed and fussed with the sleeves then tugged at the front of the dress that hung low on her. "How is it that I got less boobs than you? I made you."

"Boobs are a pain in the ass."

"You only say that because you have them."

Nudging her aside, I reached for the top shelf of my closet where I kept some of the things she'd left behind the last time she blew in. I handed her the hot pink tank dress and one of her flowy button down shirts. "Here."

She flipped my dress off and left it on the floor. "That's where this went." She shimmied into the dress and tied the shirt around her hips. "Much better."

I sighed and bent to pick up my tone-on-tone sunflower dress. "I just put five-hundred dollars in your account last month."

"I know, sweetie. I appreciate that. I bought some primo undyed wool. Wait until you see the hanks I made up with madder root. They're this rich raspberry color." She made a chef's kiss noise. "I figured out some new colors with a cotton I got from some mill ends for real cheap." She rushed over to her hemp bag. "I used some of it to knit a summer coverup."

She came back and held it up in front of me. "Look at that juicy red color. It would look amazing with your hair." She curled the netting around my hair and tilted her head. "Oh, I could make hair wraps."

Off and running with something feeding that crazy brain of hers, she muttered to herself about stitches. Naturally, she left the summer weight wool around my neck. It was still too hot, especially since I'd been loading the washer with her frigging clothes. I set the machine to wash.

"Did you use a natural soap?"

"Yes." *Lies.* Kind of. I'd used my usual detergents from a subscription service I'd been buying from for ages.

"Whew."

As I tugged off the half-knitted garment, the long circular needles tangled in my hair. "Ow." I shook my head as I followed her back into the kitchen.

I dropped the coverup on the table where she was scribbling madly in a notebook with one of my Blackwing pencils. I didn't even bother taking the pricey sketch pencil back when she shoved it in her bag.

She smiled up at me. "I can't wait to work on this idea. It's perfect for the end of summer." She picked up her knitting, noticing my sketchbook. "Oh, are you drawing again?"

I reached for the notebook, but she was too quick.

"Oh. Oh…" She held it against her chest. "It's so good." She went back to flipping pages. Then giggled, turning back a few. "Is she a fox or a cat?"

I took the notebook from her. "Fox."

She frowned, but then her face cleared. The one nice thing about my mother was that you couldn't out-rude her. She was fairly oblivious. "Well, I'm glad to see you doodling again. It always made you so happy when you were a kid."

My eyebrow winged up. "You noticed me drawing?"

"Of course. I kept track of all your hobbies."

Not my homework though. She couldn't have cared less about that.

"What do you need the money for, Rainbow?"

"I wish you wouldn't call me that." She huffed out a breath. "I want to spend some time with you. But I also have a booth at the Bear Mountain craft fair. Can't you get away?"

"I have a life here."

"I know, but it's just four days. We can make it a girl trip and camp out like the old days. Make some s'mores. You can help me eat some of the peach jam I made. It didn't sell like I thought it would."

"I..."

"Is there something keeping you here?"

Was there?

My phone display glowed bright, PMS's name flashing with a text.

> PMS:
>
> Where are you? Do you need help in the shower?

I grabbed my phone and held it on my lap under the table. "No. There's nothing keeping me here. I mean, I have work but I—"

"Then that's settled. We'll pack up and have a road trip!" She came around the table and gave me a hug. "I can't wait. It's going to be so fun."

I patted her arm, then glanced down at my phone under the table. "Yeah. Fun."

"Okay." She clapped excitedly. "I'll get some gas." She twisted the fabric of her skirt. "You know, if I could borrow some money first? I promise I'll pay you back as soon as I sell some of my yarn."

I reached for my purse and handed over my credit card—the one with the lowest limit. I wasn't stupid. "Pick up whatever else you need, and I'll finish up with work stuff here."

"And my laundry?"

"Yes, and your laundry."

"You're the best." She rushed forward and kissed me again. "I'll be back."

As with most things involved with Hurricane Rainbow, there was a flutter of insanity in her wake. I pulled my laptop in front of me and cracked my knuckles.

To whom it may concern:

I quit.

Officially.

Not that there's much left to the day, but something came up

with my mother and I have to leave town for a little while. She's not sick or anything, she just needs my help.

And to be honest, I think this is probably for the best.

We've been really hot and heavy for the last few days and we need—okay, *I* need—a minute to think. I can't do that around you.

I finished up the bulk of the records room project anyway. April can work on the last of it, I'm sure. She's super smart.

I really did like working with you. Never doubt that.

RYAN

I edited it and rewrote the end part about three times. I couldn't even figure out a way to sign off the note. Everything was so mixed up in my head.

I pressed send and then checked my messages on Instagram. I found a direct message from Penn Masterson buried in the non-follower section.

Ms. Moon,

I really was impressed with your drawings. I've been looking into signing some indie comics under my imprint. I'd really like to talk to you.

I know DMs are totally unprofessional and can sound scammy, but here is my phone number and my personal email. We can talk on Zoom or FaceTime so you know I'm not just talking out of my ass. Hope to hear from you.

PENN MASTERSON

My hands shook and I read it three times before I put my phone face down on my table.

No friggin' way.

I pushed away from my chaotic table full of Rainbow shrapnel and my own scattered things from the day before to pace around the room.

"Alexa, call Luna."

"Calling Luna."

"Hello?" I heard a voice, but it sounded far away and out of breath.

I turned around and stared at my Alexa speaker. "Lu?"

"Yeah. Just a second." I heard a muffled curse and then Luna's voice came closer to the unit. "Hey. What's up?"

"Did I interrupt something?"

"What? No. Nothing. I was just dancing."

"Oh. Sorry. I'd call back, but it's kind of important."

"Yeah. Totally no problem." Something was muffled, and then I heard a door close. "Okay, you have my undivided attention."

"Was someone there? Oh, man, were you..."

"Nope. All good. Nothing to see here. Was just my neighbor."

"I thought you were dancing." I curled into the drafting chair right beside my speaker.

"I was. Anyway, it's not important. You sound stressed, girl. What's up?"

I frowned, but my brain was still buzzing from...everything. "Hurricane Rainbow showed up."

"Oh, shit. Are you okay?" I heard the fridge open and her pour something. "How much did she want this time?"

I put my head down on my drafting table. "Oh, if it was only just money. So much other stuff is going on."

"Do you want me to come over?"

"No. I'm heading out with Rainbow."

"Wait, what?" A glug came through the speaker. "What do you mean you're leaving?"

"She wants to do this road trip thing, and I kinda need to get out of here."

"What the heck is going on? I knew something was up, but I figured you'd come talk to me when you were ready."

"Yeah, well, I'm not ready. For any of it."

"You're not making sense."

"I know." I blew out a breath. "I did something."

Luna was silent. "Like bank robbery? Murder?" She lowered her voice. "Do I need to bring my shovel? Go buy supplies in cash three counties over?"

I laughed and sat up. "No, there's no body."

Yet. I reserved the right to revisit that idea after I spent half a week with my mother.

Quickly, I recapped that I'd shared my comic and it had sort of gone haywire. Luna knew I'd been working on the comic for a while, and she was the only person who had ever seen it. And even then, she'd only seen a sketch of my little fox character.

I'd been guarding the comic for over a year. I didn't know how to let go of it.

How to let anyone see what was inside me.

Roz and Sylvia had been mine for so long it felt like laying myself bare even saying their names.

"So that dude you made me read—Penn Masterson—he contacted you? The famous dude?"

"Yes." My voice was a squeak.

"This is amazing!"

"No, it's really not. I'm not ready. I can't do this."

"Of course you can. You're a kickass goddess who can do freaking anything. Let me come over, and we'll talk about this. We can throw some cards and drink lots of wine. I'll be a buffer between you and Rainbow."

"Thanks. I think I just need to get out of here. Go think about it. Maybe go through my drawings and fix them up."

"Okay, I get that. But is there something else going on? What did PMS do? I'll kill him."

I huffed out a laugh. My bestie would slay any dragon for me, that was for sure. "He didn't do anything. I mean, we did a lot of stuff, but none of it was bad. Exactly."

I touched the burn on the side of my lip, and then I got up and went to my little shelf of balms and oils Luna had made for me. I swiped it over my lip as if I could erase everything that happened last night.

Sure.

My laptop dinged once, then twice. I crossed back to my kitchen and closed it without reading the email I knew was waiting for me—or would be soon, if it wasn't already. I didn't know how to answer Preston right now.

"Ry? My spidey sense is vibrating like my rabbit, girl. What's going on?"

"I need to figure some stuff out. Then I promise I'll talk about it."

"Seriously, do I need to get my shovel?"

"No. But I think we both need to have a little discussion."

Luna didn't answer, which of course was all I needed to know.

"Looks like we both have some tea to spill," Luna said finally.

"With all of the wine. I don't think tea will cover it."

"Are you sure you can do this trip with Hurricane Rainbow alone?"

"No." I laughed. "But I think I need to. I need to ground myself. I'm a freaking mess about everything."

"I hate this. You should let me come over."

"Rainbow is gassing up the Rainbow Mobile and we're heading out." It probably wouldn't be that quick, but if I saw Luna right now, I'd just turn into a blubbering mess.

"Make sure you at least text me while you're on the road, so I can make sure you're all right."

"Yeah. I will." My eyes were stinging, but I didn't cry.

There was nothing really to cry about. I just had to get a handle on the chaos inside me.

All of it.

"Take care of you," Luna said, her voice wavering.

"Take care of you," I replied.

I set my hand on top of the laptop, pushing PMS out of my head. I needed a little space from him. From him and I together especially. It felt like too much too soon. I'd known him for days. Not even weeks. Literally days and I was so damn twisted up about him.

This wasn't me. Not at all. I wasn't the girl to swing full on into...

Nope.

No.

Definitely not the L-word.

No way.

That was my mother. Not me. Never me.

I picked up my laptop and plugged it in to charge. I had things to do before my mother got back.

CHAPTER TWENTY-FOUR

RAINBOW'S VERSION of car tunes included a tape deck from 1987, and I was pretty sure most of the tapes were from about the same timeframe. Didn't CDs trump cassette tapes by then?

Not in the Rainbow Mobile evidently. I now had listened to a random mix of Bon Jovi, Whitesnake, and a detour into the 70s with some Led Zeppelin and Fleetwood Mac.

It had been a long damn trip out of the city.

Drawing on the Airstream was...interesting. I'd given up about two hours into the first leg of our trip. No amount of noise-cancelling headphones could combat Rainbow's singing. At least this was one of my favorite songs from Zep.

I set my notebook on the shelf behind the large couch that made up the back half of the space. Rainbow had ripped out most of the interior and turned it more into a little house on wheels. It was surprisingly comfortable compared to the vans I'd traveled in with her during my childhood.

At least this part of my mother had evolved.

Things were still mismatched in her flea market style. Macrame wall hangings warmed up the cold steel surfaces. She'd covered the walls in tapestries and reclaimed wood from various beaches she'd been to over the years. I kept track of her whereabouts through her social media.

She'd cashed in on the van-life aesthetic that had populated TikTok and Instagram. It kept her mostly on the road and in gas money. She could ship out her crafts and yarn from nearly any town in her travels.

But the fiber arts community converged on Bear Mountain every year just before the influx of autumnal traffic. This part of New York was beyond gorgeous, and the hiking trails were made for late summer and fall.

The Rainbow Mobile shook and the bungee cords my mother had strapped across her bookcase held back the rattling books and trinkets from falling over. I held onto the sides of the Airstream as I made my way up to the front.

I dropped into the seat next to her, and the yowling cat sing-a-long came to an end.

"Hey, baby. I thought you were working."

"I'll work when we stop. A little too bumpy."

"Yeah, there was a few summer storms. Some of the roads are covered in debris from flooding." She tucked her foot up against her butt, resting her knee against the door as she navigated the turning lane to get across the bridge.

"You know if you ever got in an accident, you'd be paralyzed, right?"

She rolled her eyes. "Relax." She bounced in her seat that definitely hadn't been original to the Airstream. It was like a freaking 70s recliner and a trucker seat had a baby. "You're way too tense, sweetheart. Look at all of this. Trees and tiny little houses jammed into the mountain as far as the eye can see."

"Those tiny houses are probably a million dollars minimum."

She shrugged. "The suits come up from the city to experience all this. Most of them don't appreciate it. Those kinds of places should be for people who would love the view."

"Not all of them ignore the view."

"I've been with tons of these suits. It's just status to have a waterfront house. They don't enjoy them."

"But you did."

"Damn right. They may have been stopgaps instead of the love of my life kinda guys and that's okay. Each of them gave me a little something."

Usually money.

Or tears.

Sometimes both, but mostly tears.

I glanced out my window as we approached the bridge. The mountains loomed with the late summer green dotted with the first hints of fall. The Hudson River widened under us snaking its way into the valley. "You always got your heart broken."

"It's better to offer your heart than to keep it locked away, baby."

I folded my arms over my middle and turned toward her. "Didn't work out for you so well."

"I'm happy with my lot in life. I have my freedom and I've had amazing men in my life. A few women too."

My eyebrows rose. "Is that right?"

She shrugged and gave me a wide smile. "Women know what women like. And then sometimes all you need is yourself."

I huffed out a laugh. "That's true."

"Besides, you know all about that." She wiggled her eyebrows.

I covered my face. "We will never speak of that again, thanks." Having my mother find my glass dildo was about as horrific as it could get.

Another thing I could thank PMS for. He'd tossed my moon-topped sex toy on the sofa, where Rainbow had found it spearing up between the cushions like a glass simulated penis.

Which had led to a fun convo about chasing your pleasure wherever and however you could, and did I need the link to her favorite lube, the one that offered both pleasant warming sensations and lots of rainbows and tingles?

I'd declined. Sparks literally shot off already from my connection with PMS. Any more tingles and a beloved body part might end up maimed.

"But I get the impression you have a man in your life."

I looked back out the window. "It's complicated."

"Is it? Is he married?"

"What? No. Definitely not. I don't go there at all."

"I didn't either. I usually found out too late when it happened. But a wedding ring isn't necessary to make a man unavailable."

"Oh, that's definitely not our problem."

I hadn't meant to elaborate. And in reality, there really shouldn't be an us. We didn't fit together in any logical sense. It was just chemistry. It had to be.

Despite what he said, I suspected PMS was looking for the perfect woman to step in and fill his house with two-point-five kids and host dinner parties. He might not even realize how well he was built for exactly that.

That wasn't me. I wasn't even sure I wanted children. I hadn't ever really considered it. But PMS had *future* stamped on his very patrician forehead. Didn't he understand we were probably just a phase?

Even if it was getting harder to convince myself of that.

Having a witch for a girlfriend was novel at first. Sex was all well and good—and mercy, we were really good at that part—but it didn't make for a lasting relationship. And if I did let him all the way in, I wasn't sure I could actually let him go.

It was better not to get used to him.

"Ahh, so it's just sex?"

"Yes—no. I don't know. We're intense, and the only reason he's into me is because we were thrown together for a week. He's April's boss. I filled in for her this week when she went on vacation."

"Why do you sell yourself short?" My mother curled her fingers tighter on the wheel. "He sees how beautiful and capable you are. Bonus points that you have a good sexual side."

"Yes, but it's too fast."

"Sometimes it happens fast."

"Yeah, and then it burns out."

"It might."

I jerked my gaze toward her.

She flipped her honey-colored hair over her shoulder. A few thin braids with wooden beads clacked together as she huffed out a sigh. "It might just be a fling. Is there a reason to cut things off? Is he moving out of state?"

"No."

"Is he dying?"

"What? No." Just the thought of him not being on this earth made my chest ache.

"Then what's the issue? Take it slow if you want. That's how relationships work, kiddo. It's not an instantaneous thing."

"Yeah. Maybe."

I pulled my phone out and found an email notification waiting for me. Part of me wanted to open it, but the rest of me swiped ignore and went to my social media apps. More shares of my little comic. A surprising number of people wanted me to post more.

I knew how things went in the land of the internet. People had short attention spans. So, why hadn't they moved on yet?

I clicked the phone's display off and tossed it on the dash. "Wake me when we get there."

"Okay, sweetie."

I wasn't sure how long I hid in the oblivion of sleep. I woke to the loud slap of metal against metal. The hard whack of metal being pounded into the ground was one I was well-acquainted with. I grabbed my phone and shoved it in my back pocket before I hopped out to help her make camp.

She already had the overhang set up—which pretty much was just four posts and a piece of canvas strung between them. I was almost sure it was the same one we'd always used for cover during the rainy seasons.

I'd been the one to waterproof it with three layers of poly because I'd been tired of either getting wet outside or living in a steam bath inside our various vehicles during the summer months.

From vans to RVs, we'd had just about all of them in my life. We'd even lived out of a car for a while when I was really young. I only remembered because it was a hideous green that looked like pea soup. It even had the ham chunks, only they were rust spots.

"What do you need help with?"

"I got it. Why don't you take a walk? There's a stream over that way. Stretch those long legs of yours."

"Are you sure?"

She nodded as she hauled a Coleman cooler out of the back storage panel. "By the time you get back, I'll have burgers ready."

"Real burgers or are you a vegetarian again?"

"I'm back to eating meat. I was always hungry."

I grinned. "Sounds like a plan."

"Wait." She held up a finger and disappeared into the Airstream. She came back out with my crossbody bag, which held all my on-the-go art supplies and my notebook. "Take these. Maybe you'll be inspired."

"Yeah, maybe."

"Come on. You used to love to sketch on the rocks all the time. I'd find you sunning on any available boulder with any scrap of paper you could find."

I took the bag from my mother and gave her an impulsive hug. "I could use a little of that."

She quickly gripped my shoulders and held on tighter. "I really missed you, baby."

My eyes stung, but I pulled back. "Yeah. Me too." Today was just a little too much from every angle. "I'll be back in a while."

"Just come back before dark." I couldn't count how many times she'd said the same thing when I went off to explore as a kid.

I wasn't exactly dressed for exploring, but I'd been smart enough to drag out my hiking boots before Rainbow had gotten back to my apartment with supplies.

I followed the signs for the creek as the sun streamed through the trees. I heard the rush of water before I saw it. The scent of it lured me into quickening my stride.

The incline had me skipping down the path, grabbing onto a few of the trees to slow my descent. Finally, the dirt path turned into large slabs of shale and smooth water-worn rocks. The stream was running fast thanks to the storms my mother had mentioned.

But there was enough of a path for me to climb up away from the water to get a good view of the endless trees and the mountains in the distance. Of all the places we'd lived, New York had always been my favorite.

Probably why I'd finally landed in the middle of the state. I'd never quite been a city girl, but I definitely wasn't made for rural life. Kensington Square was the best of both worlds. Close enough to a major city, but far enough away that I didn't have to worry about crime.

This was a helluva view though. I pulled out my phone and snapped a picture, then immediately opened my texts to send it to…

I stared at the contact name I'd instinctively gone for.

Not Luna.

PMS.

Luckily, I didn't have enough bars to send to anyone because I wasn't sure which one would win.

I took a few more photos because it was gorgeous and my phone was out anyway, and then I shoved it back in my pocket and found a flat rock to settle on.

Maybe Sylvia and Roz would enjoy some outdoor activity. Would Roz get Sylvia a cat pouch like Preston had for Smoky? Assuming he ever used it.

Hmm, could I bribe him through sensual means to wear the Pussy Papa pouch?

Not relevant now, Moon.

Moving on. Sylvia was a fox, but maybe she'd enjoy an adventure.

Maybe Smoky would too.

Ugh. Stop thinking about him. You have drawings you need to revise for Penn.

I flipped to a fresh page and began sketching out the usual windowsill that Sylvia sat at and surveyed her kingdom. Roz lived in an apartment building overlooking a street much like the bustling business district of Kensington Square. The fox often lusted after the baked goods of The Honey Pot. Of course if my comic ever did go out there in the world, I'd have to rename the bakery.

As I did quick little studies of Sylvia to get the poses down, I found myself sketching the gray cat again. The nebulous idea that kept knocking at my subconscious this last week suddenly had three legs.

I slammed my sketch book closed.

That wasn't in the plan. The comic was about Roz and Sylvia. I shoved my pencils into my bag and got up.

My rumbling stomach saved me from any more introspection. Instead, I headed back to the campsite, the scent of hamburgers pushing thoughts of Preston and Smoky to the back of my mind.

Music was playing. It was always playing when it came to my mother. She was singing along to CCR in her off-key way as she flipped corn, still in the skins, on the mini portable grill.

"Oh, there you are. Just in time. Go wash up, and we'll have some food and chat. You can help me with some of the skeins I need to make up for tomorrow."

I didn't really want to chat, but it was the price of food. Well, I'd paid for the food too, but that was neither here nor there when it came to Rainbow.

"Oh, grab your cards too," she called out. "I met this guy online. We're supposed to meet up tomorrow at the festival."

"Of course you are," I muttered to myself.

But at least doing a reading for my mother would help get a certain lawyer off the topic of conversation.

I stepped up into the Airstream. My mother had transformed the couch into a bed and set out my PJs for later like I was still eight years old. The sweetness of it got me—enough that I had to sit down for a second. I couldn't remember the last time anyone had done something for me. Even before I'd broken off from my mom, I'd had to learn how to be self-sufficient because she hadn't been around much when she was involved with one of her guys.

I pulled my phone out to put on the makeshift charger station she had on a small shelf. Just as I was about to plug it in, it rang in my hand. There were barely two bars, and I didn't recognize the number. But something told me to pick up.

At least the cell service at the camping area was better than by the water.

"Hello?"

"Is this Ryan Moon?"

"Yes..." He sounded familiar.

"I'm the vet over at Kitten Around. Grant Thorn?"

The more he spoke, the more his Irish accent flowed over the line. I could feel the tension in his voice.

"Right, from the park. With Poppy."

"Yes." He seemed relieved. "I know this is a bit forward, but I'm in a spot. I've called a few people, but no one seems to want to take on my case."

"Case?"

"You work for a lawyer, right? I think he was the one you came into the adoption clinic with."

"Right." I cleared my throat. "Yes, he was my boss."

"Was?" He sighed. "Oh."

"What seems to be the problem, Grant?"

"I don't even know if your former employer would take my case. I just..." He seemed to trail off to collect himself.

"It's okay. Just tell me what's up."

"It's my daughter."

"Poppy? Is something wrong?"

"Yes. No. I mean, she's fine, but I just got served from my in-laws. They want to take my baby from me. I can't let that happen."

"Preston will help."

I hadn't even been aware that would fly out of my mouth. But I knew he would without question.

Grant blew out a breath. "Do you think he'd take my case? Truly?"

"Yes. I don't know the specifics, but Preston is your man." Family law wasn't exactly his expertise, but I'd believed him when he told me he wanted to help people rather than specializing in divorce. He was a stand-up guy.

I rattled off Preston's direct line at work because, well, that was probably the best way to reach him since April wasn't exactly there to take his calls.

I couldn't help wincing. Nor was I.

"Call him and tell him about your problem." I made my tone as reassuring as possible. "He'll win your case, Grant."

"You don't even know the details."

"You love that little girl. That's all I need to know."

"Thanks." His voice was deeper and full of emotion.

"And I know Preston will do whatever is necessary for you to keep your child. I know him."

I did, I realized. Maybe it didn't make sense in terms of time, but that certainty was a steady glow inside my belly. I fisted my hand against it. There was so many things I wasn't sure of, but that he'd always try to do the right thing wasn't one of them.

"I'm sorry to impose and I shouldn't have dug around for your number, but I was desperate."

"We do what we have to when we're protecting our family." I glanced out the window to where my mother was hanging hanks of yarn on her makeshift racks. "Family is all we have in the end. And those who we care about the most."

"I don't know the specifics, Miss—"

"I think we can go with Ryan."

He laughed lightly. "Ryan, then. But I can tell you from personal experience that life is short. Don't waste it. When I lost my Anna, it tore me apart, but I'm a better man for loving her. Even if it was only for a few short years."

My throat tightened. His pain was palpable, but there was determination in there too. "I hope Preston can help."

I know he can.

"Thank you, Ryan. I hope you find what you're looking for."

How did he know? Was I that obvious? "Thanks. Kiss that little girl for me. And the ever-precocious Bosco."

"I will. Talk soon."

And then he was gone.

I plugged my phone in again and grabbed my deck. I shuffled and threw two cards to see what the cards had to say.

I laughed at the Three of Swords and Ten of Swords.

"Damn cards."

I turned the deck up to see what the shadow card was and found The World.

Endings and beginnings.

Then I looked at the three of swords piercing the heart. Was that my future or was I just afraid that it would be? The Ten of Swords spoke of endings as well. Of working through the pain, but with the hope of something new on the horizon.

Was PMS my new horizon or the pain I had to work through?

That was the bigger question.

"Ryan! What are you doing in there? Food is ready."

"Coming," I called.

I swiped up my cards and stuffed them in my hoodie pocket. Dealing with my mother's love troubles was definitely easier than trying to decipher my own.

CHAPTER TWENTY-FIVE

PRESTON

"You liked working with me?" In the silence of my office, my voice boomed out at a level not appropriate for the words I was about to utter.

And I. Did. Not. Care.

"You tied up my cock with my belt. That goes beyond chapter ten in the employee handbook. Goddammit."

I punctuated that statement with a kick against my desk. Then when that didn't have the desired effect, I swept my arm across the tabletop, sending papers, pens and even the phone flying.

Satisfying crunches and cracks filled my head, but it wasn't enough. I lifted my arm and was about to dispatch the computer as well when my door flew open and my brother sailed across the room, catching the computer like a firefighter swooping in to save a flailing baby.

"I was breaking that," I muttered before turning away to brace my hands against the floor-to-ceiling glass windows that fronted my prison.

But for a few days, it had felt like less of one.

And I'd felt like more.

I'd seen only possibilities. Options. Walking away from the firm was letting my father down, but I fully intended to find someone capable to take over for me. Maybe Bishop.

Maybe even Dex.

Now it seemed futile. I didn't want to be a divorce attorney any longer, but had I just quit my job only to have more time to consider what exactly I'd done?

More time to spend alone with my new cat, who much preferred she who would not be named.

My brother placed the computer back on my desk and quietly closed my office door. It was late afternoon, and I'd spent a chunk of it making phone calls so I could pace a tread in the carpet beside my desk. I'd been too keyed up, wondering where the hell Ryan was. What she was doing. If she was okay.

If *we* were okay, as lowering as that was to admit.

"I'm getting married to a stripper I met in Southampton. Will you be my best man?"

I gave him a dismissive glance over my shoulder. "Yes, as soon as I draw up your prenup."

"Is that how you view true love? I thought you were running off to embrace your inner love child or some such bullshit." He sat across from my desk, shaking his head of sun-bleached hair. All he needed was a large golden dog beside him and a surfboard to complete the look.

"Wanting to do something different has nothing to do with embracing my inner child. And get your feet off my desk, you heathen."

He didn't move a muscle. "Stop watching me in the glass and face me."

"Make me."

"You know, this whole exchange is fascinating. I'd given up hope of you engaging in baser emotions like rage and lust like the rest of us mere mortals. And here you are, in the grips of both."

I dragged my gaze away from the relentlessly sunny day to focus on Dex. He appeared positively delighted.

"I'm not enraged."

"Oh, just got a sudden yen to redecorate?" He kicked my gold pen across the floor, and it rolled over the mirrored tiles. "Gotta say, I never did like that blotter. It screams yuppy."

"Shut up." But I laughed as I picked up said blotter and stuck it standing up out of the trash. The stupid thing had cracked in half.

I dropped into my chair. "I think I got dumped."

"Your assistant quit early too." He widened his eyes with false surprise. "Oh, are those events related?"

I flipped him off.

"I got the general drift when I walked in on you screaming about her doing questionable things to a part of your body that should only be treated with love and respect. I should've guessed she was kinky." He shook his head. "You lucky bastard."

"I was." I rose to make coffee, even if it currently tasted like dirt.

I had to assume that was the direct result of heartbreak, since I knew the coffee was perfectly fine and had tasted superb yesterday when I was fresh off an orgasm high with the promise of more to come.

Now I faced an orgasm desert of indeterminate length, and even coconut-caramel coffee could not placate me.

"What did you do?"

"Hell if I know." I pointed at the K-cups I'd so lovingly arranged in the basket. "Want?"

"You know I don't drink your caramel shit. You don't know what you did?"

"Other than we were closer than we've ever been, nope." I banged the lid down on my Keurig.

He snorted. "Um, you barely know her. Closer than you've ever been in several days?"

"I don't expect you to understand."

"Do you?"

"No." I watched the coffee pour into my mug. "But I know it's real, because nothing else has ever felt like this."

"Dude, we've all had one of those. Or a couple of them if we're really lucky. The sex twists you all up into a pretzel and you're ready

313

to shave your head and take up residence in a hut somewhere if it means you can live on sweet, sweet love."

I arched a brow as I tossed the spent K-cup and returned to my desk with my coffee. "I'm curious about your sex life, brother."

"As you should be. I'm just saying, the haze clears. Those first few days or weeks, you're ready to do whatever it takes to live in blissful harmony forever. Then you wake up some morning and you realize you hate how she chews. And that's that."

"You're a strange one."

He jerked a shoulder and kicked aside the mess on the floor I wasn't inclined to clean up on his way over to the mini bar. He splashed some scotch into a short glass and leaned back against the bar, sipping slowly as he regarded me. "You're sure it's not just the 'any pussy is awesome after an endless drought' syndrome?"

I shook my head. "That is only a syndrome in your shriveled little brain."

"I can assure you it is not."

"And it had not been that long for me. A while, yes, but I dated now and then. I'm just particular."

"Must be a woman with cat's eyes and possess mystical leanings. Gotcha."

"In any case, this isn't about sex."

Dex gave me a thumbs up. "Sure, bro."

"It isn't," I insisted. "If need be, I could go without for a very long time. Not easily," I acknowledged as my brother laughed hard enough to splash scotch on his custom navy blue suit. "But I have before."

"Yeah, but you found your brand of catnip. Now you're in trouble. Much harder to resist when you've had a faceful of the good stuff."

"If you only knew." Before he could expound upon that subject, I forged ahead. "You told Dad what I said to you in confidence."

"You said a whole lot of nothing, as usual."

"Yet you told him I wanted to quit." I drank half my coffee in one throat-searing swallow. "Thanks. I appreciate it."

"Look, it's your own fault for—huh?"

"You broke the ice with him for me. I appreciate it."

Dex stared at me for a long moment, his expression puzzled. Then he set down his glass and walked over to flatten his hands on top of my desk. "I take it all back. You need to get this woman back. I have her number. I'll call her. I'm not above offering her a cash payment to put up with your annoying ass."

Only one part of that statement stood out to me. "Why do you have her number?"

He stepped back as if he was weighing his personal safety. "Company records?"

"You asked her for it."

"Maybe?"

I sighed. "She's allowed to give you her number. It's a free country."

"That it is, but when I asked for it, I didn't realize you'd had your first boner in half a decade in her direction. I haven't used it."

"Your free pass for insults is almost used up. Get your last few in before I kick you out of my office."

"Ah, yes, but it won't be yours for much longer. I'm glad you told Dad you were done with his crap."

"It depends how long it takes for me to wrap up my cases—and to convince Bishop he wants to throw his lot in with you." I pointed at him. "Use that cash payment you were going to give Ryan to wine and dine him. Unless you want to helm this ship all on your own."

He returned to the mini bar to retrieve his drink. "I'm okay with stepping up to shoulder more of the load, but I'm not prepared to carry it all on my shoulders. I enjoy divorce law for the sport it is. I also enjoy my very active personal life."

"Rub it in." I drank more coffee and debated getting another, liberally laced with scotch.

Or perhaps a scotch laced with coffee.

"She's into you, man. I saw it myself. You were all sparky."

I laughed. And kept right on laughing while my brother gazed at me questioningly and probably wondered if it was too soon to call for medical help.

A knock sounded at the door before our mom popped in her

coiffed head. "There is literally no sound I love more than my boys laughing together. I hope I'm not interrupting."

"Of course not." I rose and waved her over, kissing her cheek and accepting her hug.

Was I imagining things or was her embrace a little tighter than normal? Could've been mother's intuition or maybe she wasn't as happy with her arrangement with my father as he claimed.

Frowning at the assorted desk paraphernalia scattered on the floor, she went over to hug Dex as well. He held onto her as he gestured to me. "Your eldest son is in love. You should start planning the wedding."

I'd picked that unfortunate moment to take my last sip of coffee—and ended up spitting it out over the vest that Ryan had chosen for me that morning.

Our mother let out a tinkling laugh. "So, your pretty assistant sealed the deal already? Is she out selecting her bouquet? I was hoping to see her today. There's a tarot festival in Turnbull in a few weeks, and I was wondering if she'd like to attend with me. Maybe we could make it a threeway." She tapped her chin.

Dex shook his head. "Don't use that word with other people, Mom. It doesn't mean what you think it does."

"Like you know what I think, you big oaf." She reached up to twist his ear while he laughed.

I sank into my chair and rolled over to the garbage can to unbutton my jacket and squeeze out my tie. At least I hadn't made too much of a mess. "I thought I moved fast. You two have me married, for God's sake."

"Oh, you're moving fast? You admit it?"

"I'm not moving at all right now. She's gone."

"Gone?" our mother echoed, exchanging a glance with Dex. "How can you marry her if she's not present?"

"That is a quandary. Except we aren't getting married yet."

"Did you hear that yet? I heard a yet."

"Record it on your phone," our mother suggested. "That way, when he does his Frosty the Lawyer thing, we'll have proof he has warm feelings for her."

I rolled my eyes. Frosty the Lawyer was a nickname I hadn't heard in years. I hadn't missed it either.

"Try sizzling. You see all that?" Dex pointed at the scattered pens and papers on the floor. "He was having a mantrum when I came in here. He almost tossed his computer."

"Enjoying yourselves?" I asked mildly, settling my still damp tie back into place. I patted my vest and figured I might as well wear my coffee after the day I'd had.

"Hugely." My brother circled his arm around our mom's shoulders. "I almost hate to leave and break up the party, but I have a prior engagement."

"Blond, brunette or redhead?"

"Speaking of threeways…" He ducked when our mother gave him a stern look.

I had to laugh as I stood. "Can you meet Bishop and I at Lonegan's Sunday evening?"

"Sure. Time to wine and dine?"

"Or get stupidly drunk. We'll see how it goes."

"If you need a designated driver, I'll come get you," my mother said, making Dex pat her on the head as if she was a slightly dotty senior citizen. She was not amused.

"Of course. Or maybe you'll come and drink us under the table. Though last time we couldn't get you down off the bar."

She flushed and adjusted the big flower choker around her neck. "Oh, stop. I got down."

I pinched the bridge of my nose. Clearly, I needed to spend more time with my family—even if it would be an education I might not be ready for.

Now was as good a time as any to start.

"If you and Dad want to come…" I trailed off, feeling awkward as hell.

If they had an arrangement that worked for them, fine, but I didn't know if I could just play along. I'd have to keep trying, because my father was my dad regardless. Their choices were their own.

Even if they would never, ever be mine.

My mom's smile faltered. "No, that's for you boys. A lot to talk about, isn't there?"

I smoothed a hand down my vest. It wasn't too wet anymore. "Dad told you? Or your mouthy son?"

"Wasn't me this time." Dex mimed zipping his lips.

"I talked to your father."

"And you came to see if I'm on a ledge yet."

"Yes, to see if you're ready to put out your parachute and fly."

It made me smile. "No wonder you like Ryan."

"I love her. She has the most wonderful energy." She nudged Dex toward the door. "Go on now. Enjoy your threeway."

"If you insist, Mom." He kissed her cheek and opened the door, glancing over his shoulder at me one last time. "She'll be back. You know Shaw men are irresistible."

"Keep telling your hand that."

He closed the door behind him with a grin as I shut my eyes in horror that I'd said that in front of my mother.

Obviously, I was not fit for public consumption today. Or possibly any day until Ryan came back.

"Sorry," I muttered.

"I'm going to blow your mind, Preston. Not only have I had sex, I know what masturbation is."

"So, um, how's the plants?"

She laughed and bent to start picking up the items off the floor. "Just fine."

I rushed around the desk to help her. "You don't have to do that."

"I know I don't. But with two sets of hands, any task goes quicker —and is more fun too." From where she crouched on the floor, she pinned me with a direct look. "Seems like you've just discovered that too."

"Not just, but yeah."

"You really like her, don't you?"

I nodded, swallowing down the part where I spilled all my feelings like a jackass who'd never been in love before.

Because I hadn't. And I could tell myself it was just the jalapeños I had on the sub I'd gotten for lunch, but I knew better. I wouldn't be coming out of this so-called haze in a few weeks.

Or a few lifetimes.

"I think I'm like a penguin."

"Come again?"

I grabbed some of my fancy gold pens—all the same for visual continuity—off the floor and stuck them in my cup, also gold. "I saw this special once. Penguins mate for life. They may not find their specific bird for a while, but when they do, they don't see any other birds. It's like this one singular, specific one is the only one they want. And if their mate dies, they are destined to be forever alone. Staring off into the distance while saxophones play in the background."

My mom chuckled. "They have their own musical accompaniment. How lovely for them."

"I think it's in their contract. Anyway, I'm fairly certain I knew from the first time she insulted me via email. Which was right away."

"So, you have masochistic tendencies?"

"Obviously. I just got a cat." I took a few pens she'd gathered out of her hand. "Who also loves Ryan, by the way."

"Also? That's a very telling word."

I didn't bother to deny it. Instead, I dumped more pens in the cup and set it on the desk then started picking up the paperwork that had scattered all over.

My mom stopped me with a hand on my bandaged wrist. "What did you do?"

Rather than tell her, I peeled off the bandage and watched her eyes film over at the small tattoo.

"A moon?"

"Yeah." I tried to make my vocal cords work. "And a sun, because she's especially that for me. Ever since she's been gone, it feels like everything is cold and dark inside me. When she's here, it's easier for me to laugh. At myself especially. I just like having her around." I

319

shoved papers into a manila folder and flung it on the desk. "I don't know how it happened."

"It was time," she said gently.

"Maybe. I think it's just because it's her."

"Where did she go?"

As we picked up the rest of the stuff from the floor, I told her in mom-sanctioned terms. Nothing about outdoor sex or touches that singed or cock rings made from belts. Even if she knew about all that stuff and more, it was better for my psyche if I pretended she didn't.

"After spending such a wonderful night together, no wonder you felt blindsided. Good thing your brother saved your computer just in time."

"Yeah." I grabbed my mouse and found the mousepad under the chair before rising and putting them both on the desk. "I haven't had a temper tantrum since I was..."

"You've never had a temper tantrum, Preston. That would require an excessive display of an emotion, and we both know how you feel about those."

"It was stupid." I exhaled. "She's wary. I get that. She has reason to be."

"And you don't? You're a wealthy man." When I would've spoken, she held up a bejeweled hand with the typical stripe of dirt on the back. She almost always missed a spot. "I don't believe she's an untrustworthy sort. Just the opposite. But if you wanted reasons to turn away, you certainly have understandable ones."

"She doesn't want my money." I laughed dryly. "I thought about buying a sports car, and she acted as if she didn't know why would I do something like that. Turns out she was right."

I had an appointment for later to drop off the crotch rocket and test out a much more reasonable but still tricked out SUV. Only now I'd just have Smoky to discuss the purchase with.

He was probably even now making plans for a new speed dating event appointment, one where he could go home with Ryan.

Hell, Smoky was more likely to be informed of her current location then I was. Maybe he'd act as an intermediary.

I rubbed my aching temple. And I was officially losing it.

"She's a wise girl. I saw that right away."

"Yeah, and she was probably wise to take a minute to think. Neither of us have done that much."

"In that first burst of lust, no one does."

At my narrowed-eyed look, she shrugged and stood. "We've all been there."

I opened my top drawer and dumped the files in there I didn't want to deal with now. I'd handle them later. Then I eased a hip on the corner of the desk. "Is that how you got together with Dad?"

Immediately, her smile faded. "I told you we were going the same direction."

"That doesn't sound like lust to me. So, does that mean you know all about it with someone else?"

Not that I wanted to ask that question now or ever, but Ryan had put the idea in my head, and it had burrowed there like a thumbtack.

"I did date before your father, you know."

"And after?"

She sighed. "If I didn't know you were a superb attorney already, that tone would tell me. I've never been on the other side of it before."

"I didn't mean to put you on the spot."

"Yes, you did. I knew it was coming. Dad warned me about that too. Apparently, he protected my honor by not saying I was as culpable as he was." She brushed away an invisible piece of lint. "I just don't dine out at restaurants where my son can see."

I undid my tie and yanked it off.

"You're angry."

"No. Yes. More than anything, I don't understand."

"Be glad you don't." She stepped forward and reached up to grasp my shoulders. It took everything inside me not to jerk away. "I don't want that for you. Not that it hasn't worked out fine for me, but you're not—"

"A liar? A cheater?" I couldn't help the words, even if I regretted the look they put in her eyes so like my own. "I thought you were different than he was."

321

"He's your father." She so rarely used a harsh tone with me that it was almost a slap to hear it.

"And you're my mother. I put both of you on pedestals, so I guess it was time for that to end too."

Something like grief crossed over her face. "What is right for us doesn't have to be right for you."

"You're correct there. It isn't. Maybe that's the whole point with Ryan. We wouldn't ever make some bloodless arrangement about something that should be messy as fuck or it shouldn't exist. Period." Deliberately, I took her hands off my shoulders. I gave them a squeeze, but I released them.

This wouldn't end our relationship. I loved her. I loved my father. But I needed time.

That was Ryan and I, needing space to think.

The difference was I didn't when it came to her. With Ryan, my certainty was as steady as the energy that sparked between us.

Hot, untamable. Eternal.

"If you've found something real with her, hold onto it," my mom said hoarsely. "Give her that time she needs, and then make sure she understands."

I forced down the knot in my throat as she gripped my hand before crossing my office and softly closing the door.

I rose and went around the desk to wake up my computer. The wrongness of Ryan not being here, not driving me crazy, sank into my bones, and I gave in to the urge to rest my head in my hands.

Just for a minute though. This wasn't the end.

She wasn't going to think her way out of being in love with me, even if she didn't know it yet.

I pulled up her email and didn't bother to reread it. I knew what it said. If those penguins had been here, I could've recited it to their saxophone music.

It didn't take long to write my response.

I will wait.

I pressed send just as a knock sounded at the door. Inwardly, I groaned. "Mrs. Donnelly, I told you not to come by today, that I'll be in first thing Monday—"

"I'm not Mrs. Donnelly, Mr. Shaw." Grant Thorn opened the door and stepped inside, his eyes wild and his longish hair whipped into a frenzy from either his hands or a sudden windstorm. He wore a tie with his sport jacket, but it looked as if it was on the verge of coming unknotted.

"Thorn, what happened?" I shot around the desk in an instant. "Did something happen to Ryan? Where is she? I'll go to her. Just tell me where she is."

He shocked me by smiling. "So, it's you."

"What the hell are you talking about?"

He shook his head. "She's fine. I don't know where she is."

The adrenaline surge through my veins crashed into something akin to despair. "Then how do you know she's fine?"

"I'm sorry, mate, I talked to her, but I didn't know she wasn't home. I called for a reference."

I frowned. My mind was still spinning, and I hadn't quite caught my breath yet. "Are you looking for secretarial work?"

"No indeed. I need a lawyer. She says you're the best, so I need you."

"You told me you didn't have a wife, so what do you need with a divorce attorney? Or let me guess." I crossed my arms. "You suddenly remembered you're actually married. There's been a lot of that confusion going around lately."

His jaw went to granite. "My Anna is dead, so you'll mind the assumptions."

I closed my eyes and held up a hand. "Sorry. It's been a day. No excuse to take it out on you."

"It's all right."

I opened my eyes again and got myself back in line as I rounded the desk to take my seat. "I'm a recently unemployed divorce attorney. I don't know what kind of lawyer you need, but there's a good chance I'm not it."

"Ryan recommended you. She told me I wanted you, needed you, in fact, and I do. I'm not above begging, Mr. Shaw. Not in this circumstance."

I gripped my mouse as I stared unseeingly at my inbox. She hadn't replied yet, but she'd recommended me. Quite strongly, it sounded like. A commendation of my work from someone like her meant a lot. She wasn't that familiar with it, but she knew me. Days and hours didn't matter. Sometimes you just knew.

She might have needed space, but she still believed in me.

I grabbed my legal pad and motioned for him to sit. "Call me Preston. Tell me what's going on."

Grant sank into the chair opposite my desk and laid it all out for me. His in-laws lived in the western part of the state, and although they'd mentioned wanting to spend more time with his daughter Poppy since their daughter Anna's death, he'd thought they'd come to an understanding.

Evidently not.

Yesterday, he was served with papers at work. They were suing for joint custody. He spent too many long hours at his vet practice and then volunteered at the shelter besides, which meant Poppy spent a lot of time with sitters after school.

"They're right, of course. I can't be in two places at once. I'd hoped when she was a little older, she might want to work at my practice after school. She loves animals, and she's so good with them. We have a dog named Bosco and..." He trailed off. "Sorry. Not important. But she's only 9 yet, and they won't give me the time." He braced his elbows on his knees and shoved his hands through his mussed hair.

More time. Never enough of it.

"You said you're recently unemployed." Thorn frowned. "Ryan didn't tell me that. You didn't lose your license, did you?"

"Definitely not. I'm still a lawyer." I toyed with my gold pen, one like the many others in my cup. "Last Christmas, I took on my buddy's custody case."

Thorn sat up straighter. "Did you win?"

"Well, the mother didn't want to take care of her child, so that

324

made it easier. But yes."

As quickly as the light had come into Thorn's eyes, it dimmed. "My wife would be so hurt by all of this. She never wanted anything more than for all of us to be one big happy family." He stared down at his hands. "I don't know why they're trying to take her from me. She's all I have left."

"They won't take her."

My vehemence made him lift his head. "Do you really think you can win?"

"I know I will." I rose. "Let me do some preliminary research, and then I'll be in touch to discuss more. You can leave your contact information with my assistant—" I sighed and held out a hand. "With me."

He stood and gripped mine, pumping it heartily. "Ah, feck." He drew me into a half hug across the desk, and I was so surprised I hugged him back with equal fervor.

Then again, he'd given me hope with Ryan. So, I'd hug the guy all day long.

Well, maybe for another thirty seconds or so.

"Reduced fee," I added as he moved back.

"Oh, you're a godsend. Truly."

I held up a hand when he swooped in again. The damn Irish. They were a touchy-feely sort. "No more hugs. We'll just call it good."

He let out a half laugh. "That we will. I appreciate this more than you'll ever know. My Anna would too."

"I'm happy to help. Someone has to stand up for what's right."

For once, that someone would be me. Thanks to Ryan.

Later that evening, I was standing on my balcony halfheartedly looking through my telescope at the night sky. I had my scotch on the railing and kept moving it every time Smoky decided to stick his face in the glass.

Approximately every two minutes.

"Only a week ago, I'd never seen Ryan in person. Yet I jerked off to her voice." I blinked as the cat swished his tail. "Pretend you didn't hear that."

He jumped down and sashayed back inside. I didn't blame him. I'd been rambling on and off for the last hour at least.

This waiting thing sucked.

I focused on Vega, the brightest star of the Summer Triangle overhead. I didn't make a wish, but I thought of how she'd appeared this morning as she looked out the telescope, her bare feet on the same spot on the floor where mine now were. Talking to the cat, who'd listened with rapt attention. All that dark hair blowing in the breeze as her husky laughter rolled out and made me ache.

God, I already ached.

My phone buzzed with a new voicemail. Shit, I'd forgotten to turn the ringer back on. I grabbed it, already grinning.

"Your extended warranty is expiring," I read aloud, scanning the voicemail transcript.

Biting off an oath, I hit the icon for the trash can.

The next time a text came in, I almost didn't succumb. The crushing sense of defeat afterward nearly wasn't worth it. But hope was stubborn.

And flared to life as I gazed at the photo of Ryan and I kissing a few days ago. She didn't say anything, but she'd sent it.

She was thinking of me too. Thank fuck.

I debated how to reply as I showered. Playing it cool was a valid strategy, but I didn't want to seem blasé.

Dex would probably send a dick pic. I definitely wasn't doing that.

I got in my bed in the dark and closed my eyes. She was everywhere. Her honeyed scent all around me. I could feel her in my arms. Her hair against my face. Her warmth an imprint against my skin.

I fumbled for my phone.

Miss Moon,

    You did not request time off from work today in advance. I would replace you, but you're irreplaceable to me.

    Sincerely,

    PMS, Esq.

CHAPTER TWENTY-SIX

PRESTON

Saturday 6 am

To whom it may concern:

I did not request time off in advance bc 1 Preston Michael Shaw, Esq. (hereafter referred to as PMS, Esq.) kept me up late fucking me. If u've got a prob w/that, talk 2 ur dick.

UNSINCERELY YOURS, RYAN G. MOON

Saturday 6:47 am

Ryan G. Moon,

If you had an issue with fucking me, you shouldn't have come 1-2-3-4-5 times during the course of Thursday.

Sincerely,

Preston Michael Shaw, Esquire

Saturday 8:52 am

To whom it may concern:
    I do not believe that count is accurate.
    Unsincerely Yours,
    Ryan G. Moon

Saturday 10:17 am

Ryan G. Moon,
    Should we bring in an independent verifier the next time I have you on your back?
    Sincerely,
    Preston Michael Shaw, Esquire

Saturday 11:06 am

To whom it may concern:
    Or I have u on urs?
    Unsincerely Yours,
    Ryan G. Moon

Saturday 11:53 am

Ryan G. Moon,
    Position optional. Ladies' choice.
    Sincerely,
    Preston Michael Shaw, Esquire

. . .

Saturday 1:41 pm

To whom it may concern:

I'm curious abt this independent verifier. Can we get Jason Momoa? I bet I could come all over the place if he was, um, counting.

Unsincerely Yours,
Ryan G. Moon

Saturday 3:55 pm

Ryan G. Moon,

You came all over the place just fine without him.
Sincerely,
Preston Michael Shaw, Esquire

Saturday 5:27 pm

To whom it may concern:

Fantasies r free.
Unsincerely Yours,
Ryan G. Moon

Saturday 7:18 pm

Ryan G. Moon,

No, they aren't, because mine about you cost me a night's worth of sleep.

Sincerely,

Preston Michael Shaw, Esquire

Saturday 9:59 pm

To whom it may concern:

Did u use that picture 4 fodder 4 inappropriate activities? I should report you to HR. Is there a HR? Maybe I'll report you 2 Daddy. That should be a fun mtg.

Unsincerely Yours,

Ryan G. Moon

Saturday 11:14 pm

Ryan G. Moon,

Sounds like you're thinking about inappropriate activities yourself. I'd report you to HR, but I don't work there anymore. Good try though.

Sincerely,

Preston Michael Shaw, Esquire

My phone rang two minutes after I hit send.

Steeling myself, I clicked the button.

"What? Are you kidding? Did you say that to get me to call? No, of course you didn't. Why? Why would you quit?"

I shocked myself by laughing. "I've never heard you say so much in one breath before."

"You barely know me."

"I want to know everything. How you sound when you wake up

and how you say goodnight. The food you pick for breakfast. How you decide which tea for the day. I want to watch you pick out a peeing llama."

I couldn't tell if the sound she made was a laugh or a sob. "Preston, you're not changing the subject."

There was no stopping my smile. "You called me Preston."

"I'm worried about your mental health."

"You should be. I'm not right when you're gone."

"Preston," she said, softer now. "What are you doing to me?"

"When you're ready to hear it, I'll tell you."

She took a shaky breath. "What if I never am? Then what?"

"I will wait."

She hung up on me. And I smiled because I knew she was thinking about what I'd said.

She was thinking about us and what we could have.

All I was asking for was a chance.

Sunday 2:49 am

To whom it may concern:

I'm folded on my side in a couch-slash-bed with my knees to my stomach. My mom is the big spoon.

Unsincerely Yours,

Ryan G. Moon

Sunday 2:54 am

Ryan G. Moon,

Does she give good spoon?

Sincerely,

Preston Michael Shaw, Esquire

Sunday 2:57 am

To whom it may concern:
    Nothing like u do. I never slept that gud in my lif.
    Unsincerely Yours,
    Ryan G. Moon

Sunday 3:03 am

Ryan G. Moon,
    Are you buttering me up to evaluate my typo tolerance
threshold? Just so you know, I can't be swayed.
    Sincerely,
    Preston Michael Shaw, Esquire

Sunday 3:08 am

To whom it may concern:
    Why did you quit? For real?
    Unsincerely Yours,
    Ryan G. Moon

Sunday 3:21 am

Ryan G. Moon,
    You forgot your abbreviated form of speaking. I almost thought
you were an imposter Goddess.
    Sincerely,
    Preston Michael Shaw, Esquire

. . .

Sunday 3:33 am

MISS MOON:

Preston, tell me.

I finally called her half an hour later. I hadn't known how to answer.

It was a hell of a thing to drop the bricks you'd carried around your whole life. To share that load with someone, knowing full well they might not want to keep toting them the rest of the way with you.

But I had to do it anyway.

"Hi," I said quietly when she answered.

"Hi," she whispered back.

"Are you going to hang up on me again?"

"Depends. If you make me cry again, absolutely."

I smiled in the dark. "Normally, I would hate making you cry. But in this case..."

"Sadist." I could hear her smile.

"Can you talk? I don't want to keep your mom up."

"She has headphones in with her Gregorian chant music. She uses that to reach her alternative aural space."

"Okay."

"That's my mother, man. She's on a whole different plane. Now stop stalling."

I released a slow breath. "I never wanted to do divorce law. Not for one goddamn day. I finally just...stopped."

She gasped. "You walked out?"

"I said I quit. I didn't say I had a lobotomy."

Her soft giggle was breathless. "Can you return the car? That's a lot of thrusters for a guy without a job."

"I never owned it."

"What the fuck, dude?"

"You know what they say about assumptions."

"I know your exceptional penis won't save you from an asskicking when I see you in person."

I grinned. "Let's hope your mom doesn't decide to kill the chanting."

"She already knows about your penis."

I choked. "Please tell me you're joking."

"Oh, no. It's a whole ritual we do when one of us has a new man. We detail it all right down to width and length. I had to guesstimate some of it, but when we salt the circle, estimates are good enough. I mean, for a first ceremony anyway."

I'd coughed so hard my eyes were still watering. "I'm almost sure you're pulling my...not penis."

"But you're not certain, are you? So, remember I know of things you can't begin to imagine, Horatio."

"Oh, I already knew that, Moonbeam." I rubbed my chest. "Look at that, my lungs still work. I thought they'd seized up on me."

"Serves you right. That means the grandpa car is still in commission?"

"Nope."

"Care to elaborate?"

"Not particularly." I lowered my voice. "So, how tight are your quarters there?"

"If you are even so much as insinuating I should touch myself while I'm in bed with my mother, you are a sick puppy, PMS. Truly depraved."

It took everything I possessed not to laugh. "Maybe just a little?"

"Not even the tiniest bit in the history of small, infinitesimal things."

"God, I miss you already. How is that possible?"

"Same way it's possible we met on Monday. Did you quit because I left?"

"No. I quit Thursday."

Her pause made me think our banter was at an end. I waited to hear the click that meant she was done talking yet again.

"I should've known you never would've slept in unless you'd already done something rash."

"Hardly rash. I'd been thinking about it for years. I just finally pulled the trigger. And you're the one who fucked me into a coma."

"I'd say that was mutual coma fucking."

"Yeah, but the belt was extra."

"And you didn't even need Jason Momoa to spot you."

"This conversation is veering into disturbing places."

"That's what happens when we're whispering at 4 am."

There were other things I wanted to whisper to her, but that would be the coward's way out. When I said the words, I wanted to say them in full sunlight with no place to hide so she'd understand that she wasn't a passing whim for me. Not a game or a flight of fancy.

Forever didn't have to take forever. Ours had happened in an instant.

"I meant it when I said I would wait, but...."

"But..." she teased.

"When are you coming back to me?"

"Yeah, you're totally patient. Grant told me what you did for him, by the way. I didn't expect you to reduce your fee."

"Neither did I," I admitted, making her laugh.

"I have to get some sleep. Rainbow's up with the sparrows."

"Rainbow." I snorted. "I'll never get used to that name."

"Wait until you have to get used to the wo—" She cut herself off. "Okay, night. Bye."

I grinned. "Night, Moonbeam."

Sunday 11:57 am

Ryan G. Moon,
    Did you dream of me?
    Sincerely,
    Preston Michael Shaw, Esquire

. . .

Sunday 12:22 pm

Who dis?

Sunday 12:51 pm

Ryan G. Moon,
   I talked to my mom on Friday. You were right.
Sincerely,
Preston Michael Shaw, Esquire

Sunday 12:57 pm

MISS MOON:

I'm calling.

Out on the balcony, I glanced down at Smoky, who was batting a catnip palm tree with halfhearted interest as he eyed the phone in my hand. When her call came through, he sat up straight, all pretense of playing forgotten.

"She's not calling you," I informed him.

He promptly turned around and showed me his butt.

"Hey." I leaned back against the railing and crossed my ankles with a casualness I so didn't feel. "How's things with Mom?"

"Tell me what happened."

"No foreplay, got it." Idly, I scratched my stomach through the baseball jersey I'd put on to wear to dinner at the bar with Bishop and my brother later. "I asked her straight out if she'd been with anyone else after my father. She indicated yes."

Ryan didn't reply right away. "I'm sorry."

"Me too. For them, most of all. It's a hell of a thing to live like that and to think it makes sense."

"If they're in agreement..."

"It's still crazy."

"No argument. Are you okay? I know finding out about your dad rocked you."

"I'm getting there. Did you get some sleep?"

"Yeah. A little. Hard to sleep with your mom crammed in a couch-bed, but I made do."

"Maybe try the chants?"

She laughed and I heard movement and voices around her. "We're getting more of her wares ready for the fair. She does a lot of work with textiles. Yarn and stuff. It's a huge one, lots of crafters and vendors."

"Sounds like you're busy then. I won't keep you."

"What about you? Do you have plans today?"

"Yeah, I'm meeting my best friend and Dex at the bar later. We have some business to discuss." I rubbed my thumb over my phone and tried the full disclosure thing on for size. "We're asking Bishop to take my place in the firm. No idea if he'll bite, but he's a good dude. He just got back from the South Pacific and—"

"Was there a discount going around or something?"

"Huh?"

"You know, April too. She texted me from Fiji. Said she ran into some snags, but she's on her way home."

I frowned. "I didn't even make the connection. That's odd. What are the chances?"

"Well, it's not like the South Pacific is tiny."

"No, but that it was at the same time."

"Do they know each other?"

"No, not that I know of. Bishop never visits me at work, and I've never run into April when we're out together, rare as it is."

"Typical PMS. All business."

"Until I discovered the varied uses for conference tables and desk chairs, you mean."

"Your education was lacking," she agreed. "Hang on." She muffled the phone, and someone called out to her before she came back on the line. "Gotta go. My mom can't find her bag of adult booties."

I chuckled. "Do I want to know?"

"Probably not." She paused. "We can talk more later."

"I should hope so."

"I mean about the situation with your parents. That's rough. A lot to swallow."

"It hasn't been the best. But it's done one good thing."

"What's that?"

"It's made me really firm on what I don't want...and what I do. I won't make a promise I can't keep." When she didn't respond, I cleared my throat. "I just wanted you to know that."

"I never thought otherwise. Don't have too much fun at the bar."

"Afraid I'm going to get tipsy?"

"Just wear baggy jeans or something."

I choked out a laugh. "Excuse me?"

"Your ass is entirely too pinchable."

"You think? I've never been pinched when out and about."

"I know. Later, PMS." She clicked off before I could do more than grin dopily at my irritated cat.

He leaned forward and very specifically bit my big toe in my open sandal. Then he sauntered off while I stared at his ungrateful back end.

I spent the rest of disgustingly hot and humid afternoon doing paperwork in my chaise lounge on the balcony with some music playing and chilled iced tea. I wouldn't be drinking much of the hot stuff anytime soon, but even the iced version made me think of her.

Hell, everything did.

Later, Ryan texted me a snapshot of a pair of bug-eyed llama potholders.

MISS MOON:

These screamed PMS.

338

Did you buy them?

MISS MOON:

Even better. I bartered a pair of booties for
them. You're welcome.

Smoky was sunning himself in a beam of sunshine on the railing.
At my bark of laughter, he glanced over and sneered.

Elvis came on when I was just about to head inside and get ready
to go. I grinned and cranked up the music, only to lower it again when
my phone went off.

Bishop.

"Hey, what's up? You on your way?"

"I'm still in Fiji. Shit went sideways. Needless to say, I'm not going
to be at the bar tonight. Sorry."

Only one word stuck in my brain.

"Fiji? You didn't tell me you were there. And you said you met a
woman?"

"Oh, I met a woman, all right." His tone verged on furious.

"What happened? I thought you were in love and all that."

"All that is correct. Until she ghosted me." Static filled the line, and
it sounded as if he dropped the phone. He came back on, sounding out
of breath. "If I can't find her, I'm catching a flight tonight."

"You're still looking? And um, just for curiosity's sake, her name
isn't April, is it?"

That would be very, very bad if I wanted him to take my place in
the law firm, and his new assistant had just fucked and ducked him.

I grasped the back of my neck. I did not want to think of my cool,
competent assistant in that manner. I separated church and state so
thoroughly that I'd barely even noticed she was a woman.

Didn't work so well with Ryan though, huh?

That was an entirely different scenario. She'd only been a temp.

Even consumed with Bishop's problem, I couldn't help smiling like
a fool. And now she was everything, assuming she ever stopped
bartering adult booties and came back to me.

"No," Bishop bit off.

My breath rushed out. "Thank God."

More static. "Her name definitely wasn't April. If what she told me was even her name. We only did first ones. Now I'm questioning everything."

Momentary relief squelched.

"Okay, what did she look—"

A choppy voice on an intercom crackled across the line before Bishop swore. "Sorry, man, I have to go. We'll reschedule that meeting in a few days. Whatever you need."

"Sure, don't worry about it. I'm sorry about this."

Really sorry if my sneaking suspicion was right. But what were the odds?

Then again, I'd fallen in love in the course of a week with a complete stranger. A smart, funny, beautiful one who'd opened up the whole world to me—both the logical one and the mystical.

There were a hell of a lot more forces at work than I could comprehend. All I could do was be grateful for them.

"Me too, Shaw." Suddenly, he sounded so weary—and broken. I knew too well what that felt like. And I hated my buddy losing someone he'd found a connection with after all he'd endured in the past.

We hung up.

I sat there for a while, just thinking. Wondering if there was some divine plan that made sense to someone at the controls, if such a being existed. I was more inclined to believe that now than I had in the recent past, that was for damn sure.

My phone buzzed a bit later.

DEX:

Hey, assclown, did you forget me? I'm sitting here at the bar with two women who would be more than happy to soothe my sorrows at being stood up. And they can tie cherry stems with their nipples.

Is that even English?

DEX:

Who cares? They're hot and they have nipples
and a willingness to let me enjoy them. So you
have twenty minutes to get here or I'm going to
let them take advantage of me.

I'm on my way. Don't drink all the beer.

DEX:

Not what I intended on sampling first, but fine.

I shook my head as I stuffed papers from the Donnelly case into
my file folder. My brother was a horndog to the nth degree.

Hmm, maybe I should hand him Mary Donnelly to deal with. He'd
said he could help out more. This divorce was only in the early stages,
and Mary had warned me she had new "bombshell" allegations that
were going to "fry that sucker." Not exactly my preference, and Dex
enjoyed the game of all of it far more than I did.

Because it wasn't a game. These were real people and real lives
being shattered.

But if Dex was willing to take on additional cases, why not ask him
if he wanted to wade into the fray? I'd just have to get him drunk
enough to feel amenable. It shouldn't be too hard. Mary and Harvey's
estate was valued in the high seven figures, and she claimed the fucker
—her term not mine—was hiding even more funds offshore. Dex
would be more than handsomely paid for his trouble. I just didn't
want the hassle.

I fed Smoky and gave him fresh water and futilely tried to get him
to sit on my shoulder like he did with Ryan. The only thing that made
him warm marginally toward me was an extra helping of Chunky
Beef Tips—and my lie that Ryan would be home soon. At that, he gave
me a head bonk and an actual rumbling purr.

It lasted approximately thirty-eight seconds, but I wasn't choosy.

On my way to the bar, a text came in.

MISS MOON:

My mom found my dildo.

I almost drove off the road. Since I was in the dealership's SUV for a weekend test drive, that would not have been good.

I waited to respond until I pulled up next to Dexter's sleek vintage Mustang at Lonegan's.

> PMS: Did you tell her it was ornamental?

> MISS MOON:
> Like ur fountain?

> Sure. Both utilize moisture.

> MISS MOON:
> U r an actual pig. A cute one, but a pig.

> You should see if she could knit you a sock for your moon.

> MISS MOON:
> Actually, that's a good idea. She does sleeves 4 the rl thing. They r a hot ticket item.

> WHAT?

A picture came through of a knitted cylindrical-ish pouch in hot pink with a bulbous bottom...head in lime green.

> That's worse than a Pussy Papa. Also, who the hell buys that?

> MISS MOON:
> You're sure you don't want one? Pretty please?

> No.

I pocketed my phone as I walked into Lonegan's and bumped fists with my brother.

No women were in sight. At least anywhere near Dexter.

"Well, well, look who has a big-ass grin on his face. Is all fixed on the path to insanely fast true love? Did I mention insanely?"

I slid onto a stool beside him at the bar and motioned to the bartender, our old friend Callahan Brinkley. Tossing a towel over his shoulder, he smiled and held up a finger before gesturing to the customers he was serving.

"We're making progress."

Dex put a hand next to his ear. "Is that bells I hear?"

"Jealous?"

"I'm happy for you. You deserve a good woman, Pres. I mean that." I clapped his back. "Thanks, man."

The corner of his mouth ticked up. "Plus, she's imminently fuck—"

At my arched eyebrow, he smiled smoothly. "Fucking fantastic."

"Mind yourself."

"Minded. Sorry, not used to you settled down, since it's only been a week and all."

Callahan chose that moment to slide up to us and start pulling my usual Harp. "Did someone say settled, Pres? In a week?"

"We are getting to know each other." I thanked Callahan for the beer I intended to nurse all night, unlike my brother who already had two empties being taken away and it was just past seven.

"In a settled way," Dex added. "Can I get another, my man?"

"Of course, if you intend to hang out here tonight." Callahan tossed back his shock of dark hair, and the studs along the curve of his ear caught the light. "Otherwise, you know you're reaching your limit."

"Why am I surrounded by boring bozos?"

Callahan just crossed his beefy arms and waited. Dex knew the rules when it came to the tight ship that Cal ran at Lonegan's. Dex just liked to bitch about them.

Added to that, Cal was a friend, so he was even more strict with Dex for his own good. Not that he usually crossed the line, but that was the thing with my brother. Occasionally, he tried to shimmy under them as if life was one big hokey-pokey.

"Yeah, I'll be hanging out with Preston for a while. His woman's on safari."

"What?" I had to laugh. My brother was an idiot, but he was amusing.

Sometimes. Especially when I was riding on a Ryan high.

"Should we do your bachelor party tonight for expediency? I heard flights to Vegas are dirt cheap right now."

Callahan's brows lifted as he ran his fingers up and down the suspenders he habitually wore with his T-shirts. "Whoa, are you serious, dude? Last I knew you didn't even date."

"We aren't getting married." I knocked back some of my drink.

I saved the *yet* for my head.

"He was damn near a virgin. You know how it is the first time you get a taste of—"

I slapped him in the back of the head, and Callahan laughed before moving on to another customer.

"No beer?" Dex sighed, but he didn't seem to annoyed at having to wait for his next drink."Seriously, man, did you guys work it out?"

"Working on it."

"She's talking to you at least?"

"Yeah. We talked all last night and part of today." I smiled as I curled my wrist around my glass. "In our way anyway."

"Jeez, you really are like a teenager in love." He shook his head. "I'm curious and mystified and a little horrified."

"Good. Then you're in the perfect frame of mind to talk business."

He groaned and dropped back his head. "Didn't you quit? Aren't you ever off the clock? And you never told me what the hell happened to Stone."

"He's in Fiji."

"Still?" He held up a hand. "Let me guess. He fell in love in a week too."

"Actually, I think he did."

"Man, whatever you guys are taking, do not give me any. I will never settle for the daily special when I can have the whole damn buffet. Yo, Brinkley." Dex cupped his hands over his mouth as he called down the bar, catching the attention of many of the other patrons with varying results. Some amusement, some interest, some irritation—the usual responses to my brother. "I need lubrication if I gotta talk biz shit with the older bro."

Five minutes later, he had his beer, and partly against his will, we were discussing the Donnelly case in much more depth than we had previously. We spoke in hushed tones and with many abbreviations so as not to be overheard.

Not that anyone in the raucous bar gave one whit what we were talking about. The Yankees were far more entertaining.

Dex knew the basics, but when I told him exactly the kind of compensation on the table, he got a whole lot more interested.

Time went by quickly as we rolled through a few of my other larger cases. Dex drank just that final beer as we went over some of the high points, and then we circled back to Donnelly vs. Donnelly. His mind was definitely operating on all cylinders once that payout was on the table.

We sat on those stools long enough that my ass went numb.

My very pinchable ass, if scuttlebutt could be believed. I was good with just Ryan taking advantage of me.

Hopefully soon.

"I've been eyeing this place on the lake," my brother mused much later, nursing his glass of ice water as if it was another beer. "It looks like a damn chalet. Has a couple levels and an outdoor hot tub and boat launch and shit. Can you imagine the pool parties? It'd be like summer all year long."

"You do remember we live in central New York. Half the year it's practically like Antarctica."

"But a hot tub, my man." He turned to vigorously clap my shoulder. And Dex worked out a hell of a lot, so he had some grip. "With enough room for like six." He smiled dreamily, picturing things in his mind's eye I did not want to guess at. "Maybe eight if it's near bikini season."

"That can be yours and more if you take lead on this."

"You really don't want it anymore?"

"No. I really don't."

My phone vibrated in my pocket and I dragged it out to see a picture of a sliver of moon and a sprinkle of stars in a dark blue sky over what appeared to be rolling hills in the distance and a long ribbon of road. Makeshift campsites covered the land off to the side.

Before I could text, another picture came in. This one had flares set upon the road and bright orange traffic cones arranged behind what looked like a large Airstream slightly tipped to one side. That might have been an optical illusion.

Or not.

> **MISS MOON:**
>
> Our shitty luck. Had to move camp & we hv a flat. We're gonna see if 1 of our new friends in the nearby camps has a towing membership or whatever. If u text and I don't get back, that's y.

> No. What? No. Is that safe?

> **MISS MOON:**
>
> Of course. Ttyl. Hope your ass is still virgin.

There had been way too much talk about my virginity tonight, in inappropriate, non-applicable ways. But that wasn't important right now.

> No, don't do that. It looks like a hippie commune. They could be on drugs or a sex brigade or I don't even know. And it's dark out. Shelter in place until daylight.

> **MISS MOON:**
>
> They knit, PMS, among other things. And there's nothing wrong with a lil recreational ganja.

> You work for a lawyer, Miss Moon.

> **MISS MOON:**
>
> I quit, remember? And I didn't say I was smoking any. I'm too busy trying these neat lil shrooms I found…

I pressed a finger to the pulsing vein in my temple. I knew I was overreacting. I could feel that I was drifting into pure ridiculousness, but I could not seem to stop myself.

Was this love? Or maybe I really was insane.

Possibly they were actually the same exact thing.

Dexter moved his face close to mine. "You all right, Pres? You look like you're going to stroke out."

"No, I am not."

"What did she do now?"

I wanted to defend her, and yet at this instant, all I could think was that she could be three or more states away and I would not know. I couldn't swoop in and save her because she was wandering around in the dark, probably barefoot, making friends with strangers and sharing questionable items with them that could be smoked or imbibed in other unknown ways.

Potentially *criminal* items to boot.

"She left me to do needlecrafts and take drugs and now she's stranded in the desert."

CHAPTER TWENTY-SEVEN

PRESTON ☕

Ryan was not in the desert, and I would have realized she wouldn't have had time to reach one in the time allotted via wheeled transport had I not been on the verge of manful terror.

Instead, it took Dex to remind me of that little logistical tidbit before he drove himself home, now sobered up after hours of dry business talk and copious amounts of water.

She was actually not all that far away. Not all that close either. I had to look up Bear Mountain Park on my GPS, and from Kensington Square to there would take about three hours if I did not get lost.

Tomorrow I had that meeting with Mrs. Donnelly first thing. Our many times rescheduled meeting.

But technically, she wasn't my client anymore. So, Dex could handle her if need be. And I simply couldn't care when I knew Ryan needed me.

Even if she couldn't admit it.

MISS MOON:

DO NOT COME HERE. WE R ALL SET.

I'm coming, baby. You don't have to be strong.

MISS MOON:

Be strong? It's a flat. I'm not afrd of the dark &
everyone is perfctly nice.

I was driving so I didn't reply. A short time later, another text
came through.

MISS MOON:

U called me baby.

Even in my darkened car, I flushed. I tossed my phone aside and
ignored it. It also was not safe to text and drive.

Then she called me.

Reluctantly, I took the call through the in-dash system.

"Yeah?"

"You called me baby."

"You misread. I typed bubby."

"Preston, I'm serious. We're fine. The flat isn't even an issue
anymore thanks to Brock. If you come here, my mom will give you
half a dozen of her hook holders that didn't sell and then what?"

I frowned. "Hook holders?"

"I mean, penis warmers."

I started to laugh. "Baby, if my penis gets warmed any more, it will
be a medical emergency. The humidity is insane. And yes, I did say
baby, and you can just deal with it. It may be heat stroke."

In the background, I heard a feminine voice say loudly, "Oh, penis
warmers! Yes!"

Ryan sighed. "I need a vacation from my vacation."

"You should have thought of that before you completed not even
one full week of work. Wages of sin and all that."

"A week was all I was scheduled for, if you recall. Because April is
your actual assistant. I was just a fill-in."

"I believe actually *I* filled, but you came through in the clutch
admirably. Until you left without permission. Now let me alone so I
can traverse these twisty as hell back roads in the dark and come
rescue you."

"Even though I expressly asked you not to?"

"Has anyone ridden to your rescue before, Ryan Genevieve Moon?"

"How do you know my real name?"

"A handy tool called the internet. I do like Goddess though."

Rustling noises came over the line and then she was in a quieter environment. "I don't want you to miss work for me. Honestly. We're fine. A lot of the people here are senior citizens and empty nesters. Definitely not the rough crowd your way overactive imagination is picturing."

"I'm not anymore."

"No? You seemed rather…incensed. In full Esquire mode."

"It's a bad habit. I'm new to being a boyfriend and very not new to being a lawyer."

She hissed out a breath. "I don't do relationships."

"Me either, since I'm still a recent virgin, apparently."

"Wow. I did not guess that. Did you learn from YouTube?"

"Another sort of You video site, but close enough." I squinted into the darkness at a huge, looming shape. "I think I just saw a damn moose."

"What? No. Holy crap."

"Or it was otherworldly. It scampered into the night. There is that road around here with the dead bride ghost. You've heard that tale? Anyway, we'll have to look for it someday." I didn't shudder, but boy, it was close. "In the daylight."

"Yeah, we'll revisit that at another time. If you insist on coming—"

"I do."

She sighed. "Then be careful, okay? No texting or phone calls. Those back roads have a lot of hairpin curves."

"Then get off my phone." I smiled. "Baby."

She hung up.

I got lost. Three times.

By the last one, she was texting me. Dare I say frantically.

I wouldn't say I grinned as the in-dash system read them to me but—

Okay, yes, I was.

Broadly.

> MISS MOON:
>
> PMS, u shouldn't be reading these. But if you are, I just want to say that u're a pain in the ass. But I like it. I like u.

> MISS MOON:
>
> I shouldn't. We don't fit. But we do. Y do we fit?

> MISS MOON:
>
> I'm sure u're prob just trying to find u're way in the dark. I've been lost on these roads too. But I have faith in u. That's y I sent Grant to u. U won't let him down.

> MISS MOON:
>
> Just like u won't let me down. U damn idiot. I told u to stay home but u won't listen.

> MISS MOON:
>
> U won't stay in the spot I want to put u. Y won't u, dammit?

> MISS MOON:
>
> TG u won't. Bc I'm already getting used to it, u big dolt. Used 2 u. Even if it makes no sense.

> MISS MOON:
>
> Dammit, Preston Michael Shaw, u better not be hurt! If you are, I will kick your ass so badly that u'll be in traction.

> MISS MOON:
>
> After I kiss your smug, stubborn face off.

> MISS MOON:
>
> Ugh, I just need you to be okay. Please. You can call me baby if you want. You can call me anything.

I saw the signs for the fair first. It took inching around a few more curves past endless buses, vans, trucks, and other moving settlements that were temporarily in one place to get my bearings enough to figure out where I was.

Then I saw her.

She was standing off to the side of the road near the Airstream in the picture she'd sent. If I hadn't seen her, I wouldn't have recognized it because there were a few of them in various configurations.

But I could've recognized Ryan anywhere. Especially when she was one of the only people out milling about in this particular area, since it was after two am.

I'd gotten *really* lost those three times, and that was with GPS. Go down one wrong back road and you ended up in a whole other county.

And then if you just kept going, not being sure of the difference between south and not south in the dark in an unfamiliar area...

It was a problem.

She was gesturing wildly with her hands as she talked to a small blond woman. Was that her mother? She looked tiny. Ryan's exact opposite.

Her mom. Christ. I couldn't do the first meet and greet with the parental unit in the middle of the night. I wasn't even wearing a suit.

Ryan had her armor, and I had mine.

I signaled and pulled over to the side of the road a bit back. It was probably mean I didn't alert her to my arrival right away, but I was entitled after her unexpected disappearing act.

Her dark hair streamed behind her as she paced away then back a couple of times. Her mother stepped up to her and gripped her arms, saying something that made Ryan drop her head back to stare at the sky.

The brief glimpse of wet on her cheeks had me climbing out. Imagined or not, I wouldn't make her hurt for even a minute more than necessary.

Never.

She turned to face me and her eyes went comically wide as she glimpsed me standing behind the open door of my borrowed SUV.

Then she started to run.

Stepping away from the truck, I caught her as she leaped into my arms, staggering under her weight as we collided into the side of the SUV.

"Shit, if we dent this thing—"

Her mouth was on mine before I could finish. Her tongue slid between my lips and my hands landed on her firm little ass to hold her tight to my instantly interested groin.

"I'm gonna fucking kill you." Each word was punctuated with a kiss. "Didn't even need to—dammit, your mouth."

"Umph." It was all I could manage as I fought to keep hold of her and simultaneously thrust upward into her soft, unfortunately covered cleft.

A throat was repeatedly cleared nearby.

Neither of us cared.

"So, you must be Preston."

"I hear a voice," I muttered as Ryan drew my lower lip between her teeth.

"Ignore her. She'll go away."

"I certainly will not. I want to get a good look at him when you get done mauling him."

Ryan slid her mouth along my jaw, dropping kisses as she went. "It's gonna be a while. Go find Brock."

That brought a modicum of clarity to my feverish brain. I managed to ease back. "Brock?"

"Her boyfriend." She rolled her eyes and huffed a breath in my face. "You can put me down now."

"You're the one who leaped at me. You should be impressed I caught you."

She studied me for a long moment before framing my face in her hands. "I missed you."

This time, I was the one who kissed her. She smelled like a bonfire and tasted like summer and marshmallows and something sweet like wine.

Home and adventure, all rolled into one.

More throat clearing.

I finally made myself extricate my lips from hers. It was exceedingly difficult.

The part of me notched so intimately between her thighs agreed.

We were both panting. And when I set her down and she tripped, she didn't even swear at me.

Either she'd thought I'd hit a misfortunate moose somewhere and was in a pile of rubble or she was about to pass out from oxygen loss. She didn't let me off that easy ever.

I rubbed my sweaty hand on my hip and shut the door of the SUV before I held out a hand to Mrs.—well, Rainbow. "Ma'am, it's nice to meet you. I'm Preston Shaw."

Ryan circled her arms around my waist from behind and put her chin on my shoulder. "PMS. It's just easier."

I gave her a look and she nuzzled my jaw.

"Call me Rainbow." She pumped my hand. "Pleasure is all mine. Not every day I get to meet my little girl's special guy."

"I should hope not."

Ryan pinched my butt. I didn't mind, but I had to tug my jersey down in a futile attempt to hide my erection.

Who didn't want to meet his girl's mom when he had a hard-on?

"Unfortunately, I can't say I've heard a lot about you." She glanced pointedly at her daughter.

"I was getting there."

"I did hear you were looking for intimate comfort for the winter months. It does get chilly in these parts, doesn't it?" She fanned her face, stirring the tendrils of honey-colored hair clinging to her neck. "Not today though. I need a fan directed right between my legs."

Dear God.

Ryan mumbled something under her breath.

Maybe a prayer. I needed one too.

"I'm going to start making a bunch built to scale. Brock said he'd model."

I went somewhere else in my head. A safe space.

"And then she can use a warmer as a sleeve for her pleasure wand too. I wondered why she'd leave it on the couch, but now it makes more sense." Rainbow looked me up and down while I wondered if it was possible to be struck down by lightning when there was no storm on the horizon. "I can't see why she'd need it with you, but toys can be fun!"

Ryan gripped my arms and towed me behind the SUV. "I need to chat privately with PMS. Be back soon."

"Oh, okay. Calling dibs on the bed though," Rainbow called after us. "Sorry, but Brock's had a long day. I have extra headphones for PMS."

I shut my eyes. "Two Moons calling me PMS. Thanks, Moonbeam."

"Trust me, PMS is an improvement over what she called you when she first saw you."

I did not want to know.

Ryan jabbed her finger into my chest. "You can't be here. You have work in just a few hours. And even if you've quit, missing appointments isn't like you. April is supposed to be back today." She bit her lip. "Back to normal."

I cupped her cheek. "What the hell is normal? I don't want it. As for April, I'm not so sure about that. Did you speak to her tonight?"

Ryan frowned. "No, why?"

Quickly, I relayed what I knew. Her frown morphed into a smile. "Nah, that's not April. She's not a fling girl. She only has sex on the fifth date, every time."

"Is it a Moon family policy to tell information others are not ready for and do not want?"

Ryan jerked a shoulder. "Probably. Just saying she didn't bang your friend and split. And while using a fake name? That's not my bestie."

"How many best bishes do you have anyway?"

"One. Luna. April's second tier."

"How unfortunate." I slipped my hands around her waist and drew her closer to bury my face in her windswept hair. Her honey and floral scent soaked into me like a song I'd never grow tired of. "What tier am I?"

"PMS—"

"I hated that you left. I wondered if I'd ever get to tell you how I felt." I eased back to see her eyes were wide and wary and so dark in the deepest part of the night.

But she wasn't running away. So, I wouldn't either.

I rubbed my thumb over her lower lip. "I wanted to say this in sunlight. It seemed important somehow. But the moon is important for us too." I glanced up at the crescent just visible through the clouds. "The moon brought you to me."

"Preston…" She swallowed hard enough for me to hear.

"I love you. I don't care if it's too fast. If it doesn't make sense to people who aren't us." I gripped her hand and brought it to my chest, holding it there where my heart beat out of control for her.

And would always.

"I meant it when I said I'd wait for you. I will. I won't rush you. I'll give you your space."

Tears gathered on her lashes, so silently that I couldn't even hear her breathing. But her fingers curled into mine.

"You can take a year or a lifetime to love me back. What's time, right? Since a week can be forever." I caught one of her tears on my thumb. "But I'm not promising I won't ever prod or push. I'll wait, but I'm impatient to live my life with you. So, maybe you can pick up the pace just this once—"

She grabbed my face in her hands and kissed me hard, feeding me her tears and her laughter and her need in equal measure.

Tangled with them all, I felt her love. She didn't say it. She didn't have to.

When she moved back, her eyes as bright as the light of the moon, I felt something else too.

I lifted my hand to the back of my head with a wince, and she shut her eyes. "Whoops."

"Will you still love me if I have a bald spot?"

She giggled and fisted her hands. "I'm wicked with a pair of clippers."

"Then again, it might have just been a mosquito." I slapped the side of my neck. "Damn summer. It's hot as balls out here."

"Try sleeping in the camper. I had to take off my bra and—" She noticed the gleam in my eyes and propped her hands on her hips. "Watch yourself or I'll measure you while you're sleeping for your Christmas gift."

I yanked her against me once more. "Maybe it's better if you give me room to…grow."

She laughed helplessly. "I have so much to tell you, and now I'm thinking about your dick."

Lightly, I rubbed against her. "I can assure you the admiration is mutual."

"It's about my art. I've been working on this comic." She grinned. "And it's kinda exciting."

All at once, I forgot my libido. "Tell me. Now."

She dragged me forward a few feet and glanced at the Airstream where her mother and a man I assumed to be Brock were now quite enthusiastically making out in the wide front seats. "Let me just get my stuff. Really, really fast."

"You're honestly ready to come home?"

"Dude, so much. Besides, I have to yell at you for scaring me senseless. I'm way overdue."

Grinning, I smacked her perfect ass as she turned back toward the Airstream. "Yes, you're egregiously late for that, Miss Moon."

FIRST CLOSING ARGUMENT

I BROUGHT my tea mug with me to look out at the endless green of Preston's property. I couldn't say it was a hardship for the nights I stayed over—which, to be honest, was most nights.

PMS was very persuasive when it came to finding ways to get me out of my dresses each evening. And yoga pants. And my favorite boxer shorts I'd started stealing.

Non-worn ones, thanks. I didn't need man funk on my lady parts. There was a distinct difference between getting wild and naked and borrowing someone's underwear.

However, in his very Preston way, he had backup packs in his handy dandy accessory panel. You know, the kind that only rich people had. I was a sucker for hidden spaces of any kind and when I'd been snooping—sue me—I'd found his boxer stash.

Now *my* stash.

Which I was wearing right now with the dress shirt I'd stolen off the chair in his bedroom. I'd had to roll up the sleeves like crazy because his arms were ridiculously long, but I was officially a fan of the richie rich finery from his closet.

I wouldn't tell him that of course.

And to be truthful, I really liked his long arms. Especially when he decided to do his workouts with his new rowing machine.

Hello.

Watching him do that full row with all the muscles moving and shifting under his tanned skin? Yeah, sign me up for that daily workout. Well, to watch it anyway.

Then again, he definitely enjoyed my yoga workouts. However, he wasn't exactly the bendiest guy in that regard. He'd tried hard to do some beginner poses, but in the end, we decided to play to our strengths.

It didn't stop him from setting up half of his workout room with yoga supplies for me. In fact, he kept doing little things that made my heart turn over.

Smoky leaped onto the kitchen table by the window.

"Well, hey there. PMS is going to freak if he sees you on the table." But I simply stroked a hand down his smooth fur. His motorboat of a purr rolled out and made me smile. He went onto his back legs and waved his paw at me.

"Shameless." But I leaned down so he could leap on my shoulder, his favorite place to be. He settled into the crook of my neck and butted his head against my jaw. Little devil. I scratched under his chin and fixed the pile of papers he'd scattered.

I paused as I realized it was my contract, the one that had a whole lot of red pen marks in Preston's slashing handwriting. Penn Masterson had sent it over the other day after he got my first batch of sketches.

Sylvia and Roz officially had a new roommate—Smoky, the tripod cat.

Our cat was a budding comic star. I rubbed my cheek against the purring furbaby, already snoozing on me.

And now that I had a lawyer in my back pocket, who just happened to have a startling ability to research and assimilate anything—namely entertainment law or his new obsession, family law —I had someone looking out for me.

I was getting used to the idea.

It was weird and wonderful, even if I didn't quite know what to do with it most days.

"Did you make enough for both of us?" His voice rumbled behind me just before his big hand slid under my shirt to find skin.

I sipped from my mug and nodded toward the teapot his mother had gifted to me when we'd gone to the tarot festival a few weeks ago.

"I'm not sure what kind of magic you add to your tea, but I ordered more of this stuff for our new office."

"Your office," I corrected him.

"Mmm."

I rolled my eyes. I was not going to be working for him again. I wasn't.

I was pretty sure.

I lifted Smoky off my shoulder and settled him on one of the chairs at the table. We'd stashed one of his half-dozen cat beds there so he could sit with us when we ate our meals. Because of course Preston wasn't the kind of guy to eat on the couch like I usually did.

Smoky huffed out a sigh and settled after I gave him another few pats.

"I saw the contract."

"Masterson can do a lot better than that boilerplate nonsense."

"I'm an unknown, PMS."

"It doesn't matter. You have a year's worth of drawings—"

"They have to be tweaked with Smoky. They're not all done."

He blew on his tea in the llama mug I'd given him. I couldn't stop grinning especially since he was wearing the matching llama sleep pants I'd bought for him. Then again, the ripple of abs shifting as he leaned against the counter made just about anything appetizing.

"Hungry?"

His dark eyes went all heavy-lidded sexy times. "Always."

"I need sustenance first."

"Protein?"

I drilled a finger into those distractible abs. "Maybe later, ace."

He lifted his mug for a sip. "Suit yourself."

I went around him to the fridge and found the fixings for my version of Moons Over My Hammy. It was our favorite Sunday treat. Sometimes in the middle of the week too when PMS was feeling wild. Or sometimes a midnight snack after we needed a little fuel.

For such an uptight lawyer type, he had a very intense sex drive. I wasn't complaining. I'd never actually been with a man who could keep up with me.

I set the broiler to preheat then started cracking eggs. PMS came up behind me, his hands slipping back under my-slash-his shirt once more. Long, warm fingers trailed over my midriff and down into my shorts. "Smells delicious," he said against my ear.

"I haven't started cooking yet."

"Wasn't talking about the food." He nuzzled my ear, nipping the shell before kissing his way down my neck.

I shivered, then hissed out a breath as his very clever fingers found their way between my thighs.

"Are you really hungry?"

"Yes." I had to concentrate on how to use a whisk. The man was ridiculously dangerous for my mental acuity.

The ultra soft cotton of his pants slid across the backs of my thighs, and a decidedly happy Preston was rapidly firming against my backside.

Hello, sir.

Deft fingers teased along skin that was still sensitive from his beard action last night before he dipped two fingers inside and tucked his palm against my clit. His other hand cupped one of my breasts.

"I love when you wear my clothes, but I wouldn't mind if you left some of your own here."

My brain short-circuited as pleasure and new data tried to merge. I dropped my head back against his chest as he flicked his thumbnail over my nipple while pulsing inside of me with his other hand. "Clothes?"

"Mmm-hmm. I made space in my closet, if that was something you were interested in."

"Right." I rolled my hips into his touch. "Wait? Room for what?"

"Your clothes, Ryan. Merging with mine. You know, in a closet kind of way."

Another swipe from his thumb, then he gentled his touch until my skin was awash with the familiar buzzing of energy right before I started speaking gibberish ending in his name.

He lightly trailed his fingers away from my breast and down my belly. "Make sure you make a little extra. I worked up an appetite last night." He slid his fingers out of me, nipping my neck before he licked them. "I'll go grab a quick shower. Think about what I said."

I gripped the counter. "Okay, good."

Think about what? I was currently scrambled as the eggs in the bowl before me.

He walked away whistling as I relearned how words worked on the various packages in front of me.

I frowned down at the ham steak. Had he just asked me to leave clothes at his house?

I jumped as the oven beeped to let me know the broiler was ready. Well, that made two of us.

Damn him. He was always sneaky about nudging me into doing what he wanted. "Lawyers," I muttered and put the ham steaks in to broil.

I washed my hands and heated a pan for the eggs just as my phone rang.

Since no one actually called me, I hurried over to make sure it wasn't just a spam number. Surprised to see Luna's name on the screen, I picked up and put her on speaker.

"Hey, girl. What's up?"

"Ry? Are you home?"

I frowned and turned off the pan. It wasn't like Luna to sound panicked. "No. I'm at Preston's."

"Oh."

"Is everything okay?"

"No. Yes. Yes and no. Oh, goddess. One second."

The phone clattered onto something. "Lu? Luna, are you okay?"

I heard water running and a groan before she came back on. "Ugh.

I swear, I don't have anything in my body to throw up, and yet it still keeps coming."

"Oh, hell. Are you okay? Do you have the flu? I can come over and bring broth or stop at Georgia's shop for supplies." Luna's superpower was making her own elixirs from our friend's apothecary.

"No, I have something a little more permanent."

"I don't know what that means."

"Of the demon spawn variety. Freaking teacher. Imma kill him. He's never known the hex that I'm going to put on him. His ancestors for a thousand years will hate him."

"I don't understand."

"Ugh. One more second." The phone hit the table or the floor—I couldn't be sure which one.

I rushed over to the stove and pulled out the ham before I burned down Preston's very nice kitchen. I slammed the pan on the stovetop and waved away the smoke. "Shit."

I ran over to the window and opened it to get the smoke out. The cat, who was obsessed with the window, hopped up and started cleaning his leg.

"Ry?"

"Here," I yelled and ran back to the phone.

"What's going on?" Preston came running in, wearing just a pair of jeans. "Is that smoke?"

I waved to him and he saw the overcooked ham. He flicked on the overhead fan and gently pushed me to go sit down.

"What can I do?" I asked Luna.

"I need somewhere to crash for a bit."

"She can stay here," Preston said. "She's family."

My eyes instantly filled. I had to swallow down the lump. I quickly hit mute on my phone. "You don't even know what the problem is."

"It doesn't matter." He crossed to me and rubbed my arms. "Tell her to pack a bag, and I'll go get her."

"We will."

He kissed my forehead. *"We'll* go get her."

I unmuted my phone. "Lu? You can stay here with us." I pressed my lips together. Us was getting a lot easier to say. "Preston offered up one of his guest rooms. He's got a ton of them."

"With its own bathroom, maybe? I don't mean to be greedy, but the porcelain throne is my new best friend."

Spawn. Throne. The pieces slid into place. "Oh."

"Yeah. I'd handle it myself, but I just need a spot to think for a little bit."

"Anything you need. Always. You don't have to handle it alone." I grabbed Preston's hand. "We got you."

Luna sniffed. "I love you."

"I love you too, girl."

"I need to take a shower and clean up."

"Okay, we'll be there in a little bit. Take care of you."

"Take care of you," she parroted back in our usual goodbyes.

I held my phone against my thigh. "You didn't have to do that."

"When are you going to get it, Ryan? Your problems are my problems. It's just the way it is. And I love Luna just as much as you do."

I stared at the middle of his chest as everything blurred. "She sounds so scared. That's not like her."

"Whatever it is, we'll help her. I promise." He gathered me close.

I looped my arms around his waist, one hand still clutching my phone. I pressed my cheek to his chest. "No one has ever stood up for me before. And you've done it quite a few times now."

"And I'll keep doing it. One of these days, you'll trust that I always will."

I held onto him tighter. "I do believe you. I'm sorry it takes me longer to trust."

He pressed a kiss to the top of my head. "I know. Doesn't make me love you any less."

I shifted away enough to go up on my toes and kissed him gently.

He cupped my face and wiped away my tears with his thumbs. "Now let's go get our girl. I know just the room to put her in."

"One that's not too close to ours, right? I mean yours."

He grinned down at me. "No, opposite end of the house."

"Good." I twisted my fingers in his belt loops. "Maybe we could stop at my place first. I'll get some stuff."

He grabbed my hand and squeezed hard. "You got it."

I glanced over at our massacred breakfast. "And maybe we can pick up the real Moons Over My Hammy?"

His lips quirked. "You got it, Miss Moon."

EPILOGUE
FOR REAL THIS TIME

It was just past the lunchtime rush, and foot traffic was at its lightest on Kensington Square. Delivery trucks chugged their way down the side streets, and busy moms were doing last-minute errands before school let out.

I loved this area. Fall was in full swing, changing the park from lush green to leaves tipped in red and gold. Japanese maples with their glossy purple leaves stood sentry along the sidewalk to prove the town could have beauty and commerce side by side. The ever-changing storefronts dotted with crazy colors were jammed next to traditional mainstays like Connor's Drugstore with its sturdy air of responsibility and Jimmy's Pizza with its sharp, spicy sauce scenting the air.

Kensington Square was wild and messy, comforting and stable, city and town all at once. The perfect community. Now there was a new kid on the block, and I was heading his way.

The wind whipped my hair around. My boots clicked on the sidewalk, and a whiff of burning leaves mixed with the crisp cold air. A few people bustled around me, huddled into sweaters and hoodies as they hurried into shops. The sunny day had just enough bite to remind everyone of the brutal winter ahead. I preferred to embrace autumn's changeable whims.

I hugged my future against my chest, along with a little something for my resident sweet tooth.

Ahead, a small black and red sign stuck out from the freshly whitewashed brick building. We'd fought over the spray gun last weekend while painting the building he'd bought.

Bought, for goddess's sake.

Normal people rented space in Kensington Square, but not my guy. Nope. He'd bought the building and jumped headlong into renovating it. I hadn't even known he knew how to use a hammer.

Then again, was there really anything PMS couldn't do?

He got me to date him, didn't he?

Date. Ha.

There was no dating that man. I'd been assimilated. I should hate it. In fact, I should be running the other way. Instead, here I was, in front of that little red sign that read: *Preston M. Shaw, Esq. Family Law. est. 2021.*

He'd actually done it.

He had told me he was leaving his family's law firm, but I hadn't really believed he would actually take the leap. Even more, he'd gone after what made him happy. He'd made *me* believe in stepping out of my own box. One I hadn't even known I was trapped in.

A witch who believed in fate and the universe as the cornerstones of my practice never actually put those things to the test.

I'd used it as a cloak. A sparkly one disguised as giving myself to my clients and my community through podcasting and social media. Dishing out advice and words of wisdom about doing the work to heal when in reality, I'd used *them* as a buffer.

I could dish it out, but I really sucked at doing my own work. I focused on external gratification instead of looking within to figure out exactly what I needed.

I'd never truly believed in anything until Preston.

I turned toward the wide window framed in glossy black paint. PMS was pacing the length of his office while speaking on the phone.

He'd lost his suit jacket and rolled up his sleeves over his delicious forearms, leaving him in one of his vests that drove me crazy.

However, there was one distinct difference. He may have appeared a little harried, but excitement crackled around him. I didn't have to hear the conversation to know he was drilling point after point into some poor person's ear.

Fighting the good fight for a client he truly cared about.

He ripped at his tie, loosening the red silk as he hung up the phone but kept speaking as he flipped through papers on his desk. Speaker phone. Whomever was on the other end of that call was in serious trouble.

I was aware I drew a perverted pleasure from seeing PMS riled up. I was good with it.

Grinning, I ran up the three steps. I tapped on the tiny key and bells I'd hidden in the wreath on his steel-enforced red door for a little added protection and to dispel any negative energy hanging around. I'd also painted sigils into the doorways as well. Most people wouldn't notice them since I painted black on black, but family law came with a lot of high emotion and I liked to give him as much of a leg up as possible.

It also let other witches know this was a safe space. A few friends from Luna Falls had already sent people his way who were in need of a sharp lawyer.

I slipped inside to see Preston with his knuckles planted on his desk as he loomed over his phone. "I don't care if the judge is on the back nine talking to the President of the United freaking States. I want that child out of protective services and with his mother by tonight."

The voice on the other side of the line sighed. "I'll see what I can do."

A little shiver skated down my spine at the power in his voice. I unzipped my jacket, but had to adjust it to cover my chest so he didn't see the headlight action I had going on. Or the fact that I may have stolen one of his shirts again.

I couldn't help myself. I was getting addicted to the finery, and filching clothes from his closet was becoming a habit. I also didn't mind that he liked to steal them back—off my person.

He looked up from the desk, and his eyes had that far-off look like when he was in full-on lawyer mode. His brain was in overdrive as he tried to puzzle out whatever problem he was facing. But then his quick smile dispelled all that crackling energy.

Too bad.

"Miss Moon, did you come bearing gifts?" He came around his desk, those long legs eating up the hardwood floors so he could reach for my box of donuts.

"The romance is over—" I yelped as he dropped the box, as well as my other gift, on the U-shaped chairs we'd purchased from Kinleigh's Attic. Before I had a second to react, he hauled me up on my toes for a hot kiss. When my brain came back online, I settled my hands on his chest. "Well, hello."

"You are exactly what I needed this afternoon, Moonbeam." He grinned down at me.

The whole tie askew thing was going to be the death of me. I stroked my hand down the red silk. "Hard day, dear?"

His eyes went all smoldery. "I was worried I wouldn't have anything to do on my first day, but it's been non-stop calls. I'm trying to find an assistant, but they're all inadequate."

"All of them?"

He slipped his hands under my jacket. "None of them are you, Miss Moon." He frowned. "Wait, is that my shirt?"

"Maybe."

"You know the rule when you wear my clothes."

"I wear your clothes almost every morning," I reminded him.

"And I usually take them off then too." He pushed my jacket off and tossed it on the chair as well. Then he groaned when he got a better look. "Did you forget a few buttons?"

I glanced down at where his fingers were. "Will you look at that?" The charcoal shirt was open with a sheer black tank under it. And because it was so long, I'd added a thin black belt around my middle.

He dragged the backs of his knuckles over my very braless state. He parted the shirt with a groan. "My shirt has never looked so good."

My lips twitched. "You don't have your back office set up yet, sir."

He traced the pad of his finger around one tight nipple. "I don't care. Your breasts are a miracle."

I swallowed a laugh. "That's a helluva big window. I don't think that's exactly the way you want to drum up new business." I gave a throaty laugh as he picked me up to scrape his teeth over my lower lip.

I leaned in to deepen the contact. Coffee and caramel-flavored kisses were my favorite.

While he was still holding me, he strode to the door and locked it.

I gripped his shoulders and wrapped my legs around his waist. "PMS, it's the middle of the workday." I put a little extra breathy Marilyn in my voice.

"We have yet to christen this space, Miss Moon."

I should not still get chills when he used *Miss Moon*. "Um, we most certainly did. When we put up the drywall, when we painted, when we put together the bookcases." I punctuated each instance with a kiss on his very stubborn, very delicious mouth.

He gripped my ass and pressed me up against the little alcove-slash-vestibule. If one could call it a vestibule when the space was about three square feet. "It doesn't count until opening day."

"Is that right? I hadn't heard that rule." My words came out with a groan as he attacked my neck. Goddess, where did he learn how to do that?

He tipped his hips, and the very hard length of him tucked itself right where I liked him best. He caught my mouth in a long, slow kiss and rocked against me, then fumbled along the wall with one arm.

"What are you doing?" I asked against his lips.

He shimmied us to the left, and then a shade started coming down over the large picture window.

"Well, isn't that clever?"

"I'm a clever man."

"Leave a little sunshine. I like it on my skin."

"You're going to be the death of me." But he stopped the motorized

371

shade a few inches from the bottom before he gripped my ass. "I like this skirt thing. Doesn't really seem your style."

"Stole it from Luna. The waistband didn't fit, and she was trying to throw everything out in a tantrum. I knew she'd miss it though."

"Her loss is my gain."

The leopard print, ankle-length skirt swished behind me as he carried me back into the main part of the office. Eventually, this space would be the front office and Preston's space would be at the back, but we had more sheetrocking to do and he was impatient to open.

He set me on his desk, shoving the blotter, phone, and files aside to make room.

I went for his belt, and he did the same for mine. We were both laughing and tripping over each other's fingers until we finally both switched to undoing our own.

He pushed his shirt over my shoulders, then bent his head to my breast, sucking my nipple through the sheer fabric. I raked my nails along his scalp to cup the back of his head.

He slipped his hand under my skirt and hissed out a breath as he peered up at me. "No panties, Miss Moon?"

"Oops."

"*Oops?* You drove over here—"

"Walked."

His nostrils flared as his cock got even harder against my thigh. "You walked over here sans panties and bra?"

I bit the inside of my cheek and nodded.

He kicked his chair out of the way. It rolled over and banged into the bookcase full of his old law school books.

Damn, I loved when he got all growly and intense.

He crouched before me, bunching up the frothy fabric of the skirt an inch at a time. "This thing is practically see-through."

"Is that right?"

"Fuck." He dragged his nose along the inside of my thigh. "Were you thinking about this? Will I find you wet and ready for me?"

I swung my legs a little, gripping the edge of his desk. "Maybe."

"Part your legs, Miss Moon."

I transferred one hand between my thighs to stabilize myself. "Like that?"

"Don't block my view."

I slipped my hand closer to my pussy. "Should I tell you if I'm wet?"

His hands clamped on each of my knees, widening me even farther. "Yes."

I dragged my palm over my center and hissed out a breath. Wet didn't cover it. Even with just a few kisses, I was definitely ready to go.

Because his dark eyes were near-black with lust, I dragged my fingers through the slickness waiting there.

"Let me taste." His voice was hoarse.

I lifted my hand to his mouth and he sucked my two middle fingers, his tongue scraping every last bit of me away.

I let out a shaky breath and drew my wet fingers out of his mouth to cup my breast. I leaned back a bit and hooked one knee over his shoulder. "More?"

"Everything." He pulled me closer, stretching me so he could get to every part of me. I arched my back and cried out his name as he twirled that clever tongue around my clit before closing his mouth around me to invade.

Fingers, tongue, breath—he used every tool he had but one.

By the time he was done with me, I'd slumped onto my back and the heels of my boots had taken a chunk out of his desk. I was a quivering shell of my former self. Breathing was optional, but a very self-satisfied male was grinning from between my legs.

I draped my arm over my face so I didn't kick him. As usual, he'd flipped the script. I'd come here ready to seduce, yet I was the one trying to remember how to use words. "Smug bastard."

He stood and peeled open his dress pants. "Maybe."

Yeah, he'd earned his smug bastard status. Then I was getting hauled up to a seated position.

"This will no longer be my assistant's desk—unless you're the assistant."

"You deliberately tried to muddle my brain before you asked that question again." Not that it was in the form of a question, damn him. He'd been trying to get me to work for him since he'd inked the papers on the building.

I *was* going to work for him, but he didn't need to know that part yet.

He nudged my legs open again and lifted my skirt puddled between us. I released a slow breath as he stroked the head of his cock along my wildly sensitive center. "I would never do such a thing."

Then he was sliding forward, filling me like no one else ever could.

Ever would again.

I lifted my legs so I could bring him in closer, then tightened around him inside and out. He groaned against my neck. His fingers dug into my hips with each pulsing mini-stroke. I wound my arms around his shoulders, locking us tight.

His head rose and our gazes crashed together. Lust and that all-consuming love filled his endlessly fascinating eyes. Believing in that love still felt like stepping off a cliff, but he made me want to fly.

Slow, leisurely strokes built until his jaw went to granite with tension.

I knew he was close.

Knew his body almost better than my own. I wanted to watch him go over. I needed to.

I tipped my hips and nearly made my own eyeballs roll back into my head. There was something to be said for a man who was very proportional. Especially when it benefited me so much.

"Don't make me go alone."

"Never alone. Not ever again."

His eyes went wide just before I wrapped around him—my legs, my arms, and I sealed my mouth over his. I swallowed his groan, accepted that he was mine, and offered him the same.

He trembled in my embrace, his release so complete that we both melted off the desk on to the floor.

I giggled as all six-feet-four of him took up the entire Aubusson rug. He was splayed out on his back much as I had been on his desk a few minutes ago. This time, I was laying over half of him.

I'd lost my borrowed shirt somewhere, but PMS still wore his. I dragged my nail down his chest and snickered at the missing button on his vest. "Not sure when that happened."

He lifted his head to look down at himself. "Worth it." His large hand covered mine.

I laid my cheek against his chest. His racing heart slowly synced up with mine until we were breathing together. With his other hand, he played with my tangled hair.

"Ry—"

"I love you, Preston."

"What?" His head came up so fast, he rapped it on the underside of his desk. "Ow!"

I laughed. "Are you okay?"

He rolled us until we were face to face, both of our heads under the desk. Sunlight slashed across the floor, gilding part of his disheveled dark hair and highlighting half his face. "Say that again."

I brought my hand up to cup his jaw. "I love you."

He covered my hand. "You're not just saying it because I gave you four orgasms, right?"

"Okay, pal. It was more like two."

"Definitely three."

I rolled my eyes. "I've never said the words in post-coital bliss." I looked down at his mouth. "Never said them to any man, actually."

He nudged up my chin. "No one?"

I blinked away the sting of tears. "No one mattered enough to give the words to. Not until you."

He tried to sit up and whacked his head again. "Fuck." He inched back, dragging me with him.

"Hey, watch the rug burn, PMS."

"Sorry. I just can't have this conversation under my damn desk." He fixed his pants and dragged me into his lap, straddling him. "Let's try this again."

"I'm not going to offer up a soliloquy."

"I wouldn't expect one. But you've truly never said it to anyone?"

"Well, my mother and few select friends of course."

"I am not select friends."

The acid in his tone made me laugh. "That's for sure." At his narrow-eyed growl, I could do nothing else but frame his face with my hands. "You gave me time and I appreciate it. You gave yourself freely. No games, no strings, and no power plays. Okay, maybe a little strong-arming in getting me to do what you want sometimes, but I don't mind that part so much."

His eyes were rimmed with red, but he didn't say a word. Sometimes he was smart enough to know that it was my turn to talk.

"Twice today, I got news, and all I wanted to do was tell you. The first thought I had was, *PMS will absolutely go crazy when I tell him this.*"

"Tell me what?"

"It's not important."

He sighed.

"I mean it is, and I'll get to that. But the important part is that all I wanted to do was share my news with you. I've been on my own for so long. The only person who ever truly supported me was—"

"You."

"Yes. Luna and April have always been my girls. And I'd never discount that, but it's different. I always thought it made me weak to need someone. But you made me see that it's more powerful to have a connection like ours." I stroked my thumbs over his cheeks. "I believe in us. Believe this is exactly where I'm supposed to be forever. With you, wherever we are."

His arms tightened around me. "You can't take back forever, Moonbeam. You realize that?"

I laughed and didn't care that a few tears tumbled down my face. Relief unfurled inside my chest. I'd trapped those words inside the cage of my heart for so long. "Yes. I'm okay with that."

"I love you so goddamn much." He kissed me until we were both breathless and wincing from our position on the floor.

Finally, I slid off his lap and stretched my legs.

"Now about that news."

I laughed. "Hang on, let me get it."

"I'd get up, but I think you may have put me in traction. For real this time." He twisted his back before rolling his shoulders.

I crawled over to the chair where he'd tossed my gifts.

"You have the finest assets in this building, Miss Moon."

I glanced back to find him on his side, with his head propped on his hand. He waggled his eyebrows at me. Playful Preston was taking some getting used to, but I liked it. I grabbed the box of bear claws and honey glazed donuts as well as my other bit of news.

"I'm enjoying the show. Please keep crawling this way."

"Pig."

"Indeed."

Then I realized that I was only wearing my sheer tank top and showing all my wares. I shrugged and offered up the box.

He flipped it open and took out one of the honey glazed.

I selected a bear claw and tapped it against his. "Cheers."

"So, what kind of news did you have?"

I took a big bite of my confection. I'd forgotten to eat today. I'd been in meetings with Penn Masterson and his team for most of the day. "Penn's lawyer sent back the contract and accepted your revisions."

"Excellent." He reached up one long arm to his desk drawer and pulled out a small package of wipes. He washed his hands and offered me one. "I knew he was lowballing you."

I took one and cleaned up. "Well, after the site went down today from Roz and Sylvia's debut, I think he realized that."

"That's wonderful." He scooted over to me. "Can we get up and sit in a chair like civilized people?"

"You're the one who dragged me to the floor, ace."

He rolled to his knees with a groan. "I'm glad I splurged for the nice rug, but I'm getting too old for this business." He held out his hand to help me up. "What do you have there?"

I held the frame against my chest. "A little something to say thank you."

He smoothed my hair over my shoulder. "You don't have to thank me."

I looked down at the professionally matted comic strip. "This one won't be out for probably a year—maybe never." I brushed my fingertip over the new addition. "When I came up with the idea for Roz and Sylvia, I thought I knew exactly what the comic would be. Then you came along." I traced the little gray cat's face in the first box of the strip of illustrations.

His small face was pressed to the window, rain dripping from his torn ear. The little white fox, Sylvia, had the hair on her back up, her face in a snarl. In the next box, her human Roz was opening the window for the three-legged cat, letting it inside their home.

In the third box, the two animals were face to face, with the gray cat bumping his head under Sylvia's chin, offering affection. He wore a tiny red collar with a bell. Sylvia was giving him some serious side-eye.

In the final box, the cat and fox were curled together in a soft bed, their bodies making the yin and yang symbol.

"At the time, I was fighting against Roz and Sylvia getting another roommate. I dreamed of this nebulous little animal in the window. I resisted it, but it kept on coming back."

He tucked a lock of hair behind my ear. "Stubborn...cat."

I pressed my lips together against a smile. "Now I know it was my subconscious trying to let you in. Dreams are weird, especially for a witch. But then when you found Smoky—"

"*We* found him." His voice was soft as he covered my hands on the frame.

I huffed out a half laugh. "We found Smoky. And I knew something a little bigger was happening. I really didn't want to face it. But love has never been easy for me. Even though the universe kept giving me nudges your way."

"For that, I'm forever thankful."

"I know you don't believe in the things I do."

He raised my chin with his finger until our eyes met. "We ultimately make our own choices, but I would never discount a higher power showing me the path to you."

"I would be fine without you." He stiffened and I placed my hand on his chest. "Just let me finish. I would be fine without you. And my comic would have been fine without Smoky."

His brows furrowed, but he held his tongue though I knew it was killing him.

"But I'm so much better with you." I dashed away a tear. "My work is richer because of that feisty cat. I'm grateful for you, Preston. And loving you just makes everything better. I'm sorry it took me so long to say it."

"We've been on fast forward since we met. Waiting for you to catch up was worth it." He lowered his mouth to mine. "Every minute," he said against my lips. "I'd wait as long as you needed."

He was so sure. No doubt at all.

It made it easier for me to believe him. To believe the echo of the love he offered and realize it also lived in me—and that it was growing by the day.

I set the frame on his desk and kissed him back. "Oh, and about that assistant position? It's permanently filled."

We appreciate our readers so much!
If you loved the book please let your friends know. If you're extra awesome, we'd love a review on your favorite book site.

WANT TO KEEP UP TO DATE WITH US?

Please visit our website, tarynquinn.com, for details!

So...April was MIA. Wonder what kind of trouble she got into on vacation?

But wait! What about Luna? We got you covered there too.

Turn the page for a special sneak peek of MY BOSS'S SECRET & WRONG BED BABY now!

MY BOSS'S SECRET
KENSINGTON SQUARE BOOK #2

APRIL

Fiji

"You know what you need, bunny?"

Ignoring my grandmother and her so-called helpful advice, I tugged at the bodice of my perfectly cute halter dress. At least it had been before we went on vacation. Now the flared sixties' style looked blah. Boring. I'd gone for sedate blue instead of island appropriate. But I didn't do tropical flowers. Or plunging necklines. Or anything too revealing—

"You need a good, hard bounce."

"I have a decent mattress," I said distantly, reaching behind myself to temporarily tighten the bust area.

I wasn't one to be showy, especially when it came to my overly large breasts, but I'd gone a size too big. With my runner's body, it wasn't logical to have breasts one pint of Ben and Jerry's away from tipping into Ds.

Still, baggy fabric didn't help hide anything, just made me look saggier than I was. Maybe I needed a new bra. I'd gotten the one I was wearing on sale forever ago.

"April Anne Finley, look at me." My petite grandmother stepped in front of me and leaned up to grab my shoulders. She was only almost a foot shorter I am. "You're on vacation. Do you know what people do on vacation?"

I frowned down into her sparkling denim blue eyes. "Party like a rockstar?"

Something I had no clue how to do. I even had trouble partying like an office assistant, who one day might be a paralegal if I finally signed up for that program.

She laughed. "You could do that too, but I meant have a fling."

"Like sex?"

"Don't look so shocked," she chided, patting my cheek the same way she'd done when I was ten and baffled by some boy kicking my chair at school. "You don't have to sign on the dotted line to have some fun, baby girl. You desperately need more fun in your life."

"But I'm on vacation with you, aren't I?"

"Under duress, and don't tell me you wouldn't have been relieved if that codger boss of yours had pulled rank and said you couldn't go."

"Codger?" I had to snort. "Preston may be uptight sometimes, but he's 34. Far from a codger."

And I'd also been told by Colleen in computer support on the floor below us that he was hot, which I supposed I could see objectively. If I closed one eye and squinted and tried to forget he signed my checks with a flourish every week.

"In any case, you know you didn't really want to be forced to have fun on this trip."

"Well, no one mentioned anything about fun." My grandmother laughed and the sound made me grin despite myself.

Other than my two best friends in the universe, Ryan and Luna, no one made me smile more than my grandmother. When I'd been knee high to a grasshopper, as she used to call me, she had been the only person capable of drawing me out of my crusty shell.

I'd learned far too early that people couldn't be trusted, and letting down your guard brought heartbreak. Until she'd brought pure sunshine into my life.

I'd been trying to repay her ever since.

"Okay, okay. Fine. I'm game for some fun. What do you have in mind?" I waggled a finger in her face. "No bouncing."

"Maybe not for you, but I have a date."

"A date?" I tried not to sound let down.

It wasn't as if I'd needed Grams to accompany me every minute. Our vacation was half over already, and we separated every afternoon after lunch to explore and to enjoy the hotel's amenities.

But if I had to have unplanned fun, surely she wasn't going to abandon me in my time of need?

Note to self: if Preston is a codger, so are you, toots.

"Yes. Surely you remember what those are like? If not, we have to remedy that."

"Never mind me. What about this date of yours?"

"He's tall, dark, and dreamy." With a wink, she skirted around the needlessly enormous bed in my room to retrieve her big white bag from the nightstand. She took out a compact and dusted her nose. "His name is Pedro." Her nose wrinkled as she dusted her chin. "Or was it Pablo?"

Only my grandmother. Or maybe Luna. Right now, Grams was exhibiting some post-heartbreak, decidedly Luna-ish free-flowing sexual energy.

And...*ick.* I mean, good for her, but for my mental picture reel? Definitely *ick.*

What did it say about me that my sixty-nine-year-old grandmother could get some on vacation when I hadn't even rated a second look from any of the many hot men we'd seen on the island?

Unleash the Kraken in your bra, and you won't have to wait long.

My inner voice was a brazen hussy. She was also horny as hell.

I wasn't keeping track, but it had been a long time since I'd been anything remotely close to naked with a man. Any day now, I expected dust to fly out of my hoohaa. The esthetician who'd given me my Brazilian wax before vacation—*thanks, Luna, for inviting me to such torment*—had been the only one to see my lady garden since all my flowers had been replaced with dandelions.

"Is Pedro or Pablo a responsible man?"

Even before my grandmother coughed out a laugh, I winced. Yeah, it was not my place to be asking such questions. It would probably be more enjoyable for my grandmother if he wasn't.

"You're sure he's not a serial killer? On Asher Wainwright's podcast, he profiled a murderer who preyed on vulnerable seniors on vacation who—"

"Since you've been abstinent since the dawn of time and don't like 'unplanned fun', I will allow you to get away with lumping me in with vulnerable seniors. But just once." She jabbed a finger in the air in my direction. "Try it again and I'll salt your granny panties."

I giggled, and the sound was as foreign to me as it was to Grams from her startled expression.

"You need to laugh more, bunny. It's such a lovely sound."

"I laugh."

"You do, but not enough." Her voice was gentle as she dumped her compact back in her bag and slung it over her shoulder. "Go have something exotic for dinner. And when you come back, I'll have a surprise here for you."

"You know I don't like surprises."

"Exactly why you need more of them." Hurrying over to me, she arched up to kiss both of my cheeks then headed for the door. "Don't take it all too seriously. Just remember: any guy you meet here, you'll never see again. So, feel free to be anyone you want."

"But I'm me."

"Sure. But you can try a new you on for size. Just for fun. No pressure." She grinned and shut the door behind her.

Her words echoed in the silence of my spacious room as I cast another disparaging look at my reflection in the mirror.

Regardless of this whole fun thing, I definitely needed to ditch this dress.

I went down to dinner at the hotel's dining room, one of our favorites spots to eat. I decided to try the lovo, a traditional Fijian meal typically for special occasions. Hot coals were placed in a pit in the ground to cook the meats and fish, which were bundled in banana leaves. The process took a few hours, so I enjoyed people watching and listening to the local guitar group.

Although some neurotic part of me worried about food safety, everything was delicious. And at the end, one of the men who'd helped to prepare my meal placed a plumeria in my tightly bound braid, and I found myself touching it over and over as I meandered back to my room.

He was a kindly older gentleman, but imagine if he wasn't? If he was my lover and he'd put a flower in my hair...

Dammit, Grams, stop giving me ideas.

I wasn't used to thinking fancifully and I didn't like it one bit.

Nor did I like stopping at the end of my bed to find a backless short siren-red dress waiting for me.

Backless. Siren red. A neckline that dipped way low in front.

Way, way low.

I held it against me in front of the mirror then stepped out of my halter dress to swap it for this one. Technically, this was a halter too, but it was much different.

I couldn't wear a bra. And when the silky, snug fabric wrapped over my curves and my nipples beaded, I didn't want to.

The vision in the mirror could *not* be me.

I undid my braid and shook out the wild waves over my shoulders. The dress swished against my thighs and tiny crystals glittered along the sides of the neckline, drawing the eye down my body.

The woman in the mirror wasn't too curvy up top and too angular in other spots. Everything just seemed to fit together perfectly, as if this dress had been made with my body in mind. All I needed was shimmering shoes to complete the transition into Cinderella.

I spun around a few times to feel the airy material float around my thighs. Grinning, I hurriedly sent my Grams a note.

Thank you! It's so perfect. You knew just what I wanted, deep down. You always do.

Immediately, a text zinged back at me. It was just a bunch of laughing emojis. The next one at least was actual words.

Safety first! I figured rainbow was best. You know, so you can go with the mood.

That was my Grams, always speaking in complete sentences in messages. I was no better. But that wasn't my main concern right now.

What do you mean rainbow? It's red. Solid red.

She sent back more laughing emojis interspersed with a few devils.

Oh, is that the vibe for tonight? Hmm, I didn't think of one of those. I assume those are a personal choice in any case. Have fun, bunny! Gotta go. Don't stay out too late.

Then a minute later...

Actually, yes, stay out very, very late. Like tomorrow.

Many hearts followed.

I glanced at my bed. A bright flash of color beneath my pillow caught my eye. I rushed over to pick up the item, which turned out to be a strip of condoms.

A very long, very colorful strip of prophylactics.

I dropped the strip as if it had singed my hand and pressed my palms to my burning cheeks. Oh my God, Grams had bought me condoms.

A *lot* of them.

A laugh spilled out of me, and I doubled over for a full minute until I got ahold of myself. Then I gazed down at my already beloved dress and smoothed my hands down my hips. Maybe she was just messing with me.

She had to be, right? Where else could this have come from?

I hadn't made any friends on the island. Not yet. Probably not ever, because I tended to stick to corners and shadows, always observing. Always wishing I could be brave and flirty like my two best friends until I reminded myself that hey, at least I was comfortable. Maybe I wasn't taking big chances, but I wasn't risking too much either.

My life was safe. Predictable. *Boring.*

Though it wasn't as if Ryan or Lu had found their forever guys yet either. Not that they were looking. I'd been the one everyone figured was born to settle down, and I almost had—until I'd made a mistake and lost everything.

But that didn't explain where this dress had come from.

Maybe it had been delivered to the wrong room. My heart sank. God, would I have to give it back? That was the right thing to do. I was honorable. Always. Except for that one time.

Apologies didn't make a difference when you screwed up the best thing you'd ever had.

The only *real* thing.

I sucked in a deep breath and forced myself to go to the room phone on the nightstand. I called down to the desk and asked the question I profoundly did not want to.

"Was something sent by mistake to my room?"

A pause. "Mistake? No, ma'am. The gentleman was very insistent."

"What gentleman?" I gripped my throat and stared at the door I'd closed and locked behind me as always. "What was his name?"

"He didn't give his name. But he said it was to be delivered to the lovely blond in 42. That is you, is it not?" He seemed to hesitate. "April Finley?"

"Yes, but there must be some mixup. I don't know any man. There's no one." For an illogical reason, tears prickled behind my eyes.

He started to reply but a swift knock on the door startled me. Quickly, I thanked him and hung up.

I rushed to the door and then stopped with my hand on the knob.

What if I was being stalked by a serial killer with exceptionally excellent taste and a healthy bottom line?

What if I was the vulnerable one being preyed on now?

Another knock sounded. "I know you're in there. Open up."

I clutched my throat again. He'd been watching me. Following me. Buying me sexy dresses.

Maybe he wanted to debauch me. It wouldn't be hard. Missionary sex seemed like the ultimate indulgence right now.

Forget sampling my watermelon sugar.

The door had a peephole, so I used it. And gasped. Loudly.

Of course I had to meet a serial killer who was stunningly handsome. Even if his head was distorted by the optical glass in the peephole.

His rough chuckle went well with his bedroom voice. I hadn't known that was a thing until just now. "I saw you go in. Now I hear you. Do I pass inspection?"

I shut my eyes and dropped my forehead to the door. "Who are you, mystery dress man?"

"Names don't matter. I just want to see you in that dress." Somehow his voice dipped even lower. "Did you try it on yet?"

This conversation was bizarre. He was obviously a stalker and potentially dangerous to boot.

Did I say any of that? No, of course not. Instead, I asked something totally not relevant.

"How did you know my size?"

"So, it fit." The pleasure in his tone did something entirely not right to my dormant nerve endings. Specifically, the ones below my waist.

I cleared my throat. "It fit."

"You're about the same size as my baby sister, so I guessed. She's tall and lean like you. At least most of you is."

My face heated again. He'd checked me out then. Even in my too-big halter dress. But he'd bought an extremely revealing dress for me, so he had to have paid attention to my...dimensions.

Dear God, what was I supposed to do now?

"Just let me in, okay? I promise I'm not dangerous."

He had a baby sister that he spoke of with fondness. Surely that indicated he wasn't psychopathic. "Isn't that what every dangerous man has said since the beginning of time?"

"I'm persistent but I'm not a threat. I'm a man of the law, in fact."

My eyebrows reached for my hairline. "Complete with your dime store badge?"

"Not that kind." He laughed again. "I saw you two days ago. You were browsing in one of the shops, and you tried on this frumpy big hat."

I recalled it immediately. "It was not frumpy. I thought it was chic."

"Whatever. But you kept hemming and hawing, touching everything, buying nothing. So tactile. I wondered if all textures fascinated you, or just the ones you adorn your body with."

I was pretty sure that was sketchy sex talk. My nether regions offered a weak pulse of confirmation. "Watching people who aren't unaware is dubious behavior."

"If I'd approached you, you would have run. I saw you do it several times when men glanced your way."

"No one looked at me." I hated that my chin trembled. "No one ever does."

"Oh, beauty, you're so wrong."

Going from instinct, I opened the door. And nearly gasped again.

He was gorgeous. Tall and tanned with tousled golden-brown hair pushed back by his sunglasses and expressive eyes of indeterminate color. They might've even been green.

He was dressed casually in typical island wear—thin linen white pants, floral Hawaiian-style shirt opened just enough to show a smattering of dark chest hair, and sandals. The relaxed attire somehow showed off his broad shoulders and muscular chest even more.

"You're stunning." His voice was gravelly sex as he stepped forward to touch one of my loosened curls.

And I let him. I didn't move. Didn't say one damn thing.

I never took risks anymore. But I was risking this because I couldn't remember when I'd ever needed anything this much.

Then his gaze dropped to my hand and the long strip of brightly colored condoms I still clutched.

The corner of his sinful mouth tipped upward. "If you're game, so am I."

MY BOSS'S SECRET, NOW AVAILABLE!
See our tarynquinn.com for details!

Turn the page for a sneak peek of Luna's book, WRONG BED BABY!
NOW AVAILABLE!

WRONG BED BABY

MOVING SUCKED.

Moving because your bachelor pad for half a decade was being torn down by Gavin Forrester, the hotshot big time developer in town who wanted to build more condos, *really* sucked.

But getting a hefty payment to help compensate for the inconvenience of moving helped ease the pain. Slightly.

"You gonna get a move on or just keep staring into the back of this SUV like it holds the answers to good sex?"

I didn't even glance at my best friend Lucky. I knew he'd be looming over the back of my vehicle to show off his biceps to maximum advantage, just in case any ladies happened to wander by.

"I know the answer to that," I muttered. "And it involves me and a glass of merlot."

"That's how you warm yourself up? You sound like a chick, but hey, do what works for you, man."

I had to laugh. "Shut the hell up, Roberts, and grab the other end of this hutch."

He elbowed me out of the way. "You might prefer group activities, but I can handle this one on my own, son." He hefted up the handcrafted oak piece built by my older brother August with a grunt.

The sound made me grin as I stepped back and waved him toward the propped open door to my apartment building. "By all means. I'll just stand here and cool off with a refreshing beverage." I popped open the cooler and grabbed a can of lemonade before flipping open the top. "Ahh. Tastes good," I said as I took an exaggerated swallow.

In a truly spectacular feat, Lucky managed to flip me off before hauling the hutch toward the open door.

Music suddenly spilled out, loud and unrepentant. It wasn't something you'd hear on the local station either. This was a sinuous, exotic beat, the kind that brought to mind warm breezes, a gorgeous sunset, and an even more gorgeous woman belly-dancing with a colorful snake wrapped around her upper torso.

I took another drink. Or maybe that was just me.

Lucky didn't seem to pay it any mind as he barreled through the doorway and headed up the stairs with his latest bulky item of furniture.

I turned toward the back of the SUV to take stock of what was left. In short, it was a lot.

This wasn't the first trip I'd made over here, but we were in early innings. My new apartment was still mostly a barren wasteland. I'd skipped hiring a moving company, considering I hadn't had far to go and could call on a number of fit dudes like myself to help out.

Oddly enough, most of them had become suddenly unreachable despite knowing for weeks the days I'd planned to move. August would be over later after work, but I couldn't count on any of the rest of the slugs I knew. As if wives and children and gainful employment could keep them *that* busy.

Whatever.

Lucky, however, used any attempt to show off and looked at carrying heavy furniture as the best opportunity going. So far, his plan had not borne much fruit, although a couple of the gooey-eyed young baristas at Macy's coffee shop had come out a few times to offer us refreshments. Lucky hadn't been too keen on any of them, since most of those girls were barely legal.

He had some standards. Not a lot, mind you, but some.

He jogged up beside me as I was dragging out the small bookcase that doubled as a nightstand in my bedroom. "Dude, there's some kind of chick party in there, and I think they're stripping."

I snorted and set my bookcase on the pavement. "I think heat stroke has finally warped your brain." I swiped my forearm over my sweaty forehead and grabbed for my already sweating can of lemonade. "It has to be ninety out here."

"Ninety-five," he informed me, flashing me his smart watch. "Not that you've been doing much to get sweaty, you lazy fuck."

I shrugged. "Conserving energy for when the help is gone is a valid strategy. We both know you'll only stick around as long as there's a chance you'll get laid."

He waggled his brows at me. "I didn't know that was on the table."

"Not in your fondest dreams, pal. I don't care if you unload every piece of furniture by yourself and decorate too."

"I don't fucking decorate. That's what sisters and girlfriends are for. You've got one."

"A sister? Definitely. Not that she has enough time for that shit. She's not even around right now, remember?"

My baby sister Ivy was in LA with her husband and their baby daughter Rhiannon for a week, which had been a tactical error on Ivy's part since we were smack dab in the middle of a heat wave. Her ice cream truck Rolling Cones would've made a killing if she'd been open for longer than the banker's hours she kept the truck operating on while she was away. She had a good crew to help her, but she preferred shorter shifts when she wasn't around to manage things. If she'd been able to stay open until 10 pm on these sweltering nights as she usually did, she probably could've funded Rhi's college education.

Not that her fancy rich husband needed any help with that.

I wasn't bitter, toiling away on a teacher's salary. Mostly because I loved my kids. I enjoyed their curiosity and enthusiasm and sometimes even their mischief-making. Aug claimed my affinity for children came from the fact that I hadn't matured past twelve myself, but I would've said at least thirteen. Maybe fourteen on a good week.

In any case, I was happy with my lot. I wouldn't have minded a bit more green to grease the wheels, but then again, who would?

Lucky tied back his long hair, swatting away the sweaty pieces sticking to his neck. "Yeah, Ivy's getting used to that high-rolling life. Next thing you know, she'll move out there. Probably get a pad on the beach. That'd be something to have a place to crash at on the west coast, huh?"

I didn't say anything. My family was close. Sure, we had our occasional spats like any other. Now and then, we didn't speak for days at a time. Life got busy.

But I didn't want to lose my sister across the damn country. I definitely didn't want to only see my niece on FaceTime and for occasional vacations. I was her favorite uncle. The fun one who'd hired a clown for her last birthday—Lucky, of course—and helped her whip up and down the sidewalk on her tricycle. She'd had a small accident and busted open her lip on account of the raised lip on the sidewalk, but she'd healed fine, right? And she had a hell of a story for the kids at playgroup. You know, for when she could talk coherently.

She was a sentient toddler now, so I was enjoying my little RhiRhi more with each passing month. But infants were another story. My other niece, Vivian, was a bit younger, so we were still working on communication beyond *goo-goo gaa-gaa.*

I wasn't one for babies. Nope, never. Not my bag. I preferred kids once they got past the drooling and excessive pooping stages.

Lucky straightened and grabbed a soda for himself, popping the top. "Well, if Ivy can't help, then you gotta get your mom involved. They live for that stuff."

"Are you kidding me? She's on like fourteen town committees. She barely has time to sleep, when you factor in her work at the gallery. Besides, who says I need a damn decorator? I didn't at my old place."

He laughed and took a long drink. "Yeah, and it looked great. *Not.* Most of the rooms didn't even look lived in. You can't do that in a swank place like this, man. Forrester's taken all these apartments up a notch." He let out a belch. "When you invite over that sexy chick who strips for tuition, you don't want to make her sit on the floor. Then again, if you do, I have a better chance." He nudged my shoulder. "I still owe you one for the Sanders' sisters."

He'd imparted so much in that barrage of information, I didn't even know what to unpack first. "Uh, the Sanders' sisters were almost a year ago."

"Hell no. They were this spring." He frowned and drank more. "Weren't they?"

"Try last fall. And I didn't hook up with both, just Judy. You just didn't like that they both weren't immediately bowled over by your baby greens."

"Says you. What happened with you guys?"

I shrugged. "We went out a few times. We're still friends. Just no spark."

"But she's smokin'. Doesn't that count for something?"

I shrugged again and finished off my lemonade, feeling like a class A chump. How could I tell him I was developing an aversion to casual dating? Not because I wanted something serious. Hell no.

Lucky and I were Crescent Cove's original bachelors. When all the single men around us tumbled like timber for the whole marriage and babies scene, we stood strong. We didn't want any of that. Pleasures of the flesh were enough for us, thank you.

No commitment. No stress.

No way, not in baby central anymore. How could you possibly enjoy a no-strings hookup in a place like the Cove? We'd become known across the northeast for ease in procreation. The damn town bird might as well have been the stork.

I gestured to the remaining items left in the back of my SUV. We'd packed that sucker like a Tetris game, taking advantage of every millimeter of space. "You going to help me with this stuff or what?"

"*Help?* I've been carrying most of it while you stand around out here sipping lemonade like a southern belle." To show off—as usual— he picked up my bookcase under one arm and grabbed another small shelving unit with his other hand. Then he winked at me before heading inside.

Since I knew quite well his posturing probably had to do with the woman he'd mentioned probably innocently dancing in her own apartment, I grabbed a couple of small end tables and followed him toward the sexy music.

After we went upstairs, I stepped around him to open the door to the hallway before we continued on toward my apartment. The music only grew louder as we walked.

Apartments branched off in two directions. There were only a few on each floor, and for now, there were three levels. There was still room for more on the very top floor, but Forrester was taking his time there, gauging interest, before he decided to make it one big place or split it up like the other ones. On the roof, there was a communal gathering space for all the tenants' use.

This property right across from the lake was in a prime location, what with Macy's Brewed Awakening on the bottom floor and the Cove's real estate market booming. I'm sure Forrester liked being the hottest ticket in town.

"Holy shit," I mumbled as I walked into the back of Lucky, who had stopped dead outside my door.

And who could blame him, because the door across the hall was cracked open, just enough to reveal a scantily clad blond winding around a pole that had been drilled into her floor. Or attached there somehow, well enough to support the gyrations she was doing around it.

To it.

"Told you," Lucky said smugly, panting slightly from what he held. He appeared to be glued in place and had not set it down yet.

"Does she realize the door is open?"

I was fervently glad that it was, even if I felt a bit like a pervert watching her. Her eyes were closed as she moved to the music, so she didn't know we were out here, but she *was* dressed—albeit in a minuscule way.

When Lucky didn't reply, I tried again. "Since the door is open, maybe she wants us to see?" It was a mostly hopeful question.

My conscience was screaming now. I had a sister and a niece and of course a mom. I taught kids. Spying on her wasn't kosher.

Unless she had some exhibitionistic tendencies and didn't mind if we peeped on her. At least she wasn't naked.

I would just keep telling myself that.

"I cracked the door open a little, wanting to see where the music was coming from," Lucky admitted, voice low. "She hadn't latched it though. I'm not *that* bad."

"Asshole." I jabbed the pointed corner of one of my end tables into his back.

He grunted and dropped the bookcase on his toe. His unholy bellow of pain made the gorgeous blond stop dancing, just as I set down my furniture and moved toward her door to firmly pull it shut.

Well, that had been my intention anyway. I didn't make it all the way to closing the door, because her face fucking slayed me.

I could admit I hadn't noticed it before, as occupied as I'd been with her fluid movements. She was seriously coordinated. Flexible. Hot as fuck. But then she just had to have a stunning face to match, with fiery eyes—color undetermined from this distance—and full lips and enough cleavage to kill a man who'd been abstinent for, oh, close to eight months now.

The last woman I'd asked out had ended up engaged to the sheriff within weeks. So, that kind of gave a reading on the state of my love life.

"What in the goddess are you doing?" she demanded, lowering the music and marching to the door at a rate of speed sufficient to make all the dangling threads from her top flutter over her abs.

She had a twinkling jewel in her navel. I was reasonably sure the beam of light from it had rendered me cross-eyed. Possibly altered some of my bodily functions as well.

That was as good an excuse as any for my current...pants predicament.

"Eyes up here, pal." She tapped her forehead. "Were you breaking in?"

"Hardly. The door was open. I was shutting it for you. Never know who's around."

"Wind did it," Lucky muttered from behind me.

I glanced back to see him leaning against the wall, gripping his foot. His boot was lying sideways on the floor.

I probably should've felt guilty, but he knew better than to pull stunts like that. Nudging a door open wasn't cool. She didn't know us. The last thing we wanted to do was scare her or make her feel uncomfortable. And I was her new neighbor, for fuck's sake. If he made things weird between us, *I'd* be the one dealing with the fallout.

"Look, we apologize." I cleared my throat. "The music lured Lucky to your apartment, and the door wasn't latched, so he made an ill-advised decision to open it. *We* apologize," I repeated, glancing back at my best friend, who nodded with a sigh.

"Sorry, ma'am."

"Ma'am?" She frowned and crossed her arms. "Just how old do you think I am?"

"Barely legal?"

She arched a brow at my quip. "Since I suspect that's your attempt at flattery, I will say you're both wrong. I'm not old enough to be called ma'am, though who is? And I'm also not young enough to remember having a fake ID to get drinks. Although I rarely imbibe to excess." She flushed. "Well, unless bestie service calls."

"How do I call you through that bestie service?" Lucky pulled on his boot and flashed her a winsome smile. "Truly, you won't meet a friendlier guy in all of the Cove."

"She's new in town. Don't scare her off already. At least I assume." I gave her a smile of my own. One far less toothy than Lucky's.

"I'm fairly new to actually living in town, but I've worked here since last year." She squinted at me. "Are you sure we haven't met before?"

"Unless I was drugged unconscious, there is literally no way I could forget meeting you." It was probably the most sincere thing I'd ever said, but Lucky snorted out a laugh just the same.

She just kept squinting. "I've seen you before. Are you—" She snapped her fingers. "August."

I scowled. "I'm definitely not August. If you think I am, I'm leaving." Not that I could go far.

Across the hallway. Yeah, that would soothe my wounded ego.

"His reputation as the hotter brother is on the line," Lucky informed her. "Mind you, the only one who ever said he was hotter was Caleb himself, when he was preening in the mirror."

"Caleb." She rolled the name around in her mouth as if she was tasting a fine wine. "I definitely can tell the difference between you."

Was that a subtle dig? Or maybe not so subtle? I threw back my shoulders and puffed out my chest. I didn't think I was the equivalent of a body-building male model like my best friend, but I cleaned up quite well.

I'd definitely never gotten any complaints.

"August has a picture of you guys on his desk," she continued. "You two and your sister."

"How do you know August?" I wasn't over being compared to him, even if it had happened my entire life.

I wouldn't have said I suffered from middle sibling syndrome, but I had to admit I got testy sometimes. August was one of those guys who did everything well. He was a supremely talented craftsman, a good friend to practically the whole town, and now he had a perfect little happy family with Kinleigh and their baby.

But that was neither here nor there.

"I work for him. Well, technically, I worked for Kinleigh, before their stores and everything else merged." She spun a damp curl around her finger. "They're so happy. It's lovely to see."

I grunted. As did Lucky when he picked up the furniture he'd dropped, along with my end tables, and somehow managed to heft them all into my apartment in one trip. Then he banged the door shut.

"What's his problem?" she asked.

I turned back to her and sent up a silent apology to Lucky. Technically, he'd spotted her first, even if that spotting had been through shady means. Bro code and all that.

But I was the one who was moving into this building. She was my new neighbor. I was honor bound to chat with her and get to know her while she looked so attractively sweaty.

Okay, so side benefit.

I lifted a shoulder. "His paper plane has been unexpectedly grounded."

"Don't think its made of paper. Unless he's one of those who stuffs toilet paper rolls in his jeans. Do guys really do that?"

I had to grin as I leaned against the jamb. "Guys really do a lot of things, though I think socks are more common." I shrugged. "Sorry, can't say definitively."

"Oh, right, because of course you've never needed to do anything like that."

I didn't bother to hide my smirk. Hey, she'd continued this particular line of conversation, not me.

"If I was the ogling sort, I'd just look to see myself. But I prefer a little mystery."

"What's your name, Mystery?"

"Luna."

"Nice to meet you." I held out a hand and she clasped it after a moment. I waited for sparks. Expected them, for some weird reason. When there was nothing, I frowned. "Do you have a last name?"

"Nah." She released my hand with a satisfied smile. "I'm like Madonna. Who needs more than the first?"

"Us ordinary people who teach school, for one. I don't want my students calling me Cal."

"But that's what the hip teachers do, isn't it?" She smiled again, this time in a much less practiced way. "What do you teach?"

"Second grade at the Catholic school."

Her expression warmed exponentially. "It's Hastings."

"What?" Why was she so damn beautiful? It shouldn't be legal.

"My last name is Hastings."

"Mine is Beck." I rubbed the back of my neck as Lucky turned on the music in my apartment and started singing along loudly.

Since when did he like Sinatra? Or like butchering Sinatra, because wow.

Her lips twitched. "I know that. You know, August and all. But thank you for the confirmation."

When I lingered in the doorway, not wanting to leave just yet, she arched a pale brow. "Since you're just moving in, you can't need a cup of sugar."

"Oh, you'd be surprised what I might need. You don't happen to have any children you'll be enrolling at school?"

"No."

"Any husband to help you make those nonexistent children?"

She glanced over her shoulder at her fully furnished apartment. I couldn't see much with her blocking my view, but the place felt relaxed and serene. Much like the woman herself. "Appears not."

"How about a boyfriend?"

"Are you auditioning?"

"I'd like to know what the audition consists of before I sign up. If it involves that shiny pole over there..." I gestured into her spacious apartment, which seemingly had the same layout as mine. "Regrettably, I'll have to pass."

"Let me think about it and get back to you."

I knew a brush-off when I heard one. I needed to seal the deal. "Why don't we discuss it over lunch tomorrow? I'll cook," I offered, before remembering that my apartment was half empty and the rest was a disaster zone.

"A second grade teacher who cooks," she mused, tapping her irresistibly glossy lips. "In the package of an outrageous flirt. Very interesting."

"I wouldn't say I'm outrageous. Exactly. More like persistent." I flashed her a grin. "So, what do you say?"

Now Available

For more information go to www.tarynquinn.com

CRESCENT COVE

Have My Baby

Claim My Baby

Who's The Daddy

Pit Stop: Baby

Baby Daddy Wanted

Rockstar Baby

Daddy in Disguise

My Ex's Baby

Daddy Undercover

Wrong Bed Baby

Lucky Baby

Daddy on Duty

Cop Daddy Next Door

Protector Daddy

Baby, Be Mine

CRESCENT COVE STANDALONES & SHORTS

CEO Daddy

Mistletoe Baby

Taming the Boss

For more information about our books visit

www.tarynquinn.com

KENSINGTON *Square*

His Temporary Assistant

My Boss's Secret

Her Billionaire Bargain

Winning His Case

Standalone Titles

Desperately Seeking Kitty

His Favorite Mistake

For more information about our books visit

www.tarynquinn.com

We also write rockstar books together.

Lost in Oblivion

Winchester Falls

Found in Oblivion

Hammered

Rock Revenge

Brooklyn Dawn

OTHER SERIES

Tapped Out

Love Required

Boys of Fall

For more information about our books visit

www.tarynquinn.com

USA Today bestselling author, Taryn Quinn, is the bestie combo of bestselling authors Taryn Elliott and Cari Quinn. We've been writing together for years and decided to combine forces under one name.

Do you like...

✓ Ultra sexy romance with a side of sweet and funny.
✓ Quirky characters.
✓ RomCom shenanigans that usually involve crazy families.
✓ A crazy baby town that has exploded into a few side series.
✓ Office romance.
✓ Rockstar romance.
✓ And one BIG promise. If you love found families, you're guaranteed to find ones you wish were your own by the end of our books.

☕ Pour a cup of coffee and join us. We're glad you're here.

For more information about our books visit
www.tarynquinn.com
Email us: tq@tarynquinn.com

facebook.com/TarynQuinn
instagram.com/tarynquinnauthor

KENSINGTON SQUARE CHARACTER CHART

BEWARE...SPOILERS APLENTY IN THIS CHARACTER CHART. READ AT YOUR OWN RISK!

Kensington Square's office park is a hot bed of sizzling legal briefs, occasional dick-tation, and lots of hot sleepless nights! Never know what will happen in this small town romantic comedy series, but beware of the steam fogging up your glasses...

Adrienne "Dre" Robbins: Owns The Honey Pot Bakery

April Finley: Executive assistant at Shaw & Stone Family Law, LLC
Married to Bishop Stone, mother of Adeline, friends with Ryan Moon and Luna Hastings

Avery Thomas: Designing Women - Landscaping
Friends with Shelby Wilde, Dahlia McKenna, and TJ Parks

Bishop Stone: Partner, Shaw and Stone Family Law, LLC
Married to April Finley, father of Adeline, brother of Key and Michaela, friends with Preston Shaw and Dexter Shaw

Callahan Brinkley: Owner of Lonegan's Bar

Friends with Dexter Shaw
Dexter Shaw

Clintondale 'Clint' Hauser: Veterinarian at Thorny Paw
Married to Katherine Armitage, father of Brian, brother of Theo, Felicia, Fletcher, and Corwin, Melodie, and Emmaline, friends with Dexter Shaw

Dahlia McKenna: Designing Women - Design
Friends with Shelby Wilde, Avery Thomas, and TJ Parks

Dexter Shaw: Lawyer, Shaw, LLC
Involved with Shelby Wilde, brother of Preston Shaw, best friends with Isis Jenkins, friends with Callahan Brinkley, Clint Hauser, and Jimmy Greer

Eli Turner: Associate Lawyer at Shaw, LLC

Elizabeth Finley:
Grandmother of April, friends with Bess Wainwright

Emmaline Hauser: Event Coordinator
Involved with Mason Brooks, mother of Adriana, sister of Clint, Theo, Felicia, Fletcher, Corwin, and Melodie.

Grant Thorn: Veterinarian, Owns Thorny Paw Clinic, volunteer vet at Kitten Around Clinic
Father of Poppy Thorn

Isis Jenkins: Executive Assistant at Shaw, LLC
Best friends with Dexter Shaw, friends with Shelby Wilde

Issac Shaw: Started Shaw, Shaw, and Shaw, LLC
Father of Preston Shaw and Dexter Shaw

Jed Knight: Ex-Detective and current Romantic Suspense Author
Involved with Peyton Pryor

Jimmy Greer: Crescent Cove Police Officer
Friends with Peyton Pryor

Katherine 'Kitty' Armitage: Book Doctor - Romance Editor
Married to Clint Hauser, mother of Brian, business partners with Magnus Roberts

Key Stone: Landscaper
Brother of Bishop and Michaela

Luna Hastings: Works at Kinleigh's Attic,
later known as Kinleigh and August's Attic, tarot card reader
Married to Caleb Beck, mother of Milo, sister of Xavier, friends with Kinleigh Scott, Gina Ramos, April Finley, and Ryan Moon

Magnus Roberts: Book Doctor – Fiction Covers and Formatting
business partners with Kitty Armitage

Michaela 'Mickey' Stone: Student, works at Sugar Rush
Sister of Key and Bishop

Peyton Pryor: Rockstar
Involved with Jed Knight, friends with Jimmy Greer

Preston Michael Shaw: Partner in Shaw and Stone Family Law, LLC
Involved with Ryan Moon, brother of Dexter Shaw

Rainbow Moon: Artist
Mother of Ryan Moon

Ryan Moon: Artist and tarot card reader
Involved with Preston Michael Shaw, friends with Kinleigh Scott, Luna Hastings, and April Finley

Shelby Wilde: Designing Women - Interior Designer

Mother of Alice 'Berry' Anne, involved with Dexter Shaw, friends with Dahlia McKenna, TJ Parks, Avery Thomas, and Isis Jenkins

TJ Parks: Designing Women - Carpentry
Friends with Shelby Wilde, Avery Thomas, and Dahlia McKenna

as of 12/04/2023